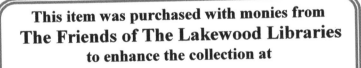

R. M. Meluch's
TOUR OF THE MERRIMACK:
THE MYRIAD (#1)
WOLF STAR (#2)

WOLF STAR

Tour of the Merrimack #2

R. M. MELUCH

DAW BOOKS, INC.

DONALD A. WOLLHEIM, FOUNDER

375 Hudson Street, New York, NY 10014

ELIZABETH R. WOLLHEIM

SHEILA E. GILBERT

PUBLISHERS

http://www.dawbooks.com

First Printing, January 2006

1   2   3   4   5   6   7   8   9

DAW TRADEMARK REGISTERED
U.S. PAT. OFF AND FOREIGN COUNTRIES
—MARCA REGISTRADA
HECHO EN U.S.A.

PRINTED IN THE U.S.A.

To Jim, of course.

PART ONE

Scorpion Sting

1

"**O**CCULTATION, NINE BY TWENTY-FIVE by eighty-eight," the tech at the sensor station sang out. "Vector twelve. Velocity five c."

Which brought the command deck to a coffee-spilling scramble at stations for confirmation. A bogey. An FTL bogey.

Lieutenant Glenn Hamilton was Officer of the Watch for the middle watch. She instantly ordered, "Go dark."

Dark mode locked down the battleship's gunports, took the force field to complete opacity, and adjusted the deflectors round the engines to mask the ship's hot stern from the bogey.

In moments came the report from the systems specialist, "We are dark, sir."

Glenn Hamilton gave a single small nod, to herself more than anyone, and ordered, "Sound general quarters, dark mode." Then she opened her direct com. Before she could speak his name, Captain Farragut's voice sounded from the open com, "Hamster, what are you doing to my boat?"

"Captain, we have company," Glenn answered. "FTL bogey at fifty-nine light-seconds. Looks like we saw him first."

"Them!" the tactical specialist loud-whispered a correction at her. "It's a *them*!"

"Them," Hamster amended her report to the captain. "We have multiple bogeys."

"I'm coming up," said Farragut. Sounded pleased.

Glenn clicked off. She turned to the specialist at the tactical station, Marcander Vincent, a man really too old to be there. Most of the specialists and techs on board *Merrimack* were baby-faced youths paying off their college educations. "Who have we got scheduled out here, Mr. Vincent? Any authorized traffic?"

"None, sir. Target is in the no-fly corridor."

That could not be an accident. No one meets anyone out here by accident. Even when ships were actively hunting, chances of finding were long. Astronomically long.

The battleship *Merrimack* had been patrolling deep Scorpion space to the galactic west of Fort Ike for weeks now, scouring the vastness between stars for just such a bogey—a needle of uncertain existence in this most vast of haystacks. Actually tripping over it took the hunters by surprise.

The only thing not unexpected was that it happened during the middle of ship's night. It was a saying on board *Merrimack*: if something was going to happen, it would happen on the Hamster watch.

"Sir, shall I request IFF?" the com tech asked.

"Negative," said Lieutenant Glenn Hamilton as she passed the log to the XO, just arrived on the command deck with a silent signal for Glenn to carry on. "Maintain dark. Move us into shadow vector."

"Shadow vector, aye," the helm acknowledged.

Captain Farragut arrived on deck like a weather front, all bright crackling bluster, still buttoning his sky-blue uniform jacket. Waved down the call to attention. "Thanks, Hamster," he acknowledged little Glenn Hamilton. The captain stood a full foot taller than his lieutenant.

He moved to the tactical station and landed a hand on the shoulder of the man seated there. "Mr. Vincent, what am I looking at?"

"Multiple-body FTL bogey, Captain. Conga line of them. Quick and dark."

John Farragut's blue eyes flickered back and forth across the readings on the tactical display. He could only see what the sensors interpreted for him. At FTL no one *saw* anything. Farragut glanced to his tall, striking XO, Commander Calli Carmel. "Stalker?"

Calli, who had not been on deck long enough to know, deferred to the Officer of the Watch.

Lieutenant Glenn Hamilton hesitated on a twinge of doubt. "I like to think *we're* the stalker, Captain. Commander. We picked them up on the skew. *We* are shadowing *them*."

The tac spec had all parts of the bogey plotted now. The plots appeared on the display strung out like beads on a necklace, spaced two light-minutes apart.

"Look up here." Calli's long forefinger landed on a plot far ahead of the rest.

"That would be the point man," said the tac spec.

John Farragut nodded. "Has that look."

The look of ships sneaking through space they ought not be in.

Farragut tapped the screen. "Can we get any better picture than this without bouncing something off 'em?"

"Negative," Mr. Vincent reported. "They're buttoned up real tight. Not much in the way of emissions. Unless we get closer, this is as good as it gets."

"Did we get a res scan?"

Mr. Vincent nodded. "Not helping."

Resonance had no location, existing everywhere at once. Even narrowed to a finite target, a resonant sounding came back like a Picasso, and sorting the returns was an art.

Nothing could hide from a res ping. But you could muddy the return. "How bad is the reading?"

"Sir, if this is what we think it is and they peed in the pool, this is what it would look like."

"Okay. Let's tiptoe in." Farragut checked with his officers, "Are we dark?"

"Yes, sir."

"Take us closer," said Farragut.

Calli issued the orders that would edge the battleship into a position at the rear of the dark train. From behind was the only way to get a good passive read on an FTL target. To move in between the plots would put *Merrimack*'s own ass on show to the next plot in line. The command crew had to assume from the way the plots were deployed—presenting the smallest possible profile to their most vulnerable angle—that they did not want to be seen.

Merrimack's slow, incremental progress gave the ship's exec moments to read the log summary of the last hours, and to get her very long chestnut hair brushed and tied back out of the way.

Though the XO did look like she had been summoned here in the middle of the night, she still looked spectacular. Calli Carmel was an extraordinary beauty, which she never pretended not to know. Just never seemed to much care.

At last, *Merrimack* slid into the tail position, where the ship's sensors could pick up the target's infrared print. At FTL, the signals came at you in a Lowrentz splat. It took a computer program to pull the readings apart into a recognizable picture.

Recognizable and familiar.

The sensor tech gave a low whistle, and Marcander Vincent at the tactical station sat back with his arms crossed. "Well, glory be and surprise surprise, we got ourselves a Roman convoy."

"I'll be damned," Captain Farragut murmured.

Exactly what they were looking for.

Earth still used the old geocentric mapping system by which space was defined in relation to Earth, in named wedges fanning out along boundaries of constellations as seen in the Earth sky.

Palatine maintained the same convention despite the Roman home world's off-center location in the constellation of the Southern Crown—because the Roman Empire still recognized Earth as their true home world. Terra, the Romans called it.

A home world to be reclaimed.

Both Earth and Palatine used the same names for the galactic spiral arms: Perseus for the outer arm, Sagittarius for the inner one, with the Orion Starbridge connecting the two.

Earth's solar system was located near the inner edge of the Orion Starbridge. And though traveling the Starbridge would eventually take you to the Sagittarian arm, it did so on a wide sweeping diagonal in relation to the galactic center. A direct route from either Earth or Palatine toward the galactic hub led across two kiloparsecs of thinly starred space popularly called the Abyss.

Two kiloparsecs made for a very long shortcut.

Palatine's solar system lay to the galactic south of Earth, and closer to the hub. The Romans claimed everything beyond Palatine—including the galactic center—as the property of the Roman Empire.

Both sides knew that was all wind. No one truly recognized anyone's claim to any planet which the claimant had not physically flagged. That set Palatine and all the nations of Earth on a planet-stabbing race to all promising star systems in all directions.

Palatine had the early jump along the Orion Starbridge toward the Sagittarian arm of the galaxy. Rome's colonies effectively blocked Earth expansion along that course. And toward Sagittarius was the favored direction.

Being older and denser than Orion space, the Sag arm promised the discovery of older civilizations and the possibility of contact with more advanced technologies. The U.S. was not about to cede that frontier to the Romans simply because a great region of settled and defended Roman Empire barred its path.

For a long time the only alternative to trespassing in Roman space, if one wanted to reach the Sagittarian arm—and the U.S. very much did—required U.S. ships to slog across the Abyss between galactic arms—an unprofitable dark voyage of three months at threshold velocity. So it had seemed the technological prizes of the Sagittarian arm were destined to belong to the Roman Empire.

The balance abruptly shifted fifty years ago when the U.S. pulled off a colossal coup in their successful activation of the Fort Roosevelt/Fort Eisenhower Shotgun.

A ten-year project of staggering concept and undisclosed cost, the Shotgun could displace entire spaceships—crew, cargo, all—from Fort Ted in Near space to Fort Ike in the Sagittarian arm—thus leapfrogging the two-klarc gap between galactic arms and reducing the three-month voyage to an instant.

Fort Ike lay well in the Deep End, on the far side of the Roman frontier. Fort Ike cut off Roman expansion eastward in the Sagittarian arm.

But from that moment fifty years ago when the U.S. proved displacement on a gargantuan scale was possible, the danger became that Palatine would build its own Shotgun and box U.S. settlements in the Deep End between Roman zones.

The U.S. had mandated such a thing would not be. The U.S. unilaterally forbade Palatine to construct its own Shotgun—a demand as absurd as Palatine's claim to the galactic hub and just as likely to be respected.

Of course the Romans would try. They must. Word on the wind spoke of a project named *Catapulta,* catapult, a term too akin to "shotgun" for comfort—the concept of hurtling something over a great distance.

Such a project would require two stations: one in Near space and one somewhere out here in the Deep End—which two hypothetical Roman installations the U.S. called the Near Cat and the Far Cat.

The Near Cat would be too close to Palatine and its home guard Legions to make an assault practicable. No one beat Rome in its home field.

As for the Far Cat—Intelligence said the Far Cat would be under construction out here in Scorpion space where the galactic Via Romana of the Orion Starbridge spilled into the Sagittarian arm.

And, lo and behold, here was a Roman convoy—one battleship, two Strigidae, and five Accipitridae riding herd on a long train of heavy cargo cars moving stealthily through a declared no-fly corridor.

Intel got it right.

"What are the odds?"

"Battle stations."

2

MERRIMACK REMAINED DARK, a malignant shadow to the unwary Roman convoy. Of what the *Mack* would do, there was no question. Strike without warning. Rome had already been warned.

The Roman battleship was not quite peer to *Merrimack,* but the two somewhat smaller Strigidae presented a problem. Each Strix carried a bludgeoning lance. Strigidae were built for one purpose—to hit hard. And the five Accipitridae were quick, nasty; you could see these were packing morning star warheads outboard.

Scuttling the cargo carriers then running seemed the logical course of action here for *Merrimack.* That would be the best way to derail the Roman mission. And, as Tactical put it, "That's real snotty escort."

But Farragut told his exec, "I need a timed strike. We deploy our fighters dark, one flight per Accipiter, and a squadron per Strix if we can. The *Mack* takes a position behind the battleship— Who is this? *Trajan*?"

"The *Valerius,* sir," Tactical supplied. "Captain at last report was Diomede Silva."

"Okay. When *Merrimack* is behind the *Valerius* and all our fighters are lined up behind a Strix or an Accipiter, we deliver one blast right up their engines, everyone on the mark. Then get out. Parting shots at the cargo carriers. Calli, get the numbers and make this happen yesterday. TR, get your wing in their fighters. Brief 'em in their cockpits. We have *no* time."

Navigation calculated the course. The pilot was already maneuvering the *Merrimack* toward the front of the Roman convoy. Tactical timed out the intervals for a silent deployment.

It was a touchy operation. *Merrimack* was to breach her force field and push out flights and squadrons of Swifts at timed intervals. The little fighter ships would glide into position on inertia only, and without IFF.

The IFF *sync-up* was resonant and so undetectable without a precisely tuned harmonic chamber. But an IFF—Identify Friend or Foe—*signal* itself was, by necessity, traceable. With an IFF signal on, the Romans would detect the Swifts' presence. The problem with turning the signal off was that, without IFF, the fighter pilots would be as alone and dark as a human could be. And vulnerable to their own mother ship's fire if something went wrong before everyone was in place.

At the end of the countdown, each fighter would have drifted into the Roman line, directly behind a heavy Strix or a quick Accipiter. Only then would *Merrimack* turn the IFF signal on at the same time as all ships fired hard ordnance into whichever Roman engine was directly in front of them.

They could only use hard ordnance. Beam weapons were no good firing forward at FTL. And firing anything backward into the next ship in line was probably a wasted shot. Any ship normally kept the strongest part of its inertial field presented in the direction of travel.

"All hell breaks loose here," Flight Sergeant Reg Monroe read from the briefing.

Got Kerry Blue's attention. Flight Sergeant Kerry Blue had been dozing, strapped into her cockpit, waiting in the queue with the other Swifts on the flight deck, half listening to Reg Monroe, Alpha Three, reading their orders over the com.

Kerry clicked on: "It *says* that?"

"Baby doll, you know I don't make this stuff up," Reg sent back, her little voice going awfully high.

A deeper, more proper voice next: "I suggest you read the mission briefing yourself, Flight Sergeant Blue." Flight Leader Sewell there. "You can read, can't you?" Hazard Sewell could be a real hard-ass sometimes. "This is not a milk run."

"Oh, yeah?" Kerry transmitted to everyone in her flight *but* Hazard Sewell. "So far sounds like we're sitting on our hands."

Alpha Two offered: "Hey, Kerry, you can sit on *my* hands."

"Shut up, Dak."

Instructions flew about *Merrimack*'s narrow corridors, all without going through the intelligence officer. The little IO stalked onto the command deck. "You are hitting the *escort?*"

Colonel Oh had not addressed anyone, but she was glaring at the captain. It was the XO who answered, "Colonel Oh, thank you for the extraordinary intercept. Now stand aside and let us do our job."

The IO spoke past her, "Captain, I should be consulted on how best to proceed here."

Captain Farragut kept his eyes on the tactical display. "Colonel Oh, that probably works real well back in Washington, but every second we sit here analyzing options is a second the wolves could spot us and blast our best options to holy hell."

"You are giving away our best option!" Colonel Oh scolded. *Scolded.* "You *must* hit the cargo carriers! They're the whole reason we're out here! They're carrying the heavy equipment to build the Roman Catapult. The cargo cars *must* be the primary!"

"The cargo carriers aren't powered up," Farragut said, information, not argument. He might explain himself to Lu Oh but he could never be said to argue with her. "They're coasting. We'll get a second shot at them. But at the first scent of our presence, those gunships will twitch and we'll have *no* shots at anyone."

Twitches at these speeds put megaklicks between you and your target before your thoughts could travel across a single synapse.

And they had reached the point of no return. Commander Carmel was already requesting go/no go. Captain Farragut said go.

"We are crossing the Rubicon."

Chrons started. T minus 500 seconds. *Merrimack* retracted her force field under her starboard wing for her first drop. More of a push, really. The battleship flung the Swifts of Alpha Flight on a trajectory that would bring the fighters into the Roman convoy directly behind the lead Accipiter in 498 seconds.

Merrimack fell back, letting the cargo cars move past. Wholly black, the cargo carriers appeared on the monitors as ghostly renegade skyscrapers. Carrying equipment for building the forbidden Roman Shotgun, *Catapulta*.

Not for long. Only for another 440 seconds.

T minus 440 brought the second drop. Green Squadron was thrown out on a course calculated to insert the fighters into the Roman line behind a stout, brutish Strix.

The edgy watch dragged. Seconds ticked. Seconds grew long when one held one's breath.

The Roman convoy's silent glide processed. Any moment now the Roman lookouts could detect *Merrimack*'s presence and run. Or detect the Swifts in their midst and extinguish them.

T minus 300. Drop Baker Flight behind another small, fast Accipiter.

Odds against this operation climbed. The more ships out there, the more chances for the enemy to detect an occultation.

Tactical counted down the seconds to the next drop. The com tech suddenly cried, "*Radio breach*! From one of our Swifts!"

An eruption of curses on deck, and Commander Carmel demanding: "Who did that!"

Colonel Steele, CO of the Fleet Marine Wing growled, "I'll kill him." He stalked to tactical's station to look over the tech's shoulder.

The com tech held his breath at his station, as if his added quiet could make up for the escaped noise.

"Reaction from the convoy!" Farragut demanded of Tactical.

"No change. No change," Mr. Vincent reported, breathing too hard, unsteady relief in his voice. "No change. They didn't pick it up." Vincent turned from his tactical display to look the captain in the eye, "We got lucky, sir."

Farragut cocked his head. So much for the vaunted Roman vigilance. He wondered if he were not so much in awe of Roman might and technology that he had overestimated them.

He had got away with a mistake he should not have got away with. One he should not ever have allowed to be made.

Tactical uncertainly continued his drop countdown, "Six, five, four—" glancing all the while to the command officers for an abort order. Got none. A rolling signal from the captain said *Keep going*. "Three, two. Drop shields. Drop Charlie."

Charlie Flight away. Safely.

Merrimack's force field resealed.

The countdown continued softly—a long count to let the next Accipiter pass, the Marine Wing lacking fighters to cover them all as thoroughly as Captain Farragut wanted.

Commander Carmel returned to the matter of the radio breach. "Do we have a mole?" One hundred fifty years after the exodus, Roman spies still burrowed deep in U.S. society.

"No," Steele answered, glowering at the tactical display. At the source of the errant transmission. Alpha Seven. "We have a cowboy."

Alpha Seven. Flight Sergeant Jaime "Cowboy" Carver. Shining star of his own universe. Loose cannon. Big mouth on the com.

Calli demanded, "Who did he signal?"

"Tight beam, ship to ship within his own flight," the com tech answered. "It was a very small leak."

"*We* saw it," said Calli.

And Farragut, "Who is Carver talking to?"

"Alpha Six. That would be—" the com tech checked his manifest.

"Flight Sergeant Kerry Blue." Steele filled in the gap quicker than the com could look it up, then demanded flatly, "She answer him?"

"No, sir. She didn't."

A grunt. Might have been approval. Clamped his jaw tight as the last Accipiter glided by, and tactical counted down to Delta Flight's launch.

Seconds stretched.

Voices sound as if at a distance. "Drop shields. Drop Delta."

Delta Flight away.

Could hear his own pulse in his ears as the count ran down for the last drop.

Dropped Delta Flight. All the fighters of TR Steele's Marine Wing were out there now. Small, lightly shielded craft. The Swifts would be easy pickings if the Romans spotted them before the attack clock ran down.

It was *Merrimack*'s turn now, maneuvering into place on elephantine tiptoe. She measured four hundred feet across the wings, and four hundred feet topsail to bottom sail. Her fuselage measured eighty-four feet on the beam and five hundred seventy feet bow to the leading edge of her six massive engines, which added another ninety feet to her stern.

Mr. Vincent had come to the final countdown: "T minus eight, seven, six—"

The engine lights of the Roman colossus hove into actual view.

"Five, four, three—"

Everything could change in the heartbeats between counted seconds.
"Two—"

And on top of *one,* Calli ordered, "IFF on! Fire Control: Away all
missiles! Fire! Fire!"

Merrimack discharged her weapons and immediately broke away
to avoid getting hit with the wreckage.

Wreckage that did not come.

Couldn't see them. Hell, no one can see snot out here. Bloody space
was some kind of hell dark and Kerry Blue was bolting through it
faster than her own neurons. Couldn't see what light there was out
here. Had to rely on the monitor to paint her a picture she could
understand.

She understood it. She just didn't believe it.

"Kerry! You hit anything?" That was Carly on the com.

"Gots! I hit gots!"

Missiles that could not possibly miss, missed. The Accipiter was
still dead ahead in Kerry's sights, but her missiles had hied off to deep
space like deserters.

Could hear Cowboy on the com. He'd spewed all the words he
knew and now he was just making them up.

"Cowboy! You hit anything?"

"Vacuum! Lots and lots of fig pucking vacuum!"

"Roger that!" Carly had come up empty, too. "Boffins must've uffed
the missile tracking system. *Frazzit!*" She jinked hard. She had become
a target. "Let's get the fork out of here!" Carly swerved back toward the
Mack.

Kerry's breath got big in her chest. She had to heave it in and out
like water. No. *No.* She was not going back to tell Lieutenant Colonel
Steele and that pinched-up little Intelligence Officer Colonel Oh that
she'd got *this* close to a Roman Accipiter and *missed.* Not acceptable.
Cannot *be.*

She circled back.

Of course it wasn't really a circle—so the techs kept trying to tell
her. But it felt like a circle. Looked like a circle on her readouts. Drove
like a circle as she cranked the stick around. Circling was not what was
really happening.

Nothing was intuitive at FTL. You don't circle at FTL. How many times had they tried to tell her? Once your forward momentum drops, you are no longer traveling FTL.

But the Swift's instruments integrated the pilot's intuitive dog-fighting motions into the intended result. They built Swifts easy, "So even a Marine can drive one."

Carly's voice came worried over the com: *"Chica linda, a donde vas?"*

"I am going down*town!*" Kerry drove her Swift head-on at a big fat Strix. Too mad to be scared.

Probably only lived because the Strix was busy targeting the *Mack* as Kerry came flying in chicken-wise, running straight up the Strix's nostrils. She barely heard Flight Leader Hazard Sewell screaming in her headset, "Kerry! Break! *Break! BREAK!"*

She drowned him out with her own shouts, "Gotcha Gotcha Gotcha, you rucking—" Squeezing the trigger, *"Dammit!"* Her Swift slid up—felt like up—and over the Strix.

The cannon of Kerry's Swift still carried a full load. She had fired nothing. *"Mack! Mack! Mack!* Alpha Six coming in. My crate is uffed! It thinks the Roman Strix is a *friendly!"*

But it wasn't just Kerry Blue's crate. It was all the Swifts who were failing to fire.

Cowboy on the com: "Something's wrong! *Merrimack,* we're getting our noses blown out here!"

"Tactical, what is our status?"

"We're getting pounded, Captain."

"I can hear that." The Roman shots hammered and hissed against *Merrimack's* defensive field. Farragut had to shout over the noise. "What's our score? What percentage hits?"

"Zero."

"Say again."

"Nada," said Mr. Vincent. "Nil. Zilch. Ninguno. No strikes, sir."

Farragut moved in, caged the man in his station, one hand on his chairback, one on the console, and hovered over his shoulder to see for himself. "We were *this* close. How could we miss?"

Mr. Vincent pointed to a screen showing a replay of their attack run, slowed down to something the human eye could follow. Farragut watched *Merrimack's* shots slither past the Roman ships.

"Looks like Palatine's got some kind of new deflectors. Look at that." Vincent's fingertip traced the arcing path of a missile swimming purposefully *around* its target.

"Doesn't explain the guns balking," said Farragut.

"No, it doesn't," Vincent agreed. Had to rethink this.

A voice from the battery shouted over the intercom: "A hit! I got a hit!"

Tactical tilted his head in interest at his readouts, footnoted for the captain: "Sir, that was a dumb shot that got through."

It was strictly against standard practice to use dumb shots in a crowded firefight. It was too easy for a dumb shot to hit a friendly. Dumb shots did not respect IFF.

Calli caught the meaning in a moment. *Dumb shots don't respect*—"Rome has our IFF!"

Colonel Steele bellowed, "Change the IFF signal!"

Wasn't Steele's order to give, and Calli ignored him. The IFF *was* changing. Constantly. Which was why no one could quite believe Rome was sending the same signal. The signal altered at machine random—which was not truly random. Machine random was a coded sequence, calculated from an initial seed signal.

"They have our program," Mr. Vincent concluded.

Captain Farragut nodded. "Rome knows the song. Let's make 'em lose their place in the hymnal. Signals!" He spun round to the signals tech. Young kid. Big ears. "Stand by to reseed the IFF program on my mark."

"Signals, standing by."

Colonel Steele turned purple wondering why they were not re-seeding *now*. Right now.

"TR, stand by to give the 'all stop' on Mr. Carmel's mark."

Steele opened his com link to his fighter wing. Waited for the signal.

"Helm, stand by to stop, on Mr. Carmel's mark."

"Helm standing by, aye."

"Mr. Carmel. Mr. Steele. Drop us out of this party."

Calli gave the word. *Merrimack* reversed thrust, as Colonel Steele barked to his Marine pilots: All stop.

A momentary quiet fell as the pounding of Roman ordnance against *Merrimack's* inertial field ceased.

The stars reappeared. The Swifts reappeared.

And in a moment, the Romans reappeared and the pounding redoubled. At sublight speeds, beam weapons were back in play. They sizzled against *Merrimack*'s field.

The enemy craft, visible now, had become cocky, fearless, feinting rams, veering away at distances of mere meters. Acted as if they were bulletproof. The Romans did not seem to notice anything suspicious in *Merrimack*'s drop from faster-than-light travel.

"All stations, here is the sequence: The instant—and I mean the *instant*—that we reseed the IFF signal, the Roman craft will no longer be identified as friendly, and *Merrimack* will feed every torpedo, missile, beam, cannon she's got up the *Valerius'* stern."

Calli acknowledged, satisfied, grim, and Colonel Steele gave a ferocious, "Aye, aye, *sir*!"

"Stations, report. Signals!"

"Signals ready. Standing by to reseed IFF."

"Fire Control."

"Fire Control ready, aye."

The gunners of the Marine Battery reported in, ready. "Oh yeah, ready. Aye."

Farragut propped his fists on his hips, with a broad smile, angry: "Send seed. Fire!"

"All stations: Execute!"

You heard the gun crews shouting, "Fire! Fire!"

And braced for the sensation of the ship's coil and discharge, for the torpedoes' hiss and cannon boom, for the victorious cries from the ship's gunners and Marine Battery and from the fighter ships over the com.

Heard instead from Fire Control: "Balk! We have a balk all banks!"

An oath.

The balk was confirmed on all banks. The battleship's guns and the Marine Battery's cannon alike refused to fire on the designated targets.

Steele was bellowing into his com to his fighters, "Wing! Report!"

"We got gots! Negs! Negs! No hits!"

Too stunned even to demand *say again*? Steele breathed, "Damn. God damn."

Calli turned to the signals tech. "Did the change of seed transmit?"

"*Yes,* sir." The kid's big ears were crimson. "The Roman ships changed IFF the instant we did."

"The *instant?*" said Calli.

"*Any* lag time?" said Farragut.

"None, sirs."

And Tactical confirmed, "Enemy is singing in tune. Right on the beat."

Calli and Farragut met gazes. Instant understanding passed between them.

"Then it's not a mimic," said Calli. "It's a direct feed. Off of *us.*"

The same signal that sent the new seed to the Swifts also fed it to the Roman gunships.

"Can't be," the signals tech said. "The signal we sent was resonant. For Rome to pick that signal up would mean—"

"It means *they're on our harmonic!*" Farragut roared.

The command crew were trying to absorb the magnitude of the disaster when a voice on the com, Flight Sergeant Cowboy Carver's, crowed: "A hit! I got a hit! Blew that frigging cargo car to fragging bits!"

And so he had. Because the cargo carrier was empty.

All the cargo carriers were.

And the situation became altogether clear, hideous.

Merrimack had not just happened upon a cargo train carrying equipment to build a Catapult. *Merrimack* had been led to find a train of empty boxes under a heavy escort.

Farragut surveyed the battle that had gone to hell. *No one ever meets by accident out here.* "I was so busy feeling lucky I forgot to feel stupid! It wasn't luck. It was *bait!*"

And he had bit the hook.

3

CALLI WATCHED THE captain's face smooth in amazement, his eyes wide with surprise, and something else. Admiration? Like a brawler in a fistfight knocked over double might give a breathless gasp: *good hit.* Staggered but not down. Never down. The day John Farragut didn't get up would be the day *Merrimack* gave him a U.S. flag blanket.

An easy man to fight for.

The signals tech mumbled, stunned, at his station. "How can this be happening?"

John Farragut took up that question to the res operator without the despair. "How *can* this be happening?"

Resonance exists outside of four dimensions. It does not follow spatial limits and so is impervious to time. A resonant pulse exists in the instant, the now, and then does not. It has no echo, no persistence. Unless your res chamber was tuned to that unique harmonic and waiting for a signal, the pulse may as well not exist in your universe.

Rome had *Merrimack*'s harmonic.

"There are infinite res harmonics," Farragut spoke what everyone knew, then what everyone wondered, "How could they get *ours*?"

"Espionage," Colonel Lu Oh answered before anyone else could. Calli heard the accusation in it. Did not have to look to know which way Colonel Oh was facing when she said that.

Calli's education at Palatine's prestigious Imperial Military Institute had been equal parts help and hindrance throughout her career.

Her training there had made her an exceptional officer, but it left her loyalty forever suspect.

Colonel Oh was not the first CIA skakker leech to set her hooks into Calli Carmel's back.

Calli kept her voice soft, hard. "I suggest you turn those eyes elsewhere, Mr. Oh."

John Farragut turned to the signals tech, "*No* signal lag? None at all?"

"None, sir," the signals tech confirmed, woeful.

IFF itself was not resonant. Could not be. Resonance had no location, and an IFF signal source must be locatable in order for friendly ordnance to avoid it. However, resonance was the only way to synchronize signals between ships light-seconds apart. *Merrimack* had sent the seed to the fighter craft via resonance, so all ships would receive it at the same instant.

"In that case it's not just our harmonic," said Calli. "They've got our IFF code *sequence*. We only fed a seed change to the Swifts." The seed started the program at a common point. From there the IFF signal changed according to the "random" program.

And the Roman IFF changed along with it.

"Captain, they've got our master code," said Calli, the only possible conclusion.

Blue eyes rolled as if heaven were still the direction opposite artificial gravity's pull. "Oh, for—" Farragut interrupted himself. "Note to file: the moment we get out of this we warn *Monitor*."

Monitor shared much with her sister ship, including codes. One gets cut, the other could bleed, too. "Aye, sir." Calli gave a sharp nod.

Marine pilots screaming on the com in their Swifts were audible across the command platform. Orders, warnings, curses, sometimes a cry that abruptly ceased.

Colonel Steele, white and rigid as a block of ice, died every time one of his Marine's plots blinked off the tactical screen. "Shut off the IFF!" came out of his mouth like an order.

"*Belay that!*" Farragut's counterorder brought him an ice-blue glare of utter betrayal.

Before Steele could say something else ill-advised, Farragut grabbed hold of Steele's sleeve, and said in a whisper, "TR, we *can't*. The Romans are right up in our faces spitting. What is more predictable than for us to power off our IFF? I've bit this hook, I'm not fixin' to swallow it."

A thick muscle bulged at Steele's square jaw with the clenching of his teeth. He could not argue. Farragut was right. Why the man was the captain.

"It's such an obvious thing for us to do," Farragut said softly. "They have to be ready for it."

Calli picked up the logic trail from there. "So if we were to cut out IFF, what would be the Roman countermove?"

"Don't know. Don't care. We're not playing their game. What *we're* going to do is send the recall. Make the Romans think we're fixin' to tuck and run."

"Are we?" Calli asked.

"Thinking about it. And while I'm thinking—God *damn!*" Broke off at the sight through a porthole. A Roman ship so close he could see it. *See* it. See its interior lights winking through its torpedo tubes.

Merrimack's recall signal brought the Swifts swarming back toward the battleship's docks on either wing.

But the Swifts could not get close.

The battleship *Valerius* belched forth fighters of its own to intercept them, while *Valerius,* the two Strigidae and the five Accipitridae continued to hammer the *Merrimack.*

Merrimack's field groaned and rasped with every strike. The battleship's violent jinking to deflect the Roman salvos from her engines also kept the Swifts from lining up any kind of safe approach.

"This is a loss, Captain," Intelligence Officer Lu Oh, advised. "Do not hand the enemy its objective."

She was telling him to run.

Colonel Steele's white face, his bulging muscles, his blanched fists were as loud as a shout: *No!*

Captain Farragut nodded. "We *should* run. I hope the Romans don't wonder why we're not doing that."

"Are we done thinking about it?" Oh prompted. "Do we have a plan now?"

"We do—"

The artificial gravity gave a burp that brought stomachs to throats, rising on a wave and not settling back down. Lights browned down, brightened up.

The systems monitor reported a flux in Engine Three. Contained. Stabilized.

Farragut kept speaking through it with no change in voice, "—If we can switch on the IFF transponder in that Wren we liberated back at the Abyss." And to his XO's uncomprehending stare he filled in, "That little Roman spyship we commandeered last month. Wearing French colors."

"*That* one," said Calli, lights going on.

"That one. Where did we put it?"

"The boffins are dissecting it in the maintenance hangar. Starboard wing."

Lu Oh spoke skeptically, "You're suggesting we send the Wren's signal to the Swifts instead of our own IFF?"

"Not *instead* of ours," said Farragut. "*With* ours."

The signals tech had to speak. "Sorry, sir. I don't get it. What will that accomplish? The Romans will just pick it up and mimic it. Apparently, whatever we feed to the Swifts' IFF sounders, we feed to the Romans' IFF sounders."

"That's why we're not going to feed the Wren's signal into the Swifts' IFF sounder. We're going to feed it into the Swift's *emergency* sounders."

A distress call, like an IFF signal, was meant to be heard, and be traceable to its source.

"A false SOS is against all conventions of war," Calli advised, very softly.

"We're not sending an SOS. We're just using the emergency equipment. All my ships will be sending two discrete signals. And the instant we activate the Wren's signal, our guns are going to target *Merrimack*'s IFF signal."

Calli's neatly shaped eyebrows lifted. She motioned to one of the techs.

Already poised on the seat edge, the young man flew from the command platform. His boots clanged on the deck grates all the way to the starboard maintenance hangar.

Steele, a brave man but not a scientific one, missed the connection that everyone else on deck seemed to be making. "What keeps *Merrimack* from shooting my Marines?"

Or were his pilots forfeit here?

Farragut answered him. "We code a NOT operand into our targeting system and direct all ordnance to hit Mack's IFF but NOT the Wren IFF."

Steele was unconvinced. "What keeps a missile from carrying out the 'hit our IFF' command before it gets to the 'don't hit the Wren IFF' command?"

Farragut caught his balance against a deck tilt, and answered his doubting Marine commander. "If I remember right, the NOT operand has precedence in computer decisions. In machine language NOT means absolutely NOT, while in human talk it's usually negotiable." He looked to the signals tech and targeting specialist who were coordinating the program over the com with the tech in the maintenance hangar. Lifted his brows for confirmation.

"Uh, yes, sir," the signals tech hesitated. "It does. NOT has precedence. Within its own statement it does."

Targeting added, "If you get your NOT outside the right statement, it'll negotiate like hell."

"Then let's get it in the right statement and get it there quick. I don't want the Romans to think we've got anything left in the bull pen."

The ship's field hiccupped. Pressure quit. Boxed the ears with its sudden return.

Tactical mumbled assurance, "We don't look like we got skat." He yawned wide to pop his ears.

Colonel Steele paced a trench into John Farragut's narrow command deck. Screams over the com bludgeoned the big man's stony nerves. The fighters, trying to return to the battleship, could not possibly dock with a bucking target.

"TR, send a verbal recall. Insist your pilots get back here right now."

Merrimack's pilot, intent on letting nothing line up anything on *Merrimack*, heard that. "Do you want me to let them approach, sir?"

"Hell, no."

And to Colonel Steele, who looked like he'd been stabbed in the gut after dutifully relaying the impossible order to his desperate Marines, Farragut said, "I'm just feeding their arrogance."

"You're feeding them my Marines." Steele whispered that, so as not to be heard arguing with the captain on his own command deck.

"Rome doesn't want to erase your dogs, TR. Those Accipiters could have mopped them all up by now. They want the *Mack*."

Steele paled in realization. "Hostages."

Farragut nodded. "The Romans won't kill all of our Swifts. They baited us. Made us come to them with our boats out. Gave us something to lose. Rome wants us to stay and try to rescue our fighters—because Rome can't afford to get into a footrace with the *Mack*. That big battle heap of theirs can't accelerate fast enough to catch us if we run."

"The Accipiters can," Tactical advised.

"Those Accipiters don't want to catch the *Mack*." Without their heavy hitting comrades, the light Accipitridae were no match for *Merrimack*.

"We aren't running without my Marines!" Steele hadn't meant to say that aloud to his captain. Waited for a rep.

But Farragut said firmly, "No, TR. We are not. Targeting! Status!"

"We are loading code to target *Merrimack*'s IFF, and waiting for the Wren code to load the NOT command before transport to the active library."

Farragut clicked on the intercom. "Maintenance hangar! This is Farragut. Get that code NOTted and up here *yesterday*."

The ship shuddered around them. Beyond the hatch, a crewman spilled into view, half falling from an upper deck. He dangled from a ladder rung, flailing for his footing. Recovered and scrambled back above deck.

A crewman in a space suit.

The XO had not ordered the crew to suits. To wear one without orders won you a rep at least, hard time more likely. Wearing a suit meant you saw a high chance of dying.

Wearing a suit against orders meant you knew you were as good as dead already.

Calli snapped to the nearest MP. "Brig that man."

Farragut was on the intercom again: "Maintenance hangar! Farragut. Tell me something."

"Maintenance here! Wren code ready to load, sir!"

"Targeting!"

Targeting picked up the cue. "Loading code, aye."

"Com, what is your status!"

"Com has the Wren IFF ready to send into all ships' emergency sounders. Com standing by."

Calli turned to the captain. "Priority of targets, sir?"

Captain Farragut answered at once, "The battleship's engines. Any open gunport. Get the *Valerius*. Ignore the little skat."

Calli had to shout instructions over the thunder roll of a heavy salvo hitting *Merrimack*'s field.

"Targeting! Status!"

"Targeting ready, sir."

"Fire Control, stand by!"

"Fire Control, ready and standing by, aye!"

"Signals, stand by!"

"Signals standing by, aye."

"Com, stand by to feed Wren signal into the Swifts' emergency sounders."

"Com standing by. Aye."

Farragut met his exec's gaze. "Ready, Cal?"

"On your word, John."

They waited. Calli nodded at the sensor display, at the Roman battleship looming, all its gunports gaping. "Here he comes."

Desperate sounds filled the waiting. A Swift on approach cracked against *Merrimack*'s field. Over the com, his flight mates shouted after him. A flight leader cried out, forlorn, betrayed—why won't *Merrimack* let them dock?

"Oh, for Jesus." Farragut signaled Calli, "Call it."

Calli ordered: "Com, send Wren IFF."

"Sending Wren IFF, aye."

All U.S. ships' emergency sounders began chirping with the Wren's IFF signal.

And immediately after, "Fire!"

Merrimack opened up everything. Techs braced themselves against the nothingness of another balk, another failure.

Blessedly, they felt the ship's power bunch and deliver. Heard, felt, the screech of ordnance leaving *Merrimack*'s barrels. The angry smell filled the corridors.

Merrimack's force field opaqued with overload of sudden luminosity.

The tactical display reimaged in a moment, showed the Roman battleship *Valerius* heave. *"Got him!"*

Voices on the com—several of the fighter pilots at once—crowed, "Yeah!"

The command deck erupted with jubilant cries, all the techs on their feet, shouting.

Farragut ordered, jubilant, "TR, cancel the recall. Have your dogs beat the blue peaches out of 'em!" Though he scarcely needed to; the Swifts already raking up the Roman fighter craft in a shredded cloud.

"Aye, sir!"

Celebration quickly subsided as the scene on the monitors rolled out. Watched in a kind of horror as the Roman battleship convulsed, twice, from within. Had the look of internal explosions.

The shimmering aura of Valerius' force field flickered, snuffed out. Another heave. Smoke belched from her gunports. And the great ship went silent and dark.

4

"THEY'RE HURT."

Farragut lunged forward, gripped the console, wide-eyed. "Oh, for Jesus. We *hurt* 'em."

Out came the white flags, stiff and unfluttering in the vacuum, on the Roman ships.

Over the com from a Marine Swift: "Delta Leader here. This skigspawn Strix is showing white! Do I have permission to shoot his ass!"

"Stand by," Farragut sent.

"Stand by?" Cowboy Carver from Alpha Flight there. "Stand *by*?"

Colonel Steele got on the com. "Stand fragging by, Marine!"

Farragut again: "Marine Wing. This is Captain Farragut. Collect the bricks."

Oxygen in solid form was often towed outboard of long-range vessels rather than waste habitable space on board. And because hydrogen could be acquired anywhere, a ship's oxygen bricks were also its water supply.

"You may acquire your targets, but do not fire unless fired upon." Farragut clicked off, murmured to the white-flagged battleship on his monitor. "Your turn."

Valerius appeared to be listing, as if it had lost its orientation in space.

And came the hail from the Roman commodore. He announced himself as Decurion Diomede Julius Silva of the Imperial ship *Va-*

lerius. He already knew his foe's name. "Captain Farragut, your assistance, if you please."

Farragut returned: "Commodore, strike your colors and show me your sincerity."

The Roman eagles reeled inboard from the *Valerius*. The escort Strigidae and Accipitridae followed suit, but their force fields stayed lit.

The Swifts buzzed round them like suspicious hornets.

"Captain Farragut, will you back off your fighters?"

"No, sir," said Farragut.

In the delay, the Swifts requested permission to fire. The small Roman fighters had all gone inert. Perhaps because they had been under remote control, but perhaps not. The Roman fighters were not showing white, so Farragut gave the Marine Wing permission to take them out.

At length, the force fields of the Strigs and the Accipiters winked out. The Romans were completely at *Merrimack*'s mercy.

Now John Farragut leaned over the com on straight arm and asked, "What do you need, Commodore?"

Coughing and a blaring alarm sounded behind the Roman's stoic voice. "I request evac and decontamination."

"You got it," Farragut sent. And to his XO, "Bring 'em over and tank 'em."

Farragut expected no treachery from his prisoners. Surrender in space was, by necessity, cordial. Vacuum was merciless. To run up a white flag in deceit was unconscionable. Only pirates—stupid ones—and terrorists tried it. God help everyone if space warfare ever degraded to that. Combatants of civilized nations were always aware that next time it could be you or your brothers in arms under that flag.

The rules were strict. Between each other, Palatine and the United States abided by all conventions, written and unwritten, of ships in distress and ships in surrender.

The Strigs and Accipiters, though intact, did not attempt to turn the situation. Nor did they run. As suspected, those ships were running lean, little more than gun platforms with engines. Without their mother ship or their oxygen bricks this deep in Scorpion space, they could only run as far as their cold, slow deaths.

The Roman commodore transmitted helpfully, "To facilitate evacuation I should tell you, Captain Farragut, we do have U.S. LDs and collars on board."

"Oh, *really*?" Now there was an unhappy surprise. Landing disks and displacement collars were not equipment the armed forces left lying around for the taking.

"They are correctly coded to your displacement chamber," the decurion added.

"I don't doubt that," Farragut said, less than pleased.

"We had intended to board you, sir. Though not like this."

In ten minutes the displacement engineers reported having received thirty-five Roman crew in space suits.

This was going too slowly. The *Valerius* was going toxic. "Bring over the rest of them," Farragut urged haste.

"I'm advised that is all of them," the displacement tech reported.

Farragut hailed the Roman commodore. "You running a light crew over there?"

The decurion's tight silence told Farragut he had not been running the *Valerius* light. Silva spoke at last, "If you could scan for survivors, I would be personally obliged. I am told you are a compassionate man when not being ferocious."

Hell, when he wasn't shooting at you, John Farragut was the Easter Bunny.

"I can do that. Get on your disk, Commodore."

The decurion allowed himself to be displaced from his crippled ship to the enemy battleship *Merrimack*.

The thundercrack brought to *Merrimack*'s displacement chamber a broad man, weary, older. Silva had twenty years on Farragut. He wore a sidearm so he would have something to hand over to his adversary.

A Colt .45. Antique weapons were often used for ceremony. Farragut turned it over appraisingly. "My Daddy has one of these."

Marines escorted the captives to *Merrimack*'s detention compartments. Honor dictated they not attempt escape until they made landfall, but it would not do to tempt them.

There were terribly few of them from *Valerius*. *Valerius* was built like a chambered nautilus, its chambers locked and segregated in battle to save the crew from total annihilation in case of a breach. As it was, the annihilation was *only* eighty-five percent.

Com open, Farragut overheard his decontamination team's exchanges as they surveyed the interior, searching for trapped survivors. A specialist breathed in his suit, "Good God, we gutted her."

TR Steele stayed clear of the prisoners. He was a bad winner and a bad loser. To TR Steele's mind, the good Romans were back in the *Valerius*.

Steele proceeded down to the hangars to receive his returning fighter pilots, those who had survived this debacle.

He was descending the ladder as Cowboy Carver jumped down from the cockpit of Alpha Seven and slung his helmet at the little intelligence officer who waited there. "Hey! Oh! Why didn't Intelligence have a clue here?"

Colonel Oh caught the helmet. Let it drop. "You will report to Ops for debriefing, soldier."

Still on the ladder, Steele shouted, pointing at Cowboy way on the other side of the hangar deck. "I get that man first!" Steele jumped down the last rungs of the ladder and started across the deck with great strides.

But another Marine pilot got to Cowboy first. Kerry Blue. Cowboy, seeing her coming at him, opened his arms for her, tilted his pelvis forward, and gave a bedroom grin. "Hey, you, beautiful bitch babe, come to your hot dog!"

Kerry folded him on the deck with a hard kick in the balls. She spun away and blundered straight into Colonel Steele. She backed her face off the wall of Steele's chest, looked up at his marble frown. She anticipated his next orders and acknowledged, "I'm walking the down decks for two weeks. Yes, sir. Aye, sir."

Steele's pale blue eyes flicked toward the groaning figure on the deck, back to Kerry Blue. With a very quiet growl he said, "One week if you do it again."

Not one to question orders, Kerry immediately stomped on Cowboy. Then lifted a salute to Colonel Steele. "Thank you, sir."

"Get out of here."

"Debriefing, soldier!" Colonel Oh barked. In Oh's reedy grating voice, the bark was closer to a yap.

"Not her!" Steele bellowed, more forcefully than he meant to.

Lu Oh, not terribly observant for an intelligence officer, didn't seem to notice anything odd about it. Must have thought Steele was merely giving his punishment order precedence over Intelligence's interrogation.

And, if challenged, Steele would be hard pressed to explain to himself why he was shielding Kerry Blue. He didn't have a good reason. He just didn't want that spider woman near his Kerry Blue.

Once she was safely out of sight, Steele caught himself shaking. Shaking.

What Antarean grughole ever let women serve on a battleship anyway?

Captain Farragut invited Commodore Silva to dine with him.

A detached sort of man, Silva. The true enormity of his loss seemed to have bounced off his weathered hull.

Typical Roman, he hadn't the same notion of the sanctity of human life as most Americans. The planet Palatine had no state religion. Not that the practice of religion was forbidden, but most Romans prided themselves on their rationality. The saying went, "Adam was a Roman." Meaning that Rome, like Adam, had chosen the apple of knowledge, science, law, and order over blind obedience to a shepherd god long ago.

"They told me you were brave, Captain Farragut," said Silva, sampling the captain's Kentucky bourbon after dinner, before returning to confinement. "They did not tell me you were especially cagey."

Farragut agreed he was not very sneaky.

"Then why did you not turn off your IFF?" Silva asked.

Farragut gave a sideways nod. Could not exactly say why. "Got the feeling you wanted me to."

"I did," said Silva. "Quite counting on it, I was. You were tipped off?"

"No, sir," Farragut chuckled a bit at how wrong that guess was. "*No, sir.*"

"How many moves ahead do you play the game, Captain Farragut?"

John Farragut creased his brow, not sure. "Depends on your batting order."

"Chess, captain. I was speaking of chess."

"I don't play chess."

"You don't say." Silva set aside his glass. Surprised, interested. "I had taken it for granted that expertise in chess was a prerequisite of the strategist."

"Baseball. I play baseball. You were expecting heat. I got you to swing at a change up. You going to tell me how you got our recognition codes?"

"Are you being coy with me, sir?"

"No," said Farragut, perplexed. As if he had just asked the Roman something obvious. He had discovered the hard way that Rome *had* his codes. He certainly did not know how Rome got them. "I told you I'm not sneaky."

Hidden things smoothed Silva's haggard features. He indicated the MPs, "I think I shall have these young men show me back to my quarters now."

There was still another play left in the game.

A message from the Joint Chiefs sat on top in the com queue, coded within codes. It said Palatine was calling for pickup of prisoners of war; can you respond?

The time of the message predated *Merrimack*'s battle with *Valerius'* flotilla, so John Farragut was puzzled. "They wouldn't even have known we have prisoners to exchange."

"The Roman message is not an exchange offer," the com spec said. "It's just a 'Here they are. Come get 'em.' "

Farragut read the message for himself. Palatine had given the Pentagon coordinates of a space buoy, which purportedly contained a small number of U.S. prisoners. The buoy was equipped with life support for five days beginning yesterday. The message said, in effect: Come get them or let them die.

"Is this addressed to the *Mack*?" Farragut scanned the header.

"No, sir. Palatine sent it to the Pentagon. The JC relayed it on the common band to any U.S. ship. We're in the neighborhood."

"I don't like it," said Farragut.

"It's a bad neighborhood," his exec agreed.

"Can this be a false message?" Farragut asked the com tech. "We know Rome has our harmonic and our IFF sequence. Do they have our encryption codes, too?"

"I guess that's always possible, Captain. But it squares with all the cross-checks, and the message doesn't ask for us. Anyone could respond," said the tech. Then, "It still smells like bait."

"Given that we're one of the few ships in the neighborhood, yeah."

Farragut checked the chron. Four days. The prisoners—if there really were prisoners—had four days. "But you can't bait with a Red Cross. Calli, respond to the JC on the LRS Marine harmonic."

The Long-Range Shuttle had brought relief soldiers to the *Merrimack*. Its recognition system operated on its own discrete harmonic. "Accept the mission on behalf of Lieutenant Popovich." Popovich was an accepted code name when you had reason not to identify yourself.

"You're going to walk into another trap?" said Colonel Oh, more accusation than question.

"No," said Farragut. "I'm going to send the LRS into the trap."

"And whom are you sending on the shuttle?" Oh's voice made it clear it would not be her.

"I'll go," Hamster volunteered. Lieutenant Glenn Hamilton was a young officer eager to make her bones with something dramatic and maybe shake off that too-cute nickname.

"Not you," said Farragut, not even considering it. And to Lieutenant Colonel Steele, who had lifted a hand as if making a bid, "TR. You're in."

Lu Oh, dumbfounded at the eagerness of these fish to snap at another hook, did not even try to speak again.

Prisoners. Where had Rome taken prisoners *from* out here? Farragut reread the message for clues. "Wonder who they've *got*."

Call-ins were infrequent. The *Merrimack* was isolated in her secrecy. The crew was never sure what was happening across the stars. The Long-Range Shuttle had just made the difficult rendezvous to bring replacements, but even the replacements' news was two months old.

The LRS wore U.S. Marines colors. Nothing about the shuttle connected it to the *Mack*. It was a generic transport, the kind that regularly ferried troops between Earth and the Deep End. It would serve perfectly for this mission.

And Lieutenant Colonel Steele was the perfect man for the job. Trust TR Steele not to trust a Roman. He would make sure to have the prisoners deloused of any Roman motes and other surveillance devices before delivering them to the *Mack*.

But it was going to kill TR Steele to obey the rules of exchange. Steele hated wearing a Red Cross almost as much as he hated wearing League of Earth Nations' green. Under either flag he was obliged to take no offensive action. The directions to the space buoy were specific. Variation from the approach route would not be tolerated.

Steele kept his fists clenched as if physical bonds were biting into his stout wrists. Yet he would not have sent any of his Marines on this mission without going himself.

His LRS obediently entered Roman space on the specified vector. The shuttle's scanners picked up the Roman spotter ships hanging back at a lawful distance. The Romans could not buzz an invited rescue craft. Steele could tell they wanted to. As much as he wanted to lob a few rounds at them.

Against all natural impulse, Steele stayed on the beacon. Ready for any trick. Ready for any treachery. Ready for anything.

Anything but this.

The nature of the trap became clear as soon as the air lock opened between the buoy and the LRS, and Steele saw the prisoners.

The gift itself was the trap. It was a strike at U.S. morale.

His Marines' morale went straight to their toes and kept on going to down decks.

"Oh, Jesus. Jesus God. Oh, Jesus."

"Shut up."

"Sir."

Steele raised a wooden, mortified salute to the ranking prisoner of the three.

The man seized Colonel Steele's sleeve, the insignia on it. "Marines," he croaked at the mastiff badge of the 89th Battalion. Meant Steele would be attached to the Third Fleet. The officer asked in horror, *"What ship?"*

Steele, already very fair, turned stark white. He could not answer the man. He motioned toward the shuttle's hatch. "This way, sir."

The displacement tech on board *Merrimack* who was logging in the displacement collars and LDs confiscated from the *Valerius* discovered that the equipment was not of Roman make. This equipment was U.S. issue. No wonder it worked so perfectly with *Merrimack*'s displacement chamber.

"So who were you stolen from," the tech murmured to a collar, checking its serial number. "Who's your mama?"

Serial number began with P29ZG. The tech did not need to read any further. He dropped the collar and ran to find Captain Farragut. Findings this explosive had to be reported in person.

The captain was on the port hangar deck awaiting the arrival of the LRS which carried the freed POWs. The displacement tech hesitated, afraid to approach him. Too many people on deck. The shuttle was already on its way down the elevator from the landing dock.

The information burned sour in the displacement tech's throat. He held back, shifting foot to foot, mentally willing the LRS to hurry.

Clamped down, the shuttle opened its hatch. Colonel Steele was first down the ramp. He threw up a salute without meeting the captain's eyes. Then stepped aside to make way for the three rescued POWs.

Gasps sounded all around the hangar.

The displacement tech withdrew. Captain Farragut just found out where the stolen collars and LDs came from.

The men filing down the ramp were well known here. Captain Matthew Forshaw, Commander Napoleon Bright, and Lieutenant Commander Jorge Medina.

Command staff of a battleship.

There was no one on deck who did not want that deck to open up and swallow them.

"God Almighty, Rome has the *Monitor*!"

PART TWO

Turnabout

5

GAVE THEM BACK. Just gave them back. High officers, thrown out like space bilge. The tactic was outrageous, insulting.

And in arrogance beyond arrogance, they had given Captain Forshaw a medal—the crimson-and-cobalt Caesar Cross, for great service to the Empire. As if Matthew Forshaw had willingly handed the *Monitor* over to Palatine.

The medal remained where the Romans had pinned it to Matthew Forshaw's uniform. It hung like an albatross he could not take off. For even if he physically removed it, it would still be there. It would never ever be gone.

It took a whole lot to make Captain Farragut angry. He was spitting mad. He grabbed the damned thing, tore it from Matty's tunic, stuffed it in the annihilator, kicked the container shut, and mashed the control button with his fist.

He breathed, terribly softly, "No excuse for that." Straightened up, clasped Captain Forshaw's right hand and hauled him in for a fierce hug and a hearty thump on the back. "Good to see you, Matty. *They* have made a *mistake*!"

Some color returned to the faces on the hangar deck. Good to see John Farragut on the offensive again.

Farragut released Captain Forshaw and grasped the hand of the *Monitor*'s XO, Napoleon Bright—a tall man, standing woodenly, his face all the more pale for the blue-blackness of his hair. "Brighty! How are you?"

"Been a whole lot better, sir."

Farragut's left hand joined their clasped right hands, warmth and strength in his grip. "Get up, Brighty. Get up so we can kick their nuts in."

Brighty nodded. "I'll be there."

Then Farragut welcomed Jorge Medina. The lieutenant commander's normally olive skin was a cadaverous gray.

Farragut looked round for the fourth, who ought to complete this set. "Where's Sophie?" The senior engineer Sophia Soteriadis was not here. "Is she alive?"

Commander Bright said, "They kept her."

John Farragut had some foul words to that.

Rome had kept those who made the battleship run—its techs, its engineers—further negating its commanders to inconsequential.

More pressing than the insult was the danger. Sooner or later, Rome was going to figure out that they could use *Monitor* to operate *Merrimack*'s systems by remote.

Farragut turned to his chief, Ogden Bannerman, "Chief, pull the plug on any system that can be accessed by remote command."

The Og grunted, "Aye."

And to his senior engineer, Ariel "Kit" Kittering, "I need a full assessment of our exposure in two hours. Include a report on any messages our captive ships got off when we bagged them."

"Two hours? I can't possibly—"

"One hour."

"Two hours, aye."

Farragut opened his direct link to the command deck. "Calli, prep a courier missile to apprise the JC of our situation. Get it off to Fort Ike best speed. And move us."

"Course, sir?"

"Don't give a rip. Anywhere but here."

"Aye, sir."

Farragut told the quartermaster to find some compartments appropriate for his guests. Then turned to the freed prisoners, "Matty, Brighty, Mr. Medina, y'all free for dinner?"

Waiting for Captain Forshaw in the Mess, John Farragut chatted with Brighty—or rather chatted at Brighty, who was understandably reserved.

Lieutenant Commander Medina showed up at the captain's table, his face and white shirt spattered with red. "I, uh, regret to inform you that Captain Forshaw will not be joining us." He listed a bit as if he would faint.

Napoleon Bright frowned. "Are you okay?"

Medina's eyes were in outer space. "No. I don't think so, sir."

Farragut came round the table. "I don't think so either. Stay here. Don't touch anything explosive or pointy." He grabbed a fistful of curly black hair on the back of Medina's head, as a big animal might grab a cub. "You'll be okay. That's an order."

And ran to meet the medics in Captain Forshaw's quarters.

Calli Carmel, overseeing a refit of the *Merrimack*'s control systems with Kit Kittering, was startled to see Captain Farragut in his dress trousers, jacket abandoned somewhere, his shirtsleeves rolled up, and him hunkered down in a maintenance pit with the techs.

In motion was Captain Farragut's natural state. However, hands-on grunt labor was a little outside the norm.

Calli stood at the edge of the pit. "What happened to dinner?"

"Not hungry," said Farragut doing battle with a stubborn bolt. "Matty went good Roman and Lieutenant Commander Medina is half in the tub."

"Good Roman" meant suicide. Romans used the term because a good Roman would rather die than live in dishonor. Marines used it because, as far as they were concerned, the only good Roman was a dead Roman.

The normal method was to open a vein in a tub of warm water and fade away. There were no tubs on *Merrimack*.

Calli stammered, "Did he— Did Matty—*succeed*?"

Farragut muscled a spanner round. "Oh, yeah." Paused to wipe moisture off his upper lip with the back of his wrist. He sat back on his heels. "I should have known. I should have done something."

Calli's long legs folded into a crouch by the pit, so she could speak softly. "Your brain doesn't work that way, John."

"It should have. God bless it, it should have! I'm the only one who could have talked him down." He gave the ratchet another snarling turn. Let it dangle. "Hell, Cal." He sat back again on thick haunches, gave a graveyard grin up from the pit. "We got ourselves another fine mess."

Calli was still too incensed to smile. "They took us down, they kicked us, they pissed on us, and, oh, Lord, they know everything there is to know about the *Mack.*"

"They will." Farragut tugged on the spanner. "As soon as they finish dissecting *Monitor,* you bet they will."

Calli took off her own jacket, climbed down into the pit to help pull. "John?" she said. Grunted.

"Yeah, Cal?" Grunted back.

Calli let go the spanner. Pushed a long stray hair out of her face. "This is all defensive."

John Farragut was an aggressive fighter. "Them's fightin' words, woman."

She nodded. Asked, speculative, "Where *is* the *Monitor?*"

Farragut saw wheels turning behind Calli's brown eyes. And he was desperate for wheels. He dared a guarded smile. "What's on your mind?"

"You said the Romans will know everything about *Monitor.* You're right. They will. But they probably don't *yet.* They'll need more time to take *Monitor* apart and analyze her."

"And?"

"Let's grab her back before they learn any more."

Farragut let the spanner drop altogether. He propped his elbows back on the edge of the pit. "Oh, yeah. Grab her back. Just grab her back." He tried out the preposterous sound of it. Allowed, "It does have improbability in its favor. What else does it have to say for itself?"

"I'm serious, John. Just do it. Quick. Dirty. Before they can think."

"Before *we* can think."

"While they are still defending a captive ship about which *we* know *everything!* We will never be in a stronger position."

"That's a scary thought right there."

"Why are we even thinking defensively? We are afraid they'll use *Monitor* against *Merrimack.* So let's use *Merrimack* against *Monitor.* We're sitting here figuring out every possible thing they could do to us with what they learn from *Monitor.* Let's do it first. While we know the field and they're still reading the playbook."

"I like the attitude, Cal."

A reedy voice intruded from above: "She learned that on Palatine."

The disheveled captain and exec looked up at the intelligence officer standing at the edge of the pit, her little hands neatly folded.

Lu Oh was always neat. She was such a tiny figure that Calli and Farragut had never looked up at her before. From this angle, Lu Oh's narrow nostrils, her slitted, slanted eyes, and her heart-shaped face made her look like a predatory insect.

"Mr. Oh, I could get real tired of that tone," said Farragut. And to Calli, "Mr. Carmel, let's go talk to Brighty."

Commander Bright was not a useful source of information. On questions of where *Monitor* had been operating, on what mission, and the battleship's last known location, he was peculiarly uncooperative.

Farragut was losing his very long patience, when the intelligence officer intervened, "He can't answer you, Captain Farragut. You are asking for classified information."

Farragut felt his eyes grow huge. They had to look like blue-yoked eggs. "He can't tell *me*?"

"Given the nature of what you intend, absolutely not."

"Oh, bullskat. Brighty!" Farragut implored.

Brighty maintained a sullen silence.

"We don't need him, John," said Calli. "We can back figure a rough window of when *Monitor* was captured. It can't have been long, or the JC would have red-balled us by now. Since the Romans dropped Matty, Brighty, and Jorge in the Deep End not too long ago, *Monitor* had to have been captured in the Deep End.

"In the time since *Monitor* was taken, the Romans did enough analysis to get our harmonic and our IFF sequence and our location. That takes more sophisticated equipment than ships carry on board. *Monitor* can't land, so they have to be dissecting her at a space dock.

"Palatine has a limited number of space docks big enough to accommodate a battleship with the right technical resources to do what they had to do. And only one of them is in striking distance of the Deep End. That's Daedalus Station on the galactic Via Romana."

Napoleon Bright registered mute surprise. He would neither confirm nor deny her conclusion, but his expression told it all.

John Farragut considered Calli's line of reasoning. Said at last, "So, tell me, why do I need an IO at all if I have you?"

"Because *I* work for the United States," said Lu Oh. Implied that Calli Carmel didn't.

Farragut ignored Lu, still talking to Calli. "You know this idea is still half-cocked."

"Half-cocked is better than dickless," said Calli.

"The situation could fast become thoroughly cocked," said Lu Oh.

Calli put it to the captain: "Go? No go?"

John Farragut had a dangerous gleam in his eyes. "Go."

Napoleon Bright broke his silence. "What? What are you planning to do here?"

"Get *Monitor*."

"Get—? You are actually considering doing this?"

"No, I'm past considering and well into planning it now."

"Sir. Reconsider. I have recently acquired a real respect for Roman cunning and resourcefulness."

"Calli's had that respect for a long time," Farragut assured him.

"No one is questioning Mr. Carmel's respect for Rome," said Colonel Oh. "Can you be absolutely certain Mr. Carmel is not delivering to Rome the complete matched set of *Monitor* class battleships?"

Calli countered, "Brighty, can you be absolutely certain your ship fell to Roman cunning and not to the blundering of an intelligence officer? Talk to us. Brighty, this is *me*."

Lu Oh pressed, "Captain Farragut. Roman Imperialists hid underground like a festering boil for two millennia. And when they surfaced in the year 2290, there were millions of them. Millions, and no one ever suspected. It is probable to a certainty that there are *still* Roman moles among us, highly situated."

"If there are, you couldn't find them if they were wearing name tags," said Calli.

Farragut tried to make peace. "I can't go around suspecting all my own people, Lu."

"Not all of them, Captain. But as far as I'm concerned, anyone who speaks Latin is suspect."

"I speak Latin," said Farragut.

Lu's voice dropped, witheringly, "Captain Farragut. You don't speak Latin."

To which Calli added in a near mumble, "You don't, John."

"*Et tu,* Calli?"

Calli's eyebrows canted up at the center, apologetic. "You're really bad at it."

And Lu Oh announced abruptly that she wanted out.

Out? John Farragut withheld a smile and asked amiably, "You want to walk, Mr. Oh?"

"I am taking the LRS and our Roman prisoners back to Earth."

Farragut blinked in surprise, unused to people challenging his command. They might question him, but never bypass him. John Farragut was as easily ignored as a freight train.

To Lu's self assignment, he said simply, "No, you're not."

Lu Oh rose from her chair. "Sir, I am."

"Colonel Steele, detain Mr. Oh."

Steele nodded to his MPs posted at the hatchway. They advanced with unholstered sidearms.

"You have no authority over me," Lu Oh declared. As if standing within a force field. "CIA."

So now she runs up her true colors. Farragut had known for quite some time. "Mr. Oh, you are on my ship, wearing the uniform of a Navy Intelligence Colonel. No one of authority has told me you are anything else. As a Naval officer, you are either delusional or mutinous. This is my ship. That's my insignia on your sleeve. You are destined for my brig." He nodded the go ahead to his Marines. "Mr. Steele."

"Aye, aye, *sir!*"

"Less enthusiasm, if you please, TR."

"Sir."

The great squared white-blond boulder that was TR Steele could have picked up the stick figure that was Lu Oh and broken all her little bones. Not entirely without intelligence, Lu Oh offered no physical struggle.

6

THE BOUNDARY BETWEEN U.S.-controlled space and Imperial space was a spongy thing, especially in the Deep End. No one guards a vacuum. And no one recognizes a claim you have not tread on or flagged. The present war had begun when Palatine drew a line in the stars and the U.S. crossed it.

Still Daedalus Station lay in undisputed Roman territory in the Orion Starbridge.

Fortunately, space was unimaginably wide. No one really ever ran into anyone else by accident out here.

Getting to Daedalus Station was not the problem. Getting at Daedalus Station could be suicide. There would be guard ships around Daedalus, and a garrison within.

Lieutenant Commander Jorge Medina, only slightly more cooperative than Napoleon Bright, did manage a nod to that. There were many guards and a garrison at Daedalus. Approach would be impossible.

Calli proposed pulling the numbers off of *Merrimack* and hauling her in under apparent control of the *Valerius* and the Strigs. If detected, she would either look like the *Monitor* in tow, or the newly captured *Merrimack*.

"Well and good," said Farragut. "Unless they know that my *Mack* blew the blue peaches out of *Valerius*. I've got to believe Decurion Silva got off a 'We're going down' message before he surrendered."

"He probably tried, but it didn't go," said Calli. "Kit says *Valerius'* res chamber boiled down at our first strike. There are no such messages in the communication logs of any of the other captive ships. Which makes sense, because it's *Valerius'* place to send that call."

Jorge Medina offered cautiously, "Don't Romans often have—what do they call them—spotter craft? They hang back and watch and run home to give reports. There could have been one at your battle with *Valerius*. Rome will know everything."

Calli conceded, "There's a chance there was a spotter craft we missed, but without confirmation from *Valerius* that signal will be suspect."

Farragut considered this gravely. "I don't like that chance, Cal."

Calli would not be turned, "In the Empire, no one is going to pass on news like that until it's confirmed. Assume the worst case scenario—there was a spotter. He sent the message. To *whom*? Not to Daedalus Station. Daedalus is a maintenance site, not a battle platform. Especially in Rome, dishonor is not news quickly shared. And not with the techs, it's not."

Farragut rephrased what she had just told him, dubious, "We are gambling that the wrong people don't know the outcome of our encounter with *Valerius*. What are the odds of that?"

"Good, actually. Roman security is constructed like a chambered nautilus, just like its ships. Everything is compartmentalized, encased in fire walls. Keeps them from the kind of informational hemorrhage we're suffering now because *Merrimack* and *Monitor* are in sync. Also keeps their left hand from knowing what their right hand is doing." She had graduated from the Imperial Military Institute. No one knew Romans better than Calli Carmel. "It's a good shot, John."

Jorge Medina was shaking his head, his mouth pressed tight shut, looking frightened.

Farragut said, "It's thin, Cal. If they see *Valerius* at Daedalus Station, we won't be the ones doing the grabbing back. I wish I could try it. I think I want it too much. I'm sorry, I can't run this nag."

Throughout the narrow corridors and tight compartments of John Farragut's battleship, technicians reworked control circuits, codes, and frequencies. Captain Farragut arrived at his command platform, glanced to the signals board where the normal IFF indicator was benignly blinking. He ordered, "Turn that off."

"IFF off, aye."

In a moment, Farragut asked the signals tech, "Mr. Remi, why are we still chirping?"

"I—I don't know, sir. It's off. We are not generating this signal."

Farragut bounded down to the signals station to see for himself as Mr. Remi explained, "It's our IFF code, but we're not generating it. It's being relayed through our res chamber from an outside source."

Farragut could not remember ever feeling more shocked. What he had been dreading was already happening.

"Monitor."

He stared at the sounder, seeing now the trap he had *not* stepped in. The near miss. A sensation like a bullet singeing his eyelashes.

During battle, when he had realized that the Roman ships were deflecting *Merrimack's* ordnance by sending *Merrimack's* own IFF code, the logical countermove on Farragut's part would have been to shut off *Merrimack's* IFF.

Rome would have expected that.

And because *Merrimack's* captain was known as an aggressive fighter, Rome might also have expected Farragut to launch ordnance targeting *Merrimack's* IFF code at the very moment he shut his ships' IFF down.

The Roman answer to that ploy was here flashing on Mr. Remi's signal board. By remote control from *Monitor,* Rome prevented *Merrimack* shutting off her own IFF.

If this had happened during the battle, Farragut would have shot his own fighters.

But we never cut IFF, so that is not how it happened.

He wondered aloud, "Do they know we know?"

"They'll know that we just now tried to cut our IFF," said Remi. "They are monitoring us, so to say."

Monitor was on *Merrimack's* resonant harmonic.

They think we're killing ourselves right now.

"Okay, let's die."

"Sir?"

"Disable the res chamber. Take it apart." And he sent an order to the maintenance hangars to pull all of the Swifts' res chambers as well.

An invisible link severed. The IFF sounder went silent.

A sudden sense of deep isolation closed in. Space seemed vast and dark. *Merrimack* was utterly alone.

For several moments no one spoke. As if mourning their own death.

"Hamster, tell my XO we're going to Daedalus Station."

Merrimack moved toward the Orion Starbridge without meeting any resistance. The war had a wide front, and neither side had enough resources to defend all its strategic points.

Napoleon Bright showed up on John Farragut's command platform like a ghost without a castle. "Captain Farragut, I cannot take part in this operation."

"No, Brighty, you can't," said Farragut. "Neither can I. Someone would recognize us."

"And they *won't* recognize Mr. Carmel?" said Brighty.

"She's not as famous as you or me. I just hope Cal doesn't run into anyone from her school days."

Calli was arranging the insignia on her Roman uniform. She said, "We are going to the armpit of the Empire. Graduates from my school don't end up at Daedalus."

"You sound pretty proud of the Imperial Military Institute," said Brighty, a touch of suspicion in that. More than a touch.

"It was very useful," said Calli. "Know your enemy. You should at least try to learn Latin, Brighty."

"I refuse."

Jorge Medina seconded the refusal.

"Jorge!" Calli said in surprise. "You don't speak Latin?"

"I speak Spanish, and I'll thank you not to call that a Latin tongue. I am an American. Here. For your disguise." He produced a Roman campaign badge. "I took it from one of our guests. It looks very impressive. It goes here."

"Latin should be easy for you, Jorge," said Calli, as Jorge pinned the campaign badge under her left pocket. "It's something educated people know."

"No. It's something the bad guys know."

"Romans aren't all bad," said Calli.

"No. Yes. Yes, they are," said Jorge. "They are bad. They were born bad. They are bad. That is why we have to shoot all of them we can before someone can call another truce."

"Amen," said Brighty.

"That's a Latin word," said Calli. And to John Farragut, "How do I look?"

"Screechin'," said Farragut. She looked head to toe a Roman decurion.

A black jumpsuit from *Valerius* had been altered to fit Calli's very slender form. She had liberated a set of Silva's commodore's eagles for her collar. She fastened her hair back with a decorative set of bronze Aldebaran scarab cricket pins borrowed from a deceased Roman crewwoman.

"Those fancy bug pins regulation?" Farragut nodded to the hair ornaments.

"No," said Calli. She knew which rules to bend and which to obey.

"I should like to go with you," said Lieutenant Commander Medina. "I know the ship. They won't recognize me. I will keep my mouth shut."

"*I* know the ship," said Calli. *Monitor* was *Merrimack*'s older twin. "You won't know when someone is talking to you, Jorge, and you don't know this is a campaign badge from the Aliquidor siege." She unpinned the badge Jorge had given her. "I was in kindergarten during Aliquidor." She handed the flashy badge back to him. "Thanks anyway, Jorge. Don't worry. I'll get your ship back."

Her handpicked attendants reported to the hangar deck, honor guard sharp, worthy of Arlington duty, only they wore Roman black and marched to a Roman cadence.

"Oh, Gawd," said Farragut with a horrified laugh, impressed. The men looked authentic as hell. "Get out of here before I brig the lot of you."

Calli lifted an Imperial fist to her chest in salute. "Domni." *Sir.*

Merrimack continued onward with *Valerius* in front of her, the Strigidae and Accipitridae surrounding her on all sides, high and low. When their flotilla tripped the Roman perimeter net on slow approach to Daedalus Station, Calli Carmel was on the command deck of the *Valerius* to receive the hail. A bank of floods illuminated the Roman craft and the dark *Merrimack* erased of all insignia.

"What ship?" came the demand.

"What ship?" Calli shot the demand right back in crisp aristocratic Latin. "Get that infernal thing off me, skakker. We are not here. You see nothing."

A very long pause followed, stretched long. Marines, huddled at their guns in *Merrimack*'s battery, got tired holding their breath. One whispered, though there was no point in whispering, "This isn't gonna work. No way this can work. They're checking. They're calling reinforcements."

"No way this would ever ever fly on Earth," said another, ready to shoot his way out of this.

But they were not dealing with Earth. After fifteen minutes the floodlights went off. The Roman guard ships wore away.

Calli Carmel did not join in the expressions of shaky relief breathed by her attendants. That had been the easy part.

The *Merrimack* parked in dead space with the *Valerius,* both Strigs, and four of the Accipiters. Calli, her attendants, and a small Latin-speaking tech crew approached Daedalus Station alone in the fifth Accipiter.

Daedalus Station stood dark as surrounding space. The Accipiter's scanners picked out the familiar silhouette docked there. Like a titanic spearhead. *There she is.*

The *Monitor.*

Calli's pilot guided the Accipiter to a station dock. Her crew secured the lock, ventilated the tube, and opened the ship's hatch.

Calli and her attendants—an appropriately odd number of them, five—marched smartly up the tube, in perfect step for the surveillance monitors. Calli inserted her old Imperial Military Institute ID into the reader at the side of the locked hatch.

And klaxons blared throughout Daedalus Station.

7

COMMANDER CARMEL'S GUARDS turned pale, cold, but resisted breaking into a panicked run as the alarms shrieked. They stayed at disciplined attention, as picturesque as a president's pallbearers.

Calli appeared nothing more than annoyed. She inserted her rejected ID again. And again. She hit the reader with her palm heel in a grand show of impatience for the monitors.

The Roman sentries who came to investigate the irregularity saw, via the surveillance monitor, a very pretty decurion on the other side of the hatch beating the ID reader and spewing invectives—Latin, Anglo Saxon, vulgar English. "I—am—so—damn all—tired—of—this—programmer—iggarspit! I'll show you technology that works!" She pulled a Roman disrupter from her thigh holster and took aim at the ID reader.

The hatch hastily opened. "Decurion!"

Good thing they stopped her, because the disrupter would not have fired for her. The weapon was coded to a deceased Roman from *Valerius*.

The ranking sentry saluted, and put out his politely demanding palm. "May I?"

Calli chucked her ID at him and made to continue on her way past him.

The sentry called after her, "*Domna,* this is an IMI pass." He sounded apologetic.

"You idiot, this is—" She stalked back and seized her pass from him, looked at it angrily, and let her high outrage dissolve into chagrin. She snarled under her breath, "Balls." Threw her Imperial Military Institute ID to the deck. Patted her pockets, produced a Senate ID, and clipped that one to the outside of her breast pocket as if that put everything in order. "Where is the idiot in charge here?"

"This way, *Domna*."

The praefect was not a self-assured sort. Direct attack by a strong, angry, scenic decurion set him immediately adrift. "I don't understand. You are saying the IFF stratagem did not work?"

"You call that debacle a stratagem? We lost—" Calli interrupted herself, as if catching herself giving away too much. Finished softly, cryptically, "It had *mixed* results. I need to see—" She flipped out a palmscreen, made to consult her notes, and read from it in stilted English, "—the 'pilot override.' "

"The pilot override has nothing to do with IFF. Anyway, we haven't been able to access the pilot override. May I see what you have there?"

"Absolutely not." She flipped her palmscreen shut and pocketed it. "I am not here to answer your questions. I will see the *Monitor* now."

"At once, Decurion." And to the sentries who had brought her, he said, "May I see the decurion's authorization?"

The sentries opened empty hands. They did not have it.

The praefect extended a requesting palm to Calli, "May I?"

Calli spoke arctic steam. "I understood this was already handled."

"I'm sorry, Decurion. I'm sure it should have been, but you know how it goes."

"No. This is *not* how it goes," said Calli, cold menace.

"I—" The praefect didn't know whether to apologize or try to explain, and didn't know how. "This is a secure project, you understand. Is there someone we can contact?"

Calli gave her long chestnut hair a mesmerizing toss with a turn of her graceful neck. Her voice became silken knives. "Yes. Do. *Immediately*. Numa Pompeii." She dropped that fifty-megaton name with breathy menace, "You check with him *personally*. Tell Numa you are giving me a headache that could last for *nights*."

A threat, sexually charged. Her already tense escort struggled to remain expressionless. That Calli Carmel possessed beauty beyond any

WOLF STAR \ 55

measure was simple fact. But none of them had ever known her to *use* it. Danger arced like an ozone burn. The XO was pulling out all the weapons in her arsenal here. They were in deep trouble; Calli Carmel had fallen back on her looks.

The praefect rose.

Daedalus Station was protected in its isolation, and Palatine was light on its internal police in secure places. A Roman was sworn to the Empire, and the Empire in turn trusted its citizens. Its soldiers more so. Betrayal of that trust was repaid with extreme brutality that extended to your children and your spouse. You could trust your fellow Romans to do their duty.

The praefect assumed the decurion loved her family. It did not occur to him for an instant that she might not be Roman. "This way, Decurion."

"If you are going to send a message, use the resonator, not a bloody telegraph!"

Rufus Novo had not realized he had been tapping. He set down the stylus, apologized through the partition, and turned up some white noise for privacy.

He flipped the decurion's discarded IMI pass over and over in his hand. Tapped it.

So all standard procedures and protocols crumble in front of a beautiful angry woman. Just like that. Callista Carmel was not on any list Rufus Novo had seen. This was too irregular.

Inattention to procedure was what got Rufus Novo posted to this bunghole of the Empire in the first place.

Still, it was not for Rufus Novo to question a decurion's word.

He had run a check on the IMI pass. The pass was genuine and valid, if very old, and this Callista Carmel was the coded holder. The card reader had only rejected her access to the station, not her identity or her ownership of the pass.

He cross-checked her identity with Imperial Military Institute records, and found that, yes, Callista Carmel had attended. Graduated. *Cum laude.*

That should have stopped him, but he tried to pull up her subsequent military career history and got nothing. Novo could not find which Legion she belonged to.

Gave him a queasy feeling. She was either not on the roles, or Rufus Novo was treading on some very deeply placed toes here.

Should have stopped right there.

Got it into his head to call Numa Pompeii. (Hadn't she told him to? Immediately? Personally?)

Well, the personally part had been directed at the Praefect, but Novo decided someone ought to do it.

He located the general's calling code in the universal log. Local time zone information came up as he logged the code into the com.

Middle of the night, Isis Station.

Should have stopped right there.

It only made sense that a man like Numa Pompeii should have companionship that was the caliber of a woman named Callista. A tall beauty with wide almond eyes and a walk like a gazelle. Novo had to wonder if he were about to step on the big man's dick. And wake him up to do it.

Rufus Novo tapped.

The Numa Pompeii he knew kept his head and his dick in separate quarters.

Rufus Novo initiated the call to Isis Station.

Calli moved about *Monitor* with one eye on her palmscreen, as if she needed a diagram to find her way.

The praefect followed her. He was a gaunt man, more scientist than soldier. His name was Rubius Siculus. He had become keenly attuned to politics and what patrons could do for you or to you. "May I ask, Decurion, the nature of the problem General Pompeii has with us out here at Daedalus?"

"Strategus" was the word Siculus used. General. It was Numa Pompeii's rank. Though most people called Numa Pompeii by his most august title of *Triumphalis*.

Calli answered grudgingly, "*Merrimack* has her protects on. Someone tipped our hand. This is unforgivable."

The praefect saw that Calli knew quite a bit about the project. More than he, apparently. "That can't be. We detected first phase success. *Merrimack* shut off her IFF at—"

"—At precisely fourteen hundred thirty-one hours and fifty-eight seconds PPMT on the eighth," Calli finished for him.

The engineers of Daedalus Station quickly checked their logs. Looked up again like a lot of bobbleheads. Gave astonished nods to the praefect. She was right.

They wondered how she could know that. No one outside Daedalus knew that.

She had to be Imperial Security. Imperial Security had tentacles no one else could see.

The attitude around her abruptly transformed from guarded suspicion to deferential dread. No one barred her way to *Monitor*'s control box. By now the engineers were only mildly amazed that she opened it so quickly when they had been trying for weeks. They only asked, "How did you do that?"

"How did you not," said Calli. Not a question. Scorn rather.

She made a show of pulling Captain Matthew Forshaw's authorization from the control box.

An engineer dared a defensive grumble, "If I may say so, Decurion, we could work more efficiently out here if those who have information shared it with those with a need to know."

She gave a cold, cold glare as if reading the engineer's ID off his badge and committing it to memory for later treatment. "I will make sure your comments are shared with those who need to know."

A voice, as clear as if originating in the compartment with Novo rather than from two megaparcs away, answered from the com: "Ops. Isis Station."

Rufus Novo tried to imitate the confident brusque menace that had carried the decurion past any challenge, "General Pompeii, at once."

Didn't work. "Who are you?" the querulous voice returned.

Novo quailed. Why did she have to ask that? He wasn't anyone. "Rufus Novo. Daedalus Station."

"Rank!" the dragon at General Pompeii's gate demanded.

"I—I'm a sentry on Daedalus Station. I have been ordered to check something with General Pompeii. Personally."

"You're a *what*? Who is your CO?" The dragon was old guard Roman, with little or no love for Novos—those come-lately Romans, whose kind had not suffered through the Long Silence. "Have you ever heard of chain of command, Novo?"

"I have orders." Sort of. "I am trying to verify an authorization to a secure site."

"The triumphalis is asleep." She hung out Numa Pompeii's augmented title. Not *just* a general. An enormously successful conquering general.

"Wake him up."

A dead pause. Then, "Novo, are you tired of living?"

"Just tell me—Decurion Callista Carmel—does she have authorization to the project at Daedalus Station? Can you find that for me?"

"Hold," the voice ordered.

Novo waited in silence. Except for the sound of his own tapping.

"What are you doing now?"

A Roman engineer tried to peer over Calli's eagled shoulder as she loaded numbers into the resonator, a 160-digit harmonic code (being the birth dates of John Farragut's twenty brothers and sisters in ascending order, except for the twins, placed third and sixteenth).

Calli said only, "You *do* know that one ship can control the other, if you know what you're doing?"

"Yes, *Domna*. That's what we've been trying to do."

"I did say 'if you know what you're doing,' did I not?"

Rufus Novo waited at the res com. Tapped.

He braced himself for what voice would eventually sound over the com. Or would the answer come in the form of Daedalus Station sentries bursting through the hatch, dispatched to arrest whoever was making midnight calls to Numa Pompeii?

The clarity and immediacy of the voice made Novo jump in his seat. A familiar, crumbly, booming baritone he had heard so often on military broadcasts. Joy in it, "You have secured the *Merrimack*!"

Novo choked, his face burning, stammered, "No, Triumphalis."

The sleepiness came through now in the growl, "Then why are you calling me!"

Because I'm a bit of an idiot, Triumphalis. "It's about Decurion Carmel—"

"Callista! Is she asking for me?"

Callista. By any gods left in the world, Novo had gone and done it. *Callista.*

Novo, you just woke up a senator/strategus—a triumphalis— fourth man in the Empire, to challenge his girlfriend.

"No *Domni,* I— Does Decurion Carmel have authority to access *Monitor*'s master codes?"

Very cross, completely mystified by the question, Numa said: "I have no doubt that Callista Carmel has full authority to do whatever the hell she wants on either *Monitor* class ship. What is your question?"

Novo foundered. "That was the question, *Domni.*"

A curse. Dead air. The click of disconnect.

Novo dropped his forehead to the console. More than a bit of an idiot.

Numa Pompeii's bedchamber was a spacious compartment on Isis Station, soaring two decks high and decorated in overwrought senatorial splendor. The heavy tapestries, the muraled overhead, the ornate bronze filigree were not to his taste, but rather expected of his august rank. He settled back into the velvet-and-eiderdown comfort from which he had been roused.

Unsorted thoughts came, as they often did as he drifted toward sleep.

Callista Carmel.

He had not thought of that silly, ridiculously pretty bitch in a long time.

Didn't know who she had smiled at to get into the Institute. The only women General Pompeii trusted in the fighting ranks looked like well-upholstered tanks.

Calli Carmel had called for him. Good. He needed a laugh right now.

The general was a man of duty. He accepted the great responsibility that went with his great power and these gods-awful rich tapestries. The matter of another Kali weighed, crushing, on Numa Pompeii's broad shoulders. That pinheaded Novo had no idea.

He had chuckled when he'd thought Callista Carmel was in captivity and asking for him, as if she thought she could get any special consideration from him.

But the error was his. She had not asked.

So why had her name even come up?

Numa Pompeii had been anticipating for several weeks now a report from Decurion Diomede Silva of the *Valerius* with news of *Merrimack*'s capture. Numa had *not* been expecting a weird question from a no-ranking Novo.

Does she have authority?

Yes, Terran operations were not compartmentalized like the Empire's. Which was why this ploy—using the *Monitor* to control *Merrimack*'s IFF—ought to work. The two ships were too closely linked. Such a danger never presented itself in vessels of the Imperial Legions.

Why was anyone asking after Callista Carmel?

And why call her decurion? A clumsy, inaccurate translation of her Terran rank. Why try to translate it to Latin at all? The Novo was ignorant, but was that the all of it?

The nagging seed grew weeds in his comfort.

And Numa wondered if he had not been speaking at cross-purposes with his midnight caller.

He rolled to his com. "Gemma, get that man back on the com!"

"Who, *domni*?"

"Whoever just called me. Get him back on the com *now*."

Calli dispatched the five members of her escort, one by one, back to the Accipiter on pretext of fetching this or that, until all five were safely off *Monitor*. She muttered, apparently to herself but meant to be overheard, "What the hell is taking them so long?"

There was nothing for them to fetch, and she certainly did not want her attendants to come back. In case something went wrong now, only she would die.

Calli's Accipiter was powered up and ready to run—without her, if need be.

Calli immobilized *Monitor*'s air lock hatches, including the open hatch where the docking tube connected the *Monitor* to Daedalus Station.

Standard ship design in any modern vessel included a trigger enabling the automatic shutting and sealing of all interior hatches in case of sudden decompression. Calli disabled that feature on *Monitor*. All open hatches were now frozen open.

Personnel aboard Daedalus Station, except for those in the compartment adjacent to the docking tube, would survive a sudden separation. Anyone on board *Monitor* would die.

There was a term for it back on the *Mack*—letting the vacuum in. "What are you doing now?"

Calli stood up, faced the praefect, Rubius Siculus. "You know what? I can do *nothing* here. Some squidhead trying something very scientific like trial and error triggered all the fail-safes and has locked up everything."

Red in the face, palm out, the praefect ordered, "Decurion, I need to see what you have been working from. I insist you hand over your notes."

Calli surrendered her palmscreen. "Take it to hell." And marched away.

"Triumphalis!"

Numa Pompeii did not have a visual, but he heard Novo salute the com, fist to chest.

Numa gave a weary growl. "Is Callista Carmel trying to meddle with *Monitor*'s controls?"

"Yes, Triumphalis."

"What—" Numa pressed his hand to his forehead, trying to force this inquiry to make sense. He found he could not even phrase a proper question. "What—exactly—is she doing and how?"

"I'm not sure, *domni*. Shall I put her on the com?"

The general's silence was brief, stunned, volcanic.

General Numa Pompeii felt he'd been hit in the face with a hammer.

Put her on the com? She was *there*?

Who knew a woman with looks like that could have such balls on her? He was hard put not to laugh. *Decurion* Carmel. Did laugh. It was horrible.

Numa Pompeii thundered, "Callista Carmel is a U.S. Naval officer, you bubonic squid! Detain her!"

8

CALLI CARMEL TRIED not to look hurried as she hurried through the passageways of *Monitor*. At any tick now, *Merrimack* would summon her sister ship out of soft dock. And Calli's decurion persona, if not Calli herself, would come apart as *Monitor* tore free from Daedalus Station.

The air lock in sight, Calli checked her breathing. She must be the picture of calm crossing into Daedalus Station.

Survival instinct howled at her to run. She maintained her purposeful measured march.

Heard running steps behind her. "Decurion! Decurion!" It was the praefect, Rubius Siculus.

Calli kept walking, face forward, cursing inwardly. She shouted up, so her voice would carry behind her, in her most annoyed voice, "What *is* it, Praefect?"

Her boot sole touched the softer surface of the docking tube. Almost, almost, almost there. But not there. She pictured, very clearly, this tube suddenly flapping like a withering balloon and spitting her into space. She could only imagine that kind of cold. Wondered, chilled, how long she would have to endure it before it killed her.

She was halfway through the soft dock when the tube jerked rigid, straight flat, under her boots. It had started.

Calli caught her balance, swore, broke into an all-out run for her life. Heard Rubius Siculus stumbling after her.

She launched herself into a flying dive at the air lock. Flew through the hatch into Daedalus. She grasped at a handhold as the structural groans shook her throat. Her long hair lifted, fluttering, in the bitter cold. Klaxons blared the decompression warning. Separation was imminent. The tube was tearing. She had to get this hatch shut, now.

The docking tube bucked. The airflow became an outward roar. The praefect was right there. His fingers clawed, white, at the station hatchway.

She might have kicked him back into the tube and shut him out, none the wiser. Instead she whirled, grabbed Rubius Siculus' gray uniform with her free hand, hauled him in with strength she didn't have, and slammed the hatch shut with both of them on this side of it as the soft dock tore away and *Monitor* pulled free.

Calli had fallen to the deck of the small compartment, gasping. Eardrums numb.

Alarms sounded far away and gauze-covered. She touched her wrist to her upper lip. Drew her wrist back bloody. She had blown a sinus.

Calli rasped, (sounding alarmed was easy), "Why is that ship moving?"

The praefect pulled himself up to his quaking knees, confused. "I don't know."

Calli lifted her com to her mouth and hailed her Accipiter—in Latin—"What is happening?"

The response, keeping character, came back also in Latin: "*Domna!*" The tech refrained from thanking God Calli was alive. Said instead: "*Monitor* is moving apart from Daedalus Station. Shall we pursue?"

"Wait for me," Calli ordered. She rose precariously to her feet. Tried the inside hatch. It was locked.

All the station hatches between her and her Accipiter would now be sealed. Standard procedure in a Roman emergency. The chambered nautilus in action.

She turned to the praefect, "Rubius, can you open this?"

He seemed about to comply when his com shrieked alive: "Breach! Breach! We have a security breach!"

Rubius Siculus checked the caller's ID on his com. One Rufus Novo. Not sure who that was. The praefect shut him off with a mutter.

"Astute bastard." Alarms banged at his eardrums. Breach was damnably obvious.

He turned to Calli, locked a meaningful gaze straight into her eyes. He opened his mouth rather helplessly as if searching for words. Calli was horrified that he might be about to thank her for saving his life.

The praefect's com reactivated. Novo again, overriding the shutoff: *"Callista Carmel is a U.S. agent! Detain her!"*

Rubius Siculus, stunned, answered softly, "Was that an *order*, Novo?"

"The Triumphalis Numa Pompeii told me *himself*! Arrest her! Arrest her!"

Rubius Siculus turned wide, amazed eyes to Calli.

Calli made a droll moue, as if this were all too peculiar for comment.

The praefect clicked the com off, opened another channel. "Security. Brig Rufus Novo." And to Calli he concluded, "This Novo must be in league with those pirates making off with *Monitor*."

She nodded. "That would make sense. Distraction tactics."

The praefect signaled his station defenses, "Contain *Monitor*! The ship is in hostile hands!"

Calli spoke low, with a touch to the praefect's forearm, "Careful, Rubius. They have hostages. Not *all* those men still on board *Monitor* can be enemy agents." It stung her to say so, when she knew that exactly no one aboard *Monitor* was an enemy agent. They were all loyal to Rome, and they were all dead.

The Praefect nodded, accepting the warning.

Calli tugged at the interior hatch. "Can you override this? I need to get to my Accipiter at once."

The praefect complied eagerly. He opened all the doors that stood in her way.

Later, when he realized he had been taken, Rubius Siculus would think she had saved his life just so she would have someone to open the doors.

And that should have been the reason. But that was not why she had done it. She had not been thinking that far ahead at the moment. His was simply a life within her reach.

An enemy life, but *there*.

She had just spaced all the Roman techs left on board *Monitor*.

Death was common in war, and she had killed before, but it was always cleaner when you knew your enemy and he was shooting back at you. This made her feel like a thug. She had done it because she must. She would never brag about this one if she lived to tell about it.

Rubius Siculus opened the last door for her, and Calli escaped from Daedalus Station. Her Accipiter immediately joined the Roman pursuit of *Monitor*. Calli hailed the dead ship for show: "Those persons controlling *Monitor,* respond immediately or you will be destroyed."

Her other four stolen Accipitridae, as if answering a call for reinforcements, took up places in the rear of the pursuit group.

The heavy patrol which Calli had bluffed past on her way to Daedalus Station moved now on an intercept course to head off *Monitor*'s flight.

Monitor veered ninety degrees to the port and eighty degrees off the horizon. Showed her heels to the patrol.

"Enemy has powered up sternside weapons," someone in the pursuit group reported.

The Romans had off-loaded all hard ordnance from the U.S. battleship, leaving *Monitor* with energy weapons only. At speeds faster than light, energy weapons were only good straight back. Aft was the only shot *Monitor* had.

Which was well. If *Monitor* had only one shot, no one would wonder at her clumsy aim and, from that, figure out that the fleeing battleship was operating under remote guidance.

As *Monitor*'s rear firing weapons powered up, the chase ships flared to vacate the direct stern position, losing ground as they did.

The patrol commander ordered all chase vessels to acquire *Monitor*.

"They have hostages," Calli warned, trying to keep the chase ships from opening fire.

"Hostages are forfeit."

Calli dutifully signaled her Accipitridae, "Target enemy. Stand by to fire."

"Target acquired," her Accipitridae acknowledged. "Standing by."

The patrol commander, just now discovering that he had Accipitridae in the rear of his posse, transmitted in annoyance: "Accipitridae, are you in this?"

Accipitridae were the second fastest ships Rome had. Their speed came at the cost of their armor. The commander must have thought Calli's fast ships were cowering back there.

"Message received, *Domni*," Calli acknowledged. "We shall engage the enemy."

"At your *leisure!*" the patrol commander snarled over the com.

Calli signaled her ships: "Accipitridae, fire upon the enemy."

9

MISSILES FROM THE Accipitridae slammed into the Roman sterns.

Accipitridae hadn't much punch—morning star warheads in this case—but their targets' defensive fields were concentrated toward the fore, so the morning stars hit hard. The detonations rattled the ships' systems, and hurled the whole patrol into confusion while the Accipitridae sprinted away as only Accipitridae could and *Monitor* sprang to threshold acceleration.

At the same time Praefect Rubius Siculus at Daedalus Station called for assistance. "All ships! We are under attack!"

The patrol commander, loathe to let go his quarry, demanded, "Identify your attacker, Daedalus!"

"It's the *Monitor*!"

A horrid chill engulfed the Roman patrol. Already flinching from each other, anticipating another shot in the back, now it seemed the enemy held the secret to the unthinkable.

Monitor had been running away from them—fast. For *Monitor* to be pounding now at Daedalus' gates far to the rear could only mean that *Monitor* had displacement capability.

No ship could displace on its own.

Could not be. Must not be.

Was not.

The patrol commander looked at the ominous spearhead image relayed from Daedalus Station's sensors. The signature shape of a U.S.

Monitor class battleship. All its gunports flashing. He shouted the sudden dawning:

"That's not the *Monitor. That's* Merrimack!"

"We need assistance," Daedalus Station called. "We are under heavy attack! They—oh, God. They have *Valerius. Valerius* is opening fire on us!"

Valerius was a hollow ship, declawed and down to only one fang. But the Romans did not know that. To those looking up her torpedo tubes, the Roman battleship appeared its redoubtable self.

The patrol commander snapped back, "Lock your damned perimeter, Daedalus! You're impregnable. The enemy is not trying to take the station, you ass. They can't! They're just trying to lure us back so *Monitor* can escape."

The patrol commander was right, but it was already too late. It only took a moment's confusion for a combatant to lose contact with an FTL target in space. You cannot do battle with a faster enemy who won't stay the field. This had become a battle against a scatter of birds. *Monitor* had gained an insurmountable lead. And with that, *Merrimack* and its puppet ship *Valerius* lifted the siege of Daedalus Station and fled in two different directions.

In the Deep Empty at the fringe of extragalactic space, *Monitor* and *Merrimack* met up and traveled side by side. With no backdrop of stars and interstellar matter against which to occult, they were virtually invisible.

Captain Farragut reactivated his ship's resonator long enough to send a two-word message to the Joint Chiefs on her old harmonic: CODES COMPROMISED.

Anything further *Mack* might send on her own harmonic, Rome would detect, too, so it was worse than pointless to say more.

Then he shut the resonators back down. Outer space reverted to its primal vastness, leaving them alone and blind as wooden ships in the middle of a merciless sea.

In the captain's Mess aboard *Merrimack,* while killing a bottle of Kentucky bourbon, talk turned to fighting sails. "How far could they see, the old ships?" said Calli. "To Earth's horizon. Eighteen miles?"

"A little farther, I think," said Farragut. "If they climbed a mast."

The lower the level of bourbon in the bottle, the stronger gravity got, so they were, both of them, flat on their backs on the deck.

"How far can we see without a res scan?" Calli asked.

"Accurately? No more than a light-second." 186,000 miles.

"Oh, hell, John. We are out here."

"Aye, matey." The glasses were abandoned. They were passing the bottle now. "Ye make a fine pirate, Mr. Carmel. Here's to ye."

"To Numa," Calli countered. "I could not have done it without him."

"If you say so." John Farragut passed the bottle. "How did you know this was Numa's project?"

"Numa Pompous Ass? Had to be. Has his big thumbprints all over it. Somebody said the word 'arrogant' and I suddenly knew. Returning *Monitor*'s command staff—that was pure Numa."

The familiarity in her voice raised John Farragut's eyebrows. "Cal, you mean to tell me General Numa Pompeii himself taught you at the Imperial Institute?"

"No. He didn't. He was an instructor of several of my classes—the Institute gets the really big guns in peacetime—but I can't say he taught me. I listened to what he taught the others in the class. Me? He looked over my head. Talked around me. Ignored me. I can't say Numa ever instructed me."

"Because you're Terran?"

"That. And." She pressed her full, perfect lips into a hard, perturbed line. "I actually asked him that. I caught him in the hall. I think I had to grab him to make him stop and face me."

Farragut broke in, merrily dubious, "He's pretty big, isn't he?"

"He's very big. I was pissed. I had smoke coming out of my ears. Don't laugh at me, John."

Farragut hid his smile, but crinkles of mirth betrayed him round his blue eyes. "I've never seen you this torqued."

"You've never seen me this drunk. And I *was* mad. The man would not teach me. I finally made him tell me why."

"And Numa said?"

"Numa gave me this slow once-over look, head to ass, and with this pissy smile said, '*You* will never need to know anything.'"

"He has a point."

"*John!*" She smacked him on the arm, calling him traitor with his own name.

"Oh, for Jesus, Cal, do you own a mirror?" He had to stop her from emptying the bottle on his head. "Whoa, that's good bourbon. I never said you weren't the best exec ever to run a battleship. But he's right. You never needed to know how to tie your shoes. Much less how to steal a battleship out of a secure Roman installation in the Deep End."

Calli lay back. The compartment had become blissfully fuzzy. "I only got away with it because Lu Oh was right."

Farragut shook his head, puzzled. Lu Oh? Right? "That you're a Roman spy?"

"That my plan was lunatic. We just caught Daedalus with their trousers round their knees. They should have been better defended."

Farragut agreed. "So where are all their big guns?"

"They're busy elsewhere. On something more important."

They both let the silence gather in. Afraid to think.

What could be more important than defending Daedalus Station?

"Shotgun," said Farragut at last.

Calli nodded. "Rome's building a Catapult. You know they are. Somewhere other than where we were looking for it."

"We've got to get ourselves refit before that project goes operational, or it'll be us caught with our trousers round our knees."

They sobered as they drank, facing the peril of getting home. "The Romans have our codes," said Calli. "They have the schematics for our ships. They've forced us off our regulation harmonic and our IFF. They've got all of *Monitor*'s hard ordnance. And we made them look stupid. It would be a mistake to assume that they *are* stupid. They're going to hunt us down, John. And if they can't catch us alive, they *will* kill us. You know there's got to be a decree out there now that *Monitor* and *Merrimack* shall not see home again."

"Never paid much never mind to Roman decrees," said Farragut. Gave a leonine yawn.

As long as *Monitor* and *Merrimack* stayed out here in open space, they were safe from any hunter. They were also useless.

Their hunters would need a pinch point to make intercept.

"They'll be looking to jump us on approach to Fort Ike," said Farragut.

Fort Eisenhower was the only installation in the Deep End big enough, secure enough, to hold the battleships. The only other suitable installations lay a three-month journey across the Abyss.

Farragut nodded to himself, sure he was right: "They think we'll head for Fort Ike."

"So what we're really going to do is . . . ?" Calli left the blank for Farragut to fill in.

"We're going to Fort Ike."

Their trail split in three.

Monitor would continue on under dead tow of the Marine LRS under command of Calli Carmel. With her went *Monitor*'s two surviving officers—Commander Napoleon Bright and Lieutenant Commander Jorge Medina—and two squads of Marines. Undermanned and feebly armed, *Monitor* would be an easy target if found, but for most of the journey *Monitor* would be running where she would be impossible to find, up here in the extragalactic dark above the disk of the Milky Way. The LRS would drag *Monitor* the long way around, overshooting Fort Ike, to make their approach from the Abyss side of the fortress.

By then, Captain John Farragut with *Merrimack,* carrying all the Roman prisoners, should have reached Fort Ike on a tortuous course. Upon arrival, he would send armed chase ships into the Abyss to meet up with *Monitor* and escort her in to the fortress.

On the third path would travel hollow *Valerius* and all the captured Roman Stigs and Accipiters, unmanned, under control of a computer program. If that flotilla made it to Fort Ike, good. If they were recaptured, then at least they would not take *Merrimack* or *Monitor* down with them.

Badly as Farragut wanted to keep his captured ships, he could not afford to hold them near *Merrimack* or *Monitor* for very long. The Roman ships carried too much enemy equipment, which meant too many chances of singers, homers, snoopers, and remote detonations. Too many ways Rome might turn the situation back around again.

Anything that had been in Roman possession was a liability and must take a separate path.

Boarding *Monitor* was like boarding a mausoleum. The ship was spooky. A giant, frozen, empty *Merrimack.*

This is what we would look like dead, thought Kerry Blue. Her lamp threw hard shadows into all the black hollows.Everything was jarringly familiar, jarringly alien in its abandonment.

Commander Carmel led the way, floating up the hatch into *Monitor*'s lower sail, followed by Commander Bright, then Lt. Commander Medina, with Kerry and the dog soldiers in the rear.

Robots had already deloused the ship, making several searches for Roman bugs, traps, and screamers. Automatons had also cleaned out the remains of the Roman techs who had died in the vacuum. Those had been bagged, tagged, and loaded aboard the *Mack* for delivery home to Palatine before the ships split trails.

Still it looked like a place you would expect to meet a corpse. The boarding party's lamps made a poor substitute for ship lights, sickly illumination pushing the blackness back only as far as stark shadows.

The light, the shadows, the crust of frost made what should have been a friendly ship into a haunted place where all intruders should die horribly one by one.

The only sounds Kerry could hear were her own breathing in her suit, and the occasional observation, spoken softly, over the com link in her helmet.

Then herself, saying, "Cheese and rice, it's creepy." Hadn't meant to send that. And to Commander Carmel's turnaround glare, she added, "Sir."

Calli Carmel could dart daggers with those almond eyes. But this time the knives sheathed and the commander's soft murmur sounded in reply, "Yeah."

They floated past Carmel's stateroom. It should have been Carmel's, but the nameplate read: NAPOLEON BRIGHT. Weird and comforting at once. It didn't look right, but it was like that moment in the nightmare when you realize none of this is real. This was *not* the *Mack*. The *Mack* was whole and light and noisy, full of people and armed to the bloody teeth. This was only *Monitor*.

Napoleon Bright's stateroom stood bare, stripped to the vents. So was Captain Forshaw's, his safe drilled, emptied of all his keys and codebooks, data slips, and manuals.

The Romans had also popped the safes in ops com and in the missile control room. Kerry guessed she sort of knew they would.

The enemy techs had scoured the ship clean of any portable equipment, small arms, splinter guns, stunners. Hydroponics had been harvested to the last pea, to the last root of the last pea plant. Uniforms, boots, space suits, torpedoes, cleaning bots, bedding—the wolves had taken all of it.

And the Swifts. They'd taken the fighter craft. Kerry's chest tightened to see the slot for Alpha Six empty, where her Swift should have stood at clampdown. Hers.

Funny how the anger rose, even when she knew this was not her ship, this was not her fighter slot, and she should have known the wolves would remove the fighters from the battleship. They'd probably done that first.

The lifts were all disabled. *We did that.* But without grav it was easy enough to glide hand over hand up—*Along? Down?*—the ladder the four hundred feet from bottom sail hatch, through eight decks of fuselage and all those equipment compartments in the sails, to topsail hatch. Carmel, Bright, Medina, and *Merrimack*'s chief—the Og—eyeballed everything in between. Scanners were well and good, but most booby traps were still found by those who knew what things ought to look like and what didn't belong.

The Marines were there in case the lookers found something.

As satisfied as she was ever going to get, Commander Carmel finally ordered reestablishment of atmosphere by means of some dumb generators from the *Mack. Monitor,* of course, didn't have any.

Found out *Monitor* was not airtight either. Kerry ended up pulling maintenance duty, assigned to plugging little pea holes in *Monitor*'s hull. Damndest things. Neat, perfectly round, and there were a whole bunch of them arrayed in perfect straight lines clean through all of *Monitor*'s bulks and interior partitions. Like someone had taken a laser drill and bored three times through the entire 570-foot length of her fuselage, bypassing the engines.

Kerry pictured Roman techs shooting up the ship for sport. Maybe Rome's answer to Cowboy Carver had done this.

For himself, Cowboy was supposed to be helping patch holes, but he was too busy trying to aim a splinter through one whole row of them with his sidearm.

When *Monitor* was airtight again, Calli Carmel tried again with the atmosphere. It worked this time. And she ordered the LRS rigged to provide minimal grav. Enough to give you a sense of up and down.

Helmets came off. Commander Carmel ordered the dogs in—the

real ones, with four feet and cold noses—for yet another inspection: a bloodhound named Nose, and the chief's dog, a big, smart standard poodle named Pooh.

"What the hell is that?" Napoleon Bright's already craggy face went distastefully askew.

Someone had shaved Chief Ogden Bannerman's dog and if the Og ever found the baboon what done it, he'd nail him up by his foreskin, by God.

The baboon had given Pooh a poodle-do, with shaved face, floofed-out chest, and pom-pom ankles. Pooh had enough intelligence to look embarrassed about it. Hung his head as he passed under Commander Bright's scowl.

"That would be a dog, Brighty," Calli said.

Cowboy Carver stood there beaming like an altar boy, and Kerry Blue had a fair idea which baboon's foreskin was on the block. Would have been. But Kerry knew for a fact that Cowboy didn't have one.

The dogs did their sniffing, and at last the space suits came off. Underneath hers, Carmel wore dress-down khakis—the Navy issue color charitably called khaki—a kind of dirty sand or baby shit or dried mud kind of no color color. Didn't matter, because anything looked like a designer creation on Calli Carmel. Captain Farragut was on the real good-looking side, too, but Carmel? Carmel just wasn't fair.

If you had enough money the surgeons could make you look like Carmel, but they couldn't make you stand like Carmel, move like Carmel, *be* like Carmel.

Commander Carmel hauled on a zippered jacket as well. At the best of times—and this wasn't—atmosphere on a naval vessel was not cruise ship grade. Running on batteries, this one was damned cold, and the burbling grav made it so drafty it moaned like a haunted castle. Unsecured hatches somewhere below decks flapped and clanked like dungeon chains. One slammed shut. Boomed through the ghost ship.

Kerry was grateful for her scratchy black pullover.

Then there was Napoleon Bright—decked out for the White House—overdone in full dress blues with *all* his medals—not just the ribbons—every bauble from every dustup he'd ever been in hanging on his chest. Ten years older than Commander Carmel, Commander Bright had a lot of crap there.

Nobody dressed like that underway. Yeah, it was what he'd been wearing when the Romans threw him back like a dead carp, but Commander Bright had been given normal clothes his size back on the *Mack*. And he'd been wearing 'em. Looked really fruitcakey here in all his geegaws.

The pooch patrol returned for treats, and Carmel pronounced the *Monitor* secure. That's when the wheels came off the mission, and Kerry had to draw her sidearm.

That's when Commander Bright turned to Commander Carmel and said dismissively, "Thank you, Mr. Carmel. I will take it from here."

PART THREE

Firing Squad

10

KERRY HELD HER BREATH. That sure sounded
like Brighty had just dismissed Commander Carmel.

No one else around her was breathing either.

Calli Carmel's beautifully tapered eyebrows lifted, surprise. She
gave a bemused smile that silently said *What?*

Commander Bright ignored the look. "Lieutenant Commander
Medina, begin start-up routine."

It sounded like Commander Bright had dismissed Commander
Carmel, because he had dismissed Commander Carmel.

So there was the reason behind all his chest froufrou. The better to
look like the master of this ship. Brighty was due for captain's stars.
Overdue. He had ten years on Carmel. Nine on Farragut.

Looked like iron. Might have been handsome, but he was too hard.
Jaw of iron. Eyes of volcanic rock. His hair was black as outer space.
He could be as frightening as one of Kerry's stepdads.

Still, one thing Kerry had learned in her two years with the Fleet
Marines: you don't ever want to get on the fang side of Commander
Carmel.

Calmer than Kerry Blue would have been, Commander Carmel
said, "Belay that, Mr. Medina. Brighty, get serious."

"You are free to disembark my ship, Mr. Carmel."

Oh, hell. Oh, God. Kerry felt herself shift into combat mode. As if
she had jumped clear of her skin, and now floated above, watching,
hyper aware, moving her body by remote.

A Marine's duty altered according to the demands of the situation. Kerry's Wing had been trained on twenty-odd different scenarios.

This was not one of those scenarios.

Commander Carmel did not so much as change her breathing. She had that luxury.

She has us.

And just in case there was any doubt which side the Marines were on, Flight Leader Hazard Sewell popped his holster strap, and stepped forward with hand on the butt of his sidearm to close ranks with Commander Carmel.

May have just blown the bottom out of his career there.

Nothing like sticking your dick way out there, Hazard.

But it was decisive. That's what separated the Hazard Sewells from the Kerry Blues. There was nothing like knowing which side you were on when fur this size flies.

"Mr. Carmel, contain your Marine."

But what Carmel told Hazard was, "Carry on, Flight Leader. Patrol, fall in. We are going back to the LRS."

"Dismissed," said Commander Bright.

"Oh, no, you're coming too, Brighty," said Carmel. Like he was still a friend. Like she could pull this skat out of the fire before it ignited. And to the lieutenant commander, "Come on, Jorge."

Commander Bright struck that wide, lord-and-master stance. "Mr. Carmel, you will not give orders to my officers on board my ship."

Officers? He had *an* officer. Used to have. One. Lieutenant Commander Jorge Medina, who froze.

Carmel turned and let Brighty have it. "Commander Bright, you *lost* your ship." Then softer, to his wide eyes, "You made me say that."

"I am XO of the *Monitor,*" said Napoleon Bright flatly. "What is your rank, Carmel?"

Carmel was tired of playing this game. "Mr. Bright. This is not a battleship. It's salvage in tow. We cannot power her up. Anything that has been in enemy hands is suspect, you know that. And for that matter, you're not an active officer; you're a returning POW."

"I never surrendered," said Commander Bright. "I did not relinquish command of this ship simply by being absent from her deck for a period of time."

"Brighty, I have no assurance that you haven't been altered in your captivity."

"Your MO found nothing."

"Absence of evidence—"

"Is no evidence."

"I've got a reasonable suspicion, growing more reasonable as we speak. Anyway, Brighty, I've got my orders. This is my mission. This ship stays dark."

"You may have orders from John Farragut, but John Farragut does not have authority over me or authority to reassign my ship to you or anyone else. Lieutenant Commander Medina, begin start-up procedure *now*."

Carmel countered, "Lieutenant Commander Medina, you have my order."

There was a man with his balls in the pincers.

For herself, Kerry's duty was clear enough. She was a little fuzzy on Naval chain of command, but even if Commander Bright won this pissing match, Kerry could not sink below her nostrils in it by following Hazard Sewell's orders. She was pretty sure her chain of command didn't change just because she was standing on someone else's deck.

Lieutenant Commander Medina was in the hanged-if-you-do shot-if-you-don't seat. At those command ranks, wrong decisions were fatal. Sometimes the right ones got you shot, too.

Jorge Medina hesitated. That narrowed it down to one choice now. Since he was belaying Mr. Bright's order, he damn well better decide to keep belaying. If he decided to execute Bright's order now after a pause that long, no one would ever follow him to the head let alone into battle against a Roman legion. Officers just don't get that long to think.

Lieutenant Commander Medina spoke, "No disrespect, Commander Bright, but it is my understanding that Commander Carmel has command of this mission."

Napoleon Bright's hard lip curled into a grisly smile. "No disrespect, Jorge. I'll have you brought up on charges of mutiny at Fort Ike and have you shot."

"Aye, sir."

Carmel gave Medina a curt, "good man" type nod, then aloud to present company announced, "In the very remote event that Mr. Bright's charges have any merit, I take full responsibility for actions taken here."

"That bullskat absolves no one," Brighty declared. Made eye contact with each and every Marine, "You are sworn to the Constitution to do *your* duty—"

"Just so," Carmel cut him off. "Mr. Sewell, remove Mr. Bright."

The court-martial will be interesting, thought Kerry. *Whoever wins, we get to watch a really big kielbasa go down.*

The Marines stepped forward, hesitant to touch Commander Bright, the uniform, that formidable rack of braidage on his cuffs. To their silent question, Carmel added, "As polite as you need to be."

To be polite meant, in the words of John Farragut, "Beat the blue peaches out of 'im if you have to."

Hazard acknowledged, "Aye, *sir!*"

Dak Shepard and Hazard Sewell took up a position on either side of Commander Bright.

Cloaked in his command invulnerability, Brighty vowed, "You touch me, I'll have you mutineers shot!"

"Take him," said Calli.

Hazard and Dak grabbed the commander's arms and started hauling. That put Brighty in a position you don't ever ever want to be in—with two guys named Twitch and Cowboy at your back with shockers.

"Lieutenant Commander Medina, draw your sidearm!" Brighty roared.

Lieutenant Commander Medina's sidearm remained at his side.

"Lieutenant Commander! You fail to carry out an order of your CO in wartime, the sentence is death!"

"I am aware of my duty to my CO, sir."

Calli accepted Medina's allegiance, and signaled everyone to return to the LRS.

Kerry Blue never ever thought to be walking with her weapon trained on a back of Navy blue. Next to captain's sky, and the red, white, and blue of Old Glory, that was the color of God Almighty.

Brighty did not go as quietly as Colonel Lu Oh had. Brighty was bigger. Fell harder.

The medics on board the LRS put him under. Gave him a transfusion and a blood wash, then put his blood back in him. It didn't sweeten him up any, the blood wash didn't sift out any Roman motes. Brighty woke up just as mad as he went under.

"Put him out for the duration," Carmel ordered.

Suited Kerry fine. She knew sure as squid spit who would pull guard duty if Brighty were put in detention awake.

Carmel turned to Medina, "How are you feeling?"

"Am I being put under, too?"

"I asked how you were feeling."

"Like crap, frankly. But do you mean did the Romans alter us? I don't think so."

"They did something to Matty and Brighty. This isn't like them."

"It's not *un*like them," Medina said, a reluctant confession. "Matt Forshaw was proud and he was tough. But when he lost *Monitor*—he was dead before he pulled the trigger. He died before he ever got to the *Mack*. And the XO is an arrogant dick. I don't mean that in a bad way. That's just the way Brighty is."

"This went beyond arrogance, Jorge. Brighty just drove a class four torpedo through his foot."

"If he shows up at Fort Ike with his ship in somebody else's control, he can forget about ever commanding anything bigger than a supply barge. To a man like Napoleon Bright, that's a fate worse than death. So he had nothing to lose by trying to get his deck under his boots."

"And you, Jorge?"

"I'd like to stay awake and serve. Do you want this?" He offered his sidearm, stock end out.

"No."

Perhaps Medina did not trust himself, or did not expect to need it again, but he gave the splinter gun over to the nearest Marine, Flight Sergeant Kerry Blue, who stowed it in the weapons locker.

They shouldn't be needing weapons. As long as they kept *Monitor* dark and ran silent, the ships were as detectable as a hole in the vacuum. The voyage should be nothing but tedium from here to Fort Ike.

If anything happened underway, it was going to happen to *Merrimack*.

Something very small, very fast, belted through John Farragut's command center. The crew heard it pierce the hull, zing through and bang out the opposite side all at once. It seared the air with its passing.

"Ho! Skat! What was that?"

Farragut lifted his com. "Systems. Farragut. We just had an incident. What was it?"

The techs on the command deck came out of their stations to inspect the bulkheads. They found a pea-sized hole in the fore partition, and a matching one in the aft. Neat. Perfectly round. It had been too fast to leave any tearing in the metal edges.

Farragut bounded off the platform and into the adjacent compartment to see if there were matching holes there. There were. "Nice hole! Turn on the outside lights."

The ship's outside lights illuminated—and were visible through the lined-up holes.

"Oh, yeah." The tac specialist Marcander Vincent crouched before the pea hole in a one-eyed squint. "We blew it out our arse."

Something had ripped the ship stem to stern. Clean. Without casualties. Fortunately it was not the hull that kept the vacuum out. It was the force field that kept the ship intact, and kept everything outside out.

Kept out everything except whatever this was.

"Engines?"

"Missed all six."

Merrimack's huge power plants occupied most of her stern, so a miss of that proportion was an amazing bit of luck. Or not luck at all.

"All stop."

Acting exec Lieutenant Glenn Hamilton relayed the orders that dropped the battleship out of FTL.

"What was our speed when we took the hit?" Farragut requested.

"Twelve thousand c," Glenn Hamilton answered. "You don't think that was the problem?"

"No. But it can't be helping. Systems! Farragut. What's going on with my cowcatcher!"

"Systems are A okay. Nothing aberrant with the force field. Integrity one hundred percent."

"We took a bullet, gentlemen. Somebody want to tell me how?"

"Would love to, sir! As soon as we have a bloody clue!" Senior Engineer Ariel "Kit" Kittering had come up to the command platform. She was a well-engineered, wide-shouldered, boy-shaped young woman with a two-dimensional waist and large doll eyes, her hair in an angular wedge cut. She touched a finger to the foremost hole. "It had to be traveling well over threshold velocity. And it cannot be particulate."

"That's not possible, Kit."

"I know that, Captain." And she gave a small woof as another bang and zing ripped through the ship.

Kit looked down, blood flowing from the pea-sized hole in her uniform. "Oh, my." Kit parted her shirt to inspect her abdomen. "Oh, my." Her doll eyes rolled back and she crumpled to the deck.

Farragut ordered the MO to bag his ass to the command deck. Called for battle stations.

Only after Lieutenant Hamilton complied did she question the order in a whisper, "*Battle stations,* Captain?"

"This isn't natural. Somebody is out there. Move this boat! Somebody is shooting at us!"

Glenn Hamilton obeyed. Didn't believe him, but obeyed.

Then Marcander Vincent at tactical reported, "Occultation. We have company."

"I know that." By instinct, John Farragut had known that. "Loc?"

"Just about everywhere, sir. Barrel orbit around the *Mack.* Pacing us move for move."

"Evasion course," Farragut ordered.

"Can't evade any wilder than we are, sir. Inertials are maxed."

Any more velocity, any more severe turns, the forces would overwhelm the dampers and throw everyone through the bulkhead.

"Somebody get that gall-blessed CIA spook up here."

The hostile took another shot. A perfectly straight shot without Coriolis curve or any angle that should have accompanied *Merrimack*'s wild maneuvers. The bullet's impact to the ship's nose and the ship's tail was effectively simultaneous.

"How do we defend against this?" Glenn murmured.

"Defend?" said Farragut. "*Shoot* the bastard!"

Merrimack ran out all guns. "Where is he?"

"Right there," Marcander Vincent said, amazed, staring straight ahead.

On the forward display had appeared a small Roman Striker, in black-and-gold eagles, holding its relative position before *Merrimack*'s bow.

Black and gold. Even John Farragut knew that one. Didn't need Calli Carmel here to tell him this was *gens* kiss-my-ring God's-gift-to-the-Empire Julian.

Once upon an ancient time, a Roman's *gens* was his family. These days, the *gentes* were more like ideological or political factions.

The current Caesar was a Julian.

"Fire," Farragut ordered. "Fire everything."

From Fire Control: "Interrupt! We are not firing."

"A balk?"

"*No*, sir. We're getting an interrupt signal from somewhere."

Somewhere would be from the Roman Striker. *How?*

"He's inside our fire control system!" Fire Control called up.

"How is he getting through our force field?" Systems snarled into his console.

"Close the gunports!" Farragut ordered.

The battleship's field was most tenuous within its gunports. The force field offered only minimal resistance within cannon barrels and torpedo tubes.

Even as he obeyed, the fire control officer warned, "We close ports, we can't shoot him."

"We can't shoot him now."

"Yes, sir."

The inertial field pulled in to a tight seal. They all felt it in their ears.

Fire Control reported, "That did it! Fire controls are responsive. But now we're limited to energy weapons."

Meant that *Merrimack* could not fire forward.

Dwarfed between two MPs, Colonel Lu Oh arrived on deck. Farragut roared, "Lu! What is shooting at us!"

"That is a patterner, Captain."

"Oh, for Jesus."

Farragut had met one of these once before. Should have recognized the unreal accuracy of the shooting. This was not the same man. That one had been in Flavian colors.

This one would not be in any mood to be gallant.

"Lu, how is he shooting through our field?"

"If he knows our phase pulse programs—and he does—he can predict the pulses through all levels and weave a shot through," said Colonel Oh.

"Even a computer can't do that."

"An altered human mind interfaced with a computer can. Pattern-ers are programmed to detect patterns. They predict things. And they can send their reactions to properly interfaced control systems."

The image of the Striker hung before the battleship's bow in black-and-gold arrogance.

"Is this Kali?" Farragut asked.

Kali, the ultrasecret Roman project with the ominous code name of the destroyer Kali.

But Lu said, "No."

"Then what is Kali?"

"Calli is the name of the mole to whom you gave command of the *Monitor*," Lu Oh said dryly.

"Kali? Calli? Not likely," said Glenn Hamilton. "A little obvious."

"Of course. That would be arrogant, wouldn't it?" Oh said, sarcasm overthick.

"What is Kali?" Farragut asked again

"I don't know." And to his dubious glare, Lu Oh said, "Captain, I don't. I *do* know we are in grave danger here. I must not be allowed to be taken."

"Com. Hail the Striker. Ask him what he wants. If it's Lu, he can have her."

The com tech relayed the question.

A machine voice answered with the Roman's demand, "Surrender. Abandon your vessel."

Farragut almost laughed. That itty bitty boat was going to take the *Mack*? He jumped down to the com station, leaned over the tech's console, and answered for himself: "You expect me to unload an intact battleship?"

"That condition can be amended."

Another shot ripped through the *Merrimack*, hit an engine compartment this time. Missed the engine itself with no margin to spare.

"We were lucky," Systems reported.

"I don't think so," said Lu Oh.

"Okay," Farragut sent over the com. "What happens to my people in their life pods?"

"They will be picked up," the mechanical voice returned.

"By who? When? There's no one out here. My people will die."

Captain Farragut was stalling, of course. He had no earthly intention of abandoning ship. He just wanted the Roman to tell him if there were any other Roman ships in the region.

A patterner could probably figure out what Farragut was trying to do.

The Roman response came as a whistle across the top of John Farragut's head. Singed his hair and made him duck. "*Hel*-lo!"

Rising from his crouch, Farragut gingerly touched the top of his head. A few burned brittle strands of dark-blond hair fell away.

He wondered if that had been a miss.

The Roman sent: "Next, I will take out an engine."

Farragut turned off the com. "Ram him. Redline."

Merrimack sprang at the patterner's little Striker at full acceleration— daring him to explode an engine he was about to wear.

The Striker dodged deftly to the side, but by then the momentum of *Merrimack's* large mass carried her megaklicks into the Deep.

The charge forced the Striker to come full about, which meant dropping out of FTL and reaccelerating in the opposite direction from its previous travel.

"Evasive maneuvers, Captain?"

"No." Course deviation became impossible near threshold velocity. "Run us up to the gate."

The contained detonations in all six engines roared, muted through the dampers. Still they shook the ship. Gauges climbed into red zones on all the consoles, and the ship grew warm even with the heaters turned off.

"Where's our friend? Is he doing his electron act?" Farragut drew orbits in the air with his forefinger.

"No, Captain," said Tactical. "He's behind us. Nine hundred thousand klicks. Closing slowly."

Farragut said nothing, seemed to be listening. And all other voices on the command platform stopped. Listened, too. Waiting on the shot.

That did not come.

At last Lieutenant Glenn Hamilton spoke for all of them, "Why isn't he shooting?"

"He can't," said Farragut. "He has to be in front to shoot."

"Now how did you know that?" Lu Oh cried.

"I didn't. I found that out when we blew past him. He didn't fire a flanking shot. Everything he's sent through us has been straight front to back. All we have to do is keep in front of him for the rest of our lives."

"Or six days, which is when he will overtake us at his current rate of acceleration," Tactical reported.

Farragut nodded. He would think of something before then. Because he had to. In the meantime, "Where are we headed?"

"Galactic north northwest."

In other words, nowhere. Fast.

11

T**HE WELCOMING LIGHTS** of Fort Ike shone at a great distance.

The voyage had been long and dark. The destination, now in sight, lay just out of reach.

Where were the trace ships come to run *Monitor* in? John Farragut should have got here first. He was meant to come out and meet her.

It could not be that he could not see her. Dark as *Monitor* and the LRS were, Farragut knew exactly where to look. They had planned for this.

He was not here. Meant that *Monitor* had beat *Merrimack* to Fort Ike. That could not be good.

Calli ordered all stop, and opened visual ports. All hands gazed at the lights, their long journey almost done.

Question was how to take the last step without an escort. There had to be a Roman ambush waiting out here in the dark for *Monitor* to announce her presence.

But if she did not announce her approach, the perimeter guards of Fort Ike would start shooting as soon as they detected her.

Fortress guards could be fairly twitchy about battleships of questionable loyalty closing on the Shotgun.

The Fort Eisenhower/Fort Roosevelt Shotgun was nothing less than a set of long-distance, titanic-scale displacement chambers.

Displacement quickly became impracticable over distance. Synchronization became error bound. And with any displacement, verification necessitated three points of information—the receiver, the sender, and the thing in transit. Time distortion over distances greater than fractions of a light-second limited the use of displacement collars and landing disks for moving people.

For displacing ships, the enormity of the endeavor was beyond all but the most ambitious of imaginations. The imaginations that had conceived this.

The colossal scale still amazed. The Shotgun used resonant verification for synchronization. Two eight-cubic-kilometer regions of perfect vacuum served as its sending and receiving chambers.

The stations lay on either side of the Abyss, Fort Theodore Roosevelt on the Orion Starbridge in Near space, and Fort Eisenhower in the Sagittarian arm—the Deep End—a separation of two full klarcs.

Using the Shotgun, Earth ships jumped clean past the whole of the Roman Empire without ever spending an instant *in* it, besting the fastest courier missile by ninety-four days.

So it followed that Fort Ike and Fort Ted were the most heavily fortified outposts in the known galaxy.

How to approach it when you looked like a hostile?

In the end, Calli was more afraid of the guns of Fort Ike than she was of any Roman lurkers. She decided to betray her existence.

You come into Fort Ike lit or you come in dead.

The code she used to announce herself would probably send up the red flag all by itself: "Fort Ike. Fort Ike. Fort Ike. Commander Callista Carmel with LRS seven eight four and recently liberated United States battleship *Monitor* in possible company of unseen hostiles. Request heavy escort immediately."

The space cav came charging out, bristling. Their Rattlers were brute, brassy, Yankee-designed craft: swift, snub-nosed, and angry. They were beautiful—even if many of their heavy guns were trained on *Monitor*. They were not shooting. Yet.

The voice that answered Calli was terse, suspicious. "Stay *on* the bubble, *Monitor*. Do not deviate."

The laser path appeared for her to follow. "Thank you, Sergeant. We do know the drill."

"Adjust your speed to ten K klips."

"Ten thousand klicks per tick on your vector, aye."

Monitor followed the line. Like flying into a jewel box.

Gases and particulates from all the ships coming and going had strewn the emptiness with a tenuous veil of smog that glowed in exotic, delicate colors, and haloed all the inhabited globes and stations that made up Fort Eisenhower.

The Shotgun itself was a perfect black void, lasered to an immaculate emptiness. But that made it perfectly transparent. You never saw *it*. You saw particles blaze on annihilation as they drifted into the Shotgun's perimeter field. On days of heavy pollution the annihilations described a glittering cell of a honeycomb.

Riding the beam in, Calli wondered why she was picking up no chatter on the secure channel of patrols searching for the Roman lurkers she had reported. Then she realized they had changed the code, and those conversations were now closed to her.

Good. Unsettling, but good.

Monitor's approach shut down traffic in the crowded space lanes for the best part of an hour. Calli could hear the ferrymen complaining on the open channels.

In the absence of any explanation for the delay, the rumors germinated, bouncing about the local channels, that Spacecraft One was headed through the Shotgun.

So Calli approached the fort to the tune of "Hail to the Chief" on the Marine channel.

On Calli's advice, the *Monitor* was led under bomb squad escort to quarantine in a heavily armed sector of the Fortress, far away from the civilian spheres and the Shotgun itself.

Calli and her crew were taken to debriefing under heavy guard, where she established her identity, told her tale, and ordered Commander Bright delivered to the military infirmary.

Hours later, Calli was sitting in a bar at Station Ibex, unwinding with some old comrades from her *Inca* days (who still called her Crash Carmel) when the MPs came to collect her with sidearms drawn, safeties off.

"Hell, Crash, what'd you do?" said Vittorio Ricci.

"Brighty's awake," Calli concluded. Tossed back her shot, rapped her glass on the bar. Took her leave from her mates, "Gents."

Serious now, her friends made to stand with her, demanding to know the bullshit charge, but Calli motioned them down. "This won't take long." She signaled to the barkeep that the last round was on her, and she went quietly with the MPs. Tolerated the nudge in her back with the gun barrel.

She was thrown into detention and held under the kind of stark and brightly lit security they used for dangerous and suicidal terrorists.

She marveled a bit at the overkill. Brighty had unloaded quite a heavy shovelful to win her this treatment.

Still, the conclusion of the matter seemed obvious and inescapable, so she hadn't the sense yet to be frightened.

She waived legal representation, against strong advisement.

"No need," she said for the ninth time, this time in an interview with the stationmaster, General Paxton S. Pike of the U.S. Fleet Marine Corps. "I don't want to blow this thing out of proportion."

"You have an astonishing sense of proportion, Commander," said General Pike. The man's small eyes crowded the bridge of his nose, leaving too much face on either side of them. "I've heard megalomaniacs do."

Woke her up. Coming from a military judge.

This interview was not an investigation. General Pike had already sided with Brighty.

But there was no sense painting the man into a corner. The stronger the general declared his position, the harder it would be for him to back out of it when he realized that Brighty had taken him for an idiot.

Calli spoke evenly, "I prefer to keep this as informal as possible."

"Informality is not possible at all. Not with a charge of mutiny and treason."

"*Treason?* What hat did Brighty pull *that* from?"

"You wish to lay countercharges?"

"No, sir."

"According to your statement in debriefing, Commander Bright made a bid for command, which you assert you rightfully held. What would that be, if not mutiny?"

"That would be a mistake—which I excused on medical grounds."

"How generous of you."

"I don't think it was generous. It was reasonable."

"You think?" Small eyes gleamed as if Pike were about to play a trump card. Which he did with a folding of hands and leaning across the table, "Commander Bright passed the detox screening."

"*Oh.*" Came out with genuine surprise and dismay. And anger. "Well that *is* unfortunate." It was going to be blessedly difficult for Brighty to get a medical out without a medical excuse. They had taken away his emergency hatch. Damn them. What were they thinking? "Still, at the time, he was under a great deal of mental stress. He'd been captured by the Romans. He'd lost his ship."

"*He* lost *his* ship, Mr. Carmel?" The little eyes were positively ablaze, animated. Paxton Pike was on his feet. One more exchange like this, and he would be across the table. "*His* ship is here. *Where is yours?*"

This line of questioning was getting certifiably ugly.

Calli did not answer immediately. Sat back in her chair to reassess the man.

Rather homely, rather toadish. In an age when anyone of means could look any way he wished, Paxton Pike was defiantly homely. The sort that resented the kind of incredible beauty that never looked his way. He had walked in hating her. No use even talking to him.

"Everything is in my debriefing statement, sir. I would like to know Mr. Bright's version, if I may."

General Pike smiled. Politeness never got an impala out of a hyena's jaws either. "Just what do you think Commander Bright's *version* is?"

"I cannot guess."

"Of course you needn't guess. You were there. You gave the *Monitor* class codes to Palatine, which allowed them to capture *Monitor.* You gave them time to dissect *Monitor,* then made a big show of rescuing it. That was a daring raid, wasn't it? It was dangerous. It was impossible. Wasn't it? Not if you just walk in to Daedalus Station, say hello to your old compadres, and waltz out with the signature ship of the greatest class of United States battleship ever built. Then you arranged for *Merrimack* to fall into Roman hands while you bring this Roman-infested *Monitor* here as a Trojan Horse."

"Oh," said Calli. Then, cheerily, absurd, "I needn't have worried. That takes Mr. Bright completely clear of a mutiny charge. He's gone completely crackers."

"Did you or did you not propose a toast to Numa Pompeii. 'Couldn't have done it without him?' "

Afraid she flinched at that one. Had Brighty pressed an ear to the partition when she'd said that to John Farragut? Maybe he even had a recording, edited to her disadvantage. "To Numa Pompous Ass. Yes, I did. If Numa Pompeii weren't such an arrogant ass, I could not have retrieved *Monitor*."

"Yes, yes, you retrieved *Monitor*. Do you have anything to corroborate your weird and self-aggrandizing tale of derring-do?"

None of the men she had with her now had been on the mission to retrieve *Monitor*. "Lieutenant Commander Medina can counter certain of Mr. Bright's claims."

"A codefendant?" General Pike dismissed that suggestion.

"That does make for twice as many people telling my story as Mr. Bright's."

"Someone else?"

"No one here."

"How convenient. Especially if *Merrimack* doesn't show up."

"Jolly *inconvenient*, I'd say," said Calli.

Even *Monitor* herself was no witness. Calli had kept the ship dark and powerless. The battleship had been retrieved by remote control by means of resonant commands. *Monitor* had nothing to say for herself.

"Where is *Monitor*'s black box?" Pike demanded, following the same line of thought.

Calli let some annoyance slip. The *box* was there. It was a big red empty. "Given that the first thing you do when you capture an enemy vessel is pull its flight recorder, I feel confident in saying the recorder is in Roman hands."

"I'm confident of that as well," said Pike. "And since the first thing one does with a captured vessel is pull the flight recorder, where might be the black boxes of those eight—was it eight?—Roman ships you claim to have captured?"

"On *Merrimack*."

"Of course they are."

"My entire crew and Marine squadron can attest to the capture of the battleship *Valerius*, two Strigidae, and five Accipitridae."

Little eyes flickered at the proper Latin plurals. A red-blooded American would have said two Strixes (or Strigs) and five Accipiters. "Which you let go."

"We did not let them go," said Calli. "We programmed them to come here. It's in my report."

"Any of those programmers here? Besides you?"

She might have sighed. "No."

General Pike looked like a horse with its nostrils full of snake stench. She recognized the type. Hard-corps Marine. Conservative. Nationalistic. Loathed all things Roman and all traits associated with Rome—intellectualism, elitism. Calli's education made her one of Them.

"So, Commander Carmel, you programmed the captured ships to come here. They're not here. Where are they?"

"I don't know. The course is computer random."

"Where is *Merrimack*?"

"I don't know. *Merrimack*'s course will be John Farragut random."

"We pinged the *Mack*."

Calli started up straight in her chair. "You—!" Stopped. Settled. On first arrival she had told the debriefing officers—emphatically—do not NOT ping the *Merrimack*.

So it made sense that the first thing this baboon went and did was ping the *Merrimack*. And received no echo.

General Pike went on to report in tones of dire triumph, "We received no return echo on *Merrimack*'s harmonic." An *Ah ha!* in his voice. "If *Merrimack* is still in U.S. control, why is there no echo?"

He meant that to be an unanswerable question. Calli answered, "Because she's running dark." *You dick.*

He heard the *you dick* though she did not actually speak it.

Calli continued, "You have, however, successfully assured the Romans—who *are* monitoring *Mack's* old harmonic—that *Merrimack* has *not* arrived safely at Fort Ike. *You* just told the Roman searchers that they were still in the hunt. They will appreciate your service."

"You are speaking for Rome?"

"On that, yes," said Calli, standing up to await dismissal. This interview could not get any worse. "I can assure you of that one."

All kinds of civilian traffic came through Fort Ike, from every nation of Earth and from many of the individual League nations' seven hundred and two colonial worlds, and several of the spacefaring alien civilizations within the LEN protectorate zone. All kinds of traffic. Except Roman.

No Roman ships were allowed near the Shotgun, much less

through it. The U.S. Navy would fire upon any Roman ship detected within the LEN protectorate, and would impound any Roman trade ship in LEN space, liberate its cargo, and usually return its crew after questioning them as spies. Roman trade was not welcome at Fort Ike.

Which did not mean that Roman goods did not come through the Shotgun, as many League nations still traded with Rome.

The Marines who had accompanied *Monitor,* except for Flight Leader Hazard Sewell, had not been confined upon arrival at Fort Ike. But neither were they issued the customary boarding passes that would allow them free passage from station to station at Fort Ike. Fort Ike was an expensive place. Without the military passes, the Marines were beggars with their noses pressed against the glass of wonderland.

All the civilian delights were closed to them. They could only look out the station portholes at the jewels hanging in the sky—small artificial worlds, casinos, brothels, hotels—with the glittering space liners moving majestically in the colored clouds among them.

The U.S. stations within the Fortress were obvious for their flags. Bigger than everyone else's. No one flew more flags than the Americans. The eighty-two stars and thirteen stripes were everywhere.

You could make out the Australian station immediately—one of the oldest stations in the Space Fortress—the one oriented upside down from the rest. Always a good time at the Station Down-Under-Way-Out-Here. If only the Marines could get there.

The Marines' obedience to Commander Carmel's and Flight Leader Hazard Sewell's illegal orders had been an error in judgment, said Napoleon Bright. So he let them off with a stern, magnanimous reprimand.

"A rep? A *rep* and we're supposed to be *grateful*? Oh, he can eat—" Carly Delgado dredged her vocabulary for Mr. Bright's menu.

"Hey! Hey! Hazard don't like that kind of talk," Twitch Fuentes backed her off.

"Hazard ain't in charge here, *is* he?" Carly snapped. Wrong thing to say and she regretted it on the spot.

A somber silence fell. Then Carly and the other members of Alpha Flight immediately vowed to clean up their language out of respect for their incarcerated flight leader.

They choked on the words that rose up when they saw Brighty

running loose, glad-talking with station officers, *too* jolly, buying tall drinks and telling taller tales.

"Why doesn't Carmel charge that son of a b—eachball?"

They couldn't understand. And could not come to attention for Commander Bright when they crossed paths in a station corridor.

The Navy did not salute indoors, but soldiers of the Fleet Marine normally showed respect to senior Naval officers by coming to attention. Alpha Flight did not.

Brighty's companions looked silently askance at the Marines' lack of regard. Mr. Bright could demand their salutes, and they would have to give them. He daggered them with his gaze as they stood in a sullen, silent, glaring knot. He started to speak, then thought better of it. Moved on.

One of his companions hissed, "What the hell was *that*, Brighty?"

"*Merrimack*'s Marines. Standing by their mutineer."

"You're going to take that?"

"They are only ignorant," said Brighty. "Loyalty is a good quality in Marines and dogs, don't you think? They are a small concern."

The Marines heard that. Cowboy turned around to start after him. "Small! Why that—" Cowboy grabbed his own dick. "I'll show him small!"

His flight mates wrestled him back.

"Put it away, Cowboy. You don't got anywhere to put it," Kerry said.

Cowboy hollered down the corridor. "Talk big while you can, squidass!" Turned away, muttering, "He won't talk that way when the *Merrimack* gets here!"

Reg Monroe, the nearest thing Alpha Flight had to an intellectual (she had taken a couple of engineering courses) shook her head, troubled. "Doesn't it bother anyone that Brighty's not afraid of that?"

"What's that supposed to mean, Reg?"

Reg held her arms crossed tightly under her breasts. "*Mack* was supposed to be here. Supposed to be here a fine while ago."

"Yeah. So *Mack*'s overdue." They shrugged. "*And?*"

"You mean nobody else gots the idea that Brighty expects the *Mack* to stay overdue for something like *ever*?"

12

"**W**HERE THE HELL ARE WE?"
"Somewhere in that vicinity, Captain." Navigation gave the unfamiliar coordinates. They didn't sound real.

Running. *Merrimack* had been running for days. The Roman Striker edging closer by the day.

Running out of days.

Apparently the only shot the Striker had with his force-field-piercing bullets was in *Merrimack*'s line of travel.

Merrimack could not afford to let the Striker get in front.

It was down to a footrace now. A race *Merrimack* would lose.

The Striker's smaller mass gave him a minutely higher threshold velocity. So he had been closing at a steady creep for days.

Black and gold. The Striker wore the infernal colors of *gens* Julian.

A Julian was not going to throw a race.

Merrimack needed to pull something out of her hat.

"So let's shed some mass," said Farragut.

"Captain, we can't possibly shed enough mass to make any possible difference."

"Can if we shed it in his face." He left the command platform to consult his engineers. He took the ladders. Farragut had no patience for lifts.

"Can we deploy a robotic arm out far enough to drop a limpet net in the Striker's path?" he proposed to his engineers.

Just dropping a bomb on the Striker would have no effect. Any simple explosive device would deflect upon contacting the nose of the Striker's force field before it had time to detonate. To counteract this effect, the limpet net had been designed to drape completely around the nose cone of an enemy ship's force field. The limpets would detonate against the ship's sides where the force field was maintained at lesser strength than to the fore.

"Captain, we are as good as hurtling down a concrete luge," his senior engineer answered. Kit was back on her feet, her middle still taped. "We can't extend the force field a micron, much less stick a pseudopod as far as we would need to get a net in the Striker's way."

"I don't intend to extend the force field at all. Can we stick a bare arm out the side?"

"Unprotected?"

"Why not? We're not exactly passing through asteroid fields out here."

The engineers consulted at some length. Ran the numbers. Came back, "Don't know."

Earthly instinct made one expect that something hung out the side of a vessel moving very fast would snap off or drag or flap. But this was extragalactic vacuum. There was no air. No drag. What inhibited the *Merrimack* from exceeding threshold velocity was her inertial field. Naked matter hadn't the same limitation.

Question was if poking the proposed mechanical arm through the force field was feasible. If so, dropping the net in the Striker's path should present no problem.

Whether a patterner could avoid the nets or withstand the limpets remained problematic.

"At the end of the day: I don't think we can destroy him that way, Captain," said Kit.

"Destroying him would be nice," Farragut allowed. "But I just need to slow him down. Would it slow him down?"

"If we can get something on him or make him twitch, hell, yeah. But he'll just make up the lost ground in time."

"Then we do it again. We can maintain a dead run longer than he can. If I can keep him from passing, we can run all year."

*   *   *

Calli Carmel had not been desperately surprised to be in confinement at Fort Eisenhower. Her experience on Palatine made her a natural subject of suspicion. But she had been investigated—exhaustively— several times in the past. Her past was an open book.

The U.S. intelligence community did not like the book.

During most of the last peace, Calli had grown up in the U.S. Embassy on Palatine, where her father had been a Marine guard.

When her parents' marriage was breaking up, Calli's father was reassigned to a place where he could not care for her, and Calli's mother—who only had Calli because she used to be in love with Calli's father—did not want her.

Calli's best friend, the ambassador's daughter, begged her parents to let Calli stay with them. She need not have begged because the Aartens dearly loved young Calli, and she was good company for their Martine.

Years later, when Martine Aarten left to study music in Salzburg, back on Earth, Calli stayed behind. Calli had inherited her mother's maternal drive and her father's pride in the military. She applied to the very elite Roman Imperial Military Institute on Palatine. She had made acquaintance with many influential Romans by then, and with the ambassador's sponsorship, she was accepted.

Her classmates included two of Caesar Magnus' offspring—Claudia and Romulus. Romulus fully expected to be the next emperor of Rome. Calli admired Caesar Magnus, but the nuts had fallen and rolled way out of shouting distance from the tree.

Friends she had many, and lovers a few, but she remained one step outside Roman society. You really weren't anyone in Rome without a *gens*. She had two offers of adoption, but that required renouncing her U.S. citizenship and she declined both.

By the time she graduated, the peace was already crumbling. Calli and her friends understood that their kisses good-bye meant that next time they met could very well be in battle. And understood that neither could expect any hesitation on the guns. Romans understood things like that.

Even some of her old friends thought—hoped—that Calli was a Roman mole. That she was just forbidden to tell them.

They would still have to shoot her if they came against her in battle.

Calli Carmel was pulling chin-ups in her solitary cell in Fort Eisenhower when a guard asked if she would see a visitor.

"As long as it's not General Pike," said Calli without breaking rhythm.

A very tall, very young, long-limbed reed of a man with a distinct starboard list, owing to the weighty satchel hanging from his shoulder, entered Calli's cell. A space lawyer. Good-looking in a scruffy way. Too young.

Calli peered at him from over the bar. "Does your mom know you're here?"

The young man let his satchel flump to the deck, straightened to full height minus an inch or two for sloppy posture. Said cheerfully, "I'll take that as a compliment."

Calli paused on the downstroke to hang from her bar like an ape. "No, I mean it. Are you old enough to drink?"

"I'm actually only a year younger than you are, Commander. I'm your attorney. Rob Roy Buchanan."

Calli let go the bar to accept his outstretched hand. "You *are* a drink. Do you know what the court got you into here?"

"The court didn't appoint me. I volunteered. Campaigned for it is more like it." His smile was genuine, disarming. "Okay, I begged." He needed a shave. The face fur didn't age him any.

"Look, Robby, you're cute as hell, but you better stay in the shallow end for your first case."

"I'm not that young, Commander."

"You said."

Sweat patched a vee down the front of her gray shirt. Rob Roy's opaque brown eyes made a quick foray there, then looked away, somewhere—anywhere—else. Dove into his satchel. "I wish you had let me on the case sooner."

She propped her hands on her hipbones. "There shouldn't *be* a case."

"I could have done something about that if I'd been at the hearing." Rob Roy glanced up from his excavation of his satchel.

"It wasn't a hearing. It was a barbecue."

"I know. I know. General Pike appointed himself case administrator." Rob Roy straightened up with a raft of papers. "Pike was Napoleon Bright's sponsor to VMI."

"Good," said Calli. That solved everything. "Demand he recuse himself." If the judge was biased, bounce him off the case. Simple.

"The time for that was before you ran him up the yardarm," said Rob Roy. "I made the request. He refused."

"The holes in Brighty's 'case' are big enough to shove Uranus through. Paxton's a purblind idiot not to see that."

"That attitude is not helping your case, Commander."

"It's not hurting it either, Robby. That man had the verdict in before he met me."

"So what's your strategy?"

"I don't have one, Robby. I assumed just because I was right, that rightness would be obvious to a purblind idiot."

"It *is* obvious. To me. But innocence is not enough. It seldom is. The hard—really hard—proof isn't here. For witnesses you've got a co-defendant, and a bunch of Marines who didn't see anything that we need them to have seen, and a brain-dead *Monitor.*"

"Get the charges dismissed because they're based solely on one man's say-so."

Rob Roy winced. "But there is the point of damnation. The one man. Your innocence comes only at the cost of Napoleon Bright's ruin. You are guilty because, in the eyes of Paxton Pike, you *must* be guilty. The alternative is unthinkable to him."

"Then he has to learn to think harder."

Rob Roy brought his hands together before his lips as if praying, thinking. Then countered with a hypothetical, "Commander, if you asked John Farragut to swallow a whale without a shred of evidence to convince him that he should, would he? On your say-so alone?"

"Don't mention John Farragut and Paxton Pike in the same breath, Robby." Of course Farragut would.

"General Pike is suffering from the selective vision of partisanship. The old school in which you back your boy right or wrong. The wrong is apparent, but he's your boy and he's right because he's your boy."

Calli had to accede to his line of logic. She'd seen it before. "That kind of thing is rampant on Palatine."

"Well, it's not unknown here either. Men see what they want to see. What they need to see."

"Leaves Pike with a very flimsy story. It's propped up with spit. It can't hold up in a court-martial."

"Oh, it's pure argle bargle, but it'll make haggis of our defense," said Rob Roy. "We got nothin'."

"I'm still innocent until proven guilty."

"No, you're not. Because your innocence means Napoleon Bright's guilt. When the verdict is in, either you or Napoleon Bright has to be a treacherous monster. The truth is one or the other. I know which side the truth is standing on, but when push comes to shove, you don't want to be standing by an air lock, Mr. Carmel. As for the other judges, they will come down on either you or Napoleon Bright based on the evidence, however thin."

"Thin? There isn't any."

"Bright's argument is based on missing evidence. He's making the missingness strategic. It'll stand because Pike has to make it stand."

"He's case administrator! *He* shouldn't be in this at all. You sure this isn't your first case, Robby?"

"Arrogance kills. People are arrogant in the Deep End."

She was about to say something else, something about General Pike and his arrogance, then did a double take. Realized, "Me." This child-faced lawyer had just called her arrogant. "You mean me."

"Especially you."

She sat down. "I am not participating in any more kangaroo proceedings until I subpoena witnesses."

He sat down next to her on the spartan cot. Opened a notescreen. "Who do you want?"

"John Farragut."

Rob Roy Buchanan rolled his cute brown eyes. "He'd be my first choice. He's not here."

"I'll wait for him."

"How long?"

"Till doomsday."

"General Pike will let you do that." He eyed the confines of her cell. The best that could be said for the small, stark, unprivate space was that it was clean.

Calli rose, jumped up to grab her chin-up bar. "Then you'd better bring me some books, Robby."

*   *   *

The Striker gained ground by the hour as *Merrimack*'s engineers designed and built the robotic rig by which to hoist the limpet net into the Striker's path.

They ran the numbers over and over, calculating what effect pushing the robot arm out through *Mack*'s inertial field at threshold velocity would do to the ship's integrity. *Attempting* to calculate, more like. The physics of *threshold* were imperfectly understood. Having no hard numbers, the engineers got no hard answer. The proposed procedure had never quite been done before.

With the contraption installed and ready to deploy came the moment of decision: go/no go.

Captain Farragut turned it back on the engineers. "I'll put it to y'all first: Do you want to wait to be executed or do you want to try to escape out a tunnel you dug which might cave in on you?"

Tunnel. They nodded to each other. Yeah. Definitely. Tunnel was good.

Kit nodded before the captain. "Tunnel. I like tunnel. I think."

"Tunnel's got my vote." Farragut winked a bright blue eye, ever cheerful facing a dare. He called it: "It's a go."

Glenn Hamilton summoned the ship to battle stations out of the edgy, monotonous high alert in which they had existed for days. The waiting was over. It was time to live or die.

The robotic arm pushed a counterphase shaft incrementally outward through the field's phase layers. Tonal changes in the field had an ill sound. The engines rolled a low, rocky thunder.

It was in the nature of threshold velocity that it required constant acceleration to maintain it. So the *Merrimack*'s six engines were already running at capacity. Had been so for days. A notice over the intercom from the systems techs warned of an engine spike. The engineers acknowledged. Slowed the deployment of the robotic arm.

The robotic arm with the limpet net approached the outer shell of the force field.

Came a moment in which no one breathed. The robotic arm, the limpet net, extended through *Merrimack*'s inertial field.

Lights dipped. The deck dropped. Stomachs lifted toward mouths. Ears popped. "Balk!" Systems reported. "We have engine balk! We are on auto shutdown!"

Shit! "Override!"

"Too late!"

The Striker shot past.

Her engines down, *Merrimack* hurtled forward on inertia only—which meant she fell off threshold velocity.

"Striker's in front!" Tactical reported.

"Sound blast alarm. Prepare for impact."

13

TIME PASSES SLOWLY FOR those who wait. What seemed like days to the traveler near to light speed could be years to those at home.

It made no sense for Farragut to travel as slowly as light, for it took extreme energy to do so, but traveling near light speed could be the only reason *Merrimack* was taking forever to get to Fort Ike. While Calli waited.

She had been speaking flippantly when she told Rob Roy to bring her books. But he brought them, and she read them. Interesting choices. He checked in on her often. Was good company, intelligent, cheerful, and easy on the eyes.

On New Year's Eve, he bundled into her cell, bright-eyed, merry, and smelling strongly of Scotch. "I tried to bring you a drink," he said, slumped on her cot, pulling an empty plastic glass from the deep pocket of his long trench coat. "They were searching visitors. So I drank yours, too." He tugged out another empty glass. "Happy New Year."

"Happy New Year, Robby."

"Don't call me Robby."

She nodded, all right. She licked a drop of Scotch out of one of the glasses.

Rob Roy's eyes widened at the motion of her tongue. He floundered to his feet and blundered toward the door. "I gotta go." Called for the guard.

Calli caught his collar before the guard came to let him out. Said low, "Happy New Year, Rob Roy." Feathered a kiss on his scruffy cheek.

In the seconds it took to bring the engines back online, Farragut had time to wonder why he was not dead. He belayed any proposal of evasive maneuvers. Something was wonderfully wrong with this situation.

Senior Engineer Kit Kittering, moving carefully, checked the ship's integrity and cried, "Where's the net!"

Half the robotic arm stuck out there, severed, limpet net gone. It should still be attached. It was not.

"Where did it go?" Kit cried. "It's not as if it could break off in the *wind*!"

"We *got* him?" Farragut dared suggest, incredulous. "I thought a patterner would have seen that coming. We hung that net out right in front him. Where is he?"

"Ahead of us," Marcander Vincent reported from tactical. "Straight-line course. Close parallel to ours. No course deviation. But slower. He's fallen off threshold." The specialist turned round from his console to meet the captain's gaze. "Sir, could he have flamed out, too?"

Farragut gave a baffled shrug. Ordered, "Hell, if he's moving slower, *get us in front of him*!"

His techs scrambled to obey. *Merrimack* edged forward, closing the gap, klick by slow, wary klick.

The Striker gave no signs of aggression, or even of awareness.

Pulling alongside, a scant twelve meters separating them, the *Mack*'s sensors captured a clear image of the enemy. The limpet net encased the Striker's nose, all limpets detonated. But the Striker's force field remained intact.

Merrimack deployed a pair of snuffers to fly up the Striker's exhausts and send its engines into shutdown.

The missiles met no resistance, and the Roman ship's force field vanished.

Merrimack delicately hooked the Striker, without actually bringing it inside her own force field, in case the Striker should be running an auto-destruct routine.

Farragut suited up to join the boarding party, against his acting XO's protest. "Captain, you can't," Glenn Hamilton said, standing in his path, drawing herself up to her full height—fully a foot shorter than the captain. "This is a trap."

"Hamster, you've got to be kidding. This wolf is hosed." And he spoke into the intercom on the back of his hand, "Mo, join us."

"Aye, sir," the medical officer, Mohsen Shah, responded. "I am being there."

The techs established soft dock, and forced the Striker's hatch for the boarding party.

Inside the Striker's air lock, all seemed well. The emergency power was on. Atmospherics read normal.

But sensors did not read the stench. Helmets off, the boarding party knew what the sensors had not told them. The pilot was dead. Dead for a while, from the smell of it. Air scrubbers kept the ammonia levels within tolerances, but it left enough fetor of human waste to wrinkle the nose and the whole face with it. "Oh, for Jesus."

They found the pilot at his station, dead, but not entirely. His body draped over the back of his seat, arched backward, sunken eyes turned up in a dried stare. They might have been blue. His mouth had fallen open. Dried blood caked under his nose. He looked like he might have once been as fair-skinned as TR Steele, but his skin was blue now.

Cables protruded from the back of his neck, his wrists. The cables connected him to the console that was awake and blinking, waiting instruction.

Mo Shah detected the faint pulse of the comatose, but no brain waves.

The medical officer's hands motioned abortive starts round the cables, afraid to unhook the man from the machine. Mo Shah had taken an oath: *Do no harm.* "I am having no idea how to be helping this man."

Farragut read the signs, the blue-black fingernails, asked, "How long do you figure he's been like this?"

"I will be guessing seventy-two to ninety-six ship hours," said Dr. Shah.

"Four days!" Farragut cried. "I have been running from a fried vegetable for a half a week?" And immediately to the corpselike Roman, with a comradely pat on his emaciated shoulder, "Sorry, Lucius. Nothing personal." For all Romans were Lucius in the slang of wartime. Then he murmured, "What *is* your name?" Reeled up the Roman's dog tags. The chain left a beaded black bruise imprinted on his pasty blue skin. "Septimus. Mo, take Septimus here to sick bay."

"What to be doing about . . . ?" Mo Shah trailed off, faced with all the cables. "I could be killing him."

Farragut pulled the plugs from the Roman's neck. "*I* could be killing him." He tossed the cable ends away from him. Cleared for the doctor. "Do what you can for him."

Back aboard his own *Merrimack,* as the battleship slowed for turn-around, John Farragut gazed at the perfect blackness of nowhere.

His acting exec, Lieutenant Hamilton came to his side, spoke faintly the understatement, "We are somewhat behind schedule, sir."

Farragut nodded. "Calli's going to think I stood her up."

"That would be a first for her."

And Farragut challenged Glenn to a game of squash. It was well past the hour for him to be turning in, but John Farragut never slept after battle.

They had not played together in a long time. Used to be they played every day. That was before he noticed how pretty she was.

The score was more even than it would have been had Farragut kept his eye on the ball instead of his opponent. Came down to it, he thought he'd salvaged a win when he hammered a rocket off the front wall, sent it sailing across the length of the court to strike high on the back wall. Then he got to watch little Hamster try to muscle it off the back wall and just hope it had enough to reach the front wall.

The little green ball sailed weakly the length of the court, losing altitude fast. It was not going to make it.

At the last moment, the ship's gravity bobbled. The deck felt like it was sinking. The ball whimpered the last yard to touch the front and drop in a wall-hugging dribble to the deck without giving Farragut the least chance at a return.

Glenn cried out, shock and glee, a lot of yesses.

Farragut howled his betrayal, "*Merri-Merri-Merri-Mack!* How could you do this to me?" He pressed his hands to a wall, talking to his ship.

Glenn winked, with a little swagger. "Hey, *Mack* and me." She crossed her fingers tight. "Like this."

"Are you done?"

"Oh, *no,*" Glenn laughed. She jumped up and slapped the front wall. "High five, *Mack!*"

"Hamster, you can't high anything."

"Patrick, are you going to let him insult me like that?"

Farragut turned. Up in the gallery stood her husband. Didn't know how long he'd been there. Dr. Patrick Hamilton.

Good-looking in an artistic way. Women said so, as long as he kept his mouth shut. He had great intelligence, which did not include common sense. Patrick Hamilton was the kind of man who, when single, always got a first date but seldom got a second.

As tall, but half as wide, as the captain, Patrick Hamilton was in no shape to avenge John Farragut's insults to his wife.

Patrick Hamilton spoke to his wife, "Did you ask him?"

Farragut assumed he was "him," and turned to Glenn to receive the question.

Glenn looked a little embarrassed. Tried to put Patrick off, "We've been playing."

"I can see that."

"Ask me what?" said Farragut.

Glenn tried to wave it off. "Later."

"Ask me what?"

Backed into it, Lieutenant Glenn Hamilton drew herself up into as much professional dignity as she could manage in gray sweats, size five sneakers, a damp headband, and frayed ponytail. "Can I keep Calli's job?"

"No."

Glenn gave a resigned nod. Expected that. Sure wished she could have chosen her own moment to ask. It might have gone better. Looked up at Patrick. "He said no."

Patrick asked, "Why?" An edge of demand in it.

"Patrick," Glenn tried to hush him, but Patrick said, "No. I should like to know why."

Glenn masked chagrin well but still looked like she could just die. Patrick Hamilton refused to know how things were done or not done in the U.S. Navy.

Farragut spoke to Glenn, "I'll recommend you for your own command if you want."

Shut Patrick up pretty well. Lieutenants were often given command of their own small ships. The kind of ship that had no use for a xenolinguist.

"Think about it," said Farragut. Not sure whether he was hoping she would go or stay.

He looped a towel round his neck, heading for the showers, when Patrick called down again, not letting go. "She's done a great job as acting exec. She can do the job. Why not let her stay in it?"

Farragut turned blue eyes up. Fought the impulse to ask Glenn what the hell she saw in this guy. Fact was, she saw enough in Patrick Hamilton to marry him, and that was a done deed. Had even let him hang his name on her.

And fact was that Glenn Hamilton hadn't the service years and she knew it. Could not fault her for asking. Humble just didn't get the job done.

Fine officer. Just not ready. She was twenty-six. A strong professional twenty-six, but command of a ship this size wanted a longer perspective and more brutally hard knocks than twenty-six years could give her.

Farragut answered Patrick, "You *do* know that I still have an XO? Calli Carmel is still exec of this ship. Lordy, Ham, wait till the body's cold."

The drums wove into Calli's nightmare. The sound became the death march, drumming in a firing squad. That hideous cadence that had become a staple of horror movies. The sound of impending execution.

She writhed, swimming toward consciousness. She was asleep; she suddenly knew that. This was not real.

Still she heard the drums, and that confused her.

The awful last roll sounded, snapped to silence. She could have sworn she heard the fateful orders. Not the words precisely, but the traditional vocal intonation, distinct and recognizable as the drums: Ready. Aim.

The shot. Bolted her up in her cot. *That was real!*

She was on her feet instantly, yelling at the monitors: "Get me my lawyer!"

Rob Roy Buchanan was there too soon. Meant he was already on his way before Calli had started yelling.

"It's out of control, Commander." Rob Roy dropped his overladen satchel. He looked like he'd slept in his coat. "The wheels of justice have fallen off. It's time to call in markers. Biggest ones you've got. Who do you know?"

"Uh," she pushed back her long loose hair, gathering sleep-fogged wits. "Ambassador Van Aarten. But I can't ask him to—"

"I already called him. He's on his way. Who else?"

"My God." The strangeness, the speed, collided with her nightmare. Left her dizzy. "Rob, they *shot* someone. I heard a firing squad!"

He nodded. "You did. 'Fubar' doesn't describe what's happening here."

"Who?" Calli demanded.

"Who what?" said Rob Roy, not understanding the question.

"Who did they execute!" Calli shouted at him.

"Lieutenant Commander Medina."

"No," she said. She believed him. She just did not accept it. "No. It's insane."

"Good description for it." Rob Roy nodded. "On the side of the angels, they exonerated your Flight Leader Hazard Sewell. He hadn't the rank to be held criminally liable for following orders of a superior officer."

"Mine," said Calli, hollow. "My orders."

Abashed, Rob Roy was forced to confirm, "Yours."

A tremor moved her long fingers. She was astonished to see the motion. Astonished at her own terror. "They killed Jorge." It was unreal. Yet suddenly terribly real. It sank in past all her veils of certainty. She was in the hands of murderous idiots.

Rob Roy gathered himself for the rest of the news. Calli heard the difficulty in the silence. Finally, he spilled it, "They're separating out the charge of treason and moving up your court-martial for mutiny."

"What about my witnesses?"

"Pike decided Farragut's testimony is immaterial to the mutiny charge."

The words that followed sounded odd coming from a pretty woman. As executive officer of a battleship, Calli knew a lot of them.

"I told him that," said Rob Roy. "Verbatim, I think. I have a contempt cite to show for it." Produced it for her.

"How can Farragut's testimony be immaterial!"

"Pike says it doesn't matter whether Farragut gave you command of *Monitor* or not. Pike's reasoning—if you can call what's happening inside Pike's head reasoning—is that Farragut had no authority to give Commander Bright's ship—his words, don't look at me like that—to you, and you should have known it."

"I still have the right to subpoena witnesses."

"Not when they've been pronounced dead."

Calli made her fingers stop their trembling. They extended long, still, and straight. "I have been arrogant."

"Yes, sir."

"John's not dead, you know," she said, quiet, certain.

"I have to believe that," said Rob Roy Buchanan.

She looked up at her baby-faced lawyer, comforted by his presence, grateful. "How did you know to call Ambassador Van Aarten?" Suddenly she wanted badly to see Van Aarten again. He had been a second father to her. Thoughts of him were warm as a blanket by the hearth on a snowy evening.

Rob Roy answered, "He seems to have been your foster father de facto, if not legally."

"He was. But how did you know that? How do you know so much about me?"

"I'm a fan of yours, Commander. I tripped over you while I was studying Farragut's career."

"Why were you studying John? A case?"

"No." Rob Roy stood up regally with a Napoleonic pose, though he was probably close to twice Napoleon's height. "Commander Carmel, you are looking at the greatest military strategist ever to captain an armchair."

"Ah, one of those." She had to smile. If only to keep from tears.

"I'll have to tell you sometime how *I* would have won the battle of Corindahlor Bridge."

"Corindahlor Bridge was a victory for our side," Calli pointed out to him. "Or is your armchair on the Roman side?"

"No. I'm on the American side. But, you see, *I* would've won it without making martyrs of the Roman Tenth. Big mistake that part. Alamo. Masada. Thermopylae. Corindahlor. Did more for the losers than the victors."

"So why did such a brilliant military mind not try a military career for real?"

"I'm in the Navy."

"You're a lawyer."

"Know your strengths. Know your limits. As a soldier, I make a fine lawyer."

"Then win my case," she told him, dead serious.

"I will. I have to. I'm not going to lose you." Stopped, amended quickly. "This one. The case. I meant to say I'm not going to lose this one."

"No, you didn't."

"No. I didn't."

General Pike came out of his seat as if ejected when the report came in that *Merrimack* had been sighted on approach to Fort Eisenhower.

"Destroy her," said Napoleon Bright.

General Pike snapped right round.

"It's a Trojan Horse," Commander Bright said to Pike's demanding, startled stare. "We won't get another chance. You know as well as I do, we have to take her out right now."

General Pike regarded his protégé a long moment. The kind of moment as exists near light speed. The moment seemed eternal, though it was only a moment.

14

NEVER SHY OF DRAMATICS, John Farragut kissed the station deck upon safe arrival at Fort Eisenhower, sprang to his feet, clapped the grit from his hands, spat, asked lightly of the first person he saw, "Is Calli still here?"

The wide eyes he met belonged to a dockworker, who dropped his maintenance bot. "Captain Farragut!"

Farragut nodded acknowledgment. Yes, he was Captain Farragut.

"You're dead!"

"Oh? How do I look?" He grinned. Did not expect an answer to that one, so he repeated his first question. "Commander Calli Carmel. Did she get away?"

"Oh, no, sir. She didn't get away. They shot her."

The look on Farragut's face vaporized the nerves of anyone in his path. Did not abate even when he learned the dockworker was mistaken; the guns the man had heard had been for Lieutenant Commander Jorge Medina.

Calli had been released. An order was out for Commander Bright's arrest.

They caught him. But not before Brighty hit John Farragut in the fist with his face.

The stationmaster, one General Pike, ordered John Farragut to his office. Railed at him with a spray that set Farragut to blinking at every "s" and "p" and "t." Demanded to know: "What did you do with the patterner!"

Farragut blinked. "Sir?"

"The pilot of this ship!" The image of "this ship" showed on all the displays in the general's office—in section, in 3D, at all angles. This ship was the Roman Striker which Farragut had delivered to Fort Eisenhower. The little ship that had nearly taken *Merrimack*. "Where is the pilot!"

"Oh. Him," said Farragut. "I bundled him up and dropped him for Red Cross delivery."

That despite Roman insistence that the man would die if detached from his ship. Perhaps he would, but Farragut had already done the detaching, and had no intention of delivering that ship back into enemy hands.

"I suppose you gave over his dog tags, too," said Pike sourly.

"No." Farragut produced the tags. "I don't think Rome's going to have any difficulty identifying that boy."

The general glanced at the tags before he clamped his hand shut round them in a tight fist. "Septimus," he snarled. "Suggests there's at least six more of those Satan-built things."

"And it's way past time someone told me what Satan built," Farragut suggested.

"We would know *exactly* what a patterner is, if *you* hadn't handed this one back to the enemy!"

"I gave a critically wounded soldier to the Red Cross," said Farragut. "In accordance with conventions of space warfare."

"Yes, yes, yes," Pike waved away the annoying rote. "You gave up covert technology along with him!"

"The components were not exactly removable," said Farragut. "I would not stoop to that."

Pike stiffened. "You suggest I am stooping?"

"Are you, sir?"

Pike was on his feet, vibrating. "I don't know why others think the sun rises and sets on your ass, but mind you, Captain, that opinion is not shared here!" And tore the bark off Farragut's tree for the next five minutes.

At the end, General Pike said stiffly, in dismissal, "You will deliver a copy of your debriefing to my replacement."

Replacement? "You're being promoted?" Farragut asked.

"Are you trying to be funny?"

Farragut's eyes were wide in confusion. "Was I funny?"

"Not in the least."

"I just wanted to know if congratulations were in order."

"Get out."

"General Pike? I have a CIA agent in my brig. Could you arrange for her to be collected—?"

"Out!"

Farragut learned only later—sitting with Calli and her very young lawyer in Mad Bear O's space bar—that General Pike had been promoted below the bottom of the galactic birdcage for his role in Jorge Medina's rushed execution. Only because Pike had realized his mistake in time not to open fire on *Merrimack* was he not drummed out of the Fleet Marine altogether.

There were no nonhumans in Mad Bear O's. Not that they were excluded; they chose not to come. Different species tended to socialize with their own kind when out to relax. Each had its own idea of what constituted fun, relaxation, flirtation, beauty, music, stink, or noise. Where species mixed, you knew business was being conducted.

John Farragut, Calli Carmel, and Rob Roy Buchanan were here to get drunk to the strains of a jazz trio improvising in a chromatic scale.

Calli sang the blues for Napoleon Bright. She had tried to get him considered a med case. But Pike had slapped a certification of perfect health on him. Not the sort of official record you can elbow into the annihilator. Therefore, Brighty was officially sane and fully responsible for everything he did.

Calli rattled the ice cubes in her Scotch. "In the Roman army the sentence for giving false evidence is bludgeoning to death."

Rob Roy shooed a fat little beetbird off the table. "This isn't Rome."

"Yeah." Calli looked away, out the clearports, to the lights of ships coming and going. "That's why we're going to shoot him."

An expectant snare drumroll ended in a brief hesitation and a leaden thump.

Thrrrrrrrrrr *stomp*! Thrrrrrrrrrrr *stomp*!

The sound carried through the hull, through all the decks and bulks of the station. Hideous. Inescapable.

That menacing thrrrrrrrr *stomp*!

The firing squad waited, expressionless. They did not look entirely human, but Fleet law mandated they be human. And provided for one of the weapons to fire blanks so that any of those executioners might hide behind the hope that he had not killed one of his own.

The drummers advanced like windup soldiers. Thrrrrrrrr *stomp*! You could not see their eyes under the shiny black brims of their caps.

The witnesses looked unhappily human. Stern. Uncomfortable.

Brighty advanced in cuffs and hobbles. Unrepentant. He showed more anger than fear. He shot a cold black unwavering gaze Calli's way.

She did not flinch.

Her lawyer stood behind her, looking like a boy dressed up for church. General Pike had mandated, if he was going to attend a military execution, Mr. Rob Roy Buchanan had damn well better get a haircut. And a shave.

Rob Roy's uniform was perfectly tailored to his tall lank frame, perfectly clean, creased like new—because he never wore it—but Rob Roy had a boy's knack for squirming within his clothes so as to look perfectly sloppy mere moments after passing inspection.

At Calli's insistence, Rob Roy had made an eleventh-hour bid for a stay of execution on grounds that the prisoner could be under the influence of an unknown Roman contaminant.

A quick med review found nothing. No stay could be granted. But an autopsy was promised.

When the moment came, Brighty refused the blindfold. A sound like a groan or a sigh came from somewhere—from the witnesses, the drummers, or the firing squad, you couldn't tell.

It was a dare: If you are going to shoot me, you're going to have to look me in the eyes.

The drums silenced just long enough for you to feel relief at the cessation of that infernal thrrrrrrrr *stomp*! When the drums started up again, it was with what someone called the death rattle.

A command passed to the sergeant at arms. Came the litany of the end: Ready. Aim.

Brighty stared down the guns, then pivoted his head slightly to fix a lizard gaze on Calli.

If he were looking for her to crack, he would die disappointed. She showed only regal professionalism. Looked him in the eye without faltering.

Had anyone been looking her way they might have seen her hand steal behind her back, palm open, and accept the hand that slid into it—her lawyer's—and squeeze at the final command.

PART FOUR

Wolf Star

15

FORT THEODORE ROOSEVELT WAS huge. Its array of lights made the glitter of Fort Eisenhower seem provincial and dim. The star city that had grown up around Fort Ted sprawled wider than some solar systems, more populous than many colonial worlds.

The space fort lay only eighty light-years from Earth, in the direction of the galactic rim, just north of the galactic equator in the constellation of Auriga.

The Wolf Star—which was not Wolf 359 and not the third closest star to Sol—lay two hundred light-years from Earth in nearly the opposite direction from Fort Ted. You could see the Wolf Star from Earth, south of the galactic equator in the constellation of the Southern Crown.

Only two hundred sixty light-years separated the Wolf Star from Fort Ted. The Wolf Star was close enough to be a menace.

The Wolf Star's inhabited planet was properly called Palatine. It was also known as Rome, as it was the seat of the resurgent Roman Empire. The names were interchangeable. Rome. Palatine. But no one ever called its citizens Palatineans. They were Romans. They were also called wolves, lupes, and countless derogatory terms, but never Palatineans.

The Roman Empire stretched across the galactic southern plane of Near space, as far as the nations of Earth expanded across the northern plane, each trying to outflank the other.

Rome had the edge toward the galactic hub in Near space. Several Earth nations from the Asian Pacific had effectively cut off Roman *and* U.S. expansion toward the rim.

Altogether, humankind had spread over less than one-eighth of the galaxy. Expansion was somewhat self-limiting. The U.S. had not been able to hold a colony at two hundred light-years distance. At fifteen hundred light-years, most nations could consider their colonies temporary holdings. Any people it took you two months to reach were not going to pay your taxes or obey your laws. That was human nature.

The Wolf Star kept a tighter grip on its possessions and had spread its control farther—and thinner—than Earth. Only one hundred fifty years old, the Empire was vast. At first independence, Rome had launched an imperial binge that spread its reign to four hundred planets. Unlike the nations of Earth, Rome would flag any planet it got to first, inhabited or not, and did not hesitate to incorporate alien civilizations into its Empire.

To populate its colonies, Romans bred like guppies, leaving their zygotes in incubators, so that many Romans had only Rome to call their father and their mother.

The soldiers of Rome's mighty Legions numbered in the millions, including aliens, child troops, and automatons. Rome's mechanized fleets, the killer bots, were beyond U.S. counting.

The biggest force ever seen in one place had been at Rome's sesquicentennial, when fifty Legions of foot soldiers marched before the Capitoline—the mountain-sized imperial complex on Palatine—while far overhead, fleets of warships flew in precise formation before Caesar's spaceborne residence, a mountainous structure nearly as massive as the Capitoline, called Fortress Aeyrie. The gold work on Fortress Aeyrie was all real. The blue-white fire spouting from the gold griffin acroteri was hologram, as were the eagles soaring in the hologramic clouds around the gleaming fortress. When in orbit, Fortress Aeyrie's lights were visible from the planet's surface even in daylight. The Praetorian Guard, Caesar's formidable elite, kept a highly visible presence around both residences.

The Praetorian Guard traditionally wore Caesar's own colors. Caesar Magnus—born Ulixes Julian Eugenus—was a Julian, so the guard ships shone black and gold.

The show of force had astonished everyone, even the citizens and slaves of Rome.

The Wolf Star's astronomical proximity made the United States' Fort Ted the most heavily fortified place in the known universe. A siege of Fort Theodore Roosevelt would win Rome nothing but the forever quagmire of a war of infinite attrition.

Flight Sergeant Kerry Blue did not see the approach. Knew better than to try to look. You never saw anything on approach to either fort coming through the Shotgun. They shut you down to minimal life support, turned off your lights, enclosed your whole ship in a gargantuan reflective foil, which made you look like a titanic popcorn bag. Then you popped.

They say you felt nothing, because displacement was instantaneous, but Kerry always did. You popped into another giant foil bag of nothing. You didn't even make a thunderclap, the way you did when displacing into an atmosphere. They pulled the foil away from your ship and, glory be, there was Fort Teddy taking your breath away.

Kerry and the Marines had made the trip in a standard transport. The majestic battleships *Merrimack* and *Monitor* had been bagged and dragged through the Shotgun dark as dead carp. Usually the battleships' arrival attracted a lot of attention, but *Merrimack* and *Monitor* had been smuggled in quiet this time. Most denizens did not even know the big ships were here.

The Marine transport ferried Kerry's company through the historic district of Fort Ted, past clusters of antique stations that still revolved, past the gaudy districts of Chinatown and Ecstacy, and the blue ocean jewel sphere of Vwakikikik, more often called Squidville. The Marines stared through cupped hands pressed to the clearports at grand hotels and casinos of the Starry Starry Way and the transparent-sided Eros Hotel where lovers coupled in the starlight. This was a high accident area among ferryboat traffic.

Cowboy and Dak howled to their own transport pilot: Stop, stop, stop, let me out.

Cackled at their cleverness. As if every bunch of Marines to pass Eros did not yell the same thing.

Passing within visual range of a Vwakikikikik ship, Cowboy planted his full moon in the transport porthole. The transport received an immediate message from the Vwakikikikik ship, and the pilot snarled back at Cowboy as he ran the message through the translator, "You get me written up, Marine, and I'll have you serving with the squid!"

But the Vwakikikikik message only requested the name of the vision of loveliness glimpsed through the U.S. transport's sixth starboard side porthole.

No one ever saw Cowboy look that shocked. He'd been sent up by a squid.

"Squids got humor!"

He was really, really impressed. Tried to get the pilot to send back, "Her name is Dak," but the pilot was not playing.

Finally the transport docked at a hybrid station in the old town, a military core that had sprouted a lot of civilian appendages—shops, service centers, ferry docks.

The cavernous arrival concourse was a milling hive of beings coming and going, or just sitting in the middle of the deck.

Reg Monroe, carrying her few belongings, squinted at the thing parked in her path. "Is he doing what I think he's doing?"

A big hairy musinot had plopped itself in the center of the concourse, just a'strumming on his old banjo.

Cowboy Carver clapped his hand over his eyes as he veered around the musinot. "Oh, *jeez*, bucko, put on some dignity!"

Kerry was staring in a different direction, pointing, "Arrans!"

Hazard Sewell followed her stare. "Glory be, so they are."

Recognized them for their very tall willowy females clad to the eyes in soft robes, and the shorter red-brown males with their upright manes.

Knew them from the Myriad.

A cluster of three million stars in the Deep End where Roman expansion pushed into U.S. space. What a Pandora's box that had been.

Shuddered to remember *Merrimack*'s hopeless stand against two full Legions and one wicked little Striker. Felt guilty for feeling grateful for the event that spared *Merrimack* and resulted in *this*.

Here was a shuffling train of evacuees. The Arrans were to be relocated to the dead Planet Xi. Arran plants and animals were even now being transplanted to Xi with its newly restored atmosphere. The relocation was an insanely huge undertaking. But the project had a certain romantic logic and the kind of humanitarian idealism that money sticks to, so funding had, for once, not been a problem. There had been an opposition by those who did not want the ancient site disturbed, but the detractors had been outshouted by the supporters and by the simple fact that thirty million refugees had to go somewhere.

Cowboy ducked and leaned, trying to see if he could make out any sign of breasts on the females. Dared Twitch to go feel one and find out.

Just because Twitch did not talk well did not mean he was stupid. He suggested Cowboy go back and help the musinot.

The Marines stopped at a cross-course, trying to navigate through all the distractions. Cowboy turned full round to follow the progress of a truly spectacular, tall woman with eleven miles of legs and a curtain of shining chestnut hair, in the company of a sloppy, sort-of attractive, very young man. "Hey! Isn't that Mr. Carmel's lawyer?"

Reg Monroe squinted. "Yeah. That's Rob Roy Buchanan." Wondering why he'd made the jump from Fort Ike to Fort Ted.

Dak looked, too. "Yeah. That's Mr. Carmel's lawyer. And look what he caught! That's some hot—holy mother—*that's Mr. Carmel*!"

No one was accustomed to seeing Commander Carmel in mufti. With her hair down and her skirt up, she was nearly unrecognizable.

Cowboy called, "Hey! Mr. Carmel!"

Her head turned. Saw a line of male Marines raising salutes.

You didn't salute indoors, but they were just impressed as all hell.

Carmel just shook her head, a little annoyed, a little amused. Walked on.

She was no sooner out of sight when you'da sworn someone barked *Eyes right!* for the way all those jarheads snapped round in unison whiplash in the other direction.

What spun 'em round was Hot Trixi Allnight, star of the dreambox. The interactive neuron ticklers activated all the appropriate nerve centers and made long black nights passable on deep space runs of months on end. Experiences in the dreambox programs—the expensive ones anyway—were nearly indistinguishable from real encounters. Only "nearly" because a virtual babe never called you a creep and demanded you take her home right now. The Navy provided its deep running battleships with the best.

All these men knew the touch, taste, smell, and weight of Trixi Allnight, the soft buffet of her peppermint breath, the tickle of her blonde hair. The timbre of her soprano moans.

And here she was in the flesh.

The male Marines were jumping like crazed rabbits. Cowboy urgled: "It's Trixi! It's *Trixi!* And—" seeing Dak beside him, "—what the *hell* are you doing in my dreambox!"

Dak grinned stupidly. "We ain't hooked into no dreambox, Toto. We are in for real Kansas."

Of course Trixi had never seen any of them before in her life, but she was a consummate professional. She made eye contact, smiled as if delightedly surprised to see them again, and blew kisses. "Oh! Hel*lo!*" as if she knew them. Intimately.

She singled out awestruck Twitch Fuentes and gave her kittenish nose a wrinkle. "Oh, and *you. You* were *so* good!"

A shining red glow transformed Twitch, as if her saying so made it all real. The others hooted and heckled. Cowboy and Dak pummeled Twitch back to reality.

Carly Delgado and Kerry Blue, whom most of them knew well, really well, stood ignored like a pair of wet muddy boots after a long trek on a dirt world.

Carly curled a hard lip, said to Kerry, "Plastic mama ain't got nothin' on you, *chica linda.*"

Kerry appreciated Carly's effort there, but still scoffed, comparing herself to the pale-pink, fluffy-blonde confection, "Oh, yeah. Right."

"Yeah. Right," someone passing behind her corrected firmly, *not* scoffing. Sounded like he meant it.

Kerry turned, but the only man back there was Colonel Steele, quick striding away, well down the concourse, and it couldn't have been him.

Though he wasn't gawking at Hot Trixi Allnight.

Naval engineers were in a panicked rush to devise a refit that could return *Merrimack* and *Monitor* to service as soon as possible, when Admiral Mishindi announced, "We got a break. Palatine has sued for a truce."

"No!" Calli cried hard on the echoes of John Farragut's roar, "No!"

The admiral regarded the pair indulgently as a hunter might two favored hounds. "And the president and the JC have accepted."

Bringing another loud chorus of language, the kind Hazard Sewell did not like.

Admiral Mishindi weathered their outburst mildly. "I sympathize. But we need this."

"No, we don't!" said Farragut. "Admiral, we *don't*. We just got a hole blown out of our defensive net. They got our codes. They got *my* res sig, they turned two RBSs into boat anchors—"

"RBSs?" Mishindi looked to Calli for translation.

"Really Big Ships," Calli supplied.

"—They've got these cyborg patterner things that can drive pea holes through a full force field. And *they* want a truce? That means they're hurt worse than we are. We have to press the advantage now!"

"With what, Captain Farragut? You haven't the *Merrimack* to fight with. You propose to throw rocks?"

"I'll throw turnips if I have to."

"Oh. That could work."

"Just let me fight! We can't have a truce now! They'll use the time to build their Catapult and make copies of *Monitor*-class battleships to use against us!"

"And they've been caught committing war crimes," Calli added.

The report from the autopsy Calli ordered on Napoleon Bright had come in. The exam had been a Sargasson one, the kind that found things that instruments of human make could miss. The seaweedy alien race had a gift for sensing wrongness, even among beings as altogether different as humans were to them.

The Sargasson had detected cells within Brighty's brain that were "not right." A DNA analysis of the identified cells produced a near match to Brighty's code.

"Near?" Calli had said.

Near was another word for *not*. What the Sargasson found turned out to be cloned matter within Brighty's head. Dead and decaying, the cells' function could not be divined.

Calli had then ordered a Sargasson autopsy of Matthew Forshaw, but the area of Forshaw's brain that corresponded to the area of Brighty's corrupted cells was gone. It was the part of the head which the late captain's suicidal shot had blown away.

And Calli had to wonder if some subconscious part of Matthew Forshaw had known this and moved his hand.

"How did you know?" the human medical examiner had then demanded of Calli.

"Brighty was XO of a *Monitor*-class battleship," said Commander Carmel. "*We* don't snap."

The genetic tampering, the biological warfare, was a crime against humanity and a violation of the conventions of space warfare.

"They can't call a truce," Calli told Admiral Mishindi. "Not when I want to shoot the first one I see."

"That will have to wait, Captain Carmel," Mishindi said. "We'll listen to their talk and rebuild as fast as we can."

"Captain who?" said Calli.

"Oh, don't look shocked, Cal," said Farragut. "It's in the bag."

Promotion. The big one.

Calli had served as captain of ships since she was a lieutenant, but captain in fact—not a field rank—was something else. It was crossing the kind of crevasse that put you up where angels sing.

"No one announced it," said Calli.

"The formal announcement is only waiting on your assignment," said Mishindi. "And since it's now out of the bag, I may as well tell you it's hung between two—*Monitor* and *Wolfhound*. *Monitor* is, of course, the prestigious assignment—would be, if she were in any shape to go anywhere. The old wolf hunter is a bit long of tooth, but she's a tough ship and ready to go now and I want you on board her as soon as you're done here."

"I'm ready to go right now," said Calli. "What do I have left to do here?" She had no business in Fort Roosevelt.

"I'd like you to sit in on the first round of peace talks, Captain Carmel. As someone who knows Romans."

"Here?" Farragut cried. "They're coming *here*? That maxes it. Admiral!" he beseeched, all but on his knees. "Don't agree to this. They have no interest in talking peace!"

"Neither do I, Captain Farragut. It remains—we need the time."

Alarms blared fortress-wide: Roman ships at the perimeter.

Fighters and sentry Rattlers scrambled to intercept, launching with an amazing spray of hot trails that painted fortress space in Fourth-of-July-colored fire.

Fortress sentinels ordered the Roman ships to stop and they had done so.

By the time Farragut careered into fortress Ops, the Roman flagship had identified itself.

There was really no need. There was only one ship of that make.

"Oh, for Jesus, it's the *Gladiator*."

Not dark. Not trying to hide its presence. It was lit to proper menace, a dark lustrous bronze, big as the Colosseum, with the same blocky architectural lines designed to evoke awe. Romans had always a sense of style, which carried to the brute grandeur of their battleships. Even out there on a scale by which we are all puny, it intimidated.

Sentinels warned: *Gladiator* gets no closer, or we burn her.

The Romans objected to the rough treatment when they had come invited with peaceful intent.

"Peaceful intent? In *that*? They brought that here?"

"It's not getting in," Admiral Mishindi said matter-of-factly.

Even gunships of the United States' closest allies could not approach Fort Ted without high-level clearance.

And over the com Mishindi said, "Park the gunboat, Triumphalis. Do not attempt to approach the star city, or you will be destroyed."

You could hear amusement in the imperious voice as the Roman general pointed out that he was, in fact, stopped and waiting instruction.

Numa Pompeii was notified that ferries would bring the Roman diplomats in to a secure station within the Fortress.

With that, the Fortress stepped down from full alert. That left a swarm of fighters on patrol around the Roman ships, but sent back to the rack anyone whose sleep cycle was now.

Mishindi allowed himself a relieved slouch in his seat. "No shooting. Thank God."

"Amen," said Farragut. "I'd've hated to miss it if this had turned into a real party."

16

"CAPTAIN CARMEL, HOW do you say *podexes?*"
Calli looked to the Marine who had stepped forward. Others hung back, listening expectantly for the answer.

"It's *podices,*" said Calli.

"Told you," one of the hangers-back hissed to another.

Calli caught the look of alarm on Colonel Steele at his Marines' sudden interest in Latin plurals. She told him, "They just want to make sure the Romans understand them when they call them assholes."

Steele grunted, reassured, order restored to his universe. And in a moment, "What was that word again?"

Calli strode up the curving corridor of the old station, conversing with Captain Farragut and Rob Roy. A squad of Marine guards, which Colonel Steele had attached to her, marched behind.

Clearing the bend, she came face-to-face with the great, medaled boulder that was Numa Pompeii.

Everyone stopped, very still, very surprised.

The Roman general's eyes flared with momentary startlement. Narrowed. He advanced on Calli slowly, a fuming bulk, as if he might scare her from her stance. Calli held her ground.

General Pompeii reached across his body, a motion like reaching for a sword hilt at his opposite hip, but with a slight bow as if the sword had stuck.

Abruptly, he straightened up, throwing his arm wide, the weight of his body behind it, backhanding Calli off her feet and into the bulkhead. She slid to the deck, and all guns behind her pointed at Numa Pompeii.

From her sprawl on the deck, Calli lifted a staying hand to her Marines. "I earned that one." She rolled, groggily, to hands and knees, crawled to her feet. "Put the hardware away, boys."

John Farragut passed her a handkerchief. She touched it to her nose. Blood.

Numa Pompeii's heavy breaths in his massive chest exploded into thunderous speech. "*You!* Presumptuous little *bitch*! Don't you ever *think* to use—"

"Hey!" she cut him off with a sharp, light-toned bark. Surprised him to silence. "You get either the slug or the sermon. You don't get both. We are square. You keep talking, mister, I let them shoot."

The Marines' facial muscles ticked. Watched Numa's mouth. Wanted his lips to move so they could shoot him. Please, please, please, let us shoot him.

Farragut murmured aside, "Nose, Cal."

She touched the handkerchief to the drop of blood about to fall from the tip of her nose.

Numa afforded the Marine squad a contemptuous glance. No fear in it. Asked Calli, "Are you laying all of them or just him?" A sideways nod to Farragut.

"Hey!" Farragut this time. "You. Me. *Outside*."

Outside would be anywhere without military witnesses.

Farragut's bright blue eyes took on an eager gleam. Numa had half again John Farragut's considerable mass, but Farragut was ten years younger. And John Farragut could be crazy.

Then Numa drew back with a near smile and courtly apology—to John Farragut. "I overstepped. I have no off-field quarrel with you, Captain Farragut."

Numa Pompeii stepped around the Marine squad and continued on his way.

Rob Roy, who was quite white, standing flat to the bulkhead, blurted, "What was *that* about!"

"I, uh—" Calli sniffed. Daubed her upper lip to see if the bleeding had stopped. "Took his name in vain."

Her slender, intellectual boyfriend—and all the other males present—were taking measure of themselves against the Roman mountain. Coming up short. Calli overheard the edge of daunted admiration
from one of the Marines, "That was one *big*—"

"Hey, Cal, couldn't you have found someone bigger to torque off?"

"Be careful, John," said Calli. "They don't just feed those boys vita-
mins on Palatine. He would have taken you."

Farragut drew up in insult. "You have so little faith in me?"

"I know Numa."

"I can take him," said Farragut. Had to. John Farragut did not read-
ily hold a grudge, but he had one against Numa Pompeii. Owed him
for Matty Forshaw. "Get those Red Crosses and white flags out of here;
I'll take him."

Palatine had sent a number of eloquent ambassadors to Fort
Theodore Roosevelt for the talks. Some of them sounded as if they
earnestly believed they were here to negotiate a lasting peace.

And then there was Numa. A big, brawny, upholstered rock. His
voice could be deep, bellowing thunder or a quiet, authoritative baritone. Numa was in every way larger than life, a hard-living, caber-
tossing, hammer-throwing man's man, whom Romans loved and Calli
loathed. He could be charming as hell. Wielded confidence like a
steamroller. Everything out of General Pompeii's mouth was fact. The
man had no opinions. This was the voice of God.

Admiral Mishindi passed a rhetorical note to Calli during the proceedings. *What the hell is he doing here?*

Calli felt like a cheating student, sneaking a glance at the com on
the back of her hand under the table to read Mishindi's note.

It continued: *I know it's his battleship that brought the ambassadors, but what is a general doing in peace talks? Talking! Any reason
he's not muzzled?*

Admiral Mishindi, Captain Farragut, and Captain Carmel were at-
tending as observers and could say nothing. Numa Pompeii had a
speaking role.

He's a senator, Calli sent back.

Not for real? Mishindi returned.

Calli answered: *Really.*

A general AND a senator? And that's not a conflict?

Not in Rome.

Above the table, ambassadors searched for "a common dialogue." They dug at the philosophical root of the U.S./Roman conflict as if, in it, they would find the basis for lasting peace.

One emissary called the war a battle with one's evil clone. He said that part of the dispute was that neither side could agree which was the clone.

"No question there," said Amos Curtius Americanus. "Roma Eterna. We have been a state since 776 BCE."

"That Rome existed first is not in dispute," a U.S. diplomat allowed. "But the fall of the Roman Empire is also a documented fact. The United States of America became the host to that dead empire's parasitic seed. A seed that ate out our hearts and brains, and took, like a cuckoo's chick takes, our strength and our knowledge for its own ends. In the end the Empire stole our property. The planet Palatine is—and remains—a U.S. colony."

"And where do you suppose the United States came from?" said Numa Pompeii. "Accept it or not, your nation was founded by a secret society of Romans to be our government in exile. The United States was founded as a Roman colony. America was, and still is, ours."

Farragut sent under the table: *Don't give a skat who was up to bat first. Just give me the final score.*

Calli did not see Farragut's note. Her gaze was fixed across the wide, wide mahogany table on Numa as he dropped his observations into the proceedings with indolent disdain. Some of his remarks were thinly veiled barbs, the sole purpose of which were to provoke Calli Carmel.

Calli was an observer and had no leave to speak back.

Calli did not want to say anything. She just wanted to lunge across the table, grab Numa's eagles, and beat the smirk off his condescending, self-satisfied, supercilious face. She visualized blood, imagined the sensation of cartilage crunching under her fist. To someone else had already gone the privilege of rearranging his nose, but it could use readjusting. His was not now and probably never had been a handsome face.

Numa finally said one thing too many—something about Rome not decorating its stalking horses with captain's stars in reward for being good bait.

"Oh, that's it!" Calli, brand new stars and all, was on her chair and launching across the table.

But the mahogany top was wide, and John Farragut had seen this coming. He got Calli by the back of her jacket and hauled her back into her seat.

To the staring ambassadors, Farragut said, "What the captain said, I believe, is that it might be a good idea to remove the military presence from these proceedings. Is that an accurate paraphrase, Mr. Carmel?"

"Something like that," Calli muttered, tugging her jacket back into a smooth fit.

They found the door before they could be shown the door.

Out in the corridor, walking very fast to keep up with Calli's furious stride, Farragut asked, "Why are you letting him get under your guard like this?"

Calli stopped, spun on him. "He's . . . he's *you,* John. A swaggering, obnoxious, bullying you. The pack leader. The one men listen to. Men hang on his words. Women lie down for him. He owns the ground. He's *your* evil twin."

Farragut considered this a silent moment. "I'm better looking."

"You're a lot he's not. The point is: he's *the man.*"

"So what?"

"He acts like I'm not even in the war. Like I'm a dance club hostess tripped onto the battlefield."

"His problem. You can't be offended if you don't respect the one judging you."

"I do respect him. I wish to God I didn't, but he's *the man.* Spits farther, pisses farther. Oh, how could you know. The outfield backs up when you step in the batter's box."

"That's because they know I can't bunt."

"*Won't* bunt, John. There could be a man on third and we only need one run to clinch it; John Farragut would still be swinging for the fences. They respect you."

"That kind of respect will kill me. Captain Carmel, you brought the *Monitor* home. And if he don't respect that, well damn, take your base. We both read *Five Rings of Power,* 'If the stratagem works once—' "

"Do it again." Calli finished the text for him. She had used Numa's terrific arrogance once to her advantage at Daedalus. "Problem is, I can't do anything. We're at peace."

"Not for long. You know what's behind this."

She did. "Palatine's building their *Catapulta,* their Shotgun. They're stalling to get it done. But there's something else."

Farragut cocked his head, curious.

"It's been bothering me, John. *Monitor* should have been under much heavier guard. Even considering that the Roman Catapult would demand a heavy guard at two widely separated stations. They shouldn't be spread that thin. Rome doesn't have our population, but the Roman military outnumbers us. Bad."

"You think we were meant to recapture *Monitor?*"

"No. I don't think that. I think—" Hesitated to finish the thought. Did so anyway, "I think someone back-doored them."

A third combatant? Farragut hadn't considered it. *"Kali?"*

"Who knows. I don't know. You know what, John? I don't know what the hell I'm talking about. It's all gut guesswork. Come on. I'll let you buy me a beer."

"I thought your drink was Scotch these days." Meant it as inane banter. Her boyfriend Rob Roy Buchanan always ordered Scotch for her.

Shocked the hell out of him when Calli started to cry. Girl tears.

Farragut guessed he'd better buy her a beer.

17

THE SIGHT OF AMERICA from space expanded the chest and thickened the throat every time. It had been seven years this time, by his mother's chron. Only slightly less by John Farragut's.

On the approach up the long, long drive to the sprawling white plantation house, one of his sister Amanda's mares cantered alongside the split-rail fence in the bright sunshine. Mockingbirds sang in the century oaks. A kingfisher cackled in the weeping willow alongside the creek.

Mama welcomed him as if he had returned from the dead. He was not very surprised, but disappointed, that his father was not here. Justice of the State Supreme Court, the elder John K. Farragut had business in Frankfurt.

Captain John A. Farragut had made the judge wait seven years. It was a measure of power how long you could make others wait for you. Judge Farragut was never on time, and he waited for no one. His Honor was not going to drop everything and run out like one of the family dogs simply because the boy finally decided to pay his old man a call.

The dogs did—assorted coonhounds, bloodhounds, foxhounds, and beagles came running to flog his legs with their tails. There was also an ancient African gray parrot, who remembered him; a collection of uppity cats, who really could care less; and a lustrous, golden Xanthin serpent, who rose up like a cobra in delight.

There were half a dozen underage siblings still in residence at the homestead, and John knew from his mother's messages that sister Lily's marriage busted up last year and she and her seven kids were home again, so you can just forget about getting your old room back, John Farragut.

His other fourteen sisters and brothers flocked home at the eldest's return with a flotilla of their children to take over the coach house.

Congress was in session, so Catherine flew in from D.C. for dinners and jetted back every morning.

There was also in temporary residence a houseguest of His Honor's, a man called Jose Maria many-many-middle-names de Cordillera, a cultured Terra Rican aristocrat, charming, and warm enough to thaw a frozen hell.

Guests were sacred around here, and Mama just collected *Don* Cordillera in with the rest of the brood.

Family dinners had always been warm and lively. With this many Farraguts at the tables, it was a party every evening. The old dinner table only seated thirty-two with the insert, so Mama had another brought in.

On the first evening Mama just had to have an image record taken of the family all together. Sixteen-year-old John John went AWOL for that. Upstairs to his bedroom in a loyal sulk. Family image indeed. Not without his father!

Mama's "Get yourself down here right now John Knox Farragut Junior!" went ignored. As did the: "Don't make me come up there!"

It was Captain John Alexander Farragut who went up there. "Put it aside, John," he advised quietly, leaning in the doorway. "It's just not helpful."

John John glared at his brother—the eldest, the best loved, the captain, the hero. The one who could make Father madder than anyone on the planet. "I don't take orders from you!"

"No one's askin' you to. There's a higher power talkin' here. Honor thy mother." He turned to go. Added: "There's a 'Thou shalt' that goes with that, and it's not comin' from me."

When reason fails, there was always the chain of command to fall back on. Mama got her image.

She sent it to the judge, who displayed it proudly in his chambers. Messaged his wife back that he had a fine brood, and he sure wished the boy had picked a better time to come calling.

Jose Maria de Cordillera accompanied John Farragut outside after dinner one evening to walk off the meal. It insulted Mama if you didn't overeat, and both men had done their duty.

The Terra Rican was trim, wasp-waisted (Mama would take care of *that*), in his late fifties. He wore his glossy black hair long as a horse's tail, held back in a silver clasp.

Farragut noted his Spanish-style riding boots and asked if he would like to see the horses. "My sister Amy's got some decent nags here."

Amanda's Triple Crown champion, a venerable stud now, held court in the upper pasture.

John Farragut and Jose Maria de Cordillera saddled up a pair of the stables' lesser lights and rode in the pinewood, the earth deep beneath them, the sky soaring above. A blanket of brown needles muffled the horses' hooves and gave a softness to the ground, a piquancy to the forest scents—pine resin, humus, horsehide, leather tack. Grackles squawked in the green canopy.

Jose Maria de Cordillera rode a thoroughbred. John Farragut, a big man whom horses thanked to stay off them, sat astride a hulking majestic black Belgian with hooves the size of dinner plates. It put him very high, but fortunately the trees' lower limbs had atrophied in the shade of the canopy; otherwise his head would be in the branches.

"Tell me, Captain Farragut, are you related to David Farragut of the *Saratoga*?"

"No. I'm a direct descendant of Michael Farragut of the *Abraham Lincoln*."

"I hear you are doing interesting things to your battleship, young captain."

Interesting was the subtlest term for it Farragut had heard. "Most people say I'm an idiot."

On how the refit of the *Merrimack* was to be done, John Farragut had some definite ideas. He wanted mechanical and manual backups for everything—for all stages of delivering ordnance—sighting, loading, arming, launching, triggering. He wanted dumb switches and chemical fuses—nothing that could be jammed by outside signals. He wanted backup oxygen canisters with demand regulators.

The Og had asked him, "How you gonna move this boat, Cap'n? You want we should install pedals?"

Senior Engineer Kit Kittering had been interested in the answer to that one as well.

Merrimack's engines were shrouded in six discrete phase-shifting barriers. Any one power plant could muscle the ship home. If all six were compromised, John Farragut would just have to get out and push.

No, he had answered. No pedals. He would trust the engines.

He did, however, want a backup switch to initiate or override the antimatter jettison system.

It was all very *interesting*.

"You think I'm an idiot, Jose Maria?"

Dr. Cordillera had a Nobel Prize to add to his curriculum vitae. His was an opinion worth considering.

"You are a battleship commander," said Jose Maria. "I am a mere microbiologist. I assume there is a method behind the madness."

"There is. I'll tell you. When I was fourteen, the judge dropped me in the middle of Cumberland Forest with nothing but the clothes on my back and said, 'See you in two weeks.' "

Properly, John K. Farragut was a justice rather than a judge. But he had been "the judge" to John A. Farragut since he could remember, so there was no changing now.

"Those two weeks taught me the value of really low tech."

"Your father has a sadistic streak, I think."

The judge was a loud, earthy, opinionated man with a great horse-laugh and coarse charm. Had a generous streak as wide as the mean one. He kept a Bible at his bench and had been known to use a Colt .45 for a gavel.

"The judge has his own way of doing things," Captain Farragut allowed.

It was several days before Captain Farragut got around to asking his father's guest, "What brings you to the judge's house?"

"You, Captain Farragut," said Jose Maria. "Your *Merrimack*. I need to get to the Deep End."

"What makes you think *Merrimack*'s fixing to go to the Deep End?"

"You are," said Jose Maria, statement of fact.

"I hate it when civilians know more about my next mission than I do."

"I do not know your next mission. I merely related some of my observations to certain members of your Joint Chiefs, and they suggested I might like to go as an observer aboard *Merrimack* when she sets spaceward again."

Farragut bridled. Did not like being saddled with passengers. Especially unasked.

"Are you going to tell *me* these observations of yours?"

"I shall tell you everything," Jose Maria said, his smile becoming benignly cagey, "When I am in the Deep End aboard *Merrimack*."

Brought Farragut's head right round, eyes big. Jose Maria de Cordillera knew Captain Farragut intended to leave him behind.

John Farragut broke into a grin. Muttered, "Damn civilians. Can't order 'em around. Can't shoot 'em."

Jose Maria's smile remained.

"I don't travel with civilians," said Farragut.

"The Joint Chiefs said it was all right."

"The Joint Chiefs need talking to. If we get boarded and you're not in uniform, the Romans will *sell* you."

"Then I shall buy myself."

Farragut was about to point out the costliness of that proposal, when he took another hard look at the man. A crisp, understated air of extreme wealth dwelled in every detail, in the fiber of his coat, the simple styling of his clothes, the spare elegance of his jewelry. Jose Maria de Cordillera lived in a rarified tax bracket beyond even the Farraguts'.

John Farragut and Jose Maria Cordillera were in the judge's study by now, an Old Boy sort of room done in leather, scented of cigars, brandy, and gunpowder. Handsome portraits of Amanda's racehorses wearing wreaths of roses decorated the walls, along with antique fowling pieces, leather-bound law books, and other manly artifacts.

Jose Maria stood before a rack of swords. He gestured toward a single-edged Chinese blade on the rack. "May I?"

John Farragut gave a sideways nod to say he was his guest, and kept talking, "The *whole idea* of taking a civilian—a civilian of a neutral planet yet!—on a mission to the—"

The *whole idea* fell to pieces as the sword moved in Jose Maria's hand. The blade became a living extension of the man, disappeared into a flashing blur. The man himself moved like a great lean cat—smooth, fluid, aggressive—his stops so clean, instant, and complete, they defied inertia. He turned with a light, balanced pivot. Brought the sword about in the wink of an eye, as if it had displaced rather than moved through the space in between *there* and *here.*

When Farragut's eyebrows could lift no farther, he found his voice, "Jose Maria, you sure you're not a warrior?"

Terra Rica was a neutral world, and Jose Maria de Cordillera a man of medicine. He was a grandfather sixteen times over, a number rapidly multiplying as happens in devout Catholic families.

"This is not warfare," said Jose Maria, bringing the sword in from a flashing lemniscate to tuck up behind his arm at rest. "It is an art. If you want to kill someone, use a Colt .45. Or a disruptor."

"There are drawbacks to having weapons with that kind of punch and range on board a spaceship." Farragut pulled a pair of dueling sabers from the rack, scooped up a pair of V masks on the blade of one, and invited, "Have a go?"

They withdrew outdoors to stake out places at far sides of a wide, empty corral, synched their V masks, and registered themselves and their swords with the program.

The blind, dusty darkness of the mask was replaced by a large hall, occupied only by the two of them. They adjusted the mask settings until the images of each other stood within sword's length.

"Test. Test."

They extended blades to their counterimages, touched swords. Heard the tinny clank, felt the light pressure of the contact.

"Okay."

"Very good."

"Set," Farragut commanded the program. Touched his hand to Jose Maria's virtual blade. Felt the razor of pain. Felt blood hot and wet in his palm. "Reset."

The pain and blood vanished. He nodded satisfaction. Looked to his opponent. "Ready?"

"Sir." Jose Maria bowed.

Farragut cocked his saber back in both hands for a mighty swing.

Quick, too quick, Jose Maria was *there,* under Farragut's cocked elbows, and opening up his rib cage. The sword actually fell, clattered against a virtual wood floor. Farragut's hands clutched at his gushing chest. Knees hit what felt like wood.

Choked. Ripped off the mask.

Gulped dusty air deeply into his undamaged chest in the aftermath of vanished pain.

Jose Maria's voice sounded above him, solicitous, "Are you well, young Captain?"

"Yes, dammit. Embarrassed." Hauled himself to his feet. Mask jammed back on. "I want a rematch."

The second round was almost a battle, John Farragut's brute strength against Jose Maria's cat-footed finesse. The elder man became the instructor. "Do not watch my eyes, young Captain. My eyes will not cut you."

From anyone else, Farragut might have taken insult, being offered advice during a competition. But the doctor was so genuine, and so skilled, Farragut took it for the help it was meant to be.

Ended up dead again, winded and wiser. He spoke up from the ground, blinking sweat and sunlight from his eyes, "Don Jose Maria de Cordillera, would you mind working for me?"

"In what capacity?" Jose Maria refastened the silver clasp in his long black hair.

"Weapons instructor for my Marines. Or is that against the Neutrality?"

"I cannot see how it could violate neutrality unless you mean to arm your *Merrimack* with swords," Jose Maria said in whimsy.

"I do. You in?"

Jose Maria absorbed bemusement. Said at last, "I can teach martial arts. How you make use of it is your business."

"A little sophistic there, hm, Jose Maria?"

"A lot sophistic. *Mea culpa*. I shall do penance."

Something slipped there, past the man's temperate benevolence. A hostility against Rome.

And it was personal.

18

AT THE NAVAL SPACE FLEET base outside of Lawrence, Kansas, Marines ran through the shoot/don't shoot drills—or in this case, slash/don't slash drills, for they were armed with swords. The program presented friends and foes unexpectedly—colonist, Roman foot soldier, ship's dog, LEN emissary, Roman Centurion, U.S. Marine, cow.

Farragut was damn serious about this part of the sword training. If you don't pass this part of the final screening, you don't serve on board *Mack* when she flies again in anger.

And Flight Sergeant Kerry Blue wanted to serve on *Merrimack.* All the Marines did. Because John Farragut was damn serious about who got slashed and who didn't. She had to get this right.

Fortunately, racquetball had always been a popular sport on the *Mack,* so they were all pretty good at not whacking each other in close quarters.

Squash was also popular. Squash was the captain's game, because the ball was smaller, harder, and the damn thing didn't bounce. You had to smash it like hell to make it go. You give Farragut the wrong shot and he'll smash you back to Philadelphia, rocketing that little green bullet around all four walls of the court. But he'd never nailed anyone with his racquet.

Still left the problem of separating friend from foe. Neither racquetball nor squash was any help with deciding that.

"Do you slash or don't slash the cow?"

Nobody quite knew.

"It's a dumb question. Don't slash the cow," said Cowboy.

"Are you *sure?*" said Kerry.

No. He wasn't quite sure. Was pretty sure.

Not good enough for Kerry Blue, who usually passed tests by the skin of her teeth. "You gotta *know.* And you can take it from me, telling an examiner his question is dumb never *ever* works."

"I'll ask Jose Maria about the cow," Reg Monroe volunteered quickly.

"No, it's my question. I'll ask him," Kerry said.

"I'll ask," said Carly. "I speak Terra Rican."

"Like that man don't know English better than any of us," said Kerry.

Twitch Fuentes turned to the nearest Y chromosome. "Just what *is* it with the girls and the old guy?"

Cowboy shrugged. "They think just 'cause Cordillera's good with a sword that he's good with his sword."

"Could be," said Kerry with a haughty, you-can-be-replaced shift of her shoulders. "I don't think there's a soft spot anywhere on that man's body."

"He's *gorgeous,*" said Reg. "He moves gorgeous."

"Oh, yeah, the moves." Carly fanned herself with her hand, suddenly very very warm.

"He's re*fined,*" said Reg, in what she thought was a refined voice. "Something you baboons wouldn't understand. He's dynamic. Intelligent. Rich."

"Rich," Carly said.

"Rich." Kerry nodded.

"Old," Cowboy said.

"Which means his kids are grown up," said Carly. "Got that skat over with. Can he be any more perfect?"

Flight Sergeant Shepard weighed in with a mouth full of pretzels and salt crumb spray: "Okay, so what's he supposed to see in you?"

A three-way pause, then, "Shut up, Dak."

John Farragut took to the sword naturally. Disruptors, splinter guns, tag seekers, and contact stunners were really too civilized for his inner barbarian. Although he was a decent, compassionate man, once committed to killing an enemy, he found the true violence of hacking sword to bone held a savage satisfaction he didn't get from modern, sterile exterminations at long range.

He had mastered all the training routines which Jose Maria had left for him while Jose Maria trained Marines in Kansas. By the time Jose Maria came back to Kentucky, Farragut was eager to try out a new program. And Jose Maria had brought one. It was called *Nemo*.

"What's it about?" Farragut asked, loading the program into a V mask.

"You will see," said Jose Maria.

They went outside to an empty corral on the Farragut property, which had become John Farragut's usual place to practice with his sword. The corral gave him a wide space without real obstacles to interfere with his virtual training world. He shut the gates to keep out children and horses.

The new routine's space requirements called for a long, rather narrow fighting area. Farragut pictured a banquet hall, and positioned himself appropriately, away from the fences, which he would not be able to see during the simulation.

He fitted on the mask, plugged in the leads.

The sun's warmth and scents of the corral's horsey dust vanished into virtual biting cold and wet salt sting of sea spray. Nothing at all like a banquet hall. A metal deck rolled underfoot. The heavy buffet of open air nearly unbalanced him. He saw, by the flicker of lightning, that he was on the heaving deck of an antique submarine on an angry iron gray sea. Waves spilled white foam over his sealskin-booted feet. He gripped the sword in both hands.

Something rose from the spume—dark, blue-black, fantastical—like a giant beanstalk, but with suction disks. A tentacle.

File name *Nemo*. Farragut barked a startled laugh. "It's a giant squid!"

The stalk whipped about, circled Farragut's legs, constricted. And suddenly he was upside down, in midair, high above the deck. Blood rushed to his head. The thing swung him in the howling, bitter wind, dizzily high.

His stomach heaved with the drop.

Prickle of grass stubble bit into his palms. He cursed, because he'd lost his grip on his sword. Blunt solidity of compressed dirt against his back confused him. Couldn't see. His mask had gone black, blank. A horse nickered from somewhere. He must have exited the program. Had not asked to.

He pulled off the mask. Inhaled warm dust. Could not open his eyes for the bright sun stabbing from above.

Quiet crunching of grit under bootsoles neared. A shadow across his face let him open his eyes. Looked up at Jose Maria de Cordillera haloed by the sun.

"What happened?" said Farragut. "The program quit on me."

"You died, young Captain."

"Did not." Then, rather meekly, "Did I?"

"Headfirst onto the deck. Your skull split open." Jose Maria offered down a kid-gloved hand to his fallen pupil. "Death was instantaneous."

"Oh," Farragut said, disappointed. "Well, hell." Then, protesting, nearly a bleat, *"It was a squid!"*

"Yes."

"A *squid.*"

"You did not expect a squid? Well, then, fight within the moment, young Captain. Do not anticipate."

Farragut snugged the V mask back over his head. "I want a rematch!"

"I thought you might." Jose Maria reset the program, stepped out of the corral. "Do not laugh at the squid."

"Right." Farragut tested his grip on his sword, flexed his knees into a mobile, stable stance. This was a matter of pride.

It wasn't like he could expect to be fighting tentacled monsters on board his *Merrimack.*

At the Naval base in Kansas, Cowboy Carver, Dak Shepard, and Twitch Fuentes battled the giant squid in the new *Nemo* program, while the women of Red Squad were still messing with the No Guns program. Kerry Blue, Carly Delgado, and Reg Monroe weren't finished with that asymptote with the bullwhip. Hated—*hated*—that cocky, sneering, leering son of a beagle kicker. Even with the program toned down, the bullwhip hit you like a two by four. The pain seized up your chest, blotted out your vision, while that guy *laughed,* and the bullwhip sizzled the air, and there was the death stroke because suddenly you were pain free and breathing easy in the dark of your mask.

Before they left this program, the women were determined to hack that stupid whip into pieces, then yank out the guy's hose and hack that into pieces, too, before killing him.

Came the day. Bullwhip came at Carly, licking his thin, smarmy lips, and laughing at her brandished sword. Carly wasn't big, and she was bone thin, but most people had the sense to be afraid of her. Bullwhip didn't. "Little stick girl," he taunted. "You are going to take my scalp?"

"Hell, no," Carly said. "I'm taking your ears and your tail."

Literal—machine minds were always stupidly literal—Bullwhip answered, "I don't have a tail."

"The hell you say."

And Kerry and Reg snagged his bullwhip on the backswing as Carly charged in from the front and tackled him low. Kerry and Reg sliced the whip into twelve pieces while Carly choked the guy into the ground, bony forearm across his throat. She held him down while Reg debagged him for Kerry to do the deed.

Kerry froze on the upstroke, shrieked, "He don't have one!"

And everything vanished. The program ab-ended, as programs will when the parameters are exceeded.

Carly and Reg were left holding down air on the parade ground.

Kerry pulled off her V mask, yanked her sweat-matted hair free from its band. She hovered over the empty spot on the ground at her feet where Bullwhip should have been. "Well, *damn*. No wonder he was so mean!"

"So what do you do with the cow?"

"What?"

They were back to slash/don't slash drills.

"The cow," said Reg. "What's the right answer? Slash or don't slash?"

"I don't *know*," Twitch brushed aside the question, annoyed.

"Well I *gotta* know," Reg dogged him. "I'm not gonna get left dock-side for not slashing the cow when the examiner thinks we're having burgers for supper."

Twitch let his shoulders slump. Reg was not going away until he gave her an answer. He asked, "Is it mad?"

"What?" Reg wrinkled up her face.

"Is it a mad cow?"

Reg gave an angry tsk. "Cows don't get mad." Reg Monroe had never seen a live one and had no interest in livestock, but she was pretty sure from the pictures she'd seen that those tranquil stupid creatures couldn't mount a convincing mad.

"Oh, yeah, they do," Twitch assured her. And the issue became terribly funny. Cowboy and Dak started doing mad cow imitations. Devolved into sniggers.

Reg walked away, let her sword drop over her shoulder. "You guys are useless."

"Oh, *sync-up.*" Kerry fit her mask on to return to the drill.

Cowboy called from behind her, "Hey, Kerry Blue!"

Kerry spun round, sword in hand. Cowboy was there. Flying at her with a wild maniacal moo.

And ran right up her blade to the hilt. Her sword point jutted red out his back.

Hot sticky splash wet her hands. Cowboy's sagging weight dragged down her sword. "Oh, hell! Reset!" she commanded the program.

Instead of resetting, her mask went dark. The weight, the wetness, the smell remained.

Kerry ripped off her mask with a sticky hand to see what was hanging on her sword.

Howled, *"Medic!"*

Lieutenant Colonel TR Steele stormed into Internal Investigations to yank his Marine out of interrogation.

"Colonel Steele, we are not finished here."

"Yes, you are, *sir!*" Steele told the II officers. "You do *NOT* take up *anything* with my Marines without going through me!"

Yeah. Anyone kick Colonel Steele's dog, it'll be Colonel Steele, thought Kerry, standing expressionless at attention. It was an oddly comforting thought. She would choose, a million times out of a million, her chops-busting CO over these cold, desk-riding ferrets, the dreaded double-Is.

"Colonel Steele, we are not talking mere negligence here," an investigator explained. Full colonels all of them. There were no low-ranking double-Is. "There is compelling evidence that the incident under investigation was not an accident. There exists a computer record from *Merrimack* of the Marine saying quote I want him dead unquote. An incident regarding a married lover. One Jamie 'Cowboy' Carver as a matter of fact."

"I didn't know the fid-squucker was married!" Kerry cried out loud.

One big jutting forefinger and a tight-shut mouth from Colonel Steele told her to slam it.

"Internal Investigations has a duty to find the truth behind the incident," said the investigator.

"*I'll* tell you the truth behind the incident," said Steele.

Truth was Cowboy Carver was an oversexed son of a rabbit who couldn't keep his shirt on or his pants zipped. Truth was Steele wanted him dead. Truth was he was glad Kerry killed him. Truth was Steele only regretted that Cowboy hadn't stayed dead. Damn medics were too damn good. Truth was Kerry hadn't checked the V mask perameters before running the program.

And truth was Colonel Steele proceeded to lie for Kerry Blue. Steele took the fall for not controlling the situation.

Internal Investigations let Kerry go. Slapped Steele with a rep.

"One last question, if you will, Lieutenant Colonel?"

Steele waited. Posed in a silent demand: *Ask, damn you.* Knew, just knew, the double I was going to say: *So, is she any good?*

The investigator twirled a light stylus indolently. "So what *is* the proper answer to that cow thing?"

It was raining when Colonel Steele ordered Kerry Blue to get her ass out on the perimeter for sentry duty.

She'd known this was coming. Well, it beat the hell out of Internal Investigations detention.

She pulled up the hood of her slicker, shouldered her splinter weapon. "Sir?" she asked at Steele's back, the prelude to a question.

He roared, patience at an end. *"What?"*

"Why'd you take the hit for me?"

He thought she was being coy. Turned to bellow at her. But Kerry was looking up at him with honest puzzlement. She didn't know. The little idiot had no clue.

His voice dropped into the gravel, soft with restrained anguish. "Don't ask me that, Marine. Don't ever ask me that."

*   *   *

"Captain Farragut, your crew and Marine contingent have suffered more casualties during *Merrimack*'s refit—at peace, *in dock*—than any five other ships in their most recent battles."

"It's not uncommon for soldiers to suffer casualties Earthside, Admiral Mishindi."

"From car crashes and skiing! Not from sword wounds!"

"Haven't lost anyone," Farragut offered.

"Close. You came very close with that Carver fellow."

Jamie Cowboy Carver. That had been over-the-line back-from-the-dead close. "Yes, sir."

"*And* I've been receiving an ungodly number of med reports of reattaching limbs and closing deep wounds. Your blood requisition is way over budget. What I really mean to ask, John, is: what the hell are you doing?"

"We're shaking out the bugs. It's a new way of fighting for them."

"It's old! It's millennia old! What do you think you're doing making your crew fight each other with swords!"

"They're not fighting each other. They're fighting virtual enemies with swords. But they're in real close proximity to each other. Makes a difference when they can do real damage to each other."

"Yes, yes, it does. The difference is *they do real damage to each other!*" Mishindi bellowed the obvious, the whites of his eyes stark rings between the darkness of his irises and the darkness of his face.

"They're learning not to. They're getting damn good at not hurting each other. Takes time is all."

"And the value of learning to fight with swords *at all* would be? Something I can tell the JC?"

"The value is that there's no on/off switch with a sword. No signal jamming against a sword. No shooting a hole through your bulkhead with a sword. And a sword can get through an exo-suit."

"This is ridiculous. Unnecessary. Wasteful. And—*swords*! It's—it's something I'd expect out of Rome!"

"No. Funny, that," Farragut smiled. "Romans like the newest, best, highest-tech toys. They've always loved new inventions. Hand-to-hand fighting is a lost art in Rome. Of course, they all think they're hand-to-hand experts by birthright. But none of them train on it. They'd sneer at my swords like a German tank brigade would sneer at the Polish cavalry."

"I'm sneering, too."

"Difference is the tanks and the cavalry were on ground that favored the tank. I'm going to fly a Cessna under the Iron Curtain and land it in Red Square."

"Low-tech tricks don't win wars."

"And all this is my last line of defense," Farragut admitted. "This is for when I'm backed against my own bulks by a Roman boarding party carrying jammable two-stage weapons and radiation armor. I can say hello with a one-stage open-up-your-skin weapon with considerable intimidation value." He pulled a Civil War era sword off the admiral's wall and whistled it through the air with all Farragut's sizable mass and strength behind it.

The admiral jerked back on reflex. Recovered, as Farragut had come to a peaceful halt. "Possibly. Do put that back. It's quite valuable."

Farragut did.

"Not saying I approve," said Mishindi. "I don't—but I've never put a leash on you, and I've never been sorry for that. Anyone else, I'd reel you in. But you are who you are, and your alarming casualty rate *is* on a marked down-tick. So I'm going to let you run with this, John. Don't make me sorry."

Farragut saluted, awaited dismissal. The admiral held up a finger to signal pause as his com burred a red chime.

Farragut waited through the yes, yes, I see, and the thank you, to the end of the transmission. Admiral Mishindi returned his attention to Captain Farragut. Asked soberly, "How much faith do you have in your 'backup' system?"

"We're good to go as soon as the primaries are."

"The primaries *aren't*. But I need you now, ready or not."

An expectant inhale. "Rome broke the cease-fire!"

Mishindi shook his head no. Rome did not. "We did. As we speak a U.S. strike force is crossing into Roman space."

Farragut was torn between reactions. It was what he wanted. But, "They couldn't wait for *me*?"

"No. Not for anything." Mishindi folded his hands. His dark face looked rather gray. He gathered in a breath to speak the unspeakable: "Palatine has a working Shotgun."

19

THE ROMANS CALLED IT Catapult instead of Shotgun, but it did the same thing—effected huge-scale displacement across an astronomical distance.

Its first test shot gave it away. Gravitation was a weak force, but a distortion spike of that size rocked the low band across a three hundred light-year radius and woke up the Pentagon.

Sensors on several colonies immediately zeroed in on the epicenter. Pinpointed the location of the Near Cat.

The location of the second Cat was less certain. Gravitational effects dropped off quickly with distance. The low-band monitors could only be certain that the second Cat was a good two klarcs distant in the Deep End.

No matter. The U.S. need only shut down one end of the Catapult to reduce this Roman end run to a one-handed clap.

U.S. warships stormed across the Roman territorial boundary, steering a wide path around Palatine, to the Near Cat with orders to shut the Catapult down. By any and all means. The rules of engagement in this war had changed. Undisputed Roman space was now in bounds, and any Roman ship not flying a Red Cross could be shot without provocation.

It was a reflection of the desperation of the situation that the JC cleared *Merrimack* for battle—and that only because *Merrimack* could run away if she got into trouble. This was a siege on Roman ground. The Romans must stand; Farragut had the option of running away.

"And you *will* call for a tow if your ship controls get overridden," Mishindi ordered in parting. Hoped Farragut would not get a chance to ignore that order.

Captain Farragut stranded his weapons instructor Earthside, and made all speed to the Near Cat.

A space fortress surrounded the Near Cat. Rome called it a Citadel. It was a kicked hive, swarming with angry ships encased in shimmering force fields.

Force fields only shimmer like that when hit. In this beam-laced space everything shimmered with the diffuse brilliance of deflected shots.

The Fortress grid illuminated like a lightning sky. The blasts gave shape to it—a geodesic containment grid engulfing a region of space equal to the volume of the Moon. And within that, rings of armed sentinel stations guarded another grid, which housed the Near Cat itself.

Hardpoints in the outer grid bristled with guns. And those were reinforced by a net of Roman battleships emplaced within the grid, becoming, themselves, hardpoints in it. Each point maintained a section of distortion wall—a modern take on an ancient Roman tortoise. The ships had locked shields, trading mobility for combined force. So long as the ships held position, they were all invulnerable, and the Citadel impregnable.

The Roman ships at the Citadel acted in either of two discrete roles—those emplaced in the grid, and those free harriers who actively engaged the U.S. attackers.

Merrimack's approach to the hot zone met with a belligerent, fear-tinged demand for IFF. U.S. forces were touchy regarding large newcomers approaching from the direction of Palatine—which was also the direction of Earth. The guard ships confirmed *Merrimack*'s sig and let the battleship pass.

In the battle zone, the paths of mobile plots showed on *Merrimack*'s display as a tangled writhing serpents' nest of besiegers and defenders.

Farragut found his former XO already there with her aging wolf hunter, a game, sturdy little ship with a crew of thirty, *Wolfhound*.

After reporting in to the siege commodore, John Farragut sent *Wolfhound* a greeting: "Captain Carmel!"

"Welcome to the show, John. Do you see something wrong here?"

Only just arrived he'd already noticed it. "Where's the rest of them?"

Too few Roman vessels defended the target. Rome had vast fire-power. And, for as many ships as swarmed about the titanic space Citadel, there should have been more. Many more. Where were the Legions of Rome if not here? Where were its killer bots?

"End run?" Calli spoke her worst fear.

In an end run scenario, an enormous Roman force would be vaporizing Washington D.C. even now.

The problem with that scenario—from the Roman perspective—was that an attack on U.S. soil would bring the League of Earth Nations into it, and Rome would prefer to let those dogs sleep. In fact, it would serve Rome not to retaliate; this U.S. invasion of Roman space could bring the LEN into the war on the side of Palatine.

Farragut took a different guess. "Maybe there's a hundred Legions fixing to come blasting through the Cat."

In that case it was imperative to shut the Catapult down quickly, *now*, before such a thing could happen. But how?

The Roman force field was impervious to any weapon. Stronger than a solid wall, the field wall consisted of layers within layers of phase-shifting distortion screens that pulsed in erratic time.

Calli asked her engineer, Amina Patel, if her ship *Wolfhound* could weave a path through the grid layers between the pulses.

Amina assented provisionally, not very happy about it. Yes, with a stutter step, pausing, advancing, and back stepping in the correct sequence of intervals, you could possibly get a small ship through. Sideways. But, Amina pointed out, *Wolfhound* would be vulnerable to the harriers while going in, and open to the ships in the adjacent grid points while staggering through the layers.

And once through, there were the Citadel guns. And, because those guns had no one else to shoot at, "We would be the only girl at the dance."

"But the inside gunners have to tag us first," said Calli. "They can't afford to shoot and miss. Tag shots are the only safe shot they've got."

Amina had to nod. This was true.

"They're shooting in a bottle," said Calli. "A ricochet could hit just about anything in there."

A tag insured delivery of ordnance to its target and only to its target.

"And so they will launch all their tags at us," said Amina.

"What's top speed of a tag?" Captain Carmel asked. "Or more to the point—can we outrun a tag?"

"Ye–es." The two syllables held reservation.

Amina's next question was how the captain intended to get her ship out again. It required the same sideways stutter step to exit the field as it did to enter. "To avoid the tags inside, we would need to be running in circles around the Cat. We stop running to stutter step, we get tagged. And at that distance, we get tagged, we get hit."

"Then we'll burn the tags before they can touch us," said Calli. "Just get us in where we can do real damage."

"Brings us back to how to keep from getting shot while we're stutter stepping in." Amina was not arguing. She simply needed to know.

Calli got back on the com: "John, I need a favor."

Told him she intended to run at the grid and tiptoe through the grid to the inner space.

Farragut did not seem surprised. Asked, "Where do you want to penetrate?"

"Next to the *Gladiator.*"

The mammoth Roman warship held an anchor position within the grid.

Senior Engineer Amina Patel politely asked her captain if she were out of her mind. But *Wolfhound*'s XO, Lieutenant Egypt (Gypsy) Dent, was nodding as Farragut replied over the com: "Good choice."

Gypsy spoke aside to Amina, "Didn't you hear the Roman chatter when we first got here?"

Amina had heard the insults. The Romans had called *Wolfhound* "that henhouse," their term for a ship whose captain, exec, and engineer were all women.

That made *Wolfhound* a target beneath notice of the Triumphalis Numa Pompeii and his great battleship *Gladiator.*

"He never pays attention to me," said Calli. "He's too proud to shoot at us. He'll leave us to the Citadel's inner guns."

Farragut asked, "What are you fixin' to do in there, Cal?"

"Don't dare tell you, John." She didn't quite have that much faith in the security of her com link. "Can you get me in?"

"Yeah, I can pick a fight with Numa."

"He'll cut our flank," said Amina.

"No, he won't," said Calli Carmel. "He's going to watch John Farragut."

"I can get you in," Farragut repeated. "I can't get you out."

"That's all I want, John."

Calli outlined the plan to her crew. And only because it was somewhat suicidal did she ask them if they would have trouble following her orders.

No. They came here to kill Romans. Even Amina said, "Tell us where to punch it." Insulted that the captain supposed they might balk.

Touched at their faith, their willingness to follow, Calli wanted to cry. And Farragut, an expressive man, would have, but she did not.

Merrimack opened up a hammering barrage of solid ordnance at *Gladiator*. *Gladiator* picked off the projectiles with gamesmanlike ease, as *Wolfhound* began her run at the grid.

Run was too strong a word. Calli with her *Wolfhound* staggered, sidestepped, and lurched through the pulsing layers of the defensive field.

And hoped Numa Pompeii was even half as arrogant as Calli thought he was.

Pompous bastard, don't fail me now.

True to form, *Gladiator,* engaged in its shooting match with *Merrimack,* gave no indication of noticing Calli's ship.

But angry eyes opened in the imperial ship *Trajan,* the ship emplaced next to *Gladiator* in the grid. *Trajan*'s side ports opened, showed guns.

And hesitated.

Perhaps because *Wolfhound* lay in a direct line with *Gladiator.* Or perhaps *Wolfhound*'s very near proximity to *Gladiator* posed the problem.

Or maybe *Trajan* was unsure of the consequences of firing between layers of the force field.

The imperial ship did not fire.

But *Trajan*'s ports were not closing, and Farragut did not like those angry eyes following Calli.

Farragut hailed the U.S. cruiser *Edmonton,* asked a favor. "Norris, punch *Trajan*'s headlights out for me?"

"I can hit him," said Captain Norris, with no questions, even though he saw no apparent point to the exercise. *Edmonton* launched a load of crap at *Trajan*'s face.

Trajan lost interest in its side game. Turned its sights on *Edmon-*

ton. Let the Citadel guns carve up the foolish little wolf hunter passing alongside.

Farragut heard *Trajan*'s commander speaking on an open channel, meant to be overheard: "Target practice for you, Citadel. Don't hit me in the ass."

And *Wolfhound* was through! Leaping instantly to speed.

Wolfhound's visuals were useless, nonexistent, at this speed. The ship's readouts had to translate an FTL propeller blade's view of the battle. The image on the tactical display looked something like a simple model of a hydrogen atom—the computer's interpretation of *Wolfhound*'s whirling path inside the grid, orbiting the Citadel several times a second.

Tags launched from the Citadel's sentinels, clouds of them. Made the sentinels look like milkweed pods bursting open.

A tag's only function was to catch a target, latch on, and give homing ordnance an exact mate against which to detonate. Tags hadn't the *Wolfhound*'s acceleration. And despite the tags' tiny mass, they made wider turns. On an ever-turning course, in which every meter demands a course correction, the tags quickly spent their very small fuel supply, and died.

Wolfhound deployed a flurry of her own tags, targeting the stationary sentinels and the sensor stations that made the Catapult work.

Those tags that touched the vital sensors of the Catapult died on contact. Those tags that nested on the sentinels sang out their bull's eyes, only briefly. *Wolfhound* launched a salvo of homers after her tags. But her missiles met with intercept, or else lost their way as their tags were erased. Only one of *Wolfound*'s missiles tagged up and detonated—to no effect—against a well-shielded emplacement.

Numa's scorn for Calli's intrusion appeared entirely justified. She could not have supposed taking down the Near Cat could be as simple as squeezing one small ship inside the Roman first line of defense.

In her tight, whirling flight, *Wolfhound* lapped some of the tags that were chasing her. Ran into the rear of a swarm of them. Most bounced off her forward shield. One stuck.

And a Roman missile was *there,* mated with its tag. It detonated on *Wolfhound*'s bow.

From outside the grid, Farragut tried to keep an eye on Calli, though there was nothing he could do for her out here except pound at Numa and keep his own hide free of stickers. He just had to wait and see what Calli thought she could do inside the grid.

It was beginning to look like she'd flown herself into a kill jar.

He watched for Calli's ship to emerge from the blast that landed on her bow.

She should have been able to take that hit, especially taking it straight on the nose like that. But maybe the tightness of her turns had distorted her forward screens, because *Merrimack*'s sensors clearly showed the speeding *Wolfhound* putting out all her lifeboats.

20

LOSING SPEED, *WOLFHOUND* TRAILED steam and smoke. The tags, which she had been eluding, gained on her stern.

Her lifeboats were not properly boats. They were very basic, very temporary, survival pods; flimsy tissue-foil sacks equipped with minimal air, a rebreather, and an uncomfortable heater.

Calli kept the life pods close to the ship, inside *Wolfhound*'s shield, instead of launching them clear of her ship, until *Wolfhound* bubbled all over with foil blisters, wearing the lot of them outboard like a mama spider carrying its young.

A Citadel gunner sent an inquiry to General Pompeii: "Cease fire?"

"No," Numa returned, emphatic. "If *Mister* Carmel thinks Rome won't take out her life pods, she is sadly mistaken. Until she surrenders, or her ship is destroyed, those pods are targets. If she's going to hide behind her lifeboats, then tag them. Tag them all and shoot them."

On board *Merrimack,* Marcander Vincent reported from his tactical station: "Sir. Roman gunners are launching tags at Captain Carmel's lifeboats. She's losing speed. They'll make contact in another minute."

Farragut nodded. "I think she's counting on it."

The command crew looked to Captain Farragut in surprise.

"Sir?" Lieutenant Glenn Hamilton asked.

"I just hope Numa doesn't see what I'm seeing," said Farragut.

Numa Pompeii refused to know Calli. Still, he must see what she was up to, if he was looking.

"Launch a planet killer at Numa."

Lieutenant Hamilton ordered up the planet killer, then said, "It won't do anything, sir."

The planet killer would create a huge, expensive light show, and momentarily blank out everyone's clearscreens. It would have no effect on the grid.

"It'll make him look," said Farragut. "At me."

Instead of?

Hamster took another look at Calli's fleeing *Wolfhound* wearing its coat of lifeboats.

The life pods were tissue thin, opaque, but so filmy they concealed little. Normally you could make out the shapes of people inside, like larvae in a cocoon. Hamster did not see anything at all pushing at the foil sides.

Where were the elbows? The knees? The hands? The butts?

Calli's life pods were neat sausage balloons.

Someone was going to notice that oddity in a moment and warn Numa.

"Planet killer armed and ready, Captain!" Hamster reported.

"Fire."

"Fire planet killer!"

The planet killer smashed into the grid, lit it up like a white dwarf star. Filled the com channels with curses and Roman scoffing.

Another spume of smoke belched from *Wolfhound*'s stern.

Wolfhound's shields flickered out. The ship lost more speed, and a whole flock of tags caught up and latched on to every available surface.

Because the wolf hunter was entirely encased in life sacks, the tags latched onto the life sacks.

The Roman sentinels launched homing missiles after them.

"They're shooting the lifeboats!" Marcander Vincent reported.

"So they are." Farragut's fingers crossed themselves.

As the homing missiles launched to mate with their tags, *Wolfhound* spun, shedding her coat of foil sacks like a snake its skin.

Because all the tags were stuck to life sacks, *Wolfhound* discarded all the tags along with the sacks.

Sending the homing missiles chasing them.

Toward *Gladiator*'s sternside engine ports.

A Roman missile will not detonate against a Roman ship, but it will detonate against a tag stuck to a U.S. life pod thrown up against a Roman battleship's stern.

Things happen quickly at these speeds. General Pompeii saw the trap as it hurtled up his battleship's engines. Emplaced in the grid, *Gladiator* could not evade. Numa shouted on the open channel: "Deactivate those homers!"

He had noticed the sacks were unmanned, but not empty. Empty, they would have been collapsed flat. These were filled with gas. Probably hydrogen because they sent fireballs exploding up his engines as the homing missiles ripped through the sacks and slammed against *Gladiator*'s stern midway through Numa's warning shout.

The great ship canted, juddered, and rocked. The grid wavered.

Into that fluctuating crack in the Citadel's impenetrable shell, the U.S. ship *Gettysburg* drove three robot seeker-killers.

Trajan, moving to take up the breach, thinned out another point in the grid through which two attack ships penetrated the perimeter. While the crippled *Wolfhound* miraculously reacquired her force field, her speed, and her atmospheric integrity.

Gladiator's guns were turning round. Calli had Numa's attention now.

Farragut saw it coming. Ordered *Merrimack* to line up a saber, "On the big, fat bully."

"Targeting *Gladiator*, aye."

"Fire saber."

Nothing happened.

"This is not a balk!" Fire Control warned sharply. "Someone is in here!" An outside signal had taken over his control systems.

Not ever to be caught staring into the headlights, Farragut did not waste an instant wondering how this was happening or spare a breath to swear. Instantly he ordered computer controls shut down and called for manual overrides. "Anything that can receive remote commands— pull the plug!"

Flight Sergeant Kerry Blue had been waiting in her Swift for orders to launch. Got this instead.

Popped her canopy to squawk: "Manual over—! We are doing this skat for *real*?"

Climbed out of her Swift, still squawking, because the lights had dipped, and something was for sure wrong. She pulled her Swift's remote recovery module from its compartment and tossed it into the pilot's seat to make sure her fighter wasn't going anywhere without her.

Her boots made a running clang up the starboard ramp tunnel. She scampered up the ladders three decks to the battery and shimmied into her team's gun blister, where Reg Monroe was bringing the mechanical junk to bear, jacking up the loader.

Got the shell ratcheted into the cannon.

"Okay, here's the fancy part," said little Reg, resting a moment, flopped over the black barrel nearly a yard in diameter, puffing. "How do we aim?"

"Look out the window," said Carly.

The open clearport was full—full—of bronze-colored Roman hull. "Who is that!"

"Com chatter's saying it's the *Scipio*," said Hazard Sewell.

Point-blank was an absurd term out here. In the absence of gravity, projectiles don't fall off their trajectories. Still it had become the accepted term for the range at which you cannot possibly miss.

Scipio rode—point-blank—alongside *Merrimack*. Something shimmered between them, hard, like glass. "What is that?"

"Our force fields are touching!" Hazard Sewell relayed from the command deck. "Hold your fire! We can't shoot. The shell will blow back in. Nobody fire!"

"Then they can't shoot us either, right?" said Reg. Hopeful. "Right?"

"I think," said Hazard, not comforted by that. This could not be good.

Kerry Blue pushed Cowboy away from the clearport so she could see. "So what are they *doing*?" Saw nothing but bronze hull.

The sounds were horrific. Electric groans and scraping squeals, sounds like nothing they had heard before.

Of something that had never happened before.

Scipio had matched phase pulses with *Merrimack* and was prying open her force field, like a starfish with a clam in its clutches.

"We're going to get our guts eaten," said Marcander Vincent on the command deck.

Captain Farragut, amazed, turned to his specialists on deck. "Someone want to tell me how the *hell* this is happening?"

Best they could offer him was to report that *Merrimack*'s phases had not been recalibrated during the refit. "They weren't broke, so no one fixed them."

Rome still had *Monitor*'s black box. Apparently no one considered that Rome had had the entire time span of the kangaroo truce in which to study *Monitor*'s workings and pull her phases from that.

"They did tell us the *Mack* wasn't ready," said Hamster.

"Oh, but we are," said Farragut. Called for suits and swords.

Glenn Hamilton's voice came over the loud com shipwide just before it went inoperative: "Prepare to repel boarders."

"I don't believe it," Twitch Fuentes mumbled at the sword in his hand. "I don't fragging believe it." This was for real.

Cowboy swaggered cheerfully, shirt off inside his exo suit, and sporting a red scarf on his head, a gold earring, and an eye patch. He kept repeating, "Arr arr, matey!" until someone told him to learn another letter of the alphabet.

The exo-suits were the same as the Romans wore. Except for the manufacturers' logos on the generators, the suits were identical on either side.

Mainly the suits provided deflector shields against beam fire. All were equipped with breathers in case of gas; sonic filters for the ears in case of sonic grenades; and energy dampers to protect against stunners. You could still get stunned through an exo suit, but your opponent needed to push the rod through the exo's energy layer and touch you with it, delivering the jolt right into you rather than through the exo-layer.

Because slow-moving objects could pass through an exo-suit, and because *Merrimack* carried redundancy to fanaticism, *Merrimack*'s crew wore helmets and kevlar clothing under the suit's energy shields.

The searing screeching of the force field's parting had stopped. The next sound was the clanging of the *corvus,* the Roman grappling hook, banging on *Merrimack*'s hull.

Reg Monroe crouched in place with her squad, cornered. The lights had gone, and no one turned on their headlamps. They listened in advancing horror to sounds of Them.

"Why don't they just kill us?" Reg breathed. "They could just as easy chuck a nuke in and close us up, and that would be that. Why don't they just do it?"

"They want the ship," Kerry murmured. *Thank God they want the ship.*

Hazard hushed them silent. "Listen!"

Thumps against the hull.

Hazard whispered, "Can anyone make out where they're going to force their way in?"

"Me, I'd come in the fighter shafts," Reg muttered.

And so they did—on the starboard wing—prying up the caps on the fighter lifts.

Came the hiss of atmospheric bleed out. Roman ships kept a thinner atmosphere. The breach sucked *Merrimack*'s air in with *Scipio*'s.

"They're in."

21

THE ROMANS OF THE invasion ship *Scipio* entered dark *Merrimack* warily, breathers clenched between their teeth, heads low. They used scanners in the dark hangar rather than illuminating their lamps. Did not like that they hadn't been met at the breach. Roman soldiers preferred fighting in solid ranks. They did not like this guerrilla skat.

Still, they could not expect the Americans to play to Roman strengths. When you reach into a cobra hole, you'd best expect to meet the fanged end.

A whole file boarded unopposed. Others waited for the area to be pronounced secure before committing any more troops to the enemy craft. This hangar, its crouching fighter craft, its silence, smelled more and more of a trap.

But the first troops found no one. Nothing sprang out at them. But they could not go deeper until they were sure flankers were not hiding here.

The cobra wanted them deeper in the hole. But, just as the Romans could not expect the enemy to play to Roman strengths, neither would Rome play into a U.S. trap.

Sensors could not detect the loc of warm bodies within exo-suits, and the sensors were detecting no motion other than their own. Yet the Roman captain knew the dirtlings could not be far.

They were here. They had to be here.

The Roman captain turned his disruptor on the nearest U.S. Marine fighter craft—a Swift with the Arabic numeral 6 emblazoned on its hull—and raked it bow to stern.

Worked. Flushed a dirtling out of the overhead. She dropped, screeching: "That's my crate!"

Someone crying after her, "*Chica linda,* no!"

Kerry Blue, madder than a wet zil, landed both boots on the Roman captain's shoulders, mashed him to the deck. Went down with him, disruptor fire flashing off her exo-suit. Pummeled him bloody.

She straightened up, hauling her sword edge across the advancing chest. The gushing stopped quickly with the heart's stopping. Just like in the simulators.

The hangar was in chaos. Kerry's sonic filters maxed with the din of screaming all around her, the screech of searing metal hit by deflected fire, the scattered crashes of severed equipment falling from the overhead, and triumphant shouts of "Arrrr!"

Captain Farragut, imitating a caged panther on the command deck, demanded again, "Status."

Lieutenant Glenn Hamilton hesitated to report that the battle was going well. It was going too well.

Roman boarders had breached Red and Blue docks, and the cargo hold. But Red dock was already secured, and very red.

Glenn expressed a concern that the Romans might decide to cut their losses, withdraw their bloody stump, and lob a bomb into the *Mack.*

"Then let's lob a bomb into *Scipio* first," said Farragut.

His techs pointed out that *Scipio* was shielded against *Merrimack*'s gunports. The Romans were not so careless as to leave an opening in front of any of *Mack*'s barrels, even though they had deactivated *Merrimack*'s computer controls.

"The mountain came to Mohammed," said Farragut. "Haul a cannon down to Red dock and shoot through the breach."

"*Haul?*" A thousand-kilogram cannon from the battery, three decks down, then all the way out to the starboard wing? "Uh, how, sir? We're on manual. The robot skids are not functional."

And, a sign from God, the antigrav failed.

As Hamster's hair lifted from her shoulders and her feet left the deck, she said, "I know Who loves you, John Farragut." And Colonel Steele bellowed for a Marine detail to bring a cannon to the starboard wing.

"Do *what*?" Cowboy protested, scrambling to action, fleet, agile, and upside down as a cockroach, propelling himself up the ramp tunnel, hand over hand along the overhead pipes. Kerry Blue had long suspected Cowboy had vermin in his ancestry.

Spurning the ladder, Cowboy sprang like Superman up through the hatch to the gun blister. Too hard. Weightless, he bounced himself off the overhead, banged his helmet, caromed back down, only to bowl Twitch Fuentes off the ladder.

Already in the gunroom, Kerry asked Reg, "Shell?" As Reg unhooked and unlatched the cannon moorings.

"Still one in there," said Reg. "We never got one off."

The grunting gorilla, Dak, wrenched the deck bolts loose.

Bolts off, the cannon lifted from its moorings. Kerry pushed the big gun toward the hatch, as Cowboy's head popped out of the hole like a prairie dog. "Ho—!" His head disappeared under the swinging cannon.

Kerry heard a metallic thud. She'd hit something. "Cowboy?" Kerry called down.

A lot of words she didn't know, then, "She's trying to kill me again!"

Kerry tsked, maneuvering the cannon into position to guide it down the hatchway. "Oh, shut it, Cowboy. I did not try to kill you! I *did* kill you, but I was *not* tryin'. And if you hadn't been brain dead, you'da had the sense to stay that way! This isn't gonna fit. Cowboy, Twitch, you're gonna have to take the ladder off!"

"Just push. It'll fit!"

"It will *not*!"

Cowboy pulled and Dak shoved. Between the two of them, they wedged the cannon tight in the hatch. The cannon hung up on the ladder.

"It doesn't fit," said Dak.

Cowboy said, "Kerry, don't push! Now look. You got it stuck. You got a wrench up there? I'm gonna have to take this whole ladder off."

There was a quick exchange of tools through the available gaps in the cannon-clogged hatchway to unbolt the ladder above and below. Kerry yelling, "Come on! Come on! We gotta go *now!*"

Ladder rungs clattered as Cowboy yanked it clear of the hatch. Shouted, "Move it! Move it!"

Kerry gave the cannon the gentlest of pushes. One thousand kilograms smashed into the deck below, bent the grates.

"God *bless* it!" Cowboy cried.

Kerry jumped up, pushed off the overhead and went air-swimming down the hatch headfirst to help dislodge the cannon from the deck.

Cannon mobile again, Cowboy, Dak, Twitch, Kerry, Carly, and Reg shepherded it down decks, like floating an elephant. They could not afford to get a mass that size moving too boisterously in any direction. Slight taps from it hurt, and turns were hard lessons in inertia.

The cannon crushed all the fingers of Twitch's right hand as the corridor turned and the cannon did not. Twitch kept up with the rest of his squad, crying.

Reg pointed up at a different sound. Knew that one. Usually liked it, but not this time. A Roman retreat clarion.

Kerry cried, "Oh, hell, they're going to close the doors! Move it! Move it! Move it!"

The cannon clanged, blundered, clunked, and smashed through the corridors. Made it to the ramp tunnel where it was clear sailing. Had the cannon hurtling toward the Red dock, Cowboy yelling, "Git along, little *doggie!*"

Came time to stop it, but Cowboy, Dak, Twitch, Kerry, Carly and Reg together did not come near to a thousand kilograms, and with a dearth of anything to grab onto as a brace, they skidded along with the careening mass.

Cowboy jumped in front of the cannon, hands out as if commanding it to stop.

It mowed him down—*"Cowboy!"*—and kept going. Bumped at the bottom of the ramp tunnel, bounced, like a slow motion missile, straight at a Swift.

"Not my crate! Not my crate!"

And plowed into the scorched side of Alpha Six.

Hazard Sewell with another squad of Marines—Echo Flight—was already in the hangar fixing braces in the Roman boarding hatch to force it to stay open against the sounding retreat.

Echo Flight helped disengage the cannon from Kerry's Swift, and then set it down, carriage-side to the deck. The Marines maneuvered the cannon to point at the breach; bolted it to the deck grates.

The two flights looked at each other. "We waiting on a command?"

"Com's down," said Reg.

"At will, I think," said Hazard.

Cowboy—bruised but still game—said: "Well, hell. Fire!"

The manual load fired dirty, the boom resounded to the limit of the sonic filters. The recoil ripped up the deck grates and shot the cannon backward into the bulk.

The shell found its mark, blew through *Scipio* and detonated deep within. The Marines could hear, then smell, the fire inside.

Their celebration was cut short with the flash of Roman lights signaling a decompression warning.

"They're gonna pull out without closing up!" Echo Leader motioned everyone up the ramp tunnel. "Get out of here! They're gonna space us! Go! Go! Go!"

"Captain, *Scipio* is preparing to disengage," Kit Kittering reported.

"Oh, no, you don't."Farragut spoke to his enemy, as if Romans were there on deck with him. Farragut was ready for this. During the melee, he had teams of erks weld the Roman grappling hooks in place, and jam at least one of them at the root, so *Scipio* could not just cast off the line. "You finish this dance."

Scipio had its hooks into *Merrimack* and could not get them out.

The communications tech, in some surprise, reported, "Getting a signal from *Scipio.*"

"How? Our com's down."

"It's on the radio. Captain Edward Sejanus is demanding *Merrimack*'s surrender."

Farragut laughed aloud in shock. "He said *that*?"

The com tech put Sejanus through to the captain's console so Farragut could tell him for himself, "Are you nuts?"

Sejanus sent a crackling reply, "I could destroy you."

"You're going to have to."

Destroying *Merrimack* would require destroying *Scipio* with it.

"I don't believe you, Captain Farragut. Your profile shows you the furthest thing from suicidal."

"And I'm not threatening suicide. *You*'re the one fixin' to pull the trigger, *Capita*. You go do what you think you have to do. I'm working here." Motioned across his throat for the com tech to disconnect.

Captain Farragut left the command platform. "Your boat, Hamster." He had his sword.

Farragut met TR Steele in the corridor on his way to the starboard ramp tunnel. "TR—your big guys and your crazy guys. With me."

Colonel Steele counted himself with the big guys, Serge, Dak, Ski. Gordo. And Delgado—crazy, not big, but then wolverines were only about twenty-three kilos.

Captain Farragut led the charge into smoky *Scipio*. Hacked his way forward, stormed onto the Roman command platform, and demanded Sejanus' surrender.

Sejanus came out of his scarlet-draped command chair, eyes flaring. The word *No!* came out of his mouth. Might have been an expression of horror, but it was the wrong answer to the demand. Farragut's sword stroke sent his head tumbling to the deck. And Captain Farragut accepted the surrender from *Scipio*'s second-in-command.

No ship from either side had interfered in *Merrimack*'s and *Scipio*'s single combat, not out of chivalry but because the two had been merged into one force field and neither side could shoot the foe without damaging the friend.

Sensor-blind and occupied with their own survival, no one on *Merrimack* had been aware of what had been happening in the battle for the Citadel. They had just got *Scipio*'s com tuned to the U.S. channel, and *Merrimack*'s techs were just learning how to aim *Scipio*'s guns when the U.S. recall sounded. All ships were ordered to abandon the field.

The U.S. assault force had managed to damage the Catapult, and the fleet was withdrawing.

Captain Farragut requested permission to press the attack. He was told to withdraw; the objective had been achieved.

"No, it's not! The objective has *not* been achieved. Get Mishindi on the com!" Farragut shouted, then begged Admiral Mishindi to let him continue the siege. "Damaged isn't good enough. We have to destroy it. I'm still in this!"

"Captain Farragut, you have your orders."

"We can take out the Cat!"

"Not your call, Captain Farragut."

"Please, sir!"

"Not my call either. With. Draw." Bit out two distinct words.

"Where's Calli?" Farragut asked. "Is Calli still trapped inside the grid?" Nothing would stop him from going back and getting her.

But no. Calli Carmel's *Wolfhound* was in retreat back to Earth with the rest of the assault force. John Farragut had no more excuses. Nothing to do but drag *Merrimack* back to Earth under *Scipio*'s power.

PART FIVE

KALI

22

"**YOU BLOODY MINDED APE!**" Admiral Toracelli railed at Captain Farragut. That for show in front of the LEN investigators. In private, with a near grin, he said, "John, you're a wild man."

"Yes, sir."

"*And* you were told to ask for a tow if you got overridden."

"I got a tow," said Farragut.

Toracelli waggled an admonishing finger at him. "Someday. Someday."

"What is the LEN doing here, sir?"

"Demanding a restoration of the cease-fire."

"Bull*skat*!" Farragut was volcanic.

The admiral continued calmly, "We said something to that end. A lot more roundabout and polite. The LEN are bringing the United States up on charges in the World Court for violating the cease-fire and for barbarism. Quite a speedy process, you know."

Speedy as Plutonian mud. Farragut sat. You could fight a whole war before LEN injunctions could go into effect.

"And the LEN are naming you personally for war crimes."

"*Me?*" Didn't believe it. Felt it like a punch in the gut. War crimes. "War crimes?"

"We're standing for you. Not to worry."

Farragut was not worried. He was insulted. And, a feeling man, deeply wounded. *"War crimes!"*

"The swords. All too gruesome."

"I was *boarded*. The lupes didn't ask my permission, and I sure as hell didn't grant it. I hadn't surrendered. I defended my ship."

"You beheaded Commander Sejanus. *Beheaded* him. On his own bridge."

"Was he more dead than if I'd shot him?"

"You do see the point, though?"

"No. No, sir, I do not. It was combat. The LEN is taking off points for neatness?"

"The combat part is the sticking point. Rolls us back to our being the side to break the cease-fire. You see, it wasn't a lawful combat to begin with in the LEN books."

"What do you want me to do, sir?"

"John, we're getting you out of Dodge on the first stagecoach."

"As long as that stage is the *Merrimack,* I'll be happy to go."

"The *Mack* is vulnerable."

"I think I just proved she's not."

"We still don't know how Rome's getting your codes. Carmel *was* a prime suspect."

Farragut's back stiffened. "I trust Cal better'n I trust my own mama."

"She did turn in a superb showing at the Citadel. Carmel, that is, not Mrs. Farragut."

Captain Carmel had not shown the least hesitation to fire on Romans she had known at the Institute. Nor they at her. It was a typically Roman sort of respect.

"Still, it looks like you have a Roman mole," Toracelli went on. "And I'm damned if I can find him. In its current condition, do you honestly trust *Merrimack* with your life?"

"Change her phases, I trust her with all our lives in the Deep."

"Who said you were going Deep?"

"Where else? Shotguns need two stations. We dinged the Near Cat. There has to be a Far Cat. And since a whole bunch of Roman Legions didn't displace through to the Near Cat when we were attacking it, that means there's lots of stranded Romans in the Deep End."

"More than likely," Toracelli acceded.

"Where is the Far Cat?"

"Not precisely sure."

Farragut's eyebrows skied. "Then where precisely am I going?"

The grav disturbance had given a rough plot—a stellar neighborhood. But it could not pinpoint the location, or even narrow it to a reasonable haystack in which to search.

"An adviser will brief you when you clear Fort Ike."

Oh, hell. I'm picking up another spook at Fort Ike, thought Farragut. "Not Colonel Oh," he insisted.

"No. Not Colonel Oh. She's flying a desk. Not even CIA." Toracelli assured him. "One more thing, John. Kali."

"Calli? My Calli?"

"No. K-A-L-I. Indian goddess with fangs, bloody tongue, skull necklace, dead baby earrings, walking over her husband's dead body. That Kali."

"What about her?"

"It's a Roman code word, associated with the Deep End. We had thought it was the Far Cat. But a thing named Kali—" he let the sentence hang.

"They don't build to import avocados," Farragut finished for him.

"Exactly."

Farragut sat forward, forearm across knee. "Vic. You're talking to me here. What aren't you telling me? Where am I going?"

"Honest to God, I don't know." Toracelli laughed at the bizarre sound of that even as he said it. "Our source is not talking."

"We're mole-infested and you trust this source without so much as a—" He broke off with the coming of the dawn. Who could win that kind of trust. "Oh, for Jesus."

Because suddenly he knew who he was picking up at Fort Eisenhower.

"Permission to come aboard—is that the correct way to phrase the request?"

"As if I could stop you. You're a determined man, Jose Maria."

Captain Farragut's civilian adviser boarded *Merrimack* like a houseguest, with a bottle of Spanish wine in hand and a kiss on either cheek.

"I've had easier times digging a tick out of my hide than keeping you off my boat."

"Please," Don Cordillera protested, hand to wounded heart. "The tick is a parasite. I am a symbiote. I know the location of that which you seek, and I need someone to take me there. And so." He spread his arms to say here he was, on board *Merrimack,* bound for the Deep End.

Farragut inspected the label of the bottle in his hands. A fine vintage Rioja. "This has lived way too long. Come on and help me put it out of its misery, and tell me how the hell a Terra Rican neutral civilian happens to know where the Far Cat is."

Kerry Blue. In flagrante.

Her partner jackrabbited away. Couldn't ID him from the white ass that bobbed through the hatch.

Flight Sergeant Blue shrugged her jumpsuit up over her shoulders to free up her arm and hoist a salute. Left her still unsnapped stem to stern, leaving a sliver peek of young strong spare flesh on display.

Colonel Steele, revving up to yell at her. Too mad to think of what to yell. Distracted. Kerry Blue didn't wear underwear. Left a tuft of wayward fur on show. Steele snarled, "You're out of uniform."

Kerry looked uncertain. Her salute wavered. "Uh, yes, sir." Not sure if she'd been given leave to do something about it. And because he looked so red-faced mad, she dropped from attention, snapped up, resumed her salute.

Steele growled, jerked his head in the direction of the hatch through which her partner had made his escape. "Carver?"

"No-oo!" Two or three syllables worth of no. "Not if he was the last—" Met the colonel's ice-blue eyes. Stopped. Said, "No, sir."

Too much protest. Told Steele what he already knew—that she was still stuck on Cowboy Carver.

At least she was making a real effort to try to hate him.

For Steele, hating Cowboy required no effort at all. Of all the men who had used Kerry Blue, Cowboy Carver was the one Steele wanted most dead. Cowboy was the worst. Because Kerry Blue had loved him.

Steele did not demand a name from her. He did not want to know. He paced back and forth in front of her, mad as hell, with nothing acceptable to say. Finally: "Marine, do you want to transfer out?"

Shock on her face. Her answer emphatic, "*No,* sir!"

"You are ruining morale."

Her brown eyes got very wide. Dumbfounded, she blurted, *"Sir?"*

They called Kerry Blue the morale officer. She was no Trixi Allnight, but she was here, she was real, and she was usually to be had. And she gave no reports on her studies of comparative anatomy.

"Discipline," he corrected himself. Glad his face was already a furious red. Ears felt like they could ignite his hair, were his hair long enough to touch them. The only morale Kerry Blue was crushing was his. "You're bad for discipline."

"I didn't think it was that big a deal. What I was doing."

Not to her, it wasn't. It was a big deal. To him.

Tough. Soft. Pretty, in a rode-hard way. A good-hearted tramp. Not stupid. Not smart. Not a real deep thinker. Kerry Blue lived for the moment. Open. Everything that was Kerry Blue was right out there. She would follow him to hell.

"Sir, I want to stay."

Like removing his own rib, Steele told her, "You are going back to Fort Ike on the next LRS."

John Farragut and Jose Maria de Cordillera had euthanized the Rioja as well as a respectable Barca Velha, and were halfway through a bottle of Cassiopeian Barbaresco when Jose Maria got round to answering the question of how he knew the location of the Roman Far Cat.

"My wife, my Mercedes, accepted an irresistible engagement with the Palatine government. In the nature of a terraforming."

Dr. Mercedes Francesca Diego de Seville de Cordillera was a preeminent xenoecologist, who had made many practical contributions to human colonization efforts. Her specialty was the successful insertion of Terran life-forms among native species without upsetting the natural balance, thus preserving the alien ecosystem while establishing a cohabiting system capable of sustaining human settlement.

The assignment that Palatine offered to Mercedes had been secret and long term. So secret she did not even know where she was bound until she arrived. She was permitted to record messages to her husband, which were scrutinized and sanitized before delivery to Terra Rica. Even Jose Maria was not to know the planet's—which was to say his wife's—location.

But Mercedes and Jose Maria had a code, the sort of code only a man and a woman deeply in love for thirty years could devise. And this man and this woman had stratospheric IQs so not even a Roman patterner could detect a code within their missives, much less penetrate their meaning. All their secret words were based on referents not contained in any database, things known only to two people in the universe.

So Jose Maria came into possession of the coordinates of a planet in the Deep End called Telecore, which served as the supply base for the construction of the Far Cat.

Which coordinates he gave to John Farragut.

Farragut tentatively accepted the data bubble. He admonished the Terra Rican, "This is a betrayal of neutrality."

Terra Rica was strictly neutral in any conflict between the United States and Palatine. And Jose Maria de Cordillera was a man of no small consequence. A personal violation of neutrality could put his world in a bad position with the Roman Empire.

"Apparently, there is no trust between us for me to betray," said Jose Maria. "I am trying to get to my wife. That is all. If the Romans will not take me, their sorrow if I seek help elsewhere."

"I don't get it, Jose Maria. Why do you need me? If you want to go, why not just go? Take one of your own yachts. You'd be a hell of a lot more comfortable. And you could've been there by now. Terra Ricans are allowed to use the Shotgun, and don't tell me you can't afford the toll."

Jose Maria lifted dark eyes to the low overhead with exposed ductwork. "I can afford luxury. Does not mean I need it. I prefer to go aboard your battleship, young captain."

Farragut set the data bubble aside carefully. "There is more to this story than you just told me."

"And so there is."

Jose Maria set aside his drink, continued soberly.

Mercedes had been homeward bound on board a Roman ship, the *Sulla,* when her messages ceased, and *Sulla* was never heard from again. The ship came in to no port. Its crew—Jose Maria managed to get the ship's manifest—were not to be found. He contacted relatives of *Sulla*'s crew. They were all steadfastly silent, the way good Romans could be.

If Jose Maria could get to the planet Telecore, he could backtrack *Sulla*'s molecular trail, perhaps pick up a transmission.

"Only if they were transmitting electromagnetic signals," said Farragut, which surely Jose Maria knew. "You can't trace resonance." Then thought to ask, "*Can* you?"

The Nobel Laureate shook his head no. "I cannot. But if *Sulla* met a foul end, as I believe it did, it must have transmitted by all means possible. There would be an SOS."

And any SOS was, by necessity, traceable to its source.

"Wouldn't someone have picked up the SOS by now?"

"I believe there was one. Palatine already answered, shut it off, and whited out the sphere of waves coming toward traveled space."

Opened Farragut's eyes. "*That* is quite a conspiracy theory." Jose Maria did not strike John Farragut as a paranoid man. But, "Death of one's wife will do things to your head. I know."

Jose Maria had not said that word aloud, but he did not argue it. "I am deeply sorry that you know that, young Captain."

Farragut found himself with a mouth full of foot and couldn't spit it out. He apologized, "I sure didn't mean to say your wife was—might be—" hitched on the word. Blundered on, "Dead."

Jose Maria closed his eyes, shook his head with a sad, benign smile. Refused the apology, admitting, "I believe that she is."

"No. I shouldn't ever have said that. I didn't mean it. I don't know that. You can't know that."

Jose Maria lifted bright black eyes as if finding something interesting in the piping. Let the tears drain inward, unshed. "That is the cruelty of it. The false hope. And it is false. Because I *know*."

"That's just worry talking."

"Concretization is the scientific term. But you must believe me. I know. *Sulla* met with more than an accident."

"What? Did you find something in Mercedes' last message?"

"Nothing said. Things unsaid. The silence round *Sulla*'s disappearance runs too deep. It was not long after that we began to hear whispers of Kali."

Farragut said he had heard that whisper.

"Whispers only. Nothing more," said Jose Maria. "A project the size of Catapulta—Shotgun—call it what you will—it does not lend itself to total secrecy. Too many workers. Too many specialists. Too much equipment. Too much money changing accounts. It was secret in the details, but everyone knew Rome was building a Catapult.

"I can find no one who knows or is willing to speak anything of

Kali. You can tell those who do know by the dire look that overcomes their visages at the mention of its name. And they do not speak."

"Not a warm puppy sort of a name," said Farragut. "Sounds like a name for a terror weapon."

Jose Maria gave a provisional nod. "Something terrible. Kali is the destroyer."

"I thought Shiva was the Destroyer," said Farragut.

"Kali is Shiva's consort. Consort of Time and the Destroyer. The goddess Kali was enlisted to kill demons, which she did, and drank their blood. But once there were no demons left to kill, she kept on killing across the cosmos, annihilating all in her path."

"Sounds like a Roman weapon run amok."

"I do not know. It does not do to parse Roman code names too finely. I think it is safe to say this Kali is a destructive thing. And I know in my heart of hearts, by accident or by purpose, it destroyed *Sulla.*"

23

A DOZEN OR SO LIGHT-DECADES into the Deep, someone and eight or twenty of his buddies started pounding out Farouq's Percussive Symphony Number 3 on the overhead with swords. It started that way. Had since devolved into a ship-wide 'cuss jam that was loud enough to shake the vacuum.

Someone clacked out a soprano counter line on the kirki sticks. Could be Kerry Blue and Carly Delgado. Someone else pulled an interesting *twok twok twok* out of what sounded like a cannon barrel.

And someone was way off beat. Probably that big lummox Dak, who had always been rhythm-free. Or Serge, bashing away like an orangutan on sprox.

Whoever had sleep cycle during the middle watch was S.O.O.L. because Farragut put up with the noise. Farragut was probably drumming on the hull with his usual exuberance.

TR Steele had taken his dogs aboard lots of ships. Had respected most of their captains, none more than this one. None had surprised him more than this one. Energetic. Fearless. Farragut never shrank from a dustup. And Steele's dogs loved him. Farragut could dive in and be one of them—the front liners—howling like a coyote, drum on the wastewater stack, without losing his command presence. Something Steele could never do. Could only get a headache from the boisterous 'cussing, and wish he knew how the hell Farragut did that.

Blessed the chime for general quarters that pierced the din, shutting down all the artistes, and had them running for the gun bays.

Merrimack had picked up an SOS.

Jose Maria de Cordillera beat Farragut to the command center, his heartbeat still pounding out Farouq's Third. "What ship?"

"Not *Sulla*," said the young Officer of the Watch, who knew Don Cordillera's story.

And Jose Maria was disappointed until he saw the ship.

"Holy God."

Thanked God it was not *Sulla*. The drifting husk of a ship looked for all hell as if it had been chewed. The SOS was a dormant signal.

"Dormant?" said Marcander Vincent. "Hell, it's dead."

Merrimack illuminated her floods and turned several slow circuits round the wreck, to identify what it had been—Roman make, big, a transport, nominally civilian, but the sort that often served as pack beast to the Legions of Rome.

"Cal—" Farragut started. Stopped.

Not Cal.

His hand landed on his XO's shoulder, and the captain hung his head, apologetic. "Ah, hell, Bast."

He had not slipped like that in weeks. Sense of danger made him fall back on his old faithful. But Calli was not his anymore. Wondered if the admiralty had given her the *Monitor*. He'd been rushed out of town too fast to know.

His XO was Sebastian Gray now. Same height as Cal. Same age. Not as fun to look at. Easy enough to work with. Had not shown what he had under fire on *Merrimack* yet. Deserved respect.

The captain took names seriously. The misspeak was not a minor uf in John Farragut's book. He started over. "*Commander Gray*, what are we looking at?"

A wide scan located the derelict's cargo cars strewn over several milliklicks like dead planets of a dead star. The food cars had been pillaged, the machine carriers and oxygen bricks left intact.

After multiple scans turned up no contagion and only moderate corrosives on board the derelict ship, Farragut ordered Old Glory reeled in and a Red Cross run up the yard.

He sent a medical team with a Marine guard on a skiff to board the wreck. They limpet-docked and entered through an existing hole in the hull.

It was slow work. Flight Sergeant Kerry Blue negotiated the passage gingerly through the tear, mindful of the jaggedness of the metal edges and the flimsiness of her spacesuit. The suit's material was actually rugged but unnervingly thin.

A lock of hair, come loose from her band, floated in Kerry's face. She tossed her head inside her helmet trying to puff the strands out of her mouth, her eyes. Floating ends tickled her nose. She lifted gloved hands to her faceplate on reflex, pawed at the visor.

"Something wrong with your suit, Marine?" That was Flight Leader Hazard Sewell doing a Colonel Steele impersonation.

Kerry spat. Hair stuck to her lips. "No, sir."

Black. Even the stark light of their lamps could not dispel the blackness within the dead ship. The wreckage inside had mostly found a resting equilibrium against the bulkheads. There was not much floating about loose. The ship had been this way for a while.

Torn, corroded holes pocked the corridors as if the ship itself were diseased. The clear signature of Roman beam fire scored the decks. It took some real nutsifaction for the crew to have done that to their own ship. Or maybe banshees had got hold of the weapons and gone on a rampage. Kerry had seen some weird things out in the Deep, but this was a tough read.

They discovered uniforms on most decks, shredded and darkly stained, but no bodies in or near them. No bodies at all.

They did find dog tags. Collected those. Two hundred forty. Two hundred forty-one. Two hundred forty-two. And would the frassing MP turn off his helmet mike or count to himself please?

Nothing remained of the ship's food stores. The ship's weapons were all here. All had been discharged, emplaced guns and sidearms alike. The wreck, her name was *Hermione,* had put up a fight for all she was worth.

The ship's mess was devoid of even coffee beans. Hydroponics had been harvested messily but completely. Holes with dirt trails gaped in the soil of flowerpots in the officers' quarters where houseplants had evidently been yanked out by the roots. The chief's fish tank was frozen to the overhead by its own water, its artificial plants encased in the ice, but not the fish. The fish were MIA.

Computer banks waited, unscathed, for a command. The pattern of mayhem spoke of rage and perhaps hunger, but not of human intelligence. Knowledge was power, and the attacker had left *Hermione*'s knowledge behind like so much junk.

Kerry found pieces of shoes—soles, grommets, and laces, but not the rest. She recognized the Roman military type. The missing parts would have been leather. Also missing was the wool lining of a very nice ylene jacket.

The Romans were keen for woodwork, but Kerry hadn't seen any real wood on board.

A floating milky gleam caught the light of Kerry's headlamp. She gathered in a couple of the pearly beads, stilled them in her gloved fist, then opened her hand for a look.

Yelped. Flung them away.

"Marine?" Hazard's alarmed inquiry sounded in her helmet.

"Teeth!" she screeched. "I got teeth!"

"Fangs?"

"No, you dwit! Somebody's teeth!" She rubbed her gloved hands on the nearest surface as if something were stuck on them that could be wiped off. The teeth had been terribly clean. That didn't matter. There was teethness on her hands. She danced off the bulk, altogether creeped.

Merrimack hailed the med team. The unfamiliar voice that sounded in Kerry Blue's helmet had to belong to Commander Sebastian Gray: "Survivors?"

"Negative." Kerry Blue recognized the answering voice as the MO's. Mo Shah was about five paces away from her, methodically collecting floating teeth. "Personnel are being gone. Probably being dead. They are not being here."

Kerry was not sure which nightmare was more hideous, that the crew were dead or that they were alive somewhere, in some state, naked and without teeth.

"Then haul on back to *Merrimack*." Captain Farragut's voice this time. "We've just been pinged."

Kerry joined the orderly scramble for the skiff.

A hail of something pelted the skiff. One of the somethings smacked Kerry's shoulder as she towed herself aboard the skiff. "Captain, we've been tagged!"

The Marine behind Kerry pulled the tag off her suit and chucked it out to space.

Merrimack's lookout reported, "Roman signature coming in high and hot on the eights. Single. Looks like a Fury. Closing."

A relief in a way. Anyone would rather face Romans than whatever had done this to *Hermione*.

Farragut's first orders were for the force field tech to scrub the tags. "Any homers on your screen?"

"Negative, sir."

The com tech reported, "I'm receiving the Roman's demand: Move away from the Roman ship *Hermione* or be destroyed."

"We have a Red Cross flying?" Farragut checked.

"Yes, sir."

The Roman Fury came into engagement range. Engagement range was anything within a quarter light-second, the range within which a ship's scanners perceived a target approximately where it actually was. The range was closer than the distance between the Earth and the Moon.

Farragut said, "Inform the Roman we are a rescue ship responding to an SOS."

Still the Fury approached, all weapons ports open. It deployed another flock of homing tags. Its commander called Farragut a murderer. Told him to take down the false flag. He meant *Merrimack*'s Red Cross.

"We *found* your ship in this state," Farragut responded. The Fury had to know that. The threats were all bluster and cover fire. "Stop it with the spitwads." Already *Merrimack*'s outboard lasers seared the second round of tags off *Mack*'s hide. "You can't shoot a rescue ship."

"Get away, you carrion eater."

Carrion? So the Roman knew the ship was dead? How did the Roman know that? *Did* he know that? Or was this more bellicose talk?

"Get your lice off our property, *Merrimack*." The Roman referred to the U.S. med team. "Do not touch the flight recorder. Touch nothing. You are not a rescue ship."

"Neither are you!" Farragut shot back. "Your boys and girls on *Hermione* are dead and you know it. You're a salvage scow."

A silence. To call a soldier a salvager was the deepest insult. The Roman came back with a spitting, angry, "Strike your Red Cross."

Farragut knew he'd just been dared to step out in the alley and say that. He put the com on mute and asked the Og if the med skiff had made it back aboard. Told yes, Farragut ordered his new XO, "Strike the Red Cross. Get us a firing solution on the Roman Fury and stand by to fire."

Commander Sebastian Gray's brows lifted, but he issued the orders and reported back, "Striking Red Cross, aye."

Targeting had nailed a sounder bull's-eye on the Fury, but held fire. The Roman ship flew no Red Cross, but it was still inside the rescue zone.

Very strict, tacit rules held out here. Everyone was vulnerable out here. When not part of a battle zone, hostiles observed a one light-second no-fire radius around the source of an SOS.

Farragut asked the Roman if he wanted to step outside, then moved *Merrimack* outside the radius.

He was only slightly surprised that the lighter Roman Fury took up the challenge.

Tac reported: "Roman Fury is leaving the radius!"

And because it did so, Farragut ordered, "Stand by to switch control routine."

In the natural order of things, the smaller Fury was no match for the battleship *Merrimack*. This dare was in no way even, unless the Roman was packing spare aces on board.

Merrimack's controls flickered. "There it is," Kit Kittering reported from Engineering. Expected it. "Roman Fury is attempting override."

Merrimack shut down all its code recognitions and activated the backup routine. The battleship's controls stabilized immediately. Plan B was working.

"Your mole doesn't have up-to-date information," Commander Gray commented.

"Doesn't look like it," Farragut murmured, glad to hear his new exec sound impassive. "Let 'em have it."

The XO ordered, "All stations, fire at will."

The Fury had no Plan B. At its failure to sabotage *Merrimack* by mimicking her old command codes, the enemy ship turned tail, squid-wise, to retreat at its most defensible angle.

Despite her greater mass, *Merrimack* was a powerful, quick ship. She ran down the Fury, forced it to turn, dropping it out of FTL.

The Fury waddled at sublight speed, angling for an escape vector.

Merrimack bludgeoned the Fury with broad waves of disrupter spreads—bludgeoned carefully, trying to crack the eggshell but still leave the yolk intact. Great fire sprays struck the Fury's inertial screen.

Realizing there could be no escape, and that the *Merrimack* would likely smash the yolk along with its shell on one of these salvos, the Fury ran out the white flag with the symbolic half roll. The Roman surrendered.

"Anyone get the idea Farragut is just a little disappointed we didn't get boarded?" Cowboy sheathed his sword and stowed it in Kerry Blue's locker with suggestive motions of the blade. "I think he gets off on that swashbuckling skat."

"So do you, you *boon*." Kerry Blue slammed the locker shut on Cowboy's fingers.

Interrogation of the Fury's crew—there were fifty of them—gave little clue as to what had befallen the derelict transport *Hermione*. The prisoners claimed not to know. Their insistence was too adamant. They knew. And they were afraid.

Merrimack circled back to dead *Hermione,* shut off its SOS sounder, took the hulk in tow along with the Fury, and continued on her voyage to the Far Cat.

Roman craft had a certain majesty to them. Where American ships had a belligerent beauty in the clean, brute, utilitarian lines of their equipment, the Romans added stylistic design components. Only details, but telling details. A blunt, rounded end to a metal shaft where a simple square cut-off would have done. Their colors were richer. Their objects looked more substantial. They suggested grandeur, permanence.

Lieutenant Glenn Hamilton sat on the Fury's command deck. Felt as if she were on a stage set. And she was getting into character. Ensconced in a chair like this, she had to be monarch of something or other. She was tempted to try on the cape.

Romans could also go way over the top with flashy, gaudy accoutrements of past glory—oak wreaths, capes, gold cuirasses molded with muscle, shiny greaves, boots, all kinds of boots, embroidered togas, and those leather-flanged armor skirt things a man had to have truly great legs to wear with confidence. Though the Romans' undress uniforms were very dignified, practical, and sharp, their dress uniforms could be Las Vegas flashy.

So there was a deep-scarlet command cape with embossed gold shoulder pins draped over the Fury's command seat, demanding to sit on Glenn Hamilton's shoulders. She refrained. Partly because the thing was awfully shiny—borderline, or maybe over-the-line tacky—but mostly because Lieutenant Glenn Hamilton was five foot one, and the cape would drag on the deck, making her look like a little girl playing dress up instead of a Roman *domna*.

She seldom felt short on board *Merrimack,* unless someone reminded her with the stupid nickname *Hamster*—and thanks a heap for that one, John Farragut. She was accustomed to giving orders to truly big Marines. But the dimensions of this Roman ship were overlarge. Monumental was the word for it.

She assumed an imperial posture.

She was reviewing the ship's log when the Aldebaran scarab crickets, which clung heraldically to the hatchway, let out a chorus of chirping. Startled, Glenn Hamilton checked her chron. No, it was not later than she had thought. It was the scarab crickets that were off.

Some Roman with way too much time on his hands had conditioned the insectoids from the time they were larvae to sound off at intervals precisely coinciding with the changing of the Roman watch.

The Aldebaran scarab crickets were big, at least one foot long, bronze-colored, metallic-looking, and so seldom moved they might well be fixtures. The Romans used them as architectural decorations. The scarab crickets had that grotesque elegance Romans fancied. Their distinctive lines, a popular motif in Roman jewelry, were familiar to everyone, though Glenn Hamilton had never expected to be sharing decks with live ones.

She had got used to the giant bugs, scarcely knew they were there, till they started singing out of time.

"Who wound up the gargoyles?" said the tech who was trying to decipher the Fury's navigational computer.

Glenn Hamilton turned toward the hatchway and ordered the decorations to shut up.

They obeyed every bit as well as any Terran insect would.

"God bless it!" Glenn rose from her seat, as suddenly one gargoyle detached and swooped across the cabin with a whirring of metallic wings. The deck officers ducked with wordless shouts.

"I didn't know they had wings!" one cried from under a console.

Other giant scarab crickets detached from their posts and set off in bulk-bouncing panic throughout the Fury.

Glenn Hamilton hailed the *Merrimack,* "Captain, I may have a situation here."

And immediately winced at how inept she was going to sound explaining why she was bothering Captain Farragut to report badly timed scarab crickets. No wonder she had only been "acting" exec of the *Merrimack.* Couldn't see Sebastian Gray making a misstep like this. Hoped Farragut didn't have her on the box, and the new XO wasn't listening in on her transmission.

She was rescued by an improbable coincidence. Over the open com, she heard Marcander Vincent on *Merrimack's* command deck sing out, "Occultation at four by twelve by one twenty!"

They had a situation.

24

"I SEE IT, HAMSTER. Good eye. Join up and go dark."

Lieutenant Glenn Hamilton was not about to tell Captain Farragut she had *not* sighted the bogey. That her situation had only to do with an antic scarab cricket.

"Tuck us into *Merrimack*'s force field," she ordered her skeleton crew. "Take us dark."

Her crew were some moments figuring out how to obey, unfamiliar with the Fury's controls. They must have hit something wrong—or else a timer had run down to zero—because the Roman ship suddenly went darker than they had wanted.

"*Merrimack.* Hamilton." Glenn opened the com. "We—uh—blew a fuse." The accepted term for when you accidentally uffed an entire system. "We are flying dead stick."

It was hardly unexpected that the Roman ship would have system bombs in place in case of capture. Something had cued the Fury that it was no longer in Roman hands, and the ship refused to obey any more enemy commands.

"Do you have life support?" Farragut sent.

"Yes, sir. And com, apparently."

"Suit up your crew in case there's a second bomb. We're going to hook you."

"Aye, sir." Glenn clicked off. "Crew to space suits," she ordered, then dove out of the way of a swooping scarab cricket. "And contain those gargoyles!"

One of the Aldebaran monsters alighted in her command chair, and jacked itself up on its six legs, buzzing, its eyes—all four of them—staring at Hamster in bugly rage. Or was that horror?

Lieutenant Hamilton lifted an image tablet with which to squash the scarab cricket, but she hesitated too long. Looked at it too long.

The scarab cricket's size, the quantity of whatever was inside it, the prospect of that whatever squirting out all over her magnificent chair, made her think better of the squashing course of action.

She yanked the scarlet cape off the back of the command chair, whisking it over the scarab cricket in one motion. She wrapped up the gargoyle's buzzing fury (or was that fear?), and pushed the whole bundle—scarlet yardage, cricket, all—into a Marine guard's arms. "Shove that out an air lock."

A dreadful pause. "We're dark, sir," the Marine reminded her. Opening an air lock would betray the ship's darkness. Hamster ought to know that. Worst luck in the world to get a stupid order from a commanding officer.

Worse still, Captain Farragut happened to be sweet on this particular officer, though the Hamster was the only man jack or jane on board who didn't seem to know that. And Farragut, who was usually all kinds of smart, thought no one noticed.

I just pointed out stupid to the captain's Hamster. I'm gonna get skinned twice.

But no skinning was forthcoming. Glenn Hamilton shut her eyes, admitted, "You're right. Do something with that, soldier."

The Marine tucked the red bundle under his left arm, very relieved. "Sir."

He marched out. Hamster could own up to a mistake. Captain had good taste.

"What have we got?" Farragut asked Tactical after he had sounded general quarters.

"Sphere, Captain."

A sphere was the most energy-conserving shape—having the smallest possible surface area for the volume, offering the least direct exposure to the deep freeze of space.

"LEN golf ball?"

The League of Earth Nations' round discovery vessels ranged

everywhere. Both sides, Roman and U.S., regularly boarded them as suspected spies.

"Too big," said Mr. Vincent. "Vector out of the deep Deep End."

The com tech discreetly hand-signaled for the captain's attention. A request, if the captain chose to notice.

Farragut nodded for the com tech to speak.

"Mo Shah," said the com tech, apparently having the medical officer on hold. "Wants to know if you 'are being exceptionally busy.' "

The captain took the medical officer's hail. "Am I *busy*? Just a *little*, Mo." A little irony there. "What do you need?"

"I am observing a coincidence, perhaps being worth noting," said Dr. Mohsen Shah. "A great agitation among the insectoid life in the lab was preceding the call to general quarters by moments. There is being an appearance of a connection."

The Riverite doctor professed a creed in the connectivity of all life. "Noted," said Farragut. "Thanks, Mo. Out." Clicked off, not about to press the ship's ant farm into service as the new long-range lookout.

It was not possible that the ship's insects detected anything thirty light-minutes distant. The coincidence could be nothing but coincidence.

Farragut regarded the orb on his scanner display. He probably ought to simply report the sighting to the Joint Chiefs and plot a course around it. Leave the first contact to the experts in that sort of thing.

But by now his techs could tell him more about the bogey. It was five klicks in radius, moving at one hundred times the speed of light, and sporting a low-level force field.

It was also moving on direct vector *from* the coordinates identified by Jose Maria as Telecore, the planetary base for the Far Cat.

"Doesn't look Roman, but it sure as hell smells Roman," said Mr. Vincent at Tactical.

"Move us into its path," said Farragut. "Ready to roll out the welcoming mat."

"Ready Roman welcoming mat, aye," said Commander Gray, alerting Fire Control.

"And get us a res scan."

The res scan came back altogether weird. The sphere acted like a vessel but its composition was in no way reflective of a vessel. Dense, solid, dead, and cold.

"Mr. Gray, what do you think?" Captain Farragut asked his new exec.

"I think the Roman is foxing our res scan," said Commander Gray.

"Me, too," said Farragut.

"Sir," Marcander Vincent called out. "The target twitched. Started the moment we scanned it."

He amplified the image on the display to show the sphere close up. Its surface pocked and moved.

Commander Sebastian Gray blinked. "Did you see that?"

"I'll be damned," said Farragut.

It didn't smell Roman anymore. It smelled truly alien.

"Get Hamster's husband on deck," said Farragut. Patrick Hamilton was a xenolinguist. "Have him ask this ETI where it thinks it's going in such an almighty hurry."

"ETI, sir?" said Commander Gray. That the thing was extraterrestrial was beyond question. But intelligent?

"If it's FTL, it's I," said Farragut.

Gray looked blank. "Sir?"

"If it's moving faster than light, there's an intelligence behind it. Res scan it again."

As the tech took the res shot, the sphere moved again. It definitely moved, its structure changing.

"Target is breaking up," said Marcander Vincent.

The sphere's twitches were coincident with *Merrimack*'s resonant scans. But the events could not possibly be connected.

The res scan revealed that the sphere was expanding. It was composed of cells in a honeycomb pattern except for the ice layer that coated the whole, which continued to rupture as the inner layers of cells moved underneath, expanded, dislodging the outer layers, changing.

Farragut ordered another snapshot of the new form. "Scan again."

The sphere became more agitated.

The command crew exchanged glances. What was becoming obvious they still refused to accept. That they could be observing cause and effect here was improbable to the point of impossibility. Harmonics were infinite. Nothing could monitor them all at once. And chances of this sphere just happening to share *Merrimack*'s particular harmonic by accident were nil.

The crew on the command platform watched the displays in amazement.

Sounds of men shouting and banging on the bulks and ductwork pushed to Farragut's attention. A battleship was not a soundproof place, but this noise was excessive even for *Merrimack*. He gave a quick order, "Quiet that unit down."

"Aye, sir."

The sphere was breaking up. Its surface crumbled away to the layer below, became ciliate, flailing like a titanic rotifer. Then cells of the honeycomb broke off. Hexagonal shapes became rounded, then sprouted wreaths of whip-thin tentacles and flew, as if floating in water, each cell roughly a meter in diameter, not counting the cilia, expanding in the vacuum.

Alive. They looked alive.

"Move us out of the sphere's way. Let's see where it's going."

"It's going toward *us*," Marcander Vincent said as soon as the pilot had altered *Merrimack*'s course. "The plot changed course as we did."

Farragut moved to the tactical station to look at Mr. Vincent's tactical array. "How? How did it change? Where's its power plant?"

"It has nothing," said Mr. Vincent. "I think our sensors are uffed."

"Are we sure this isn't Roman?"

"Captain, we are so unsure of anything about this thing that—look at that!"

The detached cells flitted, swarmed together like fish in a nonexistent current in the vacuum sea. They moved toward *Merrimack* in a tenuous cloud followed by the crumbling mass of the sphere.

The cells attached themselves to *Merrimack*'s force field. That, too, should be impossible. The battleship's inertial screen was frictionless. There was nothing for the things to latch onto.

"Jink," Farragut ordered.

"Jinking, aye." The pilot jerked *Merrimack* on a random jag of a course.

The things—giant spidery, centiped-like things—stuck fast as barnacles. "I think they've hooked our field."

"How the hell—" Farragut stopped, hearing background noise louder than his own voice. "I thought I ordered those men to shut up."

"It's the prisoners, sir," Mr. Gray reported apologetically. Tough to get Romans to obey orders. "They're screaming."

"I can hear that. What's their problem?"

"There's an insect in their compartment."

"And?"

Gray felt silly even reporting this. "There's an insect 'acting erratically' in the prisoners' hold."

"Aldebaran scarab cricket?" Farragut held his palms a foot apart.

"Someone's pet sicalian." Gray held his thumb and forefinger an inch apart. "For some reason that has them all screaming."

Farragut did not need to ask what the prisoners were saying. He could hear some of the words from here, some of them in English: "Run! For the love of God, run!"

Farragut looked to his displays, at the disintegrating sphere, the flailing things attaching to his force field. He asked his XO quietly, "How do the prisoners know there is anything out there to run from? Did someone tell them?"

Gray shook his head. "We made sure they knew as little as possible, sir. All they have to go on is our sound to general quarters and a deranged bug."

"And the chewed-up hull of the *Hermione*," Farragut murmured. "I'm thinking we might oughtta listen to the lupes on this one. Let's get some vacuum between us and Them."

"Aye, sir."

Gray gave orders to the pilot that took *Merrimack* up to high acceleration. The ship sprang at all right angles from its former course, five times faster than the sphere had shown ability to travel.

The sphere and the swarm of detached riders sprang along with *Merrimack,* matching speed and direction.

Mr. Vincent reported, "Looks like we're *dragging* them."

"They have a tractor on us? Unhook 'em."

"No detectable hook. I can't detect their propulsion system. Can't detect their tractor force. Can't detect what's keeping them mobile at two point seven degrees Kelvin. So there it is, Captain. This isn't happening."

Commander Gray shot Marcander Vincent a scowl, but Captain Farragut was accustomed to overlooking comments like that from his overaged tac specialist. "That's it," said Farragut. He'd run out of patience with these aliens. "Planet killer into the heart of that ice ball."

Said that just as Dr. Jose Maria de Cordillera arrived on the command deck. The doctor wore an expression of shock, not at the incredible scene on the sensor display, but at the captain's order to destroy a first contact.

Farragut turned away from Jose Maria's shocked face. Muttered, "Civilians."

Jose Maria Cordillera pulled back his dismayed expression, and kept his criticism, if he harbored any, to himself. He looked at the displays. "They can't get in. Can they?" He gestured at the black, ciliate things collecting on *Merrimack*'s force field.

"They're not *going* to," said Farragut. "Do we have a firing solution on the sphere?"

"Target acquired, sir," said Commander Gray. "Target is losing integrity fast on its own. It's going to break apart before we can blast it open."

"Fire," said Farragut.

Sebastian Gray ordered Fire Control to launch the planet killer.

"Planet killer away. Contact in three seconds, two, one. Contact. Detonation."

"Target destroyed, sir," Marcander Vincent reported.

"Mostly," Farragut said, watching the nearer of the sphere's scattered bits break apart further, sprout legs and swim toward *Merrimack*.

Jose Maria breathed something in Terra Rican in a tone of wonder. Then in English, "They *move*."

Farragut demanded, "How many of Them are there?"

"Minimum fifty thousand discrete entities not counting the big pieces. Not sure if some of those aren't made of multiple units. Sir, what *are* they?"

The crew tended to ask Captain Farragut impossible questions, as if he knew everything, as if he were God.

Farragut stared at the alien things swimming in literal nothing. He could see them now, without sensors. Could look out a clearport and see their bulbous bodies, their masses of black tentacles clinging to the frictionless energy field. Each of their dozens of tentacles opened and closed at the ends like sucking mouths, serrated at the openings, like teeth.

They had the appearance of living beings, though they had to be machines. Nothing could live out there, motile and mobile in the extreme cold. No natural being could achieve FTL by biological means.

The things were expanding. Free of their sphere, they bloated in the vacuum but did not burst.

A hum, becoming a growl, sounded from all directions at once. It was the force field under siege.

One of the ciliate things looked to have inserted one cilia *into* the force field.

No one bothered to say that was impossible. Mr. Vincent said only, "They're coming in."

25

CAPTAIN FARRAGUT ORDERED COLONEL Steele to launch his fighter wing. "Have your dogs burn those barnacles off my boat."

But the Swifts never even got out of dock. The fighter lifts stalled in their shafts as all ship's controls began to fail.

"Not again!"

"How did the Romans get our new codes!" Steele bellowed.

"I don't think this is Roman," Mr. Gray advised the captain.

"Romans are very good at not looking Roman," said Steele, who trusted Romans only to stab him where he wasn't looking.

"They've outdone themselves this time, TR," Farragut murmured, dubious.

He didn't believe it, because the Roman prisoners were scared. Beyond scared, screaming in a very un-Roman panic.

Someone said, *"Kali!"*

Farragut felt his skin prickle, gone chill.

He barked over the com to the Fury. "Hamster, displace your crew back on board *Mack,* stat!"

On receiving no response from the Fury, he notified the com tech, "Get ahold of her. Get the Fury crew back here *yesterday.*"

"Aye, sir."

Farragut took in a deep breath—as if he could not draw enough air. As if there were not enough oxygen in it. A quick check of the meters showed the ship's atmospherics reading at normal levels.

He exhaled hard to rid his lungs of carbon dioxide. Inhaled again. It hadn't helped.

Sebastian Gray, who was inhaling hard, hand to his chest, caught the captain looking at him, asked, "Is it just me?"

"No," said Farragut. He looked to the displays, at the spidery things encasing his ship with their bodies. He felt like a fly being wrapped in silk. "They're doing this."

He ordered his thunderstruck crew: "Prepare to repel boarders."

Boarders? Below decks crew and company traded mystified grimaces. There were no other ships in the area. *Boarders?*

Jose Maria watched the creatures on the force field oozing—*insinuating*—their way in.

Jose Maria murmured with a scientist's fascination. "This is fantastical. I wish my Mercedes could see—"

The sudden silence, the unfinished thought, made John Farragut look aside to see what had happened to Jose Maria.

Jose Maria had turned gravestone white. He resumed, voice dead flat, "She did. She saw this. The last thing she ever saw."

Farragut's gaze snapped back to the squashed looking things in his force field. *This?*

"They can't get in," Sebastian Gray echoed Jose Maria's earlier thought, with little conviction. "Can they?"

The chief, who had just arrived on deck, scoffed, fists on his fleshy flanks, "Without the codes? Impossible. Even God can't crack the *Mack*'s shell."

"Oh, for Jesus, Og, I wish you hadn't put it that way," said Farragut, who had a deep faith in an old-fashioned God, the jealous one.

A metallic scritching sounded from somewhere, everywhere. "What is that?"

"That's your impossibility on the hull, Chief."

"How the hell—" Og let the question hang. A display showed one of the things emerge from the force field and fall under *Merrimack*'s artificial gravity onto the hull.

An alarm sounded. The crew didn't need it. The pressure in their ears told them what happened. Hull breach.

"I *hate* that," Farragut said. Opened his jaws wide with the sudden dip in air pressure.

The ship's air rushed out the hole in the hull to fill the space be-tween the ship's exterior and its force field—a space that varied from five to twenty feet in width. *Merrimack* was a big ship with a lot of sur-face area, so it was a significant, though not deadly, event.

"They're in," said Mr. Vincent.

From the Romans in their detention hold came screams such as one might imagine from men being eaten alive. But the prisoners were in an interior hold. None of the intruders scratching at the hull could have got to them. At least not yet.

But the prisoners felt the pressure change, and they knew what it meant. This ship was about to turn into the *Hermione*.

Farragut listened for weapons' fire. Hearing none, he signaled the deck where hull breach was located. Tried several times. Then: "Hey down there. Report." The intercom was dead.

Farragut roared for the whole ship to hear: "All hands to swords! Destroy all—" hitched on the word, "monsters!"

Flight Sergeant Kerry Blue was still in her cockpit, waiting on the stalled lift stuck between decks. She heard nothing from outside. Had not felt the pressure drop.

She tried to get a read on the ambient atmosphere to see if the erks had opened the flight deck to let the vacuum in yet. She got no read-ings at all. Damn. Did not want to go out there in an uffed crate. She let out a string of language, then asked into her com, "Did anybody hear that?"

Her com was dead.

She unbuckled quickly. Had to get out of here before they launched her.

She pulled off her glove and lay a palm to the canopy. It was not cold, so she popped the canopy, using the manual spring. She climbed onto her Swift's fuselage, looked up the shaft.

Having trouble breathing. Damn space suit was uffed, too. She took off her helmet, inhaled. Wasn't any better out here. But now she could hear an awful lot of shouting. Something was wrong, wrong, wrong.

She dropped her helmet into the cockpit, put her gloves back on, and had at the lift cables, feeling like she was back in boot camp. She clambered like a monkey, up the dark shaft, swearing.

A wind from below fluttered her hair. *Oh, skat, they got the lift working again and they're opening the deck to the vacuum!*

Screamed, "Don't open it! Don't open it!"

But the cables to which she clung were not moving down to launch her Swift, and the wind was not the kind of gale that would signal her imminent death by vacuum. This was just a hull tear somewhere making the air circulate oddly.

She leaned her face against the cable, breathed relief, "Oh, frag. Oh, hell."

An odd sound came from below, a clattering scritching, something like dog toenails on metal, but moving vertically. The sound was nearing.

Kerry leaned way back on the cables to look down around her Swift.

A black shape filled the shaft. Lots of whippy legs. Rising fast.

Colonel Steele stalked down the ramp tunnel to the starboard hangar deck to see what had become of his fighters. He met an alien in the corridor. An amazing, nightmare thing in this familiar, orderly place. It had pried up one of the deck grates, and several of its many tentacles fished underneath for something dropped there.

The sight threw him not an instant. Steele drew his standard issue sidearm—the splinter gun, not the sword. The gunsights bracketing his eyes triangulated the direction and read the distance from the constriction of pupils to the focal point of his gaze. Vibration in his hand signaled target acquired.

The splinter gun fired true. The sliver penetrated the black body, which gave a violent jerk as Steele immediately depressed the second stage trigger to explode the sliver inside the target.

The alien ruptured nicely. Its punctured remains deflated to the deck. Seemed to be melting through the grate.

Steele did not stay to observe it. He had to burst open another one he saw clinging to the overhead, and another chewing through the bulk.

He took aim down the ramp tunnel to another thing galloping up from the hangar deck, its tentacles madly slapping. The sliver hit home, but the second stage detonation failed.

Steele fired again.

Detonation failed again, winning Steele only a thrashing mad alien, with two slivers in its belly, rolling up the ramp tunnel.

From elsewhere in the ship, other shouts reported weapons' failure.

The snaky mass left the deck, sprang at Steele. Steele saw it coming at him like a giant jumping spider, but with many mouths at the ends of many tentacles.

And he opened it up with his sword.

The blue-black mess spilled a brown stinging gush as it hit his torso. It shrank to the deck, sloshing its innards out.

Steele hadn't even thought about doing that. Didn't even know how the sword got into his hand. After all the drills, it was reflex now.

As the tentacles stopped their spasms and the thing went still at his feet, Steele vowed he would never, ever, question any dumb idea of Farragut's ever again.

Kerry Blue in a nightmare chase. Climbing for her life in this dark shaft from the most enormous of spiders. Could not move fast enough. Tentacles gained on her up the shaft.

She climbed as fast as she could, hand over hand, on the cables. Tendons straining, muscles burning, her own fierce grunts urging her on.

Near to the top. Almost there.

Glove touched deck as something touched her boot, bit a chunk out of it. She screeched.

With a sudden tightness in her collar, she was rising—fast—without effort, like puppy lifted by its scruff.

Colonel Steele. Hauled her up and threw her aside.

She rolled, pushed her hair out of her face to look up from the deck. Colonel Steele with a sword. Brought a Herculean downstroke to land on the black swarm of tentacled hideousness that emerged from the shaft.

The thing fell back down the hole.

A sharp yelp sounded from below. Inchoate cursing. Cries of more disgust than pain. Something loathsome had fallen on Cowboy's head.

A tentacle, severed from the monster, still lashed on the deck. Steele kicked it down the shaft.

Cowboy's gagging outcry echoed up the shaft.

From farther below, came other voices. "Shoot 'em! Shoot 'em! Shooooot!"

And the scritching of many many legs.

Colonel Steele cupped his hand to the side of his mouth to call down to them. "Splinter guns are inoperative!"

A shout returned up the shaft, "Then we're frogged, sir!"

With someone else crying, "It's over. It's all over!"

And closer, from Cowboy, who had to be climbing the cables, "It ain't over till the Cowboy's dead!"

Colonel Steele flipped his sword in the air a half turn endwise, caught it, so that he now held the blade between fingers and thumb, wary of the sharp edge. He called down the shaft. "Carver! Yo!"

Cowboy wiped brown slime off his face, squinted up. Saw what Steele held. He freed up a hand to receive it. "Ho!"

Steele let the blade drop.

Cowboy caught the sword deftly by the hilt. He swung down the cables to battle the monsters that threatened the rest of his squad.

Kerry sprang up from the deck. "Any more where that came from, sir?"

Kerry Blue had her flaws—lots of them—but indecision in battle was not one of them.

Steele signaled her go. Did not have to tell her where to go or how many swords to come back with as fast as she could. In a fight for your life, you want to be beside Kerry Blue.

26

THEY WERE GETTING HARDER, the gorgons, developing shells, making it tougher to slice through them.

Observations of the enemy passed quickly through the ship by shouts:

They dissolve when they die.

Close your eyes when you open them up. That brown slop that squirts out of them is caustic.

Hacking off their legs does NOT kill them.

Those suckers at the ends of their legs can take a chaw out of you right quick.

They're really ugly.

Thank you, Einstein.

You can't squash them.

So who tried to squash something that can squeeze through a force field?

Same idiot who tried a fire extinguisher on them.

As if something that came in from the vacuum would mind cold or oxygen deprivation.

But the swords still worked, even against the hard ones.

Kerry Blue hacked at flailing mouth-legs until her muscles were laced with fire, and she kept hacking. *I will not be eaten alive.* She was not even afraid anymore. Tired, in pain, angry, her stinging eyes watering. She had no room for fear.

At some point the main lights went back on. The air came in cooler through the vents. Kerry heard a splinter gun detonate. A lift running. Jubilant hoots. "We're back in this!"

They were guessing these gorgons got their strength in numbers. The company and crew had apparently hacked them down to critical unmass, and the monsters couldn't do their jamming tricks anymore.

With that, the bone-weary inner numbness lifted. The prey became the exterminator. *Merrimack's* crew and company fought with strength they didn't know they had left. It became sport to hunt down and kill these tentacled rats trying to leave the ship.

When she could find nothing left to kill, Kerry dragged herself into a lab, sat on the deck, and pulled the chain for the sprinkler that was there in case of chemical spills. She let the water wash over her face. Carly Delgado crawled in to sit back to back with her under the cool stream. A dog joined them.

Other Marines staggered in, pressed in with Kerry, Carly, and the dog, in a wet knot.

Kerry passed the chain around, too exhausted even to keep it pulled.

A tippy tappy skitter rushed past the lab—a stray gorgon down to a dozen legs, with Cowboy in hot pursuit with raised sword, wailing like Tarzan.

Carly cracked an eye, but Cowboy and the thing were already past. "What the hell was that?"

"Just one damn thing after another," said Kerry.

Colonel Steele found them there. No one stood up, and Steele didn't make them.

Steele stripped to boxers and T-shirt, his uniform sopping with brown slime and shredded from tentacle bites. Kerry and Carly scooted over to make room for him under their sprinkler.

Steele sat heavily, a mess, his white skin blotched with red chemical burns, his eyelids so swollen you couldn't tell his eyes were blue. The water rinsed brown filth from his white-blond crewcut, from the gold thatch on his chest. Blood from a gash on his arm thinned and swirled down the drain.

Kerry leaned against him. "Thanks, Colonel." She meant for saving her life in the lift shaft.

Steele grunted.

In a moment, "Sir?"

Steele snarled, *"What?"*

"Can I stay?"

A whole string of foul words. There was a yes in there among them.

"Hoo ra," said Kerry Blue.

Farragut strode through the corridors, talking to his crew, his Marines, thanking them for a job well done, asking them to account for all their mates, checking all decks for stragglers or wounded.

Returning to the command deck, he looked about for one not here. "Where's Hamster?"

Commander Gray said, "You mean our diminutive, redheaded lieutenant? I have not seen her."

No one had seen her.

And Farragut realized he had not seen *anyone* from the Fury.

He hailed the displacement deck. When he finally got someone on the com, it was a maintenance tech who had to check the displacement log in the computer.

"Negative, Captain. No displacements at all the last three watches."

Farragut had ordered the Fury crew to displace back to *Merrimack* when the gorgons first attacked.

That was about the time the ship's controls started to go down. Displacement required precise readings and confirmation from three discrete sources—the LD, the collar, and the displacement chamber. They must not have acquired a signal lock.

Farragut got on the com. "Fury. Farragut. Respond." And to the com tech. "Did they receive that?"

"I don't know, sir."

"Keep hailing them."

"Aye, sir."

Into the intercom, "Mo! What are your insects doing?"

The ship's medical officer was up to his elbows in wounded. An orderly checked on the captain's question, reported, "They haven't calmed down any."

To Tactical: "Get a scanner on the Fury. Put it on the display."

Farragut prowled the command deck end to end, fretting the thirty seconds it took to get an image of the Fury up. Asked anyone, "Did they take swords aboard the Fury?"

"I don't think so, Captain," said Commander Gray.

The image of the Fury appeared on the tac screen, still riding alongside *Merrimack*.

Riddled with holes chewed through its hull.

The com tech reported before Farragut could demand, "No one is responding."

"Hamster? Hamster!" Farragut called into his wrist com, shouting, as if that would help. *"Glenn!"*

Captain Farragut displaced aboard the Fury with a troop of his least exhausted Marines in space suits, armed with swords.

The Fury's command and control was choked with smoke. Farragut could not see his glove in front of his visor. He switched over to scanner mode, which threw an instrument reading onto his visor, giving him a weird sort of vision.

He left a team of technicians in C and C to try to restore the ship's atmosphere, while he and the Marines set out in search of the crew, wading through brown sludge, which they now knew to be dead gorgons. That was a good sign. Maybe.

If the crew survived whatever had killed the gorgons.

He came to a sealed hatch, locked from this side, hot to the touch. Had to be fire on the other side.

Farragut signaled his techs at C and C. "Dix. Farragut. Do we have fire suppression?"

"Negative, Captain. Controls are operative. And the fire suppression system is *spent.*"

"Roger that." Farragut hailed *Merrimack*. "Gray. Can you withdraw the force field at the Fury's midships for a minute?"

"At the hot spot? Yes, sir."

In moments, the smoky air inside the Fury began to stir. Midships had depressurized entirely, while the thick air from the rest of the Fury whistled toward the vacuum in a muddy swirl through many jagged holes in the decks, the partitions, the vents.

It was a long minute before the force field was restored. Farragut could see dimly now by the minimal light of emergency lamps.

He unlocked the hatch—it was still warm—and opened it.

A charred chamber lay utterly black on the other side. There was no smoke, but he could not see because there was no light. Had to watch the display on his visors to keep from falling through the holes. There was very little left of the deck.

Farragut and the Marines passed through several more hatches until they came to one sealed and locked from the far side. Farragut tapped out shave-and-a-haircut with his sword hilt.

The hatch unlocked and opened at once.

A lot of helmets clustered at the opening. Faces behind the visors broke into elated smiles.

One crewman rashly popped his helmet seal. Farragut guessed the Fury's atmospherics had been restored because the man was still breathing, still smiling, without his helmet. "Glory, glory, are we glad to see you, Captain!"

The rescued crewmen told Farragut that they had started the fire.

"Figured whatever wiggles at 2.7 degrees Kelvin might have a problem with heat."

And they had been right. Problem was, the amount of heat it took to kill the gorgons was enough to destroy everything else and use up all the available oxygen.

"I thought we'd cooked ourselves," said the crewman. "And when you let the vacuum in, I thought that was hell freezing over." Proudly showed his space suit's air gauge, reading dead empty. "I was down to my last sniff."

Farragut was counting up present company. Counted short. Five short. Throat tight, he asked, "Who did you lose?"

"Ximeno, Faqry, Williams—big Williams, not little Williams—and Brownie. Oh, Brownie bought it ugly."

"Where's Hamster?"

"She's not in here. We led the suckers this way and she stayed out that way to throw in the toaster and lock 'em in."

Here was the engine compartment. The crew had taken refuge behind the thickest bulk in the entire ship.

Farragut took off his helmet. "Did she find a place to hide?"

"She was going down to the magazine to jettison the bombs in case the fire got out of control, so we wouldn't blow up the *Merrimack* with us."

Farragut glanced up at the sound of scratching. "You've still got gorgons alive in here."

The Marines had brought over extra swords, passed them out to the Fury's crew.

Farragut pointed up toward the scraping noise. "Kill all of those." And he ran back the way he'd come toward the ship's munitions store.

He came to a hatch, locked from the far side. He hailed the techs in C and C to override the lock. The lock spun, and Farragut tore the hatch open.

And jumped back as a jet of flame shot from the opening, taking his eyebrows off.

A muffled gasp from behind the flame: "Omigod!" The blowtorch abruptly pointed up and shut off. Hamster's shocked face behind a visor looked to be all eyes. "Captain!"

"Oh, for Jesus, Glenn!" Farragut took off his glove with his teeth, brought his fingers gingerly to his naked brow.

Lieutenant Hamilton yanked off her helmet, her red-brown hair matted against her head. "I'm so sorry. Please say my guys are still alive!"

"Most of them."

She shrank at the sound of scratching from above. "They're still here!"

"Not for long. Dogs are hunting down the last of them. Guns are working again. But *these* work all the time." He brandished his sword. "Lordy, Hamster, I give you a ship and look what you do. Couldn't you have made a bigger mess?"

What might have started as a laugh ended in a sudden scream of pain.

Tentacles from beneath a jump cart had lashed out and taken a bite from Glenn's thigh.

Farragut kicked over the cart. Brought his sword down on the gorgon so hard the blade stuck in the deck between the dying halves.

He caught Glenn to him as she buckled. Held her close, her head tucked under his chin, his ungloved hand holding the back of her head, his lips on her hair.

When she was standing steadier he had to let her go. She wobbled a little, her weight on one leg. A lively stream of blood trickled from her thigh. Her face went very white, a shocky glaze coming over her eyes. "I'm sorry I trashed the ship."

Farragut gathered her up like a bride, carried her back to the LDs.

"Put me down, John, I'm gonna ralf."

He let Glenn get her good leg under her, and lent her balance as she threw up. Then he snapped a displacement collar on her. She felt limp and quaking as he lifted her again and displaced back to *Merrimack.*

He meant to carry her to sick bay himself, but met Dr. Hamilton on the way—looking frantic but whole, healthy, and unblooded. Xenolinguists were not on board for their fighting skills.

Farragut brusquely bundled little Glenn Hamilton into her husband's arms and went about his duties.

After both ships were pronounced secure, the lab ants gone back to their holes, and the crew fed, the relief tactical specialist called Captain Farragut to the command deck to observe a fragment of a gorgon swarm still out there, floundering in space, disintegrating into debris. As if they needed a certain number in their swarm to maintain viability.

Farragut thanked the specialist and went in search of Dr. Cordillera to run that idea past him.

Jose Maria was not in his quarters. He was not in sick bay.

People had seen him. He had been in the thick of the battle. "He was magnificent," an awestruck crewwoman assured him. Jose Maria was picturesque with a sword, and apparently devastating as well, because even the crewmen were impressed.

But no one could tell the captain where *Don* Cordillera was now.

Farragut was beginning to feel something like fear, when suddenly, quietly, he found him, Jose Maria, in a crouch, on the balls of his feet, his back resting against the bulk, his sword on the deck before him, his hands over his face. An image of remorse, but he could not possibly regret killing those marauding parasites.

He had got himself cleaned up. His clothes were immaculate, his black hair neat and glossy as a show horse's tail. An elegant and lonely figure down there.

"Jose Maria."

Still in his crouch, Jose Maria de Cordillera straightened his back flush to the wall, and lifted his wet face to Farragut. "She is gone."

"Mercedes," said Farragut. He leaned against the wall with Jose Maria, but stayed standing. "You don't know that, Jose Maria. There's still hope."

"Oh, I will find ways to deny it, too. But I know she is gone."

"How," Farragut challenged.

"I can tell you the date and the hour. I woke in the night, in sweat and terror. I sat straight up and spoke her name aloud. It was only later that I learned the *Sulla* was missing. There is no scientific explanation for what happened to me, but such things have been reported in old wives' tales for ages. I do not discount the tales of old wives merely because they appear to defy current bounds of reason. The popular record is too strong to ignore. I knew she was gone."

"You're talking clairvoyance," said Farragut, arms crossed, skeptical.

"No. I think I am talking telegnosis. I do not disbelieve what I cannot explain."

Of course not. He couldn't and still be Catholic.

"My Mercedes and I had a connection. Perhaps a resonant harmonic. She lived and I felt her presence with me always. And then, suddenly, I did not. I carry an empty place where she always was," said Jose Maria, hand to his heart. He sighed, deep and sorrowful. "You know. You *know*. And still you hope. The persistence of the human heart." Tears spilled from his black eyes. He reverted to his cradle tongue. "*Dios! Dios!* She was so scared. She died in terror and I was not there."

27

KERRY BLUE SLOPPED THROUGH the remains of the melted gorgons. Stuck her mop in the wringer. Grimaced at what came out. "Ugh."

Dak lifted another deck grate for her to mop up the sludge underneath. The muck pooled deep down here in the lower sail. "Need a hose over here!"

Merrimack carried a lot of things—a full hospital, a partial torpedo fabrication plant—but she did not carry automated cleaning equipment. That was why God invented Marines.

Captain Farragut came through without his normal buoyant cheer. His face looked unusually moody. He stopped to watch his Marines work, and his expression got positively angry. "No," he muttered, to himself it seemed. Then louder, stepping forward. "No." He yanked the mop out of Kerry Blue's hands. "You're not doing this."

Okay by Kerry Blue. Colonel Steele might not like it, but the captain was the captain, and who was she to argue with the captain?

Carly, Reg, and Cowboy looked up from their work to stare at Captain Farragut.

"Stop, stop, stop. All of you."

The Marines foundered, confused. Did the captain want them to come to attention?

"Put that *down*," Farragut zeroed in on Twitch Fuentes, who was clutching a vacuum hose, unable to believe he could be getting off this crummy detail. And right under Colonel Steele's nose, too.

"Colonel Steele," Farragut barked. "Issue sidearms to your dogs and come with me."

"Sir," Steele acknowledged.

And so off they went to the detention hold.

The hold was weirdly quiet within, and Kerry wondered for a moment if the prisoners weren't all dead. Or preparing a trap.

Captain Farragut made the MPs unlock the hatch. The instant it was open, he charged right through the hatchway, ahead of his armed escort. They scrambled after him in time to see him *roar* at a bunch of Romans standing in rigid ranks: "What the hell was that!"

The prisoners remained at parade perfect attention. They had begun the assault with such a poor showing—all that screaming—that evidently they decided to scrape their *dignitos* together and meet their fate like Romans. In disciplined futility.

Farragut must have been the last thing they expected to come bursting through the hatch.

But here he was, breathing fire. He stalked up to the front line of soldiers and grabbed one by the throat—looked like a lion with a baby zebra—and slammed him up against the bulkhead. *"You knew!"*

Kerry could see the furtive glances pass among the other Romans. Could tell from their perplexed stares that no one had told these men that the monsters were all dead.

They were slowly getting a clue, though, and they were incredulous. Looking at Farragut like a fragging archangel with a flaming sword.

Kerry would swear he had fire jetting out his blue eyes.

Farragut roared again, *"When the hell were you going to tell someone!"* Got no answers out of them other than their imbecilic, stunned stares.

Farragut dropped his baby zebra to round back on Colonel Steele. "TR. Get my boat cleaned up. *Them.*" He thrust a finger at the Roman prisoners. "Make *them* do it. Your dogs do *not* pick up any equipment that doesn't shoot!"

"Aye, *sir*!" Steele acknowledged enthusiastically.

The captain stomped out, smoking hot.

The Marines shepherded the Romans out of detention, armed them with vacuum hoses and mops and rags.

They came along tentatively. Docile. Amazed.

Kerry enjoyed poking in the back anyone who did not move fast enough to please her. She liked this detail much better. She'd been trained in twenty-four scenarios. This was another new one, but far and away the best ever.

One Roman, his hands stinging raw from the caustic slop, looked to Kerry and asked, in English, "What *is* this crud?"

"Dead monsters," said Kerry. "They melt when you kill 'em."

"Where are they? The monsters?"

"Under your stupid feet, you dwit!"

"*All* of them? Where are the rest of them?"

"We killed them. Shut your face bung and use that mop or I'll take it from you and you can use your tongue." Kerry leveled a sighter beam on the Roman's crotch.

Caught Reg, from the corner of her eye, screwing up her brow at her and mouthing silently, *Face bung?* Cowboy sniggering, "I love you, Kerry Blue." And Dak, shoulders shaking silent guffaws, working up to say something. She didn't even let him get his mouth open. "Shut up, Dak."

The prisoners mopped in silence.

Farragut came by again. Looked like God in navy blue. He supervised a moment in silent, frowning approval, then turned away without speaking.

It was not like Farragut not to say a word or twelve hundred.

To his back someone called, "Captain!"

A Roman.

Farragut turned, blue eyes raking across the prisoners. Kerry could tell that Farragut knew the speaker wasn't one of his own. Farragut knew the voice of every last one of his company and crew down to the lowest grunt. He even knew hers.

As the captain took a step toward them, the Roman prisoners all dropped their cleaning equipment. The Marines took immediate aim with their splinter guns. But the Romans were only coming to attention. Then—unbelievably—saluted.

Farragut turned his back on them and stalked out.

A service for the dead.

At times like this TR Steele was in awe of Captain Farragut. You'd never know the captain was American blue blood. He talked like just folks and could brawl like a street dog, or he could stand up there in front of God and everyone with his tear ducts wide open, and it didn't make him any bit weaker.

Steele would have looked like a sap.

Steele set his jaw hard as a headstone, just glad someone was crying for his boys and girls, because he sure couldn't.

Lieutenant Glenn Hamilton was back on her feet the next day, her leg still encased in a med sheath to restore the chunk of muscle the gorgon had bitten from her thigh.

She retreated to the hangar deck, carrying out a solitary damage assessment. She was off duty this watch, but she did not want to deal with Patrick right now. So she worked.

She hugged a memory she thought she had imagined. On the Fury, when Farragut killed the gorgon that attacked her, when he caught her falling. The feeling of safety in his arms. The way he'd pressed her to him, his hand behind her head. His lips on her hair. She'd felt that. Thought she made it up, but she *felt* that. John Farragut kissed her hair.

Farragut was always hugely affectionate to everyone. But that, *that* had been a little over the line.

John Farragut kissed my hair.

She had never seen him afraid, because Farragut never feared for himself. She had felt him afraid there on the Fury. Heard the catch in his breath, felt the tremor in his hands as he held her close to his thrumming heart. Held her as if she was a precious thing he had almost lost.

She was not even sure it happened the way she remembered it. The way she wanted it to have happened. It had shocked her. Not an unpleasant shock. It was very easy on the pride, coming from the captain of the *Merrimack,* after her own husband—one of the few men on board fortunate enough to be sharing his bed with a flesh-and-blood woman (a damn pretty one at that, Dr. Patrick Hamilton!) on *Merrimack*'s long tours—Patrick Hamilton hooked into a Hot Trixi Allnight virtual joyride.

"But she's not *real,*" Patrick Hamilton had defended instead of apologized, baffled by her hurt anger.

"*I* am!" Glenn had cried.

He did not get it.

Patrick also had trouble carrying her the rest of the way to sick bay when John had given her over to him after rescuing her from the monsters on board the Roman Fury. Glenn's one hundred pounds got rather heavy between decks, and Patrick had to set her down once to regroup.

Glenn had not married Patrick Hamilton for any brute qualities. Patrick was an intelligent, boyish, slender man, with a dry sense of humor. Companionable. Could be very sweet. Could be very inconsiderate. Hell, Patrick Hamilton could be an ass.

Left her vulnerable to dreams. That big, swashbuckling John Farragut could harbor a secret love for her was too much like a dream she wanted too badly to believe right now. It was too easy on the pride. Too easy on the heart.

She convinced herself she had imagined too much into the encounter on board the Fury.

Convinced herself she had imagined all of it.

Until suddenly she was alone with him again.

She had just made note of a couple of inoperative lamps, when John Farragut dropped out of the lift shaft. He had been doing a visual inspection of the cables—had probably been swinging on the cables, knowing John.

He looked startled to see her here. Then sheepish. Awkward, the way he had never been with her. For an indecisive instant he seemed about to beat a retreat on some pretext.

Then his expression changed. The blush was still there, but he had decided to hold his ground and own up to what he had let show. He glanced about the vacant half-lit hangar. Gave an abashed smile, as he might if caught stark naked. Spoke, embarrassed, ironic, "Hi."

His blue eyes met her gaze and did not look away.

She had imagined nothing.

Suddenly it felt dangerous to be here. Heat welled. Fear. Sexuality.

Glenn should just walk up the ramp tunnel and report the inoperative lamps to the Og.

So why am I not walking? she wondered. Suspended in the moment. Listening to her own heart pound. Watching John Farragut's eyes.

He had shown his hand. Now he was waiting for a move from her.

She ought to go. Why was she stringing this out when she had no intention of going through with—with what?

And realized she had no intention of stopping whatever was about to happen. She felt warm and longing and she was going anywhere this man wanted to lead her.

A light metallic ping of something dropping on the deck made her break her gaze. She heard its clink, plunk through the grate, and roll-spin to a stop.

John Farragut crouched, lifted up a deck grate, retrieved what had fallen beneath. Stood up with her wedding band between his thumb and forefinger. Dropped it into her palm. "Klutz."

The back of his fingers brushed her cheek before he ceded the field.

Two days after the battle with the gorgons, John Farragut came to see Jose Maria in the lab. The ship's medical officer, Mohsen Shah, was with him, puzzling over beakers of sludge. Gorgon remains.

"Machine or biological?" Farragut asked.

The doctors shook their heads. "I am having no idea," said Mo, and Jose Maria had no words at all.

"Animal, vegetable, or mineral?" Farragut tried again.

Again they shook their heads. Jose Maria lifted one of the beakers, gave it a swirl. "Fluidity," he said. "I am—I am entirely at a loss."

"But that's the dead phase," Farragut nodded at the dirty brown stuff. "Can't you reverse engineer it from that?"

"This—this—*soup* consists of common elements and unexciting compounds," said Jose Maria. "What is missing is the code of its existence. It moves itself. It moves itself at near absolute zero in total vacuum."

"Well there's another axiom out the porthole," said Farragut.

"A lot of traffic through that porthole lately, young Captain." Jose Maria let himself sit. His stately posture slipped. "We are back to square one, and I do not know where to go."

"You can come to the command deck," said Farragut. "We're approaching your wife's planet."

The planet Telecore—the construction base for the Far Cat. From there, Farragut hoped to find the Far Cat. And Jose Maria had hoped to find his wife.

"We passed through a noise zone, like scramscat transmissions," Farragut explained on the way. A Roman installation would try to mask, diffuse, scramble, and scatter its signals escaping into space to imitate natural radiation and stellar noise. "But we came out into a clear zone. The scramscat stopped."

"That is odd," Jose Maria agreed. Why scramble when you are sending nothing in the first place? "Then might the Romans have seen us coming and have shut off all transmissions?"

"I can't imagine how you could take a whole *planet* dark. I mean someone would microwave their leftovers. Something. Then again, these *are* Romans." Farragut argued with himself.

He took his ship to stealth mode, altered course, sounded general quarters. *Merrimack* approached Telecore from an overshot angle.

Still the scanners detected no transmissions from the planet.

He would have expected someone, even on a small colony, to let something slip. Activate a remote, signal a friend, forget to cancel the automatic feed from a weather satellite.

The planet they approached was dark. Physically dark, shrouded in brown clouds with little albedo.

Jose Maria moved forward, tense. "That is not the planet Mercedes described." *A blue-green jewel wrapped in white lace.* "I fear I have led you into a trap."

He'd been given the wrong coordinates. Jose Maria would have sworn to heaven, and bet all of Terra Rica, that the Romans could not have broken his and Mercedes' code.

And Farragut still believed that. "Damn peculiar sort of trap." He turned to his scan tech. "What's down there?"

"No life, sir."

"I asked what *is* there."

"Yes, sir," the scan tech said quickly, did a quick read of the major features. "There was a settlement here, all right. Ruins. Looks like Roman construction. Dead vegetation. Can't even say it's rotting. There's no bacteria."

Jose Maria jerked in physical startlement. Farragut said, "Now how the hell does *that* happen?"

The scanner looked for it. Found it: "The planet's hot! Radiation, sir! Not naturally occurring!"

Farragut nodded. Had feared, expected that. "Known signature?"

"Yes, sir," the scan tech confirmed. "There's a match in the system. It's *Roman*."

"Did someone blow up Rome's nuclear installations down there?"

"No, sir. Not that kind of radiation signature." The tech turned from his console to look up at his captain, wide-eyed. "Looks for all hell like a Roman Legion took a neutron hose to the whole world."

28

THE PLANET TELECORE SWIRLED under the high muddy winds of nuclear winter. Impact craters and scorched trenches pocked and laced the ground. A Roman sanitation crew had done a thorough job here.

Of Dr. Mercedes de Seville de Cordillera's terraforming artistry, or of anything else living, there was nothing.

"The cleaners were here," said Mr. Vincent.

No wonder *Merrimack* had met no guard ships. There was nothing here to defend.

Mr. Vincent shook his head at the readings. Bitter. Astonished. "So their Catapult goes operational and they just erase the whole base."

Rome had been known to take terrible measures to keep its secrets.

"Where are the people?" asked Jose Maria.

"They killed their workers," Vincent said.

Farragut shook his head. "Unlikely. Romans aren't as stupid, inhuman, and wasteful as they're cracked down to be."

Despite U.S. propaganda, even he knew that Romans were not comic book thugs who disposed of their servants like movie extras. "I have to believe they moved their people out first.

"Something had to turn septic for them to do this. I'm sorry, Jose Maria, we're not going to find anything down there." Farragut clasped Dr. Cordillera behind the neck and gave him an encouraging shake. "But we know your wife wasn't there. Mr. Gray, move us out."

*　　*　　*

Glenn Hamilton lay in bed, drifting uneasily near sleep, her back to Patrick, the ship on guarded alert moving through space that should be thick with Romans but wasn't.

A buzzing clamor made her jerk and sit straight up, shaking like a shell-shocked soldier.

Patrick mumbled sleepily, "That's just one of the Roman clock bugs. Aldebaran scarab crickets."

"I know what it is," Glenn snapped, shaking.

Patrick rolled over, forced his eyes open. "You okay, babe?"

"I—uh. Pavlov's dogs. I—associated the noise with something else. Sorry I woke you up. It's nothing."

That sound had preceded the gorgons' attack, so the two events had become entwined in Glenn's mind. Unconnected, of course.

Still she did not sleep.

Listened to the scarab cricket ricochet off the corridor walls.

The call to general quarters came while the ship was already on high alert. Up ahead lay a field of interstellar debris, which the scanners identified by silhouette as a fleet of dark ships. A rough count of fifty. Some had the size and aspect of transports. Some were unmistakably Roman ships of war.

Normally ships in a group will orient to a single axis, choosing a collective *up* and *down*. These had assumed a chaotic array. No doubt doing their best imitation of an asteroid field.

"Res scan the lot of them," said Farragut. "Let's see who we have and how they lie."

"And if they suddenly wake up, we'll know Rome's got our new harmonic," Mr. Vincent muttered.

But nothing woke up on being scanned.

The scan synthesis was so long in coming, Farragut demanded of Tactical, "Report."

Mr. Vincent gave an un-Vincentlike, heartfelt croak. "Oh, my God. Oh, my God." Before he went dumb.

He sent the image to the captain's display.

The command crew all moved forward as one, some with hands to mouths, some with mouths gaping uncovered, eyes huge and unblinking, or else blinking very fast against horrified tears.

Fifty dead ships. Knew they were dead and not playing at it for the ragged holes in their hulls. The sensors showed no shimmering halos of inertial shells. Nothing that might hold in the ships' atmospheres.

Farragut heard Jose Maria murmuring in Latin. Alarmed him for a moment, then recognized the words as the Lord's Prayer.

Captain Farragut ordered *Merrimack* to drop out of FTL so he could relay the horrific images to the Joint Chiefs on Earth by res pulse. Res messages at speed got very spotty on the receiving end.

"Are you getting this?" Farragut encapsulated a voice message and transmitted that.

Got a terse, single word acknowledgment back: "Receiving."

Merrimack wove a grim path through the graveyard of ships. Came upon a huddle of smaller ships, unarmed or lightly armed. Passenger types. All knotted together as if enclosed in a kill jar, surrounded by space buoys.

"What are these doing here? What is this group?"

Senior engineer Kit Kittering's voice shook. *"That's the Far Cat."*

This space was the Deep End displacement chamber of the Roman Catapult. They had tried to get out.

"Oh, for Jesus, why didn't they *tell* us?"

The command platform had become deathly quiet. Everyone staring.

Someone murmured into the silence, "There be monsters here."

Merrimack dispatched skiffs to the dead ships. Marine crews boarded the derelicts to pull their black boxes. And collect five thousand, five hundred and three sets of dog tags.

Oxygen bricks were plentiful, littering the area, abandoned. Whoever had attacked these ships had not been short on breathable air reserves. Or did not need air at all.

Merrimack did. The battleship had spilled a lot of air in fighting the gorgons off the Fury.

The Og appropriated a few tons of the solid oxygen, took the bricks under tow, and drew up a due bill payable to Rome. Even at war, *Merrimack* did not steal from the dead.

A stillness held the ship. The *Merrimack,* normally filled with raucous life, sounded like a machine and nothing more. The crew moved through her like ghosts, distracted, stunned or on the verge of tears. Spoke quietly. No one joked. They were preternaturally kind to each other.

Someone had spaced an Aldebaran scarab cricket, which had gone mad and would not shut up. Now everything hushed.

Jose Maria de Cordillera wore black.

"This is the end of the world as we know it," said Jose Maria, standing at a clearport, watching the Marine skiffs move through the graveyard of ships. "We are here thrown back to the twilight of civilization, when existence could end in a moment. When there were monsters on Earth."

"When was that, Jose Maria?" Farragut asked. He had never believed in monsters.

"Many times. The Black Death. The great earthquakes. Or even when men become the monsters. Killing without mind or mercy. When there is nowhere to hide. The death that comes suddenly and ends everything you know.

"We have returned to that elemental time. This universe we have civilized and rewrought in our own image is once again a pitiless place. We see ourselves diminished back to our true tenuous position in it. The unknown horror could strike in the night and obliterate everything we know. Or erase us entirely."

Farragut gave *Merrimack*'s bulkhead the kind of stout thumping pat he gave his dogs. Answered, "Not on my watch."

"Good lord, Dak. Don't lose your head over a little bug." Kerry ducked—from Dak, not the bee. "It's not as if it's got a stinger."

Dak swatted madly about his head, boxing his own ears trying to get at the furiously buzzing bee.

Several of the crew kept hives full of stingless bees. On a normal watch, the bees were rather cheerful, actually, and the honey wasn't bad as long as you kept them away from Suriya's murkflowers. You didn't usually see them attacking people. And not Dak, who did not smell particularly sweet.

"The bugs!" Dak's huge hands flailed. "What's with the fragging bugs on this ship?"

Concerned over the mood of his ship, Captain Farragut consulted his MO. But he found Dr. Shah as depressed as anyone.

The last thing Farragut expected. Mohsen Shah was a tranquil, philosophical man. A Riverite by creed, which made him slow to anger, and long of patience. Riverites accepted everything—transgressions, misfortunes—as part of life's flow.

"Mo, are you corked?" Farragut asked.

Mohsen lifted deep brown, red-shot eyes to Captain Farragut. Mo's looked like the face on the barroom floor. But he shook his head, no. He was not drunk.

"We of the River are not believing in endings, but I am looking at this." Mo Shah gestured at the hideous images on all the screens in his dispensary. "And I am—" His voice stalled out. Started over, "This is the end."

Abrupt. Stark. So unlike Mo's ever-flowing speech, the statement brought Farragut up short.

And Farragut wouldn't have it. He stalked around the dispensary, clicking off the displays. "Mo, I swear to you—" *Click. Click.* "Look at me, Mo." *Click.* "I swear to you: this is being no such damned thing."

He locked gazes with Mo Shah, and meant to stare him down. Would have, but a whiskermoth dove right into his eye.

Farragut's one eye screwed shut against the oily sting. Mo Shah became animated, now having a patient to attend.

Farragut glanced around the lab with his mothless eye. "Your bugs still acting up here, Mo?"

"Not still. Again. Please be opening your eye."

Farragut forced his lids apart to receive a gentle jet of liquid, washing out the moth and its irritant oil.

Mo continued, "The lab insects were finding peace again, but, as you are seeing—you *are* seeing?—the insects are being antic again."

"When did they stop? When did they start?"

"Do not be rubbing your eye."

"Mo, when did the bugs stop 'being antic' and when did they start again?"

"I am looking and will be telling you when I am finding," Mo said evenly, opening his file to consult his lab notes. Found the notation. "The time of the insects' quietude was coinciding with the destruction of the so-called gorgons. The beginning anew was happening while *Merrimack* was orbiting Telecore. Why is the captain asking?"

"The captain is having improbable thoughts, Mo," Farragut murmured, thinking back on disconnected things—

I res-scanned Telecore.

Nothing can pick up a random res harmonic.

—as he watched the ants clawing at the top of their terrarium in Mo's lab. His skin crawled right along with them.

He lunged across the lab table, slapped on the intercom, "Lookout! This is Farragut!"

"Lookout, aye."

"Watch for—" Farragut floundered for words, "What did we call that alien sphere in the ship's log?"

"Alien sphere," said the Lookout.

Farragut's brow furrowed in disappointed surprise. "We *did?*" Could have come up with a better term than that. "Scan for alien spheres."

"Aye, sir," said the lookout, then, much sooner than expected: "Sighted them, sir. Three. Four. Five. Seven . . . ."

"Where?" said Farragut. "What are they doing?"

"Nearest plot at seven hundred megaklicks. Farthest—we're still finding them, sir. What they're doing? They're all moving FTL, coming right at us."

"Battle stations."

29

CAPTAIN FARRAGUT AND HIS SPECIALISTS weighed their options against the oncoming horde. They had the luxury of discussion. The closest sphere was still twenty minutes out at its best speed. And if the specialists needed more time for discussion, *Merrimack* could outpace the aliens.

Tactical ran a comparison of the spheres' vectors. A bit disconcerting, the result. The spheres came from various directions, but all converged on the precise location from where *Merrimack* had sent her last res signal.

"You can't home on a res signal," said Farragut. "Resonance has no location."

"Tell that to *Them!*" Marcander Vincent snapped.

That man was going to ride a console for the rest of his career, if he didn't finish it out in a brig instead. Farragut said only, chiding, "Mr. Vincent."

"Sir." An apology, Vincent-style.

Farragut resumed his briefing. "Since no one told the gorgons they can't home on a res pulse, and since I'm not fixin' to run and hide from those murdering bags of sludge, I need to know the best way to kill them from as far away as possible. We learned the hard way not to let them get close."

Jose Maria, who had been invited to this meeting, asked, "Why did not the Romans learn these things? Why did so many Roman ships die the same way?"

Hamster suggested, "They probably lacked the ammo to take out all the spheres sighted so far. I know we do."

"So I'll shoot us empty, take out as many of the closest ones as I can, then go reload."

"Brings the question again," said Jose Maria. "Why did not the Romans do precisely that?"

"Dammit, Jose Maria—" said Farragut. A slight frustrated smile crept over his face. "That's a damned good question."

His techs tried to look for answers in the flight recorders from the *Hermione,* the Fury, and the Roman ships at the Far Cat, but the recorders were encrypted, impenetrable.

Farragut gathered up the recorders and took them down to the detention hold. He all but *threw* them at the Roman prisoners. "From your dead buddies at the Far Cat. Let me know if you get in the mood to share anything you learn from these."

Turned to storm out.

"Domni!"

The captain paused. Turned. Glowered through the hatchway, waiting.

The Roman spoke, "No one has ever *ever* survived contact with Them."

Merrimack was the unspoken exception.

The Roman's face twitched, wrinkled. His chin quivered. Tears fell. "You just watch the transmissions of soldiers dying, until the signals stop."

"*You're* alive," said Farragut, an accusation. "How did the Fury survive?"

A guilty sob. "We ran like hell, *Domni.*"

"Are you going to give me the code to unlock these?" He nodded at the black box recorders.

Saw the man struggle between fear of dying and fear of aiding the enemy. In the end, he was more afraid of committing treason. "I can't, *Domni.*"

Farragut left the recorders with the prisoners. "Watch some more dying." He stalked away.

Behind his back he heard Jose Maria speak to the prisoners, in Latin, before the guards could close the hatch. "I have a question."

Farragut spun, glaring at him. Jose Maria met the captain's angry glare. "If I may."

Farragut gave Jose Maria a silent, curt go ahead, wondering what in heaven the neutral Terra Rican civilian could have to say to the Romans.

Jose Maria turned back to the prisoners. "Did you destroy Telecore?"

"We?" The Roman circled with his finger to indicate we, the imprisoned company. "No. We—Rome—had to. Telecore was infested with Them."

Scorched earth was an old tactic. Older than Rome.

Jose Maria asked, "Is—was—Telecore the gorgon home world?" A hopeful edge in his voice. Perhaps the Romans destroyed the monsters' nest.

"No," said the Roman. "They came from—from out there, and started eating everything. Those things cannot have a home. If those things ever had a home, they ate it."

"What became of the people?" Jose Maria asked softly. "Rome had a thriving colony at Telecore."

"Evacuated," said the Roman.

"To where?"

The quivers again. With more breath than voice, the Roman answered, "To the Catapult."

Farragut landed on the command deck. "Let's keep this simple. Here's our strategy. Don't let them get close. We're going to shoot really big skeet. Mr. Gray, do we have a firing solution?"

"Star Sparrows lined up on the nearest eight spheres," Commander Sebastian Gray reported. "Awaiting your order."

"Warheads?"

"Incendiaries and nukes."

Farragut nodded approval. The gorgons could withstand vacuum and near absolute zero cold. They could not withstand high heat.

"Let 'em have it."

Mr. Gray spoke into the com. "Fire Control. Command Deck. You have permission to fire Star Sparrows."

"Firing Star Sparrows, aye." That was Hamster, OOD in fire control. She sent again: "Star Sparrows away."

First impact came in eight minutes. Savage cheers burst on deck as the gorgon sphere blew into burning pieces.

The second impact should have come thirty-two seconds later, but the second sphere *dodged* the Star Sparrow.

Farragut jumped at the display screen, not sure what he'd just seen there. "Targeting. Farragut. Course correct that missile."

"Correcting, aye. Target acquired."

But the sphere twitched again before Targeting was done speaking.

Mr. Gray, got on the com immediately. "Targeting. We have an evading target. Ride the Star Sparrow in."

A difficult task, given the speed discrepancy. The Star Sparrow was moving much faster than *Merrimack*. But, unfazed, a gangly V-jockey named Raytheon—called Wraith—pulled on a visor to take resonant remote control of the missile.

Relativity made for a disorienting picture in the visor. The Star Sparrow's instants were much closer together than those of its pilot back on *Merrimack*. But Wraith loved this stuff. Rode the Star Sparrow like a madman, and plunged the nuke into the gorgon sphere's black frozen heart. *"Yeah!"*

The horde swelled, burning like a nova.

Farragut blew out a breath. Exchanged glances with his XO. "We had to work for that one."

Gray nodded.

The third missile was due for contact by now, but its target had altered course also.

Wraith took over remote control of the third Star Sparrow and redirected the missile toward the target. The Star Sparrow drew nearer and near. Tactical counted down time to impact.

"Six, five, four—"

The gorgon sphere blew apart like a dull Fourth of July rocket, without burning lights, but with a wide, wide spray of black bits. What would have sparkled on the Fourth, here sprouted legs and wriggled.

Farragut lost a step there. An effect without a cause. "Did I blink?" He'd missed three, two, one.

"Mr. Vincent, did you count three, two, one?"

"No, sir."

The Star Sparrow and its warhead still showed intact on the tactical display.

"What did we hit that gorgon ball with?"

Tactical just looked baffled.

Wraith reported up: "Didn't touch it, sir. Unless you count a res sounder."

"The sphere blew up *itself*?"

"Looks that way, sir," said Wraith, and Tactical nodded, concurring.

"They can't have our harmonic," said Senior Engineer Kit Kittering.

"I would say they do," said Tactical.

"Change harmonic," said Farragut. "Synch up Targeting."

With the new harmonic established, Targeting took a res sounding to locate the target.

The target moved the instant the res signal pulsed.

"Oh, for Jesus. Is there anyone in the Milky Way who doesn't have our harmonics!"

"Captain, *we* didn't even have that one," said Mr. Vincent. "I fed in my GRE scores."

"Then we must be sending out our code as we log it into the targeting system." Farragut stalked over, jabbed a bunch of numbers into the res sounder manually, and slapped it home.

Mr. Vincent hesitated. "Sir, we don't know what harmonic you loaded. We can't target on it."

"Good. Scan with that one."

Mr. Vincent did. Of course, no reading appeared on the targeting system. Targeting had no idea what harmonic to monitor.

But when Tactical took yet another sounding with yet another harmonic, it was clear that the sphere had, in fact, changed course in between soundings, apparently in reaction to the resonant scan sent on Farragut's mystery harmonic.

"Jesus, Mary, and Joseph," someone said.

At Hamster's suggestion, the erks turned the *Hermione*'s res sounder back on and gave the hulk an FTL shove on a tangential course as a decoy.

The alien spheres ignored the decoy. As if they recognized *Hermione* as a bone they had already picked clean.

Recognized it how? "Those things can't be the same spheres that ate *Hermione*," said Mr. Vincent. "Their top speed and where we found *Hermione* don't add up. Means these things have to be talking to each other."

"And I'll bet you the Qarfin Bank they're talking in resonance," said Mr. Gray.

"Impossible," said the senior engineer.

"Kit, the weight of evidence has crushed that argument just about flat," said Farragut, and without taking a breath started shouting very fast: "*Cease fire!* Recall remaining Star Sparrows!"

Mr. Gray acknowledged, ordered the recall, then questioned his captain, "Sir?"

"We're not the only ones learning here. We're *teaching* them! That's what happened to Rome! They taught the gorgons all their weapons, all their technology, all their tactics, and *that's* how they got slaughtered."

30

JOSE MARIA LOOKED A BIT startled. Took a moment to shake off a few axioms, then nodded. These giant clots of frozen aliens separated by light-years were learning, sharing knowledge, adapting.

Merrimack's best course of action for the moment was to steer clear until someone could come up with a better one. Rome had not been able to pull back and think, damned by the same weakness that lost them the Near Cat—Rome had stationary targets to defend. A fixed site was death in a space battle.

"Sir, if we stop resonating, can we shake the gorgons off our tail?" Mr. Vincent asked, as if Captain Farragut knew everything about the aliens.

The crew thought the captain knew everything because they needed for him to know everything.

"Well, let's run a little experiment on that," said Farragut. "Mr. Gray, take us dark. Sneak us around *behind* a couple of those alien spheres then ping 'em. If we get a picture of their butts, then, Mr. Vincent, I would say the answer is yes, we can shake them. TR, you don't look real sure about this."

Colonel Steele tended to remain silent in the company of educated men and women, but his frown was speaking loudly. He cleared his throat. Hoped his question wasn't stupid. "If the gorgons home in on res pulses, why aren't there a bunch of gorgon balls headed for Fort Eisenhower right now?"

A squirm-making silence grew long, before Hamster said, "Who says there's not?"

Several sets of eyes grew very big. Commander Gray snapped fingers at Mr. Vincent at tactical, who quickly organized a resonant scan of a two-klarc radius surrounding Fort Ike.

And located the alien spheres. A lot of them. On trajectories originating from the general direction of the galactic hub. At present speed the nearest of the spheres were still six years out. But at the end of those six years, the same thing that destroyed the Far Cat would be at Fort Ike.

"We've got our own fixed site to worry about."

Rome had apparently constructed their Deep End displacement chamber farther into the gorgons' territory. If Rome had obeyed the U.S. sanction against building a Catapult in the Deep End, then it would have been Fort Ike who discovered the monsters.

Or someone else. "Mr. Vincent, scan all U.S. colonies in the Deep End. A hundred-parc radius. Find me who's in trouble out here."

Found what they did not want to find. FTL spheres moving toward every one of Earth's deep colonies. At current speed, the predators were two years out from the planet New California, and a scant six months out from the globular cluster IC9870986 a/k/a the Myriad, where the LEN were conducting an emergency evac of two lightly populated planets. That planetary evacuation's short deadline just got nine years shorter.

"I do *not* want to explain this to the LEN," said Farragut, hand over his face. "And I'd rather eat gorgon guts than tell the Archon of the Myriad. We just have to kill all these things before it comes to that."

A bee banged around the command deck, smacking off the consoles and attacking the techs, its little abdomen pumping the instinctive motion of bee rage in racial memory of a stinger.

"The insects," Farragut said following the bee's manic path. "How do the insects figure into this?"

"There is an appearance of connection," Jose Maria allowed.

"Are they ratting us out?" said Farragut. Did not wait for an answer. "Mr. Gray, space all the ship's insects. Every last cricket, bee, ant, moth, earthworm—no forget the earthworms—insects. Insectoids. All of them. Out the air lock."

"Please." Jose Maria held up a hand.

Commander Gray hesitated, looking to his captain as Jose Maria pleaded quietly, "Stay the bees' execution for a time, young Captain. The insects did grow calm in between our battle with the aliens and our visit to Telecore. It suggests the insects are reacting to the aliens rather than calling to them."

"Reacting to what, Jose Maria? Why are they bouncing around *now?* We don't have any gorgons on board."

"Do we not?" said Jose Maria.

Farragut went momentarily dumb. Would have thought that answer obvious.

Jose Maria went on, "Are the gorgons perhaps an infection that is suppressed below detection but does not quite go away? Or did we pick something up at Telecore that only the insects can sense?"

Farragut didn't like it. Didn't accept it. "I think I'd notice if we had gorgons on board. And I can't take the chance. The bugs are going out."

"There has been enough death."

"They're *insects,* Jose Maria."

"They are innocent lives. Perhaps more than innocents. Might they, in fact, be warning us?"

Farragut loved the man but was about to throw him off the command deck.

Then Lieutenant Glenn Hamilton said, "I think they are, Captain. Warning us."

"Oh, for Jesus." Farragut rolled his blue eyes. *Women and civilians.* But he ordered a shipwide search for "anything gorgonoid."

Thoughts ran more to homicide than to extermination. Colonel Steele knew he wasn't going to find anything out here. This was an idiotic assignment.

TR Steele had gone hull-walking outside the ship with F/S Cowboy Carver. Searching for gorgons. Felt like he'd been sent to fetch a left-handed baseball.

Artificial gravity was odd out here. Fluctuating. The direction of its attraction roughly inward toward the ship, but unpredictable. The shimmer of the force field some thirty feet above (beside? below?) them made the surrounding blackness surreal.

The atmosphere was feeble out here, so Steele and Cowboy wore space suits. Magnetic boots helped them keep their footing on the hull.

Didn't want to lose contact. The force field could be dangerous. You did not want to touch it.

But the boots also made simple walking more like a march through mud.

Cowboy moved with a cowboy swagger. Lean, all muscle even to the brain, Cowboy's body formed a wedge from shoulders to narrow hips. Women thought he was gorgeous. The only woman who mattered, Kerry Blue, still thought Cowboy was gorgeous. She hated him too hard. Meant she still loved him. For that, Cowboy ought to die.

Starlight shone in a red Doppler smear on this side of the ship. Lamplight took a strange bounce from the force field, brightened the gray metal hull.

"Hey, what's this?"

Cowboy kicked at *this*. A thigh-high pile of black, crusted *stuff,* big lumps of it, as if some titan forgot to clean a gigantic grill.

"Clean it up," said Steele.

"Me?" Cowboy squawked. "I didn't do it." And opened a com link, "Hey, Captain. Something odd out here. We got barnacles."

Since when did Cowboy Carver report directly to Farragut?

Farragut responded, but not to Cowboy. "TR, find something?"

"Sir, I—" Dammit. Had not meant to take this to the captain. Could not exactly tell him never mind now that crater-mouth Cowboy had opened the com. "I *think* it's molten debris blown out of the Fury stuck on the hull. It looks like big burned carbon lumps."

Cowboy poked at the pile with his gloved forefinger. It didn't give. "You know, I think this might be Kerry Blue's cookies. I just throw 'em out the airlock. So *this* is where they land."

Kerry Blue made cookies for Cowboy Carver? Steele wanted him so very dead.

Cowboy took his knife to the crusted stuff. The blade did not so much as prick the surface. "Yep. This is Kerry's bakery, all right."

Cowboy crouched down to try to wedge his blade between the black heap and the hull. His helmeted head bent over his work, intent.

Steele blinked in the peculiar light. Might be hallucinating out here. One of the crusted blobs seemed to move.

Did move. Was *opening*.

Disbelief made time stretch. A slow-motion quality to it. The solid heap took on shape, grew a pincered head. Or was that a clawed arm?

Turned glossy as a beetle's back. Pincers sharp as razors parted to encircle Cowboy's bent neck.

Blue-white flame leaped from Steele's blowtorch in a hard jet. Cowboy ducked and rolled, swearing. "Gak! What are you trying to— *ho, skatbricks!*" Dodged a fiery, thrashing pincer.

The other globules opened—briefly—under Cowboy's and Steele's blowtorches.

Over the smoldering remains, Cowboy's clap on the back of Steele's shoulder rocked Steele a step forward. "Thanks, Old Man."

Cowboy. Steele had just saved Cowboy's life. Steele snarled. "What was I thinking?"

And Cowboy laughed. Never knew Colonel Steele could make a joke.

"They weren't the same thing," Cowboy said at debriefing.

"They have to be the same thing," Steele told the officers and scientists.

"No," said Cowboy. "Gorgons got whippy bitey leggy things all over a blobby bag body. Those things out there were armed and way bigger. They got jointed legs and pincer things."

Steele rapped down a beaker of sludge on the table between himself and the investigators. "They look the same now."

One of the examiners leaned forward to sniff the beaker. "Which creature is this?"

"Yes," Steele said, sour.

The lab had specimens of melted gorgons and specimens of the creatures Steele and Cowboy had dispatched on the hull. Without labels on the beakers, no one could tell which was which.

"A red blood cell does not look or act like a white blood cell, neither of which looks or acts like a cell from a muscle or from the brain," Dr. Cordillera offered.

Farragut listening in, leaning back against a wall, got into it here: "Jose Maria, you're saying we're fighting some huge space body's white blood cells?"

"I cannot know. I am throwing out analogies from my own frame of reference for consideration." Jose Maria lifted the beaker from the table. Gave the brown sludge a swirl before his eyes. "They die the same. How is our insect life faring now?"

Farragut had forgot all about them. A quick demand for report revealed that the bees of *Merrimack* had returned to their hives, their buzzing a soft, peaceable hum.

"God Almighty."

The implications were astonishing—the two sets of monsters were the same. Insects could sense them both.

And, more significant still: "We have a warning system."

Farragut signaled the command deck: "Mr. Gray, cancel order to space the insects."

"Aye, sir."

"If I may be so bold, young Captain," said Jose Maria, a preface to advice.

"Go ahead, Jose Maria. Your guess on these things is better than mine."

"I advise disabling the ship's resonance chambers. Res pulse exists everywhere at the same instant, which means there is no effective difference between sending and receiving—one touches the harmonic either way."

"You mean if the JC contacts us—"

"I believe such contact would betray your ship's position to the predator."

The ship's res specialist agreed in theory, though he still didn't know how anyone or anything could pull a location off a res pulse. He excused himself from the debriefing to go disable the ship's resonant chambers.

Merrimack altered course, ran dark until she was in a position calculated to be well behind the gorgon spheres stalking her.

"If we don't come out behind the gorgons, that means they can track us without our resonating," said Farragut. "And it means the insects are going out the air lock."

The only way to know was to resonate.

The scan tech hesitated on the switch, warned, "This could betray our new position."

"If they don't already have it," said Commander Gray. "Execute scan."

Took a resonant scan of the area *Merrimack* had vacated. And glory be, there were the gorgon spheres, roaring blindly away after *Merrimack*'s old position.

A second scan revealed the gorgons turning hard about. Expected that, but still came as a shock "They've reversed course. They *do* locate by res pulse! They're chasing us."

Farragut was about to signal the lab to ask what the insects were doing, when an entire of swarm of bees invaded the command deck with an enraged hum.

Farragut moved carefully, so as not to crush any bees. "Let's see if we can't give the gorgons a wild goose to chase."

He ordered *Merrimack* to turn toward the galactic hub and resonate again to encourage their pursuers. Then go dark and double back, disable all res chambers.

In moments the bees quieted, settled to a placid search for anything edible in Jose Maria's ruby collar tack and in the red-and-yellow console lights before they gathered up and went home.

Steele stood uneasy on the command deck, eyes shifting, as if They were listening. Mumbled near to a whisper, "We *think* they can't see us, but we *know* we can't see them." Didn't put much faith in the testimony of bees.

"I believe we threw them off," said Commander Gray. "But, Captain, the lieutenant colonel is correct. The darkness works both ways. Tough to fight what we can't see."

Actually, Farragut could think of a few options but did not want to use any of them. "I'm not fixing to teach those gorgons one more blessed thing about us."

"That doesn't leave us with much to do out here," said Colonel Steele.

"Orders?" Mr. Gray asked.

"I'm beginning to like the Roman suggestion," said Farragut, and issued the order: "Run like hell."

"Any particular direction, sir?"

There was really no choice but to fall back, regroup, and organize a mass extermination. "Fort Ike."

Commander Gray instructed Navigation to plot a course to Fort Ike, and relayed the order to the helm. "Run like hell."

"Running like hell, aye."

"Occultation nine by fifteen by one forty-eight," the lookout sang.

Farragut had not thought there were any alien plots on this path. "Take us wide of the sphere."

"Not a sphere, I don't think, sir." Positive ID was tough with a passive scan. Then, "Occultation twelve by twenty by one thirty."

"Identify," said Farragut.

"Possibly ships. Possibly human make. Occultation eighteen by three by one ten."

Bogeys. Three of them. Something very deliberate in their placement.

No one runs into anyone by accident out here.

"Occultation eleven by eight by twenty."

"Oh, for—" Farragut pounced on the tactical station, watched the plots appear. On the left. On the right. On the up. On the down. The plots constricting like a snare. Didn't need a fine scan. "That's Roman. Pilot! Ram it to the gate! We're going through!"

As *Merrimack* sprang, the Roman ships opened fire. Their positions were staggered so each had a clear shot at *Merrimack* without danger to their counterparts on the far flank.

Merrimack ran out her guns and charged, blasting through the closing gauntlet. Did not need to take out the ships. Only had to make their field generators dip. There was no stealth in this maneuver. Just punch and speed, which *Merrimack* had. Ran at the force field barrier—

"Yeeee HA!"

—and through.

Merrimack ran full out. You could hear the engines, feel the deck throb, take savage joy in the strength of this ship. The Roman ships turned about to give chase, and you had to laugh at them, because they hadn't a prayer of catching up.

Cowboy Carver shot the moon out a sternside clearport.

The Roman ships could not catch *Merrimack.* You had to wonder why they were still back there, chasing. But they hung in, dogging *Merrimack*'s widening lead through two watches.

Merrimack would enter Fort Eisenhower's fire zone in eight more hours.

"Those ships follow me into the fire zone, I'm keeping one as a souvenir," said Farragut watching the rear display.

Then, from the lookout: "Occultation five by two by thirty."

No! The mind would not accept it.

Those coordinates were in *front*.

"Occultation five by nineteen by forty."

Elation turning to sand.

"Occultation ten by nine by nine."

From the pilot, hope descending: "That's not the space cavalry coming out from Fort Ike, is it?"

Farragut, stoically, "I don't think so, son."

Watched the tactical display, the angry lights blinking on before of them, one by one by one.

Tactical started, "Sir, it's a—"

Farragut nodded. Knew what this was. "It's a Roman Legion."

Dead ahead.

31

FARRAGUT SHOUTED OVER the intracom: "Og! Re-deploy force field. Brace for a hit from any direction." A split-moment before Marcander Vincent sang out from the tactical station, "Javelins headed toward us, from all quadrants. Nineteen of them. Twenty. Impacts in twenty-nine to forty seconds, sir!"

"Battery! This is Farragut. Target incoming javelins."

The pounding of the cannon thundered through the decks with the hiss of the ship's beam weapons discharging. The burn smell snaked through the tight corridors, carried up to the command deck.

Merrimack's force field crackled and groaned, made a sickening light show through the clearports as the ship took hit after hit.

"Colonel Steele," Farragut sent up to the battery. "I just counted fifteen javelin strikes." Five intercepts out of twenty hostile missiles. "Unacceptable, TR."

"Yes, sir," said Lieutenant Colonel Steele.

The Marine gunners' second chance was already on its way—a salvo of thirty javelins. Impact due in eighteen to twenty-three seconds.

Farragut had been in a fistfight like this once. That one had been sixteen to one. Best tactic against multiple attackers was to run. Not sure that card was still in the deck. Surrounded like this, *Merrimack* was caged in an energy field the size of a small solar system.

"Mr. Gray, we're in a bag. Punch us out of here."

"Aye, sir."

In a fistfight the first punch usually gets blocked. So Commander Gray issued instructions for a lunge forward at the oncoming Legion, a zig *down,* a zag toward the rising starboard and a charge forward again in hopes of carrying the *Merrimack* past the Legion and forcing the largest bar of this Roman cage to reverse direction.

The helm fed the course to the ship's battery so the gunners could adjust their shots accordingly, then executed the escape action.

The Legion was ready for it. They gave little reaction to all the feints, anticipated the end maneuver and went straight to countering that one. The Legion split, with the rear guard executing an immediate full reverse. One of the rear guard caught *Merrimack* a hammerball square on the stern.

Merrimack's force field fluttered. Gravity hesitated, came back hard, buckled the MPs' knees to the deck, cracked the techs' foreheads to their consoles. Farragut dropped into a linebacker crouch. Jose Maria went down like a cat.

Then a torpedo strike concussed the ship, peppered an inner corridor with slivers from the ship's own hull blown inward.

Ears popped open as air rushed out of the ship to fill the gap between the punctured hull and the inertial screen.

An erratic groaning of a force field in distress warbled through the pounding of the ship's guns. "Systems, do we have a containment field going bad on us?" Commander Gray asked.

"*Yes,* sir," the systems tech reported. "Engine Three's containment field is fluctuating. Mr. Kittering is— Go ahead." That last spoken into the tech's headset, to the senior engineer.

"Put her on the box." Farragut waved a come on.

The systems tech clicked his com link onto the speaker, through which Kit's voice became audible, "—need to space Number Three."

"Kit, this is Farragut. Is that engine critical?"

"No, sir. Just keeping a contingency plan in place. This engine is NOT going to reach critical. I won't let it."

"Kit, you might rethink that. When it comes time to jettison an engine, can you—" He paused, reconsidered what he was about to ask, pushed ahead anyway, "*Aim* it?"

Kit's voice went softly icy, as if he had suggested she cut off her arm and throw it out a porthole. Reminded him of the cost of the thing, and reminded him that the engine was *not* critical.

"Yes, I know the cost. It's one-fifth the cost of the surviving engines, which *are* going to fall into Roman hands if I don't do something drastic. Can you aim a jettisoned engine?"

"Sir, I'll—make it happen."

"Mr. Gray, coordinate this."

"Aye, sir. Target, sir?"

Farragut gave a nod at the tactical display, which had identified most of the member ships of the Legion. "Cal's buddy."

The Roman flagship.

"*Gladiator,* sir?"

"*Gladiator.* We take out Numa, or we got nowhere to run."

"May I make a suggestion, sir?" Commander Gray offered.

"I'll take any you got."

Sebastian Gray spoke in a stop-start staccato, attention divided between the com chatter on his headset, and the plots on the tactical display. "We probably won't be able to get a jettisoned engine close to any of the Roman ships, especially *Gladiator.* They'll avoid it or just shoot it. But Mr. Kittering can probably arrange the containment mix so that when the engine blows, it'll hose antimatter everywhere. Now if we can stick some *matter* onto the Roman force fields right before that—"

"Tag 'em!" Farragut roared.

Merrimack launched homer tags at all Roman vessels within range, especially *Gladiator.* Any Roman tags which might be clinging to *Merrimack*'s field were not just deactivated but scoured off. There must be no particle of matter attached to *Merrimack*'s defensive barrier when the antimatter was unleashed.

Kit, reported up: "Engine Three, ready to jettison."

"Jettison Number Three."

"Jettisoning Number Three, aye. Engine away."

Without its containment housing, Number Three's antimatter collided with its matter. The force of mutual annihilation sprayed the engine's surviving matter and antimatter in a wide, widening bubble, detonating all warheads in its radius.

The sphere of antimatter grew, reached back to *Merrimack.* Washed harmlessly over her force field.

Commander Gray on the com: "Battery! Recommence fire! Tactical! Status of the Romans!"

"All incoming Roman ordnance destroyed." Mr. Vincent reported.

"No damage to the Roman ships. Repeat: No damage. Not even any detonations against the Roman shields."

"How can that be?"

"The lupes must have cleaned the tags off their force fields same time we did."

Commander Gray looked cheated. "Now how the hell could they know to remove dead tags? Unless they saw us do it. But still. That is damn fast thinking."

"Don't beat yourself up, Bast. It was a great plan," said Farragut. "Points to Numa."

A ripping blast inside the ship slammed Farragut against the bulk. Split his lip against his teeth. He tasted blood. Heard shouts muffled by the sponginess in his eardrums.

"Systems, what was that?" Commander Gray demanded, crawling up his console from the deck.

"Roman beam shot caught one of our cannon shells leaving the barrel. Looks like the shell detonated half in, half out of the force field. Gun bay twenty-five is a code thirty-three." Fire code.

The Roman shooter was either vastly lucky or impossibly good. Either way, that was a one in a million shot. Impossible really.

Then he did it again. This one caught the shell more in than out of *Merrimack*'s force field. Ripped two gun blisters off the ship, with cannon and crew, and left the hull torn open. Only the heavy blast wall, which backed the gun blisters, kept the ship from more catastrophic damage.

Two in a million.

"Lock down!" Farragut ordered, and the shouts echoed throughout the ship, "Lock down! Close and *seal* all ports!"

Farragut turned to Tactical. "Mr. Vincent, there's a Striker out there. Find it!"

All of *Merrimack*'s guns reeled inboard, the force field solidifying over the ports.

Except one. Gun bay sixteen was stuck open.

The command officers listened to the exchange between Colonel Steele and the gun crew over the intracom, Colonel Steele roaring in some unknown tongue, but everyone understood what he was saying.

Gun bay sixteen reported, "Cannot close the gunport. We have a foreign body in the cannon."

"Can you dislodge?"

"Won't budge in or out. It's big, sir. And it's in here."

"Nature of the foreign body. Something blown back?"

"No, sir. It looks like— Sir, it looks like another gun barrel."

"Oh, for—" Farragut pulled off his headset. "Systems, get me a picture. What is he looking at?"

One of the ship's external monitors picked up the unlikely scene from the outside. "Located your Striker, sir," said Mr. Vincent, putting the image on the display.

A very small Roman ship, carrying under its fuselage a missile launcher nearly as long as the Striker itself, had thrust that launcher's 30-millimeter barrel in through *Merrimack*'s gunport, right up the cannon barrel, so that its maw was inside *Merrimack*. The Striker had managed the maneuver without sustaining any damage to itself. The precision was unreal.

The Striker's colors were not black and gold. This one was not Julian.

Farragut put his headset back on. "Gun bay sixteen. This is Captain Farragut."

"Sir! Gun bay sixteen, aye."

"Serge." Farragut recognized the voice. Big Brazilian ape. Played a mean game of squash. Could remain vertical carrying an awful lot of alcohol. And evidently never ever blinked. "Good man. Serge, can you load a shell and blow this guy out?"

"Can't load, sir. Enemy's barrel is sticking right up through the cannon breech. He is *in* here. I might be able to discharge small arms up his nose, but it might make him sneeze. Please advise."

Farragut responded over the com, "Any chance this guy has fried his brains out like our poor Julian friend Septimus did?"

"Don't think so, sir. We're in direct contact. I'm getting vibrations through the barrel. Like something moving around over there in the Striker."

And in case there was any doubt, came a strange voice, muffled, flat, not Serge's: "I live."

Farragut squeezed the com as if it were Serge's big beefy shoulder. "Get out of there, son." Took off the headset, shook his head at the damning sight on the display.

Commander Gray asked, "Is that a patterner, sir?"

"Oh, yeah."

"*Know* him?"

Farragut nodded.

An angry little ship. Red and Black. *Gens* Flavius. First patterner Captain Farragut had ever seen.

Remembered the Myriad. The *Merrimack* in a tug-of-war with an event horizon. Farragut refusing to let go of two crewmen to turn and defend himself.

Rather than take the kill shot in the back, this red-and-black Striker had made an impossible shot that set *Merrimack* free.

The Striker's parting words: *Next time, when I have a clear shot at something other than your back, prepare to yield to Rome as my prize of honor, or else die for the glory of the Roman Empire.*

Commander Gray hadn't been there.

"I owe this one my hide," Farragut told Commander Gray. "And he's come to collect."

The com tech held up a link, "Captain. Numa Pompeii, for you, sir."

The command deck became quiet, a weird oasis of stillness amid shouts of emergency, which rang through the rest of the ship. A stillness as acrid as the smoke. Whites showed full round all the eyes on deck. Everyone knew what this was.

"Let's have him," Farragut nodded to the box.

Waited for the demand.

His gaze strayed to the systems monitor screen. Number Four Engine containment field was fluctuating.

The com tech routed the Roman signal to the speaker and advised the Roman, "Go ahead, sir."

"Captain Farragut," the disembodied baritone voice of Numa Pompeii inquired.

"I'm here," said Farragut. Standing straight up. Gaze level, distant, slightly to the starboard.

"We will not board you, *Merrimack*," said General Pompeii. "Surrender or die."

How quaint that sounded. How weird that he meant it.

Farragut mentally ran through all the possibilities, thoughts racing faster than light. All scenarios came back to those two. Surrender or die.

Still, he tried, without hope, "We are carrying fifty Romans in detention. Do you want to talk to them?"

"They are Romans," said General Pompeii. Meaning Romans were ready to die for Rome. "Your decision, Captain."

A feeling like a knife in the gut. With someone else's voice, Farragut spoke, "Mr. Gray. Strike colors."

Gray nodded to the Marine guard.

With the smallest hesitation, a motion like a sob in her shoulders, the Marine obeyed, laid a reverent hand to the panel that slowly furled Old Glory and reeled the flag inboard. And because it seemed the thing to do, she extinguished the ship's exterior lights that had illuminated the colors for so long through the eternal night.

Numa's voice sounded again through the speaker, "Not enough." And he pressed the demand, "Farragut, your surrender."

"I'm choking here, Numa. Give me a second."

Numa waited.

Farragut lifted his face as if looking for God, took in a breath. He asked, a rather desperate stall, "Terms?"

"You have my terms. Surrender or die. Now."

Farragut opened the shipwide intercom, so all of *Merrimack* would know what was happening. Sounded like someone else speaking. Could not be he, because he could not even breathe. "General Pompeii, this is Captain John Farragut. *Merrimack* surrenders."

PART SIX

In Manus Tuas

32

FARRAGUT RASPED, "FORCE FIELD."

Commander Gray saw to the force fields, brought them down to minimal, presenting only enough barrier to prevent air escaping, and down to nothing around the air locks.

The Roman boarders would have no trouble getting through.

The exec also initiated capture protocol, commencing destruction of sensitive files. Asked Farragut, "Who has the CT?"

Farragut pointed to himself and spoke without voice, "I do." Then he got Lieutenant Hamilton on the com, his words escaping one, two at a time, "Everyone. Cargo hold."

Glenn Hamilton had known him a long time, so she understood him. Captain Farragut wanted his crew and company assembled in the only place big enough to hold them all.

As they congregated in the cargo hold, Farragut detoured to sick bay. Kissed his medics, laid hands on the wounded, pulled covers over the faces of his dead.

Jose Maria had accompanied him to sick bay, and there he stayed when Farragut departed for the cargo hold.

Wondered how he would speak, but he found his voice in time to talk to his crew and company as the Romans approached.

He named the dead. Thanked the living for their loyalty and courage, and their superhuman fighting spirit. "What faced us here was beyond even us. And it only proves that nothing under God is invincible.

"You know I'm not the giving-up type. But I won't sacrifice your lives to keep this ship out of Roman hands. You are far too valuable. I expect we will be separated. Should this be the last time I talk to you, I need you to know: there is no guilt in stopping your fight now. We did all we could. I have surrendered. Respect my surrender."

A ship's dog trotted in, a big-hearted mutt who sensed he was needed. He climbed up on the cargo crate on which the captain stood and sat at the captain's side.

Farragut interrupted himself, hand on the dog's head. "Reminds me. Og, have your boys leash the dogs—the four-footed ones. I don't want any of these guys getting shot trying to protect us."

He continued to the assembly, "And I need y'all to do something for me. Survive. You will—I promise you will—see your families and your homes again. And none of you dare feel bad about that. You have served your country and your world honorably. Never a better crew, never a better pack of dogs prowled these decks."

A smattering of barking crackled from the Marines, quickly quieting again to listen, for already there intruded the clanking of the Roman *corvus*. The bang of a boarding skiff coming up against the hull.

"And if I could, I would thank each man jack and jane of you face-to-face by name. But Numa's knocking at my door here—"

The deep thump of a hatch opening. Many boots tramping in unison.

"Be proud, as you have made me very, very proud."

The dog snarled, hackles lifted, teeth bared, as Captain Farragut gave over his sword to Numa Pompeii in formal surrender. Normally, the ceremonial antique weapon these days was a revolver.

General Pompeii quirked a half smile at the sword. "A little over the top. But that's you, Captain Farragut." Numa passed the blade to an attendant. "Join me for dinner, Captain?"

"No disrespect to the Triumphalis, but I am the farthest thing from hungry," said Farragut, and before Numa could press the invitation, said, "How the hell did you locate us?"

"That was easy. Once you betrayed your location at the Far Catapult, I drew a straight line from the Catapult to Fort Eisenhower. You would not be far off it. Not that you don't have sinkers and sliders in your arsenal, but you are at heart a fastball pitcher."

Know your enemy.

"Dammit Numa, you know what's out there! And you send a Legion after *me*?"

The Roman nodded. "I know what's out there. The *Merrimack* is fresh meat. And I need fresh meat, because *They* learn."

"The meat is not as fresh as you think," Farragut took mean pleasure in disillusioning General Pompeii. "In fact, it's pretty well tainted. The gorgons figured out how to shut us off."

Numa's eyes masked shock, suspicion, doubt. Rather mockingly he said, "You're trying to tell me your ship was boarded?"

"That's a surprise?" said Farragut. "The gorgons boarded plenty of Roman vessels I've seen."

"You have an intact ship and a live crew and you tell me with a straight face your systems were shut down and you were boarded."

"Here's my straight face, Numa." Farragut turned his face to the side, pointed at a fresh star-shaped scar in front of his ear, precisely describing the outline of a gorgon leg-mouth.

Numa's color darkened, his victorious shine dulled. His mouth set into a sullen line. He spoke flatly to his guard, "Show the captain to his accommodations."

There was a cot, but Jose Maria found John Farragut sitting on the deck in his solitary detention compartment, his back against the bulk.

Farragut looked up at his visitor. Jose Maria was dressed in casual aristocracy—wide black trousers, a light taupe tunic wrapped round his narrow waist, his hair pulled back in its silver clasp.

"They treating you okay, Jose Maria?"

"Very well," said Jose Maria, coming to crouch at near level with Farragut. Balanced on the balls of his feet, shod in soft, expensive galoug-skin slippers.

"Did you have to buy yourself back?"

Jose Maria shook his head. "Rome appears to have turned a blind eye to my less-than-neutral behavior."

"They don't want to get into it with Terra Rica just now."

"That would be my take," Jose Maria agreed. The focus of his black eyes traveled from the captain to the cot back to the captain on the deck. "Penance?"

"Unraveling a bit. How are my crew? Have you seen them?"

"Rebounding better than you," said Jose Maria.

The captain had lost weight, which he could afford, but without the usual fire, he looked hollow. His bloodshot eyes fixed in a barely open squint.

"They quote you often. The shock is wearing off and they are, as you would say, working up a good mad."

Farragut scowled a satisfied scowl. The news seemed to cheer him. "Good. That's good. What ship are they being held in?"

"This one. *Gladiator.*"

Farragut's brows lifted, intrigued. Blue eyes traveled the confines, searching for something conductive to rap on.

"Are you eating?"

"Sometimes."

Farragut made the guard who brought his food taste it first. If delivered by an automaton, he did not touch it.

"General Pompeii is vexed at your refusals of his invitations to his table."

"Oh, good for Numa."

"You should go, young captain. Romans do not invite losers to the commander's table."

"I don't think I could swallow."

"They say you are not sleeping."

The question struck him as odd. Brows dropped over squinted eyes. His head tilted. "You working for them now, Jose Maria?"

"Paranoia is a symptom of sleep deprivation."

"Answer the question."

Jose Maria touched Farragut's face. "No, young Captain. I am not in league with Rome."

"Sorry." Turned his face away. Breathed into his hands. "I don't dare close my eyes very long. I don't want them putting anything in my head."

"I cannot prevent them from doing as they will," said Jose Maria. "But to the limit of my ability to do so, I will tell you if that happens."

Farragut nodded. "Deal." Then seized the wide sleeve of Jose Maria's tunic, as he might the robes of a father confessor. "This, *this,* Jose Maria, is the end of the world. Not the gorgons. This. Surrender." Tears wet the expensive fabric. "I know how Matty felt."

"You *do?*" Jose Maria said, quietly alarmed. After losing the *Moni-*

tor, Matthew Forshaw had blown his brains out. "Is this a suicide watch, young Captain?"

"No. No. Just—damn, this is tough." Tears flowed freely now. "I want another shot. Reset. Go back. I want a rematch and it's not going to happen." He sat back, sighed. Calmer for the outburst. "And I think—was this what the judge was trying to prepare me for with the choke holds? He used to put a forearm right here and say, 'You gotta know if you can take it.' Was *this* what all that was for? And you know what? That's a load of jaggerskat, Jose Maria. I can choke just fine without all the rehearsals."

"You should sleep."

Farragut closed his eyes and nodded. "I should. Can you stay?"

"I shall. For as long as I can."

"Wake me when you go."

"Deal."

Guilt said he should sleep on the deck. Farragut was not the sort to haul around that kind of load. He followed common sense onto the cot and passed peacefully out.

"I begin to take insult, Captain Farragut." Numa Pompeii showed up in John Farragut's detention compartment in person to voice displeasure at the captain's latest refusal to dine with him.

Numa Pompeii was not missing any meals. The Triumphalis carried a lot of flesh on a very large frame. Farragut was down to his college weight.

"Well, that's a start," said Farragut, not bothering to stand.

"There should be respect between officers, even on opposing sides."

"Yeah, there should be," said Farragut blazing back to life. "Except that you're a swine, Numa."

"I won. You lost. The lack of civility is uncalled for."

"I had a lot of time in here to hear it calling. What you did to prisoners of war is proscribed by all conventions of war, and you're talking to me about civility?"

"I don't know what *you* are talking about, sir."

"Matty Forshaw! Napoleon Bright! What you did to them is a war crime."

Numa looked genuinely puzzled. "I let them go. And I arranged for pickup. It's not as if I stranded them in outer space. It was simple, elegant, legal. Moral. I even gave Mr. Forshaw a medal." Then, to Farragut's homicidal glare, "I admit even I was surprised to learn how hard he took it."

Farragut, stonily ironic: "You were."

"Matthew Forshaw killed Matthew Forshaw. And your people killed Napoleon Bright."

"I'll be damned if I let you do to me what you did to Matty and Brighty."

"Oh, no. You're too big a fish to throw back, Captain Farragut."

"I meant the brain alterations, you smug baboon."

"What alterations?"

"Ingenuousness doesn't look good on you, Numa."

"I am—" the general chose the next word carefully, "ignorant." Could not ever call himself innocent. "What alterations?"

"You had foreign cells inserted into those men's brains."

"No, sir. I did not. I believe that you believe what you say, Captain Farragut. But you are wrong. Do I play mind games? Of course I do. But not like that. If you know your enemy at all, then you know that is not my style of warfare."

"I thought I knew you. But I know for a fact you put something in Matty and Napoleon, you lying sack—"

"DO not shout at me, Captain Farragut. No. I did nothing to Mr. Forshaw and Mr. Bright. Someone is lying to you. Your CIA is not above slandering me to you."

"The CIA had nothing to do with it." Farragut did not tell Numa Pompeii that the autopsy had been at Calli Carmel's order. "And it's not slander. I *saw* the Sargasson autopsy."

Numa took an unconscious step back. Face betrayed little, but the concern that escaped looked real. He resumed, guarded, "Troubling, if true. If true, I had no knowledge of it."

Unlikely. And Farragut did not believe it. Just who could do something like that to Numa Pompeii's prisoners without the Triumphalis' knowledge? There was no way.

And then the thought.

Oh, for Jesus. Could it be that Imperial Intelligence was every bit as honorable and law-abiding as the CIA?

"Snakes?" said Farragut. *Spies.*

"Snakes," Numa Pompeii muttered.

Numa Pompeii had his own Lu Oh? Farragut almost felt sorry for his opponent. Not really. But he stopped trying to figure out how to kill him with his bare hands.

Numa continued, displeased: "Whatever your seaweedy allies found in Mr. Forshaw and Mr. Bright would have been the work of someone with less faith in my simple ploy than I. Someone saw fit to gild my lily."

"Your lily was a piss in the eye."

"Yes, it was," Numa admitted. Had meant it to be. "I trust Mr. Medina was not 'altered.' "

"No," said Farragut before he could wonder at the question.

Numa nodded, seemed satisfied, relieved.

Farragut spoke aloud, realizing only as he was speaking it, "Jorge Medina was a Roman mole."

Numa nodded as if the news were very old news. "For a moment I was afraid whoever gilded my lily might have butchered my own man. I do loathe snafus on that scale."

Numa Pompeii did not notice Farragut's struggle to contain his shock. Jorge Medina. Red, white, and true blue Jorge Medina who wouldn't speak Latin to save his life. Quiet, devoted lieutenant commander of the *Monitor*. It had been Jorge Medina who betrayed *Monitor*'s and *Merrimack*'s codes and harmonics to Rome.

Numa mused aloud, half to Farragut, half to himself, "I'm told that Medina never broke cover, so I'll be damned if I can figure how your CIA smoked him out."

We didn't smoke him. Farragut's mind all but whited out from all the lights going on. *It was all a huge mistake. Lord Almighty, Paxton Pike accidentally executed the right man!* It was hideous. Farragut fought down graveyard laughter, said tenuously, "Sometimes our intelligence staggers even me."

"Why the trumped-up mutiny charge, though? Why did you not simply execute Medina as a spy?"

"I—" Farragut couldn't lie. "—have no earthly idea what they were thinking when they executed Jorge."

"Useful creatures, moles. I dislike them. I am fortunate not to have been born during the Long Silence. I would have made a very bad mole."

"A very, very *large* mole," said Farragut.

"And you were no Cinderella before you stopped eating." Numa dropped a fresh uniform and a pair of spit-shined dress shoes—size large—on him. "You *will* join me for dinner."

The Triumphalis' table was on a par with that of the White House, decked in Roman splendor. The French doors opening onto a formal garden was perfect in the depth of its illusion, even to the movement of the air, and the scents of greenery and hyacinth. The cutlery was gold and had the heft to be solid throughout.

Farragut struggled through the appetizer. Finally dropped his gold fork and took up his wine goblet. "Oh, fuck it, Numa. Just keep this topped."

The general's deep rumbling chuckle sounded sympathetic. He lifted a wine decanter, but Farragut said, "What else you got back there?"

Numa Pompeii poured him Kentucky bourbon instead.

Farragut approved. "Well, that's better." Felt the burning comfort go down. "Is this my stash?"

Numa nodded. "We liberated it."

Farragut lifted a toast with his bourbon, "Here's to you being in this seat next go round."

"You threw some pretty hard language at me back there, Captain Farragut. War criminal. Lying sack."

"Baboon," Farragut added. "I called you a smug baboon."

"And you have an apology for me now?"

"No."

"You're a sore loser."

"I'm a piss-poor loser, Numa."

"Now tell me truthfully, Captain Farragut, were you actually boarded by Them? What do you call Them?"

"We call them gorgons. Among other things."

"Odd. So do we."

Not so odd. Earth and Palatine might be Cain and Abel, but underneath it all still brothers.

"And you're honestly telling me the gorgons boarded you?"

Farragut tired of the question. "Ask the crew of the Fury." He had no need to insist to this man.

"You've brainwashed the crew of the Fury."

Farragut gave a little jerk of surprise, then said, "I get it. They never saw a live gorgon. They saw a lot of sewage-looking stuff we claimed was gorgon remains. We made it all up."

"You made them swab your decks, threatened them, ignored their salutes. And they love you."

"*Do* they?"

"*Merrimack* would be the only ship ever to survive boarding."

"I've been told."

"The troubling thing is that the boarding does, as you say, 'taint the meat.' Whatever you did to combat them won't work twice."

"The gorgons that boarded the *Mack* are all dead. Who are they going to tell?"

"They're all connected somehow—which is why we call the gorgons collectively the Hive. They have a colonial intelligence."

"Across parsecs of empty space?"

"It would appear so."

Farragut was not accustomed to sharing intelligence with the enemy, and did not intend to start now. He only fished for confirmation of some of his own suspicions.

He offered a lot of nothing that could be news to the Roman general. Told him that *Merrimack* had not observed a Hive sphere travel faster than two hundred times light speed. That gorgons had no apparent means of propulsion, no apparent means of cohesion. That gorgons fall apart when they die.

Numa asked, "Ever seen an individual gorgon travel FTL without latching onto something else?"

"Haven't seen it," said Farragut. "On shipboard they don't move any quicker than a diamondback."

"Which?"

"Which what?"

Farragut learned then that the monsters came in not two, but three different forms—most common being the bundles of legs, which Farragut had assumed was the only flavor gorgons came in. Another, which must be what Colonel Steele and Cowboy met on the hull, a variety the Romans called soldiers—bigger, harder, fewer legs, viciously barbed, and they traveled in bigger spheres. And a disgusting third form Numa called gluies.

"Gluies. What's that in English?" Farragut asked.

"That *is* English," said Numa. He described white, revolting, slug-like things with nubby little teeth, and a paralytic poison. "Are you going to bring anything useful to this table, Captain?"

"Ask your patterner," Farragut said, feeling uncooperative. Surely the pilot of that infernal little Striker with its barrel stuck inside *Merrimack* could tell Numa Pompeii everything *Merrimack* knew about gorgons.

Numa Pompeii said, "The emperor's patterner is an obnoxious Flavian. I talk to him as little as possible. How do you kill them?"

"I outran one," said Farragut. "He self-destructed."

"How do you kill the *gorgons,*" said Numa, irritated. "Not patterners."

"It's like this," said Farragut. "You can develop all kinds of fancy poisons, but in any battle with a cockroach, a shoe always has the last word."

"Gorgons don't squash," Numa argued, a momentary lapse into stupid literalism.

"Numa, you're disappointing me. You don't deserve this." Farragut reached across the table to grab his bottle of bourbon.

The general quickly caught up. "Low tech. Your swords. Your damn swords."

"Which I owe to you and Jorge Medina. Thank you, Numa, for forcing me to arm my crew with swords. I think I will apologize now for everything I called you."

Numa had a lot of words for Farragut's apology.

"And gorgons burn," Farragut offered.

Numa shook his head. "Flash point is too high and they burn dirty. You kill yourself trying to fight them off a ship that way."

A sudden brassy chirruping and a frantic buzz made Farragut's skin roughen and prickle. Aldebaran scarab crickets fled their heraldic perches flanking the archway. They flew away, screeching.

Numa set down his glass, laid his linen napkin on the table. "You'll have to excuse me, Captain."

Numa rose, offering no explanation. Saw that Farragut knew the signs.

Farragut rose without prompting. "Put me in with my crew?" he asked as the guards stepped forward to collect him.

Numa nodded to the guards, granting that.

* * *

Bored stiff in captivity—Kerry Blue figuratively, the guys literally. Kerry was randy, too, but yab-yum was not a spectator sport and there was zero privacy in detention except for that curtained area, and Kerry Blue did not do toilets. Showers, yes, but there were no showers in here, and everyone stank.

She had to settle for kicking butt at poker to pass the time. They used banana chips for coin. Had nothing else. For clothes they were down to tanks, T-shirts, sweats, and deck mocs. Anything with buttons, zippers, hooks, or heels had not made it into detention. Not exactly Red Cross-approved quarters either, this meat box.

Then someone—the Hamster—heard bug noises through the partition—Aldebaran scarab crickets—which she claimed meant gorgons were stalking the ship.

Oh, good, what we need. A little panic in here. Kerry took one card. Didn't get the flush.

The hatch opened and Captain Farragut came in like daybreak. It was always good to see him. He looked good slimmed down like that, even though he was way too old for Kerry Blue. And he was the only one in this tank clean, shaved, and in uniform. Maybe thirty-eight wasn't so old.

Kerry tossed down her cards, uncrossed her legs, and jumped up from the deck. "Hey, Captain!"

And suddenly there were a lot of people talking at once. Most asking the captain if there were gorgons. It shocked Kerry when Farragut nodded, "I think we have gorgons on our tail."

Someone asked: "We're running, right?"

"I wasn't told." And the captain went round talking to everyone. Took his time getting to the Hamster, as if she were nothing to him but another officer. How the woman could be that blind to a man's interest was beyond Kerry Blue—but hel-lo. This time was different. Somebody woke up Sleeping Beauty. The Hamster was blushing, and doing little eye things, and little almost-smile things.

Kerry moved closer to listen. The captain's and the Hamster's words were all business, but the body language was saying "I want you bad and there are way too many people in here."

"*Gladiator* can easily outrun a gorgon sphere," Glenn Hamilton was telling Farragut. "Numa will run."

"Unless he's been ordered to turn and fight," Farragut said, very softly. "If Caesar orders it, the Romans will stand and die like the three hundred at Corindahlor."

"No. He wouldn't," said Hamster, dropping the flirty bit. Didn't sound like she believed herself. "Romans have never won against the gorgons. He has to run."

A ship within an inertia field gave no sense of its true motion, so Kerry couldn't guess which way *Gladiator* was taking her.

But she could hear the ship's guns erupt.

That was when Captain Farragut slapped the bulk and roared, "Dammit, Numa, run!"

Lots of pounding of outgoing ordnance. Hissing beam fire. *Gladiator* was unloading the whole rock pile on something out there.

Could be our guys coming to the rescue.

Kerry didn't believe herself either.

The lights flickered. Flickered off. Everyone looked ghastly in the yellow-green chemical glow of the emergency lamps, like they were dead already. On the deck overhead, someone's smart snappy Roman march step gave way to running footfalls. The ship's force field mooed like a dying gurzn. Kerry only ever heard a field urgle like that once before.

"We got gorgons on the screens," Kerry said to no one, anyone, in the dark.

Knew now why John Farragut was in here.

Numa Pompeii was allowing the captain of the *Merrimack* to die with his crew.

33

UNGODLY NOISES FROM THE force field told the prisoners that the gorgons were insinuating their way through the ship's defensive screen. That metallic scritching had to be tentacles against the hull. It would not be long now.

Glenn Hamilton cocked her ear to the changing sounds. "They're in."

"We're going to die in this cage!" someone cried in the crowded detention hold.

"Belay that," Farragut ordered.

After a slow, agonizing while, sounds of weapons fire diminished within the ship. Did not mean the enemy was on the run. You still heard enough scritching. Meant the gorgons were overwhelming the computer controls.

The air felt thick in Farragut's lungs.

He waited for the expected miracle. Heard it in the smallest *snick* amid the shouting and banging uproar that resounded through the big ship.

The detention hold's locks had failed.

Farragut bellowed, "Open that hatch! Look alive! Those closest to the hatch, get out and get clear! Do not block the exit!"

Kerry Blue shuffled with her squadron mates toward the hatch, inch by inch, stinking bodies pressed together—no one exactly pushing, but no one leaving any space between himself and the person in front of him.

There was just no herding seven hundred people through one hatch fast enough when your lives depended on it.

Kerry craned her neck round, looking for Farragut. Glimpsed him. Way in the back of the back. Kerry looked up at Colonel Steele, damp skin of her arm stuck to his. "Orders? When we get out of here?"

"We still have our orders from Farragut," Steele growled. "Stay alive."

The Romans made no move to stop the POWs spilling from detention, so even John Farragut, at the tail end of the file, got free of the hold. By then the Romans had switched from beam guns to ceremonial bayonets, antique revolvers, and roundsaws to combat the gorgons. Anything with a blade was in use. *Merrimack*'s crew and company found no useful weapons to be had.

Farragut sprinted to an unattended sensor compartment, and ordered his senior engineer, Kit Kittering, to locate *Merrimack* on the plotter screen. But the screen was dark and stayed dark. *Gladiator*'s sensors were all down. The only thing operative in the room full of unfamiliar equipment was the battery-powered backup lamp.

"That's why no one is in here," said Kit. "Even if *Merrimack* is out there, we won't be able to see her."

"*I* see her," said Farragut, startled, looking out a clearport.

The *Merrimack*. Right there. So close he could not take in any more than a wide stretch of gray hull. Only knew the ship was *Merrimack* because she was his.

Kit's great round doll eyes briefly widened at the featureless gray bulk. "John, that could be any ship."

"No, that's my *Mack*!" He knew her every inch, every flaw (she had none), every dimple. "She's gotta be hard docked and inside *Gladiator*'s force field to be that close. That's her port side and *Gladiator*'s got to be docked to her cargo bay two. The access will be three, maybe four decks down from here and twenty meters that way. Where would I find a vertical access in this hulk? Are you familiar with the layout of a *Gladiator* class battleship, Kit?"

"*Gladiator* is the class," said Kit. Rome had constructed only one. "I don't think the blueprints ever got out. Anyway, John, I don't think they would have the *Merrimack* right—"

Surprised shouts sounded from three, maybe four, decks down, in English: "*Merrimack!* It's *Merrimack!* She's here! She's open! This way!"

Clanging on the vents took on a distinctive Morse rhythm. Reg Monroe started spelling aloud the taps. "That's the captain! *Merrimack* is here!"

Kerry heard it, too. "Where? How do we get there from here?"

Dak came loping up, pointed with a broad, twice-broken finger. "Take this corridor to the T intersection. Go right. Take the ladder. Hard to starboard and down the ramp."

Carly wrinkled up her face at him. "Now how the hell do you know that?"

Dak nodded backward. "I asked a guy back there."

"You asked a *Roman* for directions?" Reg's voice ascended off the register.

"Yeah." Dak's big sloping shoulders shrugged.

None of his mates could believe it. But that *was* the direction all the excited shouting was coming from.

"He said we better hurry. The lupes are gonna push her off."

Reg, Carly, Twitch, Cowboy, Kerry, and Dak looked to Colonel Steele. Steele was about to give the go ahead when Cowboy yelled, "Gorgons! Six o'clock on the real fast!"

Aliens were coming up the corridor behind them—a black mass of ugly.

"Go!" Steele ordered.

As ready for combat as a clutch of rabbits, the Marines of Alpha Flight took off at a barefoot run, the hideous scritching rolling hot after them. At the T intersection the way broke right and left. Cowboy, in the lead of the retreat, broke *up* in an acrobatic leap, swung up on a pipe, kicked an access panel out of the overhead, and hoisted himself up.

Down on the deck were gorgons on all sides—a clot on the left closing in, more on the right barreling off the way the Marines wanted to go, and the mass of gorgons from behind, moving in fast. Cowboy in the overhead, hanging upside down like a trapeze artist, yelled, "Come *on!*"

Steele seized Reg by the waist and threw her upward to Cowboy, who caught Reggie's wrists and hauled her up into the vertical shaft with him.

Kerry next. Too high. Separated her ribs on the downward yank as Cowboy caught her wrists. She went up breathless, stunned with pain. Tried to climb up past Cowboy to where Reg was, higher in the stack. Could not breathe.

Carly, crowding in from below, gave Kerry a push on the ass. "*Chica linda*, some *help, por favor!*"

"Kerry's hurt," said Reg.

"She's okay," said Cowboy. Caught Twitch Fuentes. "Move it up. We're on a real deadline here."

Kerry climbed, grimacing.

Steele, down below, called, "Big load, coming up."

"Hey! Hey! Don't get personal!"

"Shut up, Dak."

Oofs from Steele, like boosting a sleeper sofa. Lots of weird sounds from Cowboy and Twitch, hauling Dak up into the shaft.

Kerry had to stop. Curled around a waste pipe. Looked down. No one left down there to boost the Old Man up. And Colonel Steele was not a small guy.

But stampeding gorgons with snapping tentacles converging on you can make you fly. Big yells, and Colonel Steele was up. Dak caught his wrists and heaved him into the overhead just as the gorgons from the six- and nine-o'clock corridors connected at the T intersection below the shaft. Looked like a snake's nest down there.

The whole snarl of them swarmed to the three o'clock and stampeded onward—the way the Marines wanted to go.

Reg whispered, "They didn't look up. Why didn't they look up?"

Kerry clenched her teeth, wrapped one arm around her rib cage. "Don't really give a squid."

"They want something bad that way," Dak said, filling the vertical access, shouldering his way up the stack.

"*We* want something bad that way," said Carly. "That's the way to *Merrimack*."

"Lupes must've slathered up the *Mack* real tasty. You think?" said Cowboy.

"Could be," said Carly. "I'd still rather be on *Mack* than here. This boat ain't exactly vermin free."

A glimmer of light returned to the bottom of the stack. The gorgons had passed on by. Steele clambered down, headfirst, for a recce, checking all three corridors.

"Clear?" Cowboy asked.

"*Not* clear." Steele twisted around upright. Sounds of gorgons' skittering toothy feet approached. "Marines, proceed up. We'll try to circle around to the dock from the next level. *Move!* Blue, you can move your ass faster than that!"

Fighting tears, nostrils flaring, Kerry acknowledged through her teeth: "Yes, sir!" Followed Reg up the shaft. Better off mad. Kept her mind off the pain.

The Marines moved like a line of rats, nose to tail, Reg leading. Reg had a sense for how ships were put together, and she brought them out on a catwalk twenty feet above the loading dock where great cargo doors lay open like parted jaws to swallow eager gorgons swarming from *Gladiator* to *Merrimack*.

The gorgons moved with a singular will. Ignored the Marines up above and the few Roman soldiers on other catwalks around the dock. Kerry crouched on the grating, arms round herself, head between her knees. The doors. The doors. Right down there. And no way to get through them.

The alien rush ebbed. There came an exchange of shouts in Latin from the dock and elsewhere, but no more gorgons.

"There's our chance!"

Carly had no sooner whispered when a ratcheting clangor filled the empty space.

The cargo doors were cranking shut.

"No!"

Cowboy leaped down the twenty feet, rolled on the deck, and up to his feet. He charged at one of the Romans at the winch.

The Roman dropped him with an easy crack of the butt of his beam gun across the side of Cowboy's head. The Romans continued cranking at the winch. Got up a rhythm. The cargo doors were clattering together easily, faster.

Dak and Steele vaulted over the catwalk railing, hung from the grate, dropped to the deck, and rolled. Steele roared at Dak, "Help them!" Of the Marines stranded above, while he, Steele, ran at the doors. He had nothing to wedge between them. They boomed shut before his nose.

Colonel Steele had been a drill sergeant once, in the dawn of his career, and still sounded it. "Open this!" he thundered in a voice that might have made even Romans obey, had they understood English.

Didn't seem to. They exchanged shouts with the upper decks. Acknowledged orders. Gave their weight to reluctant levers that creaked, budged, banged into position.

A clunking sounded from outside the hull. The sound of separation.

"Merrimack *abst!*"

Cowboy pried himself off the deck. Jumped at the doors like a caged kangaroo rat. "No! No!"

Reg stared, stunned, from the catwalk. Met the dark eyes of a Roman soldier at one of the levers. Oddly sympathetic eyes. The Roman spoke to her in English: "No tears now, pretty Yank. You didn't want to catch that ship. We're going to blow it up."

34

UPON BOARDING HIS gorgon-infested ship, Farragut
had been met by a squad of Marines at the dock, who were
passing out swords to all boarders having only two legs.
"Compliments of Lieutenant Hamilton, sir. Glad to have you aboard,
Captain Farragut."

"The Romans left these?" Farragut felt the satisfying weight of the
blade in his grip. It was good to be armed again.

"Yes, sir. We were surprised. They took everything else."

Maybe because the swords had worked once against the aliens,
Numa assumed the swords would not be effective twice. Or maybe it
was just because Numa disdained swords.

"I do love that man's hubris," said Farragut. Took possession of his
ship.

Nothing computer operated worked over here either, the ship
smothered by whatever force the alien mass exuded. Air was still
tough to draw. Numa had managed to off-load thousands of his gorgons
on to *Merrimack*.

But the gorgons here acted differently than the last swarm *Merrimack* had encountered. The gorgons of the last swarm had attacked
whatever was closest. These snubbed the easy snack in pursuit of
something irresistible.

"The Romans stowed something mighty tasty on board is all I can
think," said the Marine who accompanied Captain Farragut through

Merrimack's corridors, hacking a path through those few monsters still interested in random prey.

The captain's first order was to run out his flag.

The Romans had taken the Stars and Stripes, so someone quickly made up one and hand-cranked Old Glory out. Not perfect but just as proud and more defiant for its flaws.

"Captain on deck!" a Marine proudly announced Farragut's arrival on the command platform.

The few techs and specialists there leaped to their feet. Farragut took stock of who he had: Ben Mueller, the com tech who normally sat mid watch. Marcander Vincent, *Merrimack*'s junkyard dog of a tac specialist, scabs on his face, both his arms bandaged from a close encounter with a gorgon. Qord Johnson, the cryptotech, young guy, freckled, flat-nosed, with fuzzy rust-brown hair and amber eyes. The second-string pilot, Jul Cortez. They all cheered as if the captain could breathe life into their dead systems just by being here.

Farragut clasped their hands, embraced them, grabbed his little lieutenant behind the head and kissed her on the mouth. Under the circumstances it didn't raise any eyebrows. John Farragut was an expressive man.

A deep, ratcheting clatter made him rear back, alarmed. Sounded like cargo doors shutting, and he shouted to anyone, "Why are those doors closing! We're not all here! I am not abandoning our people on *Gladiator*!"

An anonymous voice shouted back from below: "Ready or not, yes we are, Cap'n! *Gladiator* closed first! They mean to space us!"

The ship heaved, canted. Farragut fell against a control panel.

The voice again. Pretty sure it was the Og: "We didn't do that, Cap'n! We were pushed!"

Ready or not, *Merrimack* was departing with the crew she had.

"Who is here, Hamster? Do I have enough to fly this boat?"

"Maybe half, Captain," said Lieutenant Hamilton. "Maybe."

"Colonel Steele!" he bellowed. "TR! You on board?"

"Don't think he made it, sir."

"Commander Gray?"

No one had seen the XO.

"Hamster, looks like you're acting exec again." Wanted to know if her husband had made it on board, but now was not the time to ask anyone. "Find out who we've got, and fill in the holes. I want this ship operational and all the gorgons dead. Does that uffing Striker still have its barrel stuck inside gun bay sixteen?"

With all systems fouled, he might be able to take over the patterner's demonic little ship. But the report came back from someone who ran all the way up to gun bay sixteen and back, "No, sir."

As *Merrimack* drifted apart from its captor, Farragut got a visual of *Gladiator*—coated with gorgons. Half of Farragut's crew was still on board that ship.

"Kit!" Farragut bellowed at the top of his voice. Knew his senior engineer was on board. She had come over with him. "Kit, can we steer?"

His engineer ran to the command deck to answer, gasping for oxygen. Took her a moment, hands on knees, to catch her breath. "Don't know, sir. We've got a strange mess in the back. A mad heap of gorgons—thousands—tens of thousands—outside Engine Room Six."

"What are they doing?"

Kit straightened, opened empty hands. She had no good answer. "Biting. They're even biting each other. Like there's something in the middle of them they ALL want."

"In Engine Six?"

"No, sir. In the maintenance shed right outside. And every compartment adjacent to it. God knows what's in the maintenance shed. They want it."

Captain Farragut and Lieutenant Hamilton spoke at the same time. "Bait."

Looked at each other.

"Why would the Romans put gorgon bait there?" said Kit Kittering.

"To lure the gorgons off *Gladiator*?" Hamster suggested. Seemed obvious.

"Well, it concentrates them real nice. A lot of them, anyway," said Kit. "Containment systems are functioning. Gorgons can penetrate them, of course, but it takes them time. I could seal off the affected compartments and lob in an incendiary. Take out about nine-tenths of our gorgon problem in one crack."

"No!" said Hamster.

Kit turned arctic. Knew her job better than any mid watch officer. "Just because *you* burned out the Fury, sir, doesn't mean *I* don't know what kind of bomb to use to contain destruction to only the maintenance shed." Told *her*. Captain's sweetheart be damned.

"No," Glenn Hamilton said again. Appealed to Captain Farragut. "I think there's already a bomb in there."

Farragut lifted his eyebrows—thinner eyebrows since they had grown back from his brush with Hamster's blowtorch aboard the Fury. He murmured. "What good's a lure without a hook?" And to Kit. "What do you think?"

Kit had to concede, with a pained nod. The God-blessed Hamster was right. "Got to be a bomb on board." That would explain why the Striker's barrel was absent from *Merrimack*'s gun bay. "And I bet it will take out more than the maintenance shed."

Gladiator had some systems controls back, but the intercom was not one of those, so the crew were shouting orders between decks. It was all in Latin, except for Colonel TR Steele bawling like a bull, "Pompeii! You can't do this!"

Merrimack. The Romans were going to blow up *Merrimack*.

Steele's mission presented itself—the reason God had stranded him on *Gladiator*. While TR Steele breathed, no one was going to blow up the U.S.S. *Merrimack*.

Kerry Blue never ever thought any responsibility so huge would fall into her hands—never when there wasn't some equally expendable grunt next in line to take up where she failed. Never thought she would have anything of value to offer Colonel Steele. But Kerry Blue had had lots of stepdads and had grown up learning bits of lots of languages. Kerry, Carly, and Twitch could piece together some of the Latin the Romans were bellowing for all to hear.

A lot of it was just yelling from soldiers locked in combat with the gorgons. But the voices that mattered were very loud and speaking very clearly to make their orders heard—calling for *Merrimack*'s destruction.

Kerry, Carly, and Twitch isolated three from the din.

An authoritative, high tenor voice, dubiously female, from an officer type addressed as *Domna,* giving orders.

A brassy male voice, grating. Made you hate him instantly, sight unseen. Had to be a tech in fire control, whose name was probably Bellus. He would be the one with his hand on the detonator.

And a third someone who was gauging a safe distance of separation between *Merrimack* and *Gladiator* for detonation. Reporting status updates to *Domna*.

It was going to be a hell of an explosion for distance to matter. The Romans had probably tied the device into the antimatter in *Merrimack*'s engines.

Steele pointed in the direction of the brassy one, Bellus. "That's the guy at the switch?"

"Yes, sir," said Kerry.

"You sure?"

Hated it when he asked her that. The man could make her doubt her own name when he asked her that way. Kerry was sure. She thought.

Carly answered, "Yes, sir."

Steele ordered all of them, "Take that man out."

Trying to find him in this maze was the problem. Sounds banged round the metal bulks, and became more confusing the closer the Marines got to Bellus. They listened and advanced by stops and starts, dodging Romans and gorgons at every turn.

Had to be getting close, but the brassy voice sounded from everywhere now. Right behind that partition. Or was that just an echo cracking back from the opposite direction?

"Oh, skat!" Carly hissed.

Bellus hadn't made a sound. Carly was listening to something else.

"What did you hear, soldier?"

"*Domna*'s asking for confirmation that they've reached safe distance for detonation," said Carly.

All the Marines heard a word in the tech's response to domna: *Confirmo.*

"I think I understood that one."

"Shh!" Carly was trying to listen. "*Domna*'s ordering Bellus to arm the detonator."

They all held their breath, waiting to pounce in the direction of Bellus' acknowledgment.

As soon as the brassy one opened his mouth, the Marines made a stealthy sprint in the direction of his voice. They jumped through a fire door to another section of corridor.

Now any of three closed hatches might shield Bellus. Or other Romans who would detain them. Or gorgons.

The Marines waited, listening for the voice of brass to bray again.

"Dammit, Bellus, say something!" Cowboy muttered through clenched teeth. "Can't kill him if he don't talk!"

Carly turned to Steele. "Colonel, he ain't gonna talk again till it's too late! It's too late!"

Because *Domna* had begun a sequence anybody but Dak could figure out: *"Novem, octo, septum, sex—"*

"Take a hatch!" Steele ordered out loud. "Cover all of them! Terminate any enemy on the other side. Go!"

Twitch and Carly dashed for the farthest hatch.

Reg and Cowboy took the middle.

Kerry, Dak and Steele stormed the closest one.

"—tria, duo, unum."

Steele tore open the near hatch to empty darkness. "Damn!" Skidding round.

Domna's order shouted from above: *"Fiat!"*

Let it be done.

Cowboy leaped through the middle hatch with Reg, her little hands cocked back in bear claws—

As the hand of the Roman at the console inside the compartment depressed a switch, an indicator light turned green, and the Roman reported in a brassy crow: *"Fit!"*

It is done.

35

REG'S SCREAM PIERCED the battleship.

"Ho!" Cowboy reeled back, finger in his ear. "Mind the decibelage, girl baby."

The Roman, Bellus, had whirled from his console, brandishing a bayonet. Had he stabbed or poked, Cowboy might have made a grab for the weapon, but Bellus sliced the air between himself and the Marines. Reg and Cowboy stumbled backward out of the compartment. Cowboy slammed the hatch and leaned on it to keep Bellus in.

Carly popped out of her hatchway, "What happened!"

"What the hell do you think happened!" Cowboy yelled. "He pushed the button on *Merrimack*! He got a green!"

Steele bellowed for status.

"Fubared beyond all recognition!" Cowboy hollered.

Kerry's mind went into dumb overload. *It's all moment to moment now.* Held her side with one hand. Pulled Dak from his salt-pillar stance with the other to follow Colonel Steele, who signaled the squad to fall back.

Retreated into *Gladiator*'s labyrinth of moody corridors. Following a man who didn't know the way but was decisive about it.

Stopped somewhere. Didn't know where, didn't care. Thirsty. Kerry was hellfire thirsty.

There were a lot of bushes here. An atrium of sorts. The Marines breathing hard as if from a twenty-klick forced march.

Steele gathered his Marines into a huddle.

Kerry was shaking mad, breathing through her teeth, eyes wet.

Carly a dry, hard mean.

That big lummox Dak looked like a motherless child.

Little Reg squeaking, trying not to sob out loud.

Twitch's long-lost tic had come back.

Cowboy was taking off his shirt.

Hazard—they'd lost Hazard Sewell way back at the detention hold. Hoped he hadn't made it to *Merrimack*.

Reg squeaked between sobs. "I don't hear the captain anymore. He'd be talking to us if he were here." She motioned a Morse tapping. "He must have—" Could not speak where Captain Farragut must have gone.

The captain's silence left a pall. Like God had died.

"Later, Monroe," said Steele. "Captain's order still stands—stay alive." Steele was pulling up foliage from the trees and bushes in the atrium, passing them out to his squad like ammo. Kerry wondered for a moment if their leader, their rock, their lifeline had snapped. She accepted a philodendron. Hoped Steele didn't think you could eat these.

"Listen up. Here's your new objective," said Steele. "We're going to find this ship's hangars, and hijack a transport—a fighter craft, a shuttle—anything to get us out of here. We are jumping ship."

A hearty "Yeah!" from Cowboy.

"*Gladiator* won't have deployed its small craft. They're a liability in a battle with gorgons, so all boats should be inboard."

"Sir? If we do get out—won't we be gorgon meat out there?"

"As long as we don't attack the gorgons or resonate, they might not even know we're out there."

Might. Not an encouraging word.

And the idea of not attacking the enemy was alien to the Marines. Stealing away while others fought for their lives felt like desertion. But this was not their ship. These were not their people. *Romans* could not run away from this fight.

But we can.

Getting to the hangars was going to be a problem. Since *Merrimack* detached from *Gladiator,* the remaining gorgons—and there were a lot of them—had scattered into an every-monster-for-itself feeding frenzy, eating the nearest living or once-living thing.

Steele shook a palm frond at his Marines. They were all loaded with vegetation now. "Any gorgon you meet, throw it something to eat, and run."

Clad in nothing but sweatpants, Cowboy muttered, "Hope gorgons don't pass on the salad and come for the meat."

But the tactic worked for a time. As long as the Marines had something to throw to the many many mouths, the gorgons did not feel the need to chase.

The Marines moved at a dodging, furtive run. Felt like mice when the world has gone to cats.

Avoided a contingent of Romans, ducked into a dark compartment. Held their breath.

Became aware of the bigness of the space they were in. Sensed it in the eddies of the air, in the smallness of their breathing when they finally exhaled.

Eyes adjusted from dim to only the most minimal emergency lighting. They were in a stowage area. Or a hangar. Cold. They could see their own breath rise in the eerie lamplight. Hard-edged shapes loomed, still as statues, in the mists of their frosty breath.

The shapes.

The hair pricked on Kerry's scalp. An awe so deep you don't want to move. "Those are Swifts!"

And Reg did her one better: "Those are *ours*!"

Kerry limped in to touch her beloved Six's cold, cold hull. Swifts. Of course, the Marine wing's fighter craft would be here. *Gladiator* would have harvested the useful parts before blowing up *Merrimack*. God bless their vulturous souls.

Kerry's eyes leaked joy.

Leave it to Carly to whisper, "Now how do we get out? I don't think *Gladiator* is going to lower her force field for us."

Reg hissed. She didn't dare shout. Not now, so close to escape. She motioned big. "Colonel! Over here."

Reg turned an emergency lamp on a set of hangar doors. The lamp's dim glow glinted on a crusting of ice at the seals. The doors themselves looked cold enough to stick your hand to. Reg whispered, afraid to say it, too good to be true: "The force field is down!"

It was true. There were enough gorgons left on *Gladiator* to keep the ship's computer controls suppressed. "We can get out!"

Unfortunately, the system failure extended to the Swifts as well. Cowboy was already in his cockpit trying to start up his machine. The Swifts were nonfunctional except for their most basic systems with a mechanical on/off, and the magnetic antimatter containment systems. Otherwise, they were brain dead.

"You'll have to hand adjust all life support," Steele told them. "Use your backup heaters, and the demand regulator for air."

There were no space suits. It was going to be uncomfortable. And no thrust.

"So how do we get out?"

A scratching at the inner hatch made them all hunker down, go silent.

Reg mouthed a warning: "Gorgons!"

The scratching came again. With a snuffling.

"Gorgons don't sniff," said Carly. "Gorgons don't breathe!"

Dak moved stealthily to the hatch, sword at the ready, to check out the snuffling visitor.

He relaxed, lowered his sword and let in a dog—the Chief's dog, Pooh—happy as hell to see Dak. Always a smart dog, the poodle didn't bark, only padded from Marine to Marine in hand-licking, tail-lashing, frightened-eyed joy.

Kerry expected a reaming from the colonel for wasting time with the mutt, but Steele only whispered loud, "Shut that hatch! Get the deck locks off your fighters! Push the Swifts up against these doors!" Jerked his head toward the ice-encrusted outer doors.

They had to breathe on the chocks to unfreeze them and get the Swifts' gear free. Kerry knew where this was going. *Colonel means to open the doors and let the rush of air sweep us out to space.*

She put a shoulder to her Swift. It wouldn't move. Pain stabbed her separated ribs, and folded her to a crouch. The Old Man stalked over to shove her crate flush up against the icy doors for her.

Snarled at everyone else to make 'em snug, so the Swifts won't crash on their way out.

Steele always had a sandy voice anyway, it was all gravel now. A comforting, domineering you-got-a-job-to-do-and-here's-how-you're-going-to-do-it rasp. "At some distance from the ship, you should regain systems controls. Do NOT resonate. In fact, pull your chambers out right now."

"Uh, Colonel?" Cowboy raised his hand, like preparing to ask a question of an idiot. "How are we supposed to open the hangar doors?"

Idiot question. Even Kerry knew the answer to that one. There were seven Marines here, six Swifts pushed up against the doors.

Steele ordered Alpha Flight into their cockpits.

Dak stripped off his T-shirt. Offered it to Steele. "Gonna get cold in here, sir."

Steele gave a taut nod. Put the shirt on over his tank top.

Carly and Reg took off their tops, offered them, too. The big man's blond brows screwed up at them, but before he could say something about the size, Carly said, "Mittens. You got to get the doors open wide enough for us to be sucked out before you freeze solid. You ain't dying for nothin', sir."

He accepted their salutes. Wrapped his hands in the women's shirts as Carly and Reg scampered, freezing, to their Swifts.

Dak, looking round in near panic, whispered, "Who's got the dog!"

Twitch's voice, muffled, from his cockpit: *"Yo!"*

Kerry was leaning against her Swift, one hand on the handhold, crying silently because she couldn't even lift herself into her cockpit. Steele stomped over, growling. Hauled her up and deposited her ungently into her fighter. Then strapped her in like a child into a safety seat. Fished out her oxygen mask and her regulator for her. Tugged her straps tight. Treated her like a brat child he had lost patience with.

Old Man really hates me, thought Kerry, taking it.

Hates me, and he's going to die for me.

"Clear your arms, Marine." Steele held the canopy over her.

"No, no. Wait, wait, wait."

Grimacing, like there was a nail in her side, Kerry pulled the red crowbar from her Swift's emergency hatch. Handed it up to Steele. "After you get out of this hangar, you'll need it against the gorgons."

He frowned at the red crowbar in his hand, odd, shifting expressions on his face. And Kerry reached up, grabbed his head, kissed him on the mouth. Felt a sudden warmth down to her groin. Let go.

"In case I never see you again," she said to his ice-blue eyes. "And if you do see me again, you can court-martial me. Give you something to live for."

"Get your arms in the cockpit, Marine."

"Yes, sir. *Semper fi.*"

The canopy closed over her, sealed.

She watched the colonel, a stocky figure, walking away in the dark. Never looked so small. Never looked so big.

Steele stowed the crowbar so it would not fly away, tethered himself tight to a stanchion, and took the red safeties off the windlass.

Kerry gave him a thumbs-up through her icing canopy.

Last saw him muscling the crank round for dear life.

An icy fog rose, debris swirled up, and her crate began to slide.

Ice cracked like thunder. The doors parted. Kerry's Swift tilted. Her hands gave a reflexive clutch as if she could catch herself. Her canopy rapped against the doors, made her yelp. The fighter lifted, scraping.

The outrush was a whirlwind now. Kerry's Swift banged back down, jarred her ribs so hard she couldn't breathe, and the whole crate canted over screw-wise. The canopy struck again, and she rolled.

Up. Sucked against the doors, straining to get through, a hailstorm of things clattering against her fuselage. The doors were parting slowly, slower.

Oh God, Colonel, keep cranking.

A stomach-heaving pitch and roll. Then an all hell cracking and banging. A weightless leap—

Through! And slammed back round with a dizzy swing and an awful crack. Her gear was hung on the door, her Swift flapping in the hurricane wind.

Kerry closed her eyes, teeth chattering. Helpless, cold, and going to die.

Screeching metallic tearing hammered at her ears. Felt it in her chest.

Then the end of sounds. Floating free. The Swift tumbled into the dark. Kerry's damp hair floated off her scalp.

Opened her eyes.

The only lights were those on her gunsights, implanted on either temple. Those lights were powered by her brain, so she was surprised they were still working.

She shivered, cold, the heater throwing only enough to bake her feet. Her muscles quivered in dehydration.

She groped with fluttering hands for the drinking tube. If there wasn't water in here, she was going to flat line.

She sucked on the tube, and, hallelujah, there was the most wonderful stale flat water in the universe filling her mouth.

She relaxed. Might live.

Tried to see out through the canopy. Then focused on the canopy itself.

A crack.

Fear coiled round her gut. That jagged white thread looked like a crack in her canopy.

She tried to lean forward for a better look, but Steele had her strapped in immobile. She loosened the straps, pushed herself forward in her seat.

It was a crack.

Without a force field, only one centimeter of cracked polymer stood between her and forever, hundreds of degrees difference on either side of that thin barrier.

Panic tugged, screaming, at the edges of her consciousness—the depth of space on the other side of that cracked shield. The enormity. The infinity. She was alone with her own breathing in her mask, her primitive heater at her feet.

The crack snaked longer and she flinched back. Scarcely felt the pain jerk her ribs.

She watched the crack, as if staring at it would keep it still. Breathing too hard, too deep. Tried to slow it down. Her breath. The crack.

It grew again, lancing toward the seal.

No. God, make it stop.

A loud beep. Kerry shrieked.

Console lights powered up. The force field came up round the Swift. Pressure and warmth filled the cockpit. The crack in the canopy spread seal to seal and Kerry told it to go to uffing hell.

Her com link gave a gentle buzz of life. She pulled off her regulator and yelled into her com. "This is Alpha Six! Can anyone hear me!"

"Alpha Six! Alpha Three! I am the happiest hag west of Vega!"

"Reg!"

"Chica linda! Donde estas?"

"Carly! *Estoy acqui!*"

"Where the hell is *acqui?*"

"Alpha *cinco, acqui!*"

"Twitch! Oh my God, Twitch." Kerry was laughing now.

Heard a woofing on the com that had to be the dog, Pooh.

"Yeeeeeeeee HA!"

"Cowboy!"

Reg reported that her sensors had picked up a heat trail. Big one. "Gotta be *Gladiator*. Do we follow it?"

"Follow *Gladiator*?" Cowboy squawked. "We just got out of that hole."

"Don't know about you, but I forgot to pack a lunch," Reg shot back.

"Well there won't be any food on *Gladiator* if the gorgons win," said Cowboy.

"If the gorgons win, the rest of the Legion is sure to send a robot back to collect the teeth. It can collect us, too. I'd rather be a prisoner than starve out here."

Carly put an end to the debate. Ordered the flight to form up and follow the heat trail.

Alpha Flight caught up with the heat source while Kerry was on point.

Glory be.

"That's *Merrimack*!"

Cowboy laughed like a hyena. He had seen the Roman, Bellus, on *Gladiator* send the destruct signal, had seen the light turn green on the console.

The destruct signal *went*. But: "How the hell is *Merrimack* going to *receive* the signal with all those gorgons on board uffing the systems? Did those squid-humping gits ever think of *that*?" He howled in gloating triumph.

Carly was sending: "*Merrimack! Merrimack! Merrimack!* This is Alpha Four! You have a bomb on board! Repeat message: You have a bomb on board!"

"They aren't responding," said Reg. "I guess they're not receiving that signal either."

"If they kill enough of the gorgons—and knowing Captain Farragut, they will—and someone don't disarm that bomb, their systems come back on and *Gladiator* can still destroy the Mack with the flip of a switch."

"No!" Kerry cried. *Not in front of my face. Not after all this.*
But how to warn *Merrimack*?

"Captain! I'm picking up a Morse signal!" Marcander Vincent reported, surprised. "Dead ahead. Light beacon. Claims to be Alpha Four.
Says we have a bomb on board."

Already figured that out. Still surprised, Farragut moved forward
to see the beacon. "We have *people* out there?"

"Alpha Four says *Gladiator* tried to detonate the bomb."

"Using what kind of switch?"

"Can't ask, Captain. Ben can't get a tight beam out of this gorgon
nest, and we can't send a light signal forward at this speed."

Farragut was about to order his senior engineer to the command
deck, when she appeared on her own. Ariel Kittering had never looked
quite real—porcelain skin, China-black hair, baby-doll eyes. She appeared now like a mannequin.

"Did you hear any of that, Kit? Romans have a remote detonator
that didn't work."

"Yes, sir. I—" She held an X-ray clutched tight in her fist.

Farragut knew that Kit had commandeered equipment from the
dental lab, and apparently managed to shoot some X-rays into the
heart of the gorgon swarm, which filled the maintenance shed, to get
a better look at what was inside.

"What've you got, Kit?"

She stammered a bit. "Rome took a page from our playbook. Redundancy is good. Redundancy is good. There's a backup destruct
mechanism in there—with a timed chemical ignition." She flapped the
X-ray uselessly. "And I never seen a gorgon inhibit a chemical reaction,
so the clock is . . . running."

"How long do we have?"

Kit checked her chron. "Eleven seconds."

Startled techs grasped at their consoles.

Farragut, very softly, "Kit, are you serious?"

"Nine. Eight. Seven. Six. Five. Four. Three. Two. It has been an
honor serving under you, Captain Farragut."

36

" **N**OW KIT, WHY ARE YOU scaring the royal blue peaches out of me? We're still here."

"Honest to God, Captain, I don't know what happened."

"I can tell you what *didn't*," said Farragut.

Kit checked the X-ray. "All I can think is the gorgons *ate* the *fuse*." Consoles lit up.

Barking resounded through the ship—Marines, turning the gorgon tide. The enemy was on the run.

Farragut asked if anyone had got at the bomb yet to disarm it.

"Not yet, Captain. We haven't got inside the maintenance shed yet."

Ben Mueller at the com reported, "Receiving a tight beam transmission."

"Please say that's not from *Gladiator*."

Gladiator's force field went up. Numa Pompeii congratulated his crew on their victory against an enemy against which all others had fallen. Told them to press the offensive until the ship was rid of every last gorgon.

The communications officer informed the general, "We are picking up English transmissions among unknown vessels and—*Merrimack!*"

"Sad for them they shall receive no answer," said Numa Pompeii, hands clasped behind his back.

"But they *did*, General," said the communications officer.

The *Triumphalis'* glacial calm rippled, returned. "It's a hoax."

"Quite a good one. That is John Farragut's voice." The communications officer offered General Pompeii an earphone.

Numa turned to his adjutant, deadly polite, "Kindly bring my fire control officer before me."

Portia Arrianus was a squarish woman, a long-time veteran, confident of her work, even before a scowling Numa Pompeii. "We sent the destruct signal," she told him simply. "Systems confirms it. *Apparently* the signal was not received."

"*Merrimack* is receiving signals *now,* isn't she?" Numa Pompeii pointed out.

"Yes, Triumphalis."

"So send the destruct signal again."

Arrianus never questioned orders, but the Triumphalis could not have thought this one through. "If *Merrimack* has overcome its gorgons, is it necessary to blow her up? Wasn't the point of this operation to destroy gorg—?"

"Send the destruct signal."

Arrianus opened her com link to fire control. Spoke stiffly. "Bellus. Are you receving?"

"I am here, *Domna.*

"Send the destruct signal again."

"Domna?"

Like chewing and spitting, "Send the destruct signal again."

"At once, *Domna.* Rearming destruct trigger," Bellus acknowledged. Then, "Ready. At your command, *Domna.*"

Arrianus glanced to Pompeii. There was to be no reprieve. She ordered, "Let it be done."

Waited. Waited too long.

"Bellus? Have we detonation?"

The com link remained inert.

The communications officer reported *Merrimack* was still talking. The unknown vessels *Merrimack* was talking to were apparently U.S. Marine Swifts.

Portia Arrianus saw her career shredding under Pompeii's glare. She barked into the com link: "Fire Control. Why don't we have detonation? Bellus! Acknowledge!"

Got no response.

Pompeii seized the com link, but even Numa Pompeii's roar could not wake the dead—Bellus lying on the deck, a red crowbar in his skull.

Merrimack's Marine company hacked, slashed, and clawed their way through the mass of gorgons in the maintenance shed. The killing went faster once small weapons' controls returned. And soon they were wading in the goo that was all that remained of a gorgon upon dying.

Techs disconnected the Roman explosive device from Engine Number Six and hustled it out an air lock.

With the Roman bomb safely outside the battleship's force field, the techs asked the captain where he wanted it.

Farragut was not really concerned with it once it left his ship. Space was vast. The universe could end before someone tripped over it.

"Kit! Just what the blue peaches was the ultra tasty gorgon bait Numa planted in my maintenance shed?"

"It wasn't blue peaches, Captain. It was a res sounder. We pulled the harmonic out of the chamber, but no one's told me if it's that exact harmonic that jacked the gorgons' interest or if any old res pulse would do it for them."

"Get that data to Jose Maria."

"Already done, Captain."

Glenn Hamilton reported in surprise that *Gladiator* was the only battleship in the region. The rest of the Legion must have kept running. Only *Gladiator* had turned back to repel the gorgon menace.

Merrimack hailed *Gladiator,* but the Roman ship was unwilling or unable to respond.

"Numa, talk to me or I am opening fire."

Glenn Hamilton questioned quietly, "We're attacking *Gladiator*?"

"They've got our people."

"I know," she said thickly. "And something else, John." Glenn moved in close so only he could hear. Made him lean down an ear. "They've got *all* our food."

"Are we in a day's range of anywhere?" he mumbled, glancing round at his techs.

"No, sir."

"Then to hell with him." Didn't wait for Numa to respond or not. "Give Numa back his bomb."

Merrimack slung the bomb at *Gladiator* and detonated it with a beam shot when it got close. The thermonuclear explosion hadn't much punch coming from outside the battleship's force field, but in this case it was the thought that counted.

Cowboy heeled his Swift round at the blast. "*Merrimack*'s opened fire on *Gladiator!* EeeeeeHa!"

"Cowboy, no! Alpha Seven, join up! That's an order!"

Carly might as well be shouting orders to a gorgon.

Didn't know if Cowboy knew *Gladiator* was operational. Alpha Seven ran straight into a beam cannon pulse and broke apart.

The com tech on *Merrimack* yanked his headset off at the piercing scream on the Marine channel. Knew that scream, long and anguished. Kerry Blue. Everyone knew Kerry Blue.

Farragut looked to the com tech. "You okay, Ben?"

The com tech replied laconically, replacing his headset. "Marine Swift down, sir."

"How did that happen?" said Farragut, shocked. How could he have Marine Swifts out there? Apparently there were great gaping holes in his chain of command. "Get those Marines on board! Then beat the tar out of *Gladiator!*"

Hamster advised, "*Gladiator* has run out a Red Cross."

With a string of words Farragut did not normally use, he lunged at the console and shouted into the com, "What's next, Numa? Grab a baby for a shield? Strike the false colors, and fight like a man!"

"Captain Farragut." The voice was of Numa, himself, on the com. "Run out a Red Cross of your own and come with me, please."

John Farragut sent back, "Numa, what's Latin for 'bullshit?' "

"No need to translate. I understand Anglo Saxon well enough."

"I want to make sure I'm communicating. Strike the Red Cross!"

"I can't. I am . . . choking here, Captain Farragut."

"Captain!" Marcander Vincent cried at his tactical station. "Roman Legion entering fire zone!"

Ship after ship blinked back in, all sides.

Farragut roared into the com, *"You baited me with a Red Cross?"*

"This flag is not bait, and if it were up to me, I would do as you suggest and step out alone in the alley. But it is not up to me."

Not up to him? Who could force General Numa Pompeii to run out a Red Cross against his will?

Numa said again, pained: "If you please, Captain Farragut. Run out a Red Cross of your own."

Doing so would shield *Merrimack* from Roman fire—if it were an honest Red Cross. If Rome had not abandoned all sense of human law.

"*I* can't!" Farragut sent back. "I am *not* on a mission of mercy."

"Apparently, you are. This way, please."

Gladiator moved out.

Merrimack fell in behind, but acquired a firing solution on *Gladiator*'s stern. "Numa, send food back here or I am shooting your damned flag!"

When the Romans actually dispatched a skiff, Farragut nearly shot it for a Trojan Horse. But the skiff brought only food.

Two days' worth.

"Not enough!"

Numa signaled back: "It is enough."

If Farragut had not seen the hecatomb at the Far Cat, he would not even have considered cooperating further in any way. But he had seen, and half his crew was aboard *Gladiator,* so he told Lt. Hamilton, "Run out the Red Cross."

Then ordered the helm to follow *Gladiator* on its mission of mercy. Did not know where they were headed. Was afraid of what he would find when they got there. Finally, he thought to ask his navigator, "Where *are* we?"

In the Abyss.

In transit into the Abyss, Captain Farragut collected the names of the missing. He already knew that his new XO Sebastian Gray was not aboard, but no one could say what had become of him.

Alpha Flight had returned to *Merrimack* without Flight Leader Hazard Sewell. No one aboard was sure what had become of Hazard Sewell either. Lieutenant Colonel Steele was reported dead, even though Flight Sergeant Kerry Blue swore—swore a lot—that Steele was still alive. He had to be.

Patrick Hamilton was on the list. Surprised him. Glenn had not let on. Looking back, yes, she had the bearing of someone carrying a heavy burden inside, alone. He had seen her in the ship's chapel. Glenn Hamilton never went to chapel. He asked Mo Shah to look in on her for him.

If she needed an ear, John Farragut's was the wrong one.

The journey lasted less than two days. During that time, the ship's cryptotech, Qord Johnson, tried to re-create some of the ship's information. Immediately upon surrendering to *Gladiator*, *Merrimack* had run an information destruct protocol that had vaporized the contents of Captain Farragut's and Commander Gray's safes and all the red files in the data banks.

Qord Johnson was the only man on board who could reconstruct the codes. He hummed while he worked, happy to be alive.

The captain looked over his shoulder. Qord looked up, met the captain's eyes, gave a shaky grin. "They used to shoot cryptotechs on capture, didn't they?"

Once upon a time there'd been someone on board a Navy ship who was assigned to shoot the CT if the ship fell into enemy hands.

"I heard they used to do that," said Qord.

Farragut nodded. "They still do." And to Qord's open mouth and wide wide eyes, he said, "Carry on." To Tactical: "Got a plot yet on where we're going, Mr. Vincent?"

"Not sure, sir. Possible target dead ahead."

"*Possible* target? Can I get some more information than that, Mr. Vincent?"

"Could be just a nebula. Can't get a fix on it to measure it. It's a bit nebulous, so to say. Vector galactic normal." And, like dropping one shoe: "Could be a nebula."

"Could be a refractor," Farragut supplied the other shoe.

It was a common stealth tactic, to refract electromagnetic emissions around oneself. If the scattered light up ahead was not a nebula, then someone was hiding there.

Farragut got on the com, "Hey, Numa, have you ever known a Hive sphere to refract?"

The return message came from one of the general's adjutants: "That is not a Hive sphere."

The Romans knew what it was. Farragut had to wait and see, since Rome was not telling. Not over the com.

Gladiator led *Merrimack* into the refracting field. The Legion did not follow.

The two battleships came out the other side of the scattered signals to a clear zone.

Farragut recognized the approach, but the sight that coalesced on the sensor display still came as a shock.

"Captain!" Marcander Vincent turned from his console to show the amplified image.

A fortress, built like a mountain towering above its own reflection, hanging in the dark of space. The computer-enhanced image lit it up gold. Its griffin acroteri, normally spouting blue-white fire, stood quiescent.

Glenn Hamilton came forward from her station, breathing an invocation. "That looks like—"

It looked like what it was. "That's Fortress Aeyrie," said John Farragut. Caesar's mobile palace.

Captain Farragut had just been summoned to an audience with the Emperor of Rome.

37

"**W**HAT WOULD CAESAR BE doing out here?"

The image on the display was, without a doubt, Fortress Aeyrie, Caesar's mobile residence. But Captain Farragut could not quite believe that Caesar could be in it so far from Palatine.

But then the Empire did have a crisis out here of extraordinary magnitude, so perhaps Farragut should expect the extraordinary of Caesar.

"There's no Praetorian Guard!" Lieutenant Hamilton cried a warning.

Caesar never went anywhere without his Praetorian Guard. This had to be a fraud.

This fortress had no guard ships at all—unless one counted the half Legion that had just escorted *Merrimack* here. Only a force field shell protected this place.

The real Fortress Aeyrie had a legendary force field. If Fortress Aeyrie should ever fall into a black hole, it could remain intact and self-sustaining for a thousand years. It did not really need guards. Still, it always had them. Fortress Aeyrie was never without squadrons of guards and flocks of hangers-on, lackeys, sycophants and petitioners. You never saw Fortress Aeyrie hanging alone in space.

"But that *is* Fortress Aeyrie. And those *are* Caesar's eagles," Marcander Vincent pointed out the distinctive eagle standards on the display image.

"So where is the Praetorian Guard?" said Glenn Hamilton.

"Glenn, you were right the first time," said Farragut in hollow realization.

There is no Praetorian Guard.

He was just beginning to wonder if anyone were left inside the fortress, when slowly, there appeared a break in the impenetrable field's shell and a beacon to ride in on.

"I'm not docking my *Merrimack* with that," said Farragut and got on the com. "Numa, you give me back one of my LRSs for me to pilot in myself, or I don't go."

It disturbed him that General Numa Pompeii complied.

Farragut snapped sighting brackets on either side of his eyes. Not that he would carry a gun into Fortress Aeyrie. But so that his command crew would be able to see whatever he saw. He left his com link open so the command crew would hear him also, and he could hear them.

He left the command deck. "Hamster, your boat."

Alone in his LRS, on slow approach to the wayward mountain, Farragut was struck by the sheer size of Fortress Aeyrie. Built like an iceberg, the lower mile of it housed all the machinery that served the hundred-meter-tall residence built of rich rose granite inlaid with black marble polished to a glossy brilliance. The fortress summit, normally ablaze with white-and-gold firestones, stood dormant in milky translucence.

Golden hangar doors parted for Farragut's LRS. "Not the servants' entrance," he overheard someone back on *Merrimack* say.

He rode the beam in, set the LRS down, locked down. Golden doors closed him in. The air pressure gauge turned green.

A Roman soldier, arrayed in bronze cuirass and scarlet cape came to the LRS to show Captain Farragut the way through the fortress, up to the immense double sequoia doors of Caesar's audience hall.

It surprised Farragut a little that he was not taken first somewhere to make him presentable. *Merrimack*'s captors had stripped out all of the captain's personal effects, so he was still wearing the dress uniform he had worn to General Pompeii's table, but torn now and stained with blood, sweat, and gorgon gore. He smelled pretty bad and needed a shave.

He muttered into the com link on the back of his hand, "Hamster, get ready to run. If you don't see Caesar when these doors open, get the hell out of here."

Towering twin gods flanked the giant doors—Diana and Apollo, golden-skinned and armed with bows and arrows, she in a scant shimmersilk tunic, he in less. On a twelve-foot god, the fig leaf presented at eye level, and John Farragut was glad of the foliage.

The twin gods moved to open the massive doors. Farragut locked his eyes forward. First thing he saw had better be Caesar.

Apollo and Diana stepped to either side, admitting him to the Presence.

Farragut recognized the man on the dais, though it was a shock to see him so haggard. The emperor had let himself age authoritatively, with white temples and distinguished lines in his skin, but it was unusual for a man of his wealth and resources to go to jowls like that. Julius Caesar Magnus.

John Farragut had been before kings and presidents many times before. The Presence did not intimidate. It did impress.

The hall was huge. Alabaster columns soared to the distant ceiling, under which the architrave moved in a procession of larger-than-life tribute bearers from all the worlds of the Empire.

Above Caesar's massive throne a pediment niche housed the generously figured goddess Ceres with a pregnant she-wolf at the foot of her throne and a globe in her hand, which Farragut recognized as planet Earth. Three mother images there. An unsettling grouping.

At the right hand of Caesar stood Numa Pompeii. Already a big man, dressed here in ceremonial armor, Numa looked huge.

On Caesar's left stood a lean, very tall man with an opaque gaze, who had to be a patterner, dressed in gray. He was not perfect enough to be an automaton. He had to be human, though cables ran from the back of his neck to an outlet in the shimmering wall like an ancient electrical appliance. His attention seemed entirely inward.

A very long approach bridge of snowy marble stretched from the dais to the entranceway where Farragut stood. On either side of the bridge, the floor appeared to drop off to an eternal expanse of blue sky.

Farragut glanced down on soaring golden eagles and miles of white clouds. Heights never scared him and he was in no mood to admire the beauty. He marched straight up the bridge to the Presence on his raised dais.

The Presence handed Farragut back his sword. "Captain Farragut, thank you for coming."

"I was invited at gunpoint, so I'm not going to pretend to have manners," said Farragut, belting on his sword. Lionhead finials on Caesar's throne watched him with topaz eyes.

It felt good to be armed. Farragut demanded of the great Caesar: "What do you want?"

"A truce," said Caesar.

"We're done here." Farragut turned to go back the way he came.

"Captain Farragut, we took you for a reasonable man."

"Sir," Farragut turned his head to face the emperor, his body only half turned. "I am *reasonably* sure I am holding all the high cards at this table. I've seen your hand, and I am not sitting through a hot air storm while you're holding nothing. You've got yourself a two-front war, haven't you? You want us to put *our* war on hold while you deal with that godzilla you woke up. No. No truce. You want a cease-fire, you surrender. That's my first, last, best, only offer."

Dour silence held the great hall except for the rush of the wind under the bridge and eagle wings.

"Like I said, we're done here," said Farragut. Walked briskly back across the snowy marble bridge.

"Captain Farragut."

Farragut wasn't turning this time. Did not slow his pace.

"Captain Farragut."

The second "Captain Farragut" made him stop. That the emperor had spoken his name—twice—at his back—made his skin crawl right up it. He waited for what was to follow.

Let Caesar say it to his back. "We would like to discuss—"

Started walking again.

He had reached the sequoia doors when he heard a clatter on the marble—a sound exactly like a gilt eagle scepter would make toppling down the steps of a raised dais. Then a rustle of rich fabric—like an old man standing. An abject voice: *"In manus tuas."*

Farragut felt his eyes grow huge in his head.

Into your hands.

Words of ritual. Taken from the last words of Christ. Shorthand for a last surrender: *Into your hands, I commend my spirit.*

Farragut turned round to face his nation's mortal foe.

With slow steps, Caesar descended the dais where his black-and-gold eagles lay on the floor. He opened his empty hands. "Rome surrenders."

Farragut spoke in a near whisper, "What have you got yourselves into?"

"We are a desperate nation."

"I figured that part out, sir. When the hell were you going to tell us?"

"We have no other possible choice. We are being eaten alive. Yours—and now *Gladiator*—are the only vessels to survive an encounter with Them once engaged."

"The only of how many encounters?"

Caesar did not answer. Closed his eyes.

And did he see behind those creased lids the holocaust at the Far Cat?

That vision came to Farragut in the dark.

General Numa Pompeii could not keep quiet any longer. Words exploded out of him without leave: "It is not any great talent or secret they have, Caesar! They use swords and manual controls! His ship has low-tech backup systems. We can do that! We have their great secret. You don't need to—"

Caesar held up his hand to signal silence. *"Stratege,"* he said. "Do we have their numbers?"

Numa did not answer that.

"What hands will lift those swords?" Caesar asked, fatally.

"We have colonies," said Numa. "We have numbers."

"We have willing amateurs. We have Hive fodder. They still have their best."

"What are *we?*" said Numa with a thumping fist to his armored chest.

Caesar beckoned his general in for a murmur. Said something that first slackened, then hardened Numa's face. The general turned away from the old man's whispered words, chastised.

Numa did not speak again.

Caesar spoke aloud to the patterner stationed on the other side of his throne. "Augustus. Can you show Captain Farragut the map?"

The patterner did not acknowledge the request. Did not move.

But the blue sky and the eagles vanished, and John Farragut was standing on a marble bridge in outer space. A three-dimensional star map surrounded Caesar's throne.

It took Farragut a moment to get his bearings. He was in Fortress Aeyrie in the Abyss. From there he found Palatine, Earth, and Terra Rica, in the Orion Starbridge. What he could not identify were the glowing orange dots cluttering the Abyss like stars. There were not that many stars in the Abyss. And each orange plot was labeled with a vector. The orange plots were moving FTL. Not a stellar motion.

"Hive swarms," Caesar identified the orange plots for him. "Gorgons."

Farragut felt his pulse leap. "Caesar, these spheres are going to home in on this res scan!"

"This is not a live resonant scan," Caesar assured him. "This is a recording made weeks ago, from elsewhere. The gorgons do not know where we are now. A tragedy that planets cannot run and hide so."

Farragut took a moment to assess all the vectors on the map. He saw it now—where many plots converged on a single point. "Well, hell. All roads *still* lead to Rome."

"Do not suppose they have not found you, Terran. There are hundreds of them headed for Fort Eisenhower. As for these," Caesar gestured at the monsters in the dark. "Once they have devoured Palatine, your world is next in line. And they do move in straight lines. Your terms, Captain?"

"Take it up with President Marisa Johnson and Congress," Farragut said curtly.

"I have no intention of sitting through a hot-air storm," Caesar echoed, mild and reasonable how he said it. "You are a decisive man, Captain Farragut, and I will have this done quickly. You have the authority to dictate terms on this side of the Abyss."

"I do?" Farragut blinked, spoke into his com, "Glenn, check the regs." And back to Caesar, "You want to bypass Marisa? Why?"

"President Johnson and your Congress are politicians. You are a soldier. I will surrender to your U.S. Navy. You have power to accept for the Navy and for the United States by extension of that."

Farragut was speaking into the back of his hand again: "Hamster, can I do that?"

There had been a feverish scramble for the Naval Codex back on *Merrimack*'s command deck. They had the reference now and Glenn

Hamilton's answer stumbled over the link, "Yes. Yes, sir. Actually, you can. The captain of a commissioned capital ship in the Deep End in wartime, has authority to speak for the United States."

"We're not in the Deep End. We're in the Abyss."

"We checked that, too, sir. Deep End is defined in the regs as the space this side of Fort Theodore Roosevelt."

"Oh, for Jesus," he spoke to the stars. He crossed the bridge back to Caesar, stood over the dropped scepter. "Sir, you're gonna wish you asked President Johnson. Here are my terms. Palatine maintains its internal government, but not a skatload else. All Roman military units will swear allegiance to the U.S. Constitution."

"Obedience," Caesar amended. "Not allegiance. Allegiance is already sworn and cannot be foresworn."

"Fine."

"And not to the U.S. Constitution. To you."

"I'm sworn to the Constitution and I obey the Joint Chiefs, so that still leads y'all back to the Constitution."

"If that is where that road leads," said Caesar, conceding. Then, "What will be our Trade status?"

"You're an Earth colony. Always were."

Farragut saw Caesar and General Pompeii bristle. That term was a bitter one. It threw the mighty Empire back to its colonial beginning. But Caesar did not argue. He asked harshly, "Are you done?"

He was not. "Where were all your killer bots?" Farragut demanded. "I want those under direct U.S. control."

Palatine had robot fleets, hundreds of thousands of unmanned vessels equipped with a wide variation of weaponry.

"We have only those rolling out of the factories now," said Caesar.

"No." Mama Farragut's boy was not so naive. "You've got thousands. Near on millions. Where are they?"

Caesar had just been called a liar. He stared John Farragut in the eyes. His voice was soft, brittle. "Robot ships are equipped with a kill switch. The kill switch does not just deactivate the robot; it causes the robot to self-destruct." He took a deep breath for strength, finished. "The kill switch on a robot ship has a resonant trigger."

"The Hive found your harmonic," Farragut guessed.

Resonance was instantaneous. Caesar nodded. "Destroyed them all. Everywhere. At once."

Farragut reconsidered his position. Good that Rome was without its vast automaton force, but the loss took the killer bots out of his own arsenal now.

"How many Legions are you consigning to my authority?"

A long conspiratorial pause expanded there. Secrets. Rome was accustomed to keeping secrets for millennia. Numa became like gray granite, the patterner Augustus completely inhuman and inanimate. Caesar looked grave.

Caesar answered: "Twelve."

Farragut heard gasps from his com link, his command crew back on *Merrimack*.

Farragut asked, "Where's the rest of them?"

Numa Pompeii came forward with an angry stride, offering something in his fist. Farragut put out an open palm to receive it.

Teeth.

"Sixty-four Legions?" Farragut cried. "How the hell did you lose sixty-four Legions?"

Caesar had to sit down. Explained, "Many were on board carriers when the Hive touched the killer bots' harmonic. Many others perished in the evacuation of Telecore. Thanks to *you*, our first ship evacuated through the Catapult was also our last. You destroyed the Near Cat, and marooned our people in the Deep."

"Load of crap, Caesar. Tote that guilt back where it came from. Your pride killed those people." He handed Caesar his people's teeth. "Who nuked Telecore?"

"The Praetorian Guard. It was necessary. Their last act."

"Would it have killed you to ask for help before it came to that?"

"It does kill me to do so," said Caesar. "Help us."

"Imperial 'us'?"

"All of us. All humanity."

Farragut was about to demand the return of all POWs, including the rest of his crew. A sudden thought quilled his mouth. He asked in dread, "Where are the crew of the *Monitor*?"

A bitter turn of Caesar's lips, too sad to be called a smile. Answered, "They should be safe. *Monitor*'s crew are on a slow prison boat through the Abyss back to Near Space. We were in no hurry to return them, so your people did not go to the Catapult."

Farragut lifted eyes on a prayer. Felt the nearness of death brushing by.

Heard himself saying, "What was *Monitor* doing out here?" A very odd question to be asking his enemy. It just came out. *Monitor's* mission was so secret his own country's Intelligence agency would not tell him, so he had to ask Caesar.

"Your *Monitor*," said Caesar, "was hunting for Fortress Aeyrie."

"Fortress Aeyrie is not a military target," Farragut blurted.

Made Caesar smile. "They did tell me you were a Boy Scout, Captain Farragut. That is why we offer surrender to you and not to your government." And, profoundly defeated, Caesar asked, "Do you accept our surrender?"

"Just about," said Farragut. "Now rack 'em."

"Sir?"

Farragut picked up a fallen eagle standard from the marble deck. "Make an arch."

That provoked a twitch even from the immobile Augustus. General Numa Pompeii looked about to detonate.

Farragut held out the eagle. "I insist."

Caesar recoiled, aghast. "You *wouldn't*."

"I do."

Caesar Magnus pulled in his quiet dignity, offended. "When one puts his hand under your foot, it is impolite of you to step."

"Caesar, I can almost believe you're sincere. But there can be no doubt in anyone's mind all the way down to the buck grunt on either side. Down to the kid in the street with a pipe bomb. I have to see it. So does Rome. So does Earth. So no one can say, 'what are they up to?' Rack 'em. Right here, *and* down the Via Triumphalis at the Hill."

He wanted another subjugation on Rome's home planet, Palatine, in their capital city, down their processional way, in front of the Imperial Residence.

Unspoken—heavily implied—was that John Farragut had to see if Caesar could make his soldiers and his world obey. The doubt was too rude to speak, but there it was. If Caesar could not make his remaining soldiers walk under an ancient subjugation, he could not make them honor the surrender.

Caesar closed his eyes. "So be it."

38

PEOPLE ALL OVER THE WORLDS woke each other in middle of their nights to watch, astounded. Images from Fortress Aeyrie. Of Caesar Magnus and the Legion Pompeii walking under the crosswise spear held up by Caesar's own eagles. And images from Palatine, where Roman Legions passed under racked spears on the Capitoline, the same march they had forced upon the armies of many a subject world. Watched in horror, like watching a king put on his own slave shackles.

Not until they saw it did the magnitude of the coming danger hit home.

Invoked their gods.

Merrimack reactivated her res chamber, and immediately received an incoming transmission from Earth, from the Joint Chiefs. Admiral Mishindi, near shouting: "John! Are you seeing this?"

"I'm right *here,* sir."

"This has got to be a hoax! Where's the Praetorian Guard? The Praetorian Guard would never stand for this!"

"No, sir. They would not," said Farragut.

Let the silence speak. The feared and hallowed Praetorian Guard was simply *not.*

"What is Caesar really up to?" Mishindi asked, as if there were a secret to be shared.

"He's surrendering, sir."

"Lord God Almighty."

"Admiral Mishindi, I thought you left the church a long time ago."

"I'm thinking of re-upping. Good *God*!"

There followed an urgent call from Calli Carmel. Not sure where she was calling from. She immediately cried, "John! I only see the *triarii* going under those arches! Where are the crack troops? This has got to be a sham!"

"Speak English, Cal. What's a *triarii*?"

"The reserves. I'm only seeing reserves walk in subjugation."

"That's about all they got, Cal. Look here. This is no reserve unit."

He moved his vid sender to show her Numa Pompeii striding under the racked eagles at Fortress Aeyrie.

Dumbstruck silence sat on the com. Calli Carmel saw her nemesis in utter, humiliating submission. She knew now it was real. Numa Pompeii would never walk under a rack for show. Ever.

Calli might have gloated, but Farragut heard in her silence only real horror.

Merrimack received other signals, newscasts showing people watching the transmissions from Palatine. Showed all of the people, even citizens of Earth, frozen in that universal pose of horror, eyes huge and watery, staring above hands pressed together over mouths.

Did not take long for Congress to throw a primordial fit. John Farragut had passed on the chance to end slavery, take over trading alliances, get a piece of Roman taxes, annex some of those lucrative colonies, investigate Roman bio-research violations. The list was long.

Captain Farragut was summoned before a Congressional committee via the res com.

Farragut shut them down quickly. "This is an expensive call and too late. You don't like the deal, take it up with the pinhead who put this clause in the Navy regs that gave me authority to negotiate it. My enemy, as he says, put his hand under my foot. I stepped on it. But I did not harvest the rest of his body parts, because I need him up and breathing to help me fight. Y'all are really not grasping what happened here."

"What's to say this isn't a trap." The Senator from Oaxaca there.

"Caesar is going to walk in subjugation for a *trap*? What else do you want said? No, you're right. It's a trap. The moment Caesar put his head under that arch, we inherited his war. Here it is in terms y'all might understand: Fort Eisenhower must be evacuated within six years. That means the Shotgun shuts down in six years. Palatine will be dead in one hundred thirty years. Later that same year, Earth will be eaten alive, which may be just fine for you if you don't have grand-children. But since we're all feeling human beings here, I suggest you stop dividing up the spoils of the conquered and start fighting the Hive now. Right now. Unless one of you can figure out how to start yes-terday. Having said that, y'all will have to excuse me. I have to get back to work."

Gladiator returned the captured equipment, personnel, provisions, dog tags, and teeth to *Merrimack*.

Captain Farragut composed messages to the widows, the moms, the dads, the children. Starting with his XO Sebastian Gray. Hoped like hell the last thing he'd said to Gray was *not* to call him Cal by mistake. Scarcely had time to know him. Knew he'd left behind his wife Narinda with two young boys, Terrance and Justin. A blind springer spaniel named something or other. Knew there was a pocket keettrig nesting in the attic, which Gray had to evict next time he got home. Home was Providence, one of the American colonies. Farragut guessed he ought to arrange for someone to take care of the keettrig for Narinda. Or do it himself if orders took him near Providence. No one had seen Gray buy it, so Farragut couldn't even tell Narinda that her husband had died valiantly.

Oh, yes, he could.

TR Steele had been returned to *Merrimack* in a bag. A med bag. In ragged shape but still alive.

Also returned in a med bag was some idiot, bandaged over his eyes, who kept calling over and over, "Marco! Marco!"

The MPs were beginning to wonder if this weren't a Roman plant, because of the bandaged face, because no one knew his voice, and no one knew who in blazes was Marco.

Till Lieutenant Glenn Hamilton broke out in an astonished sob-bing laugh: "Polo!"

No matter what, Patrick Hamilton could make her laugh.

Glenn Hamilton could not follow her husband to the ship's hospi-tal, where he was carried—babbling joyfully "Marco! Marco!" the whole way—until the end of her watch. When she came to his bedside, the bandages over Patrick's face were fresh.

He had taken a dying gorgon in the face. A pair of new eyes were being cultivated for him in a tank next to his cot.

When Glenn slipped her hand into his, Patrick asked, "Have I lost you to Captain Farragut?"

"What do you mean?" Could not believe how lame those words sounded coming out of her mouth.

He gestured blindly at the organ tank next to his cot: "I have eyes!"

Glenn could not speak. Could not think.

"I'm not wrong, am I," Patrick said more than asked.

"You're not right either," said Glenn.

There was a motion of eyebrows lifting under the bandages. *"Meaning?"*

"John Farragut was nice to have around when you were making me feel like—I can't even tell you what it feels like."

"Hull, do you remember what I said when I asked you to marry me?"

Her eyes stung. She remembered exactly. Tried to keep the unsteadiness out of her voice. She recited back to him: "Hull, you could do better, but I wish you wouldn't."

He nodded on his pillow. "And I was lying here thinking, and I thought I was going to offer you your freedom when you got here. But screw that. I'm fighting for you, Glenn Hull." He sat up, put up his dukes. "Let's do it. Point me at your Superman." He jabbed at the air.

"He's not here, Patrick."

"Oh, thank God." He fell back on the cot.

May as well have challenged a bull gurzn. "Glenn, I swear I'll never look at another woman."

"You don't need eyes to see Hot Trixi Allnight."

"Hot Tr—! Who wants *her?*"

"*You* did!"

Patrick's arm flopped at his side. "I just had to see what all your thugs thought was so special."

Her thugs—what Dr. Patrick Hamilton called the navvies and Marines behind their backs. They were hers because she was an officer. Patrick was just a scientist in uniform.

"And?" Glenn waited for the verdict on Trixi's specialty.

"I still don't see it. She's no Glenn Hull."

Glenn left Patrick's hospital compartment. Gasped.

John Farragut was waiting in the corridor, leaning back against the bulk, his arms crossed, as if he'd been there for some time. Regarded her strangely. Puzzled maybe.

"John?"

He straightened up. Glanced away, brow creased. Looked back to her. Decided to speak. "Okay, Glenn, here it is. He's an ass."

She dropped her gaze to the deck grates a thoughtful moment. At last looked up, looked into his eyes. Nodded yes.

"But he's *my* ass."

General Pompeii returned the captain's bourbon in person in preparation to take his leave. The gorgons would be heading to this location after the recent flurry of res transmissions. It was time for *Gladiator, Merrimack,* and Fortress Aeyrie to be elsewhere.

Farragut brooded over what Caesar had said earlier regarding *Monitor*—that she had been hunting Fortress Aeyrie.

No wonder Napoleon Bright had refused to tell him *Monitor*'s mission.

"What the hell were they going to do when they found Fortress Aeyrie!" Farragut wondered aloud. "Kidnap the emperor?"

A bit of Numa's old superciliousness returned. The general gave a disingenuous shrug of his massive shoulders. "That would be your side's information."

And Farragut understood now Rome's reluctance to ask the United States for help.

Farragut muttered softly, "God blessed tunnel-visioned schemers!"

"You blame the snake for having tunnel vision?" said Numa.

"No, I blame the snake for being a snake. Numa, what was that harmonic you stuck on board my boat to lure the gorgons?"

Numa Pompeii shook his head. He didn't know. "I got it from our snakes."

Farragut checked over the ship's manifest. "I think that's everything."

"Not quite," said Numa. "I have also been ordered to turn over to you a valuable piece of equipment, the emperor's patterner."

The phrasing gave Farragut pause. "His patterner. That's a person, right?"

Numa gave an enigmatic glower. "If you say so."

"Permission to come aboard."

"As if I could stop you."

Farragut collected kisses on either cheek from Jose Maria de Cordillera at the starboard dock along with a bottle of well-aged cognac. "I liberated this from *Gladiator*."

"Good man."

"It is good to see you restored to your ship, young Captain. A bit of a deus ex machina, is it not? As in ancient Greek plays, when all looked lost, a god stepped in and made everything right again."

"Oh, no. Everything is not right, and what's behind this is the furthest thing from God," said Farragut.

"I know that well. And I have a request, young Captain. If your mission is now to destroy this thing, this Hive, I would travel with you. I think I could make myself of use in your lab."

It had the sound of a vendetta. Farragut guessed, "The Romans told you what became of *Sulla*."

Jose Maria's black eyes glistened. He smiled tragically. "They do not know."

"I don't believe it! Where's Numa? I'll beat the answer out of him!"

"They truly do not know. They never found her. *Sulla* was the first victim of the monsters, they think. But she vanished without a trace, so they assume, but they do not know. Hope turns like a thorn in the heart, because this hope is a lie, and I know it."

Farragut made a fist, with nothing to punch. "If only Rome had asked sooner. This would have been a different ball game. Hell, Jose Maria, you're a learned man, can't you build a time machine? Do this over?"

Rhetorical, but Jose Maria answered anyway. "In theory. If one views our ten-dimensional universe in three dimensions—which is the only way we can view it—picture, then, the universe as an expanding balloon and we all dots on the surface of it. We grow farther and farther apart from each other as the universe expands, but no single one of us can be called the center."

"Where does that take us?"

"Because time and space are a single entity, in theory, to go back in time, you could circle the entire surface of our universe-balloon to bring you back where you began."

"It's a damn big universe."

Jose Maria nodded. "It is. And remember that the balloon is expanding. You would need to travel faster than light to outrun the expansion of our balloon, which, in real time, we cannot do."

"We do it all the time," said Farragut.

"We exceed light speed, that part is true. But not in real time. Mass increases as an object approaches light speed—from a sublight observer's perspective. From *our* perspective, I still measure seventy-eight kilos no matter what speed I travel. At light speed, energy is infinite, time is infinite, neither of which condition is possible in real space-time. We never actually travel at light speed. We go faster or slower, but no one has ever observed us at light speed."

"Which is another way of saying it doesn't happen."

"In effect, yes. Just as when we exceed light speed, we become irrelevant to the universe and, in effect, leave it. We become unobservable from our sublight observer's vantage. Picture us now inside the balloon. We have left the surface of the real space-time universe and are in a sense tunneling from point to point without hitting all the points in between."

"So with a deep enough tunnel we *can* go back in time," said Farragut.

"Alas, that is where reality sets back in. You would need to exceed threshold velocity to dig that kind of tunnel. As you say, it is a damn big universe. And even were you able to break threshold and reach the required velocity, the journey would last several billion years from *your* perspective. You would not arrive intact. From the observers' perspective, of course, none of it would happen at all."

"Jose Maria, you weren't with me at the Myriad. I think we *had* that kind of tunnel. Twelve billion years deep. Maybe, maybe, if I could just have stopped the Arran from going down that hole—"

"We would still be here," a strange voice finished his thought.

Jose Maria de Cordillera and Captain Farragut turned to the speaker.

The emperor's patterner. Not eager to board, he had not asked permission. He waited at the dock between Marine guards.

Augustus was now unplugged from his machines, looking only

slightly more human, rigidly tall, but pained, as if their talk struck him as exceedingly tedious and embarrassing.

"Problem?" Farragut prompted, beckoning his Roman "equipment" in past the Marines.

"To speculate on things that are not real and can never be real," said Augustus, "is a waste of energy and time."

Jose Maria smiled benignly. Jose Maria had apparently made acquaintance with the patterner while in Roman company. The patterner's brusque manner disturbed him not at all. "Good heavens, Augustus. Regretting what might have been is an ancient sport. Possibly a Roman invention, though I think Adam and Eve must certainly have played it. Can you say there is nothing you have ever done that you never wish you could have done differently, if only you had the chance?"

"There is," said Augustus, dark and distant. He turned to Farragut. "I'd have pulled the trigger on you at the Myriad."

Confirmed what Farragut already knew. He and Augustus had met before.

Augustus continued, to Jose Maria. "Yes, Dr. Cordillera. I would like to have that one back."

Farragut was afraid he must have looked hurt and personally insulted, because Jose Maria asked for him, "And what would *that* have changed, patterner?"

"In the end, nothing," said Augustus, expressionless. "Which is why this exercise is pointless. Entropy is a basic condition of the universe. The enemy are entropy incarnate. They are inevitable. Done is done. All roads lead here."

"And there you have it, young captain," said Jose Maria blithely. "There is no going back."

Augustus said, "You won."

"I won," Farragut echoed, no triumph in it.

"The only way out of this is straight ahead," said Jose Maria.

"I can do that."

Not the victory he wanted. But it was the one he had. Straight ahead at full speed was really the only way Farragut knew how to go.

Lieutenant Colonel TR Steele's new fingertips were as broad as the ones he had frozen off in *Gladiator's* hangar deck, but they were pink, girly soft, with thin, pliant nails.

The new tip of his nose did not bother him so much because he could not see it, and he'd never been much for looking in mirrors.

But those new fingers were right in front of him as he emptied the contents of the late Flight Leader Hazard Sewell's locker into a small box.

These could not be his hands. Didn't look like they'd ever fought beside this guy.

Hazard Sewell had died honorably, horribly, fighting gorgons. Better hands should be handling his stuff.

And Cowboy Carver's locker should not be allowed next to Hazard Sewell's locker.

"Cowboy got himself killed and Alpha's a better squad for it."

Should not have said that. But it was out there now, and Colonel TR Steele could not reel it back in. Left him in the awkward position of having to eat words to a subordinate. The subordinate he had a hopeless crush on.

He talked thick, through a lump in his throat. "Sorry. I know you loved him."

"I didn't," said Kerry Blue. "I never did."

And that sent Steele into giddy orbit, though it was obviously a lie. "Blue, you're crying over his empty locker."

" 'Cause I'm an idiot!" Kerry shouted through tears. "I loved someone I made up. Guy I loved looked like Cowboy, lived like Cowboy. Made me feel like I could fly. But the guy I loved loved me back just as hard. And I am so damn mad at Cowboy for not being that guy! Cowboy made me feel *this* big when he wasn't making me feel sky high." Marked off the tip of her little finger with her painted thumbnail. "Lying, cheating, married son of a— Hell, if he didn't die here, he'd a died of boredom. Sorry, sir. You didn't need to hear that."

"Not hurting me."

Kerry Blue dragged a khaki sleeve across her angry face. "I am *not* crying. Over *nothing*. Scum. He was scum. I'm not saying I'm glad he's dead. He was one of us. I'm just saying—didn't everybody always say?—that boy's gonna die young. Some things happen 'cause they just gotta happen. There's nothing of mine in here." She slammed Cowboy's locker. "Can I go, sir?"

Steele didn't want her to go. Wanted her to stay here, with her silly pink nails, that slight curl in her soft brown hair. He just liked having her near him. Tough, trashy, girl-soft and Marine-hard Kerry Blue. Talked with her whole body. A great little body. He looked at her mouth and remembered her kiss when he thought he was about to die in that black, cold hangar. Had given him something to live for. He wanted to live.

She was asking to go. And that was probably a desperately good idea.

Steele gave a gruff rasp, "Dismissed, Marine."

Watched her walk out, loose, rangy, rolling.

Keep your eyes above the neck, soldier, an inward rep. *Put it out of your head. Not going to happen. Not in this or any lifetime.*

Some things were never meant to be.